ULTIMATUM

■

R.J. PINEIRO

TOR®

A TOM DOHERTY ASSOCIATES BOOK ·
NEW YORK

ULTIMATUM

Copyright © 1994 by Rogelio J. Pineiro

All rights reserved, including the right to reproduce this book, or portions thereof, in any form.

Cover art by Wes Lowe

A Tor book
Published by Tom Doherty Associates, Inc.
175 Fifth Avenue
New York, N.Y. 10010

Tor® is a registered trademark of Tom Doherty Associates, Inc.

ISBN: 0-812-52400-4
Library of Congress Catalog Card Number 94-12923

First edition: September 1994
First mass market edition: July 1995

Printed in the United States of America

0 9 8 7 6 5 4 3 2 1

For my parents, Dora and Rogelio A. Pineiro.
Thanks for your guidance, your patience,
and your love. Thanks for the memories.
Although I've never been good at saying it
or showing it, I do love you both.

AND

In loving memory of Dr. Manuel Valle,
uncle, friend.

ACKNOWLEDGMENTS

I am especially indebted to my wife, Lory, for her eternal patience and encouragement during the writing and rewriting of this novel. I am indeed very lucky to have married such a naturally beautiful, supportive, and compassionate woman.

Thanks go to my twin sisters, Irene and Dora. Looking back at those wonderful years growing up together is always a source of inspiration.

Speaking of sources of inspiration, none beats the sparkle in my son Cameron's brown eyes. Thanks, Cam. Your daddy loves you very much.

For his assistance and valuable feedback during the early stages of writing the manuscript, I thank Gary Muschla.

I would like to thank Lt. Kate Muller from the U.S. Navy Public Affairs Office at the Pentagon for her help coordinating part of the technical assistance on this project.

Special thanks go to my technical consultants, all of whom spent a great deal of their own time reviewing the manuscript and making helpful suggestions. They are:

Lt. Comdr. Dave Parsons, U.S. Navy F-14A Tomcat Radar Intercept Officer (RIO), who flew with squadron VF-32 "Swordsmen," aboard USS *John F. Kennedy* (CV-67) during the Gulf War. In addition to his flying background, Commander Parsons is the author of a number of nonfiction military books, and he was the editor of *Approach,* the naval aviation safety review magazine.

Lt. Robert Lamanna, U.S. Navy Aeromedical and Aviation Safety Officer, stationed with Marine Aircraft Group 11, Third Marine Air Wing, in Bahrain during the Gulf War. Lieutenant Lammana was in charge of survival training, survival equipment, and aircrew defense systems, among other responsibilities. He is currently the Aeromedical Safety Officer with Commander Fighter Wing One at NAS Oceana, Virginia.

Dennis Jenkins, military aviation writer and space shuttle engineer. Mr. Jenkins has written books on the F-15, F-14, B-52, EA-6A, and the Space Shuttle, among others.

My friend Dave, who flew A-37s and F-5s as a civilian employee of the U.S. government in counterinsurgency operations in Southeast Asia during the Vietnam era.

To all four, I give my deepest gratitude for improving the technical accuracy of the story. Any errors that remain, of course, are my own.

As a Catholic, I was taught that the saint of the impossible is St. Jude (Catholics have saints for just about every occasion). Since getting published is next to impossible, I decided to pray to him a while back. I guess my prayers continue to be answered. Thank you, St. Jude.

Special thanks go to Matt Bialer, my gifted agent at William Morris, for his assistance, support, and guidance on this and other projects.

I would also like to thank Andy Zack for his thorough editorial assistance during the revision process. Thanks to his accurate feedback, clear direction, and helpful suggestions, *Ultimatum* is a better story. It is always a pleasure to work with such a pro.

Finally, I want to thank the staff at Forge Books, particularly Anna Magee and Camille Cline. Very special thanks go to Robert Gleason, former Editor-in-Chief of Tor and Forge Books, for giving me the opportunity to become published and also for pushing me to hammer out the best possible story I could.

R.J. Pineiro
Austin, Texas, 1994

We will not act prematurely or unnecessarily risk the cost of nuclear war in which even the fruits of victory would be ashes in our mouth. But neither will we shrink from that risk at any time it must be faced.

— *John F. Kennedy*

We have genuflected before the god of science only to find that it has given us the atomic bomb, producing fears and anxieties that science can never mitigate.

— *Martin Luther King, Jr.*

PROLOGUE

CRACOW, POLAND.

Wearing a dark blue overcoat over a long-sleeved shirt and blue jeans, CIA Case Officer Donald Bane slowly studied Pijarska Street, running south from the edge of *Planty,* the park ringing Cracow's old city. The park had long replaced the old walls of the town, which had been torn down in the middle of the nineteenth century. Two blocks up Pijarska stood St. Florian's Gate, which led to the old town. Next to it was the impressive Barbican, a large fifteenth-century fortress that had guarded the gate back in those days.

The crystalline, star-filled sky of just an hour ago had given way to gray clouds, which brought with them thunder and the high winds that swirled Bane's thin brown hair. Four short bugle calls from the Church of the Virgin Mary three blocks away mixed with the thunder, creating a somewhat sinister sound. Bane was glad when the hourly calls from the Gothic church stopped and he could hear only the natural sounds of the storm.

Pulling up the lapels of his coat, Bane took two steps back into the shadow of a tree by the edge of the park before placing his left hand in the coat's side pocket. His fingers curled around the stainless-steel handle of a Smith & Wesson Model 659 automatic pistol. He hoped he would not have to use it on this cool and windy night, but twenty years with the FBI prior to his current job with Central Intelligence had taught him the value of being cautious.

At six feet two and 230 pounds, Bane was a large man with a shiny square face and a broad nose. A pair of thick brows crowned Bane's alert blue eyes. His full lips and strong chin gave him the rugged appearance of a prize-fighter.

He spotted the headlights of an approaching car as the wind began to mix with a light drizzle. The vehicle made its way over the pothole-filled Pijarska, casting a yellowish glow over the four-lane street. Bane pressed his body against the tree trunk as the automobile—an old Skoda—slowed down as it approached his position. The CIA officer heard the strong bass of rock music coming through the Skoda's open windows and spotted four kids inside the vehicle.

He relaxed. Waiting for one of his agents had never pleased Bane because he felt too exposed, but as a senior case officer working for the European Division within the Directorate of Operations, Donald Bane's main job was that of recruiting agents in Kiev to spy for the CIA. Normally, Bane would have held this meeting in the Ukrainian capital, but his agent, General Vasili Krasilov, had contacted him a week earlier about a serious problem—too sensitive to be discussed over the phone —at one of the army warehouses outside L'vov, where the Ukrainian government stored key components of disassembled nuclear warheads prior to their disposal in radiation-proof containers. The general, however, had been reluctant to meet in Kiev. Because of the incident at the warehouse, Ukrainian intelligence had many high-ranking army officers under constant surveillance. Luckily, the Ukrainian air force was scheduled to participate in formation flight demonstrations at an air show in Cracow this week, and General Krasilov was among the staff escorting the pilots. It was the perfect opportunity for a clandestine meeting, and Bane had flown in from Kiev this morning.

The Skoda continued to the end of the block, where the driver turned left. Quiet returned, to be interrupted seconds later by thunder. The light drizzle gained strength, slowly turning into a downpour, and a fork of lightning streaked across the sky. Krasilov was late, very late. Bane checked his watch again.

Where in the hell is he? Did something go wrong? he thought while rubbing a hand over his coat to check a stack of one-hundred-dollar bills tucked in an inside pocket. The money was the prearranged price for Krasilov's information, assuming Bane thought it valuable enough to dish out five thousand dollars from the Kiev station's budget. Contrary to popular belief, CIA operations officers worked under very tight budgets and had to account for every penny spent to pay off agents.

Thunder came as the rain began to drip down Bane's forehead and into his eyes. He rubbed them and blinked several times to readjust his vision. The collar of the cotton shirt he wore underneath was already soaked. As he raised his hands to pull the coat's lapels even closer to his neck, he felt someone tap him on the shoulder.

Startled, Bane quickly pulled out the Smith & Wesson as he pivoted on his right foot while dropping to a deep crouch and bringing the weapon up and around. His index finger was fixed on the trigger, the tall and slim silhouette in front of him lined up between the fixed rear sight and the adjustable forward sight.

He stopped and lowered the pistol.

In front of him stood General Vasili Krasilov, wearing a dark gray raincoat. His soaked black hair stuck to the sides of his long, pale face, a few strands falling over his narrow forehead. His eyes, fixed on Bane, were as dark as the sky. His nose was as long and thin as his lips.

"You're late," Bane said, straightening up and shoving the pistol back into his coat pocket.

Eyes frightened and bulging, Krasilov scanned both sides of the street before saying with a heavy Slavic accent, "You brought the money. Yes?"

"Follow me. We're too exposed here," Bane said

before turning around and disappearing behind one of thousands of trees in the *Planty*. The stench of urine filled his nostrils. It was mixed with the repulsive odor rising off a pile of garbage to his left. A recent local strike had disrupted some of the city's public services. Since his arrival in Cracow, Bane had seen piles of garbage everywhere.

Briefly holding his breath, Bane pulled out his gun and warily inspected the trees around him. He continued walking into the park until he reached the edge of the parking lot on the other side, where a dark Fiat was parked by the treeline. Bane pointed to the vehicle.

"Is safe there? Yes?" Krasilov asked.

"This side of the park's been sanitized. We're okay," Bane responded.

Still a bit reluctant, the Ukrainian general peered out from the edge of the forest and scanned the deserted parking lot for several seconds before moving. A minute later, they sat on the Fiat's front seats, where Bane turned a knob on the dashboard. The tint on the windows abruptly changed to a much darker shade. Bane then flipped a switch under the dashboard and was rewarded with a light humming noise. All the windows of the small Fiat now vibrated at a high frequency, masking the vibrations induced by any conversation inside the car. This last measure would prevent anyone with a laser audio surveillance device from reading the vibrations off the glass and translating them to a meaningful voice pattern.

Krasilov gave Bane a puzzled look.

"Well? You said it was important," Bane said as the rain subsided to a light drizzle.

"The money?"

"You'll get it *after* the information. Those are the rules. Now, out with it. We don't have much time."

Krasilov reached into his coat and handed Bane a stack of documents in a green manila folder.

For the next five minutes, Bane reviewed the papers in silence. They were mostly copies of records from the warehouse in L'vov showing inventory levels of nuclear weapons components scheduled for destruction. His eyes scanned through the long list of stored items, paying close attention to the ones he recognized right away: plutonium cores, neutron initiators, hollow spheres of high explosive plastic. The classic ingredients of an atomic bomb.

"This shows a steady reduction of inventory, just as it should," Bane said.

Krasilov rubbed his hands before saying, "But you see, that is the problem. Yes?"

Bane looked at the old general. "But that's the purpose of this place, right? To get rid of the stuff."

"That is correct. Yes. The problem is the destruction of the components was put on hold a year ago."

Bane shifted his gaze back to the documents on his lap, quickly scanning the dates on the forms. "But . . . but these dates are from just *eight* months ago, and they show that the level of inventory has dropped significantly. What happened to the nuclear components?"

Krasilov shook his head. "They have disappeared."

"Disappeared? Where? Who's got them?"

The Ukrainian general spoke a single word: "Iraq."

Donald Bane closed his eyes. *God Almighty.*

RULES OF ENGAGEMENT

All they that take the sword shall perish with the sword.
—Matthew, 26:52

USS *RANGER*, EIGHTY MILES NORTH OF BAHRAIN, PERSIAN GULF.
Day One. 0800 Local Time.

The catapult officer held up two fingers and rotated his hand clockwise. Lieutenant Kevin "Crackers" Dalton responded by pushing both throttles to the mechanical stops. His Grumman F-14A Tomcat trembled as both Pratt & Whitney turbofans unleashed forty thousand pounds of thrust against the jet blast deflectors of number one catapult.

Watching the cat officer's hand signals, Kevin placed his flight controls in the prescribed catapult position: flaps down, control stick pulled back, and variable-sweep wings in the fully forward position. The cat officer, a tall, thin black man wearing sun goggles, the standard yellow jersey, and mandatory ear protectors, moved his head from side to side, carefully making sure his area of responsibility was clear, before glancing at the signal light on the carrier's island and verifying that it was still yellow. Then he stared at Kevin.

Although Kevin was relatively new to the ceremony, he played his part like a pro, bringing his right hand up and touching his index and middle fingers against his helmet. The cat officer gave him a jaunty salute before extending his right arm toward Kevin's Tomcat, hand flat. Kevin responded by applying afterburners.

The cat officer, with the natural rhythm of a ballet dancer, bent down and softly touched the armored deck with his right hand. At the catapult control panel on the edge of the flight deck, the operator extended both arms up in the air.

"All set?" Kevin asked his RIO over the intercom system, the ICS.

"Sure thing, Crackers," responded Kevin's Radar Intercept Officer, Lieutenant Ricardo "Chico" Delgado, sitting directly behind Kevin in the dual cabin of the thirty-ton plane. "Looks like another beautiful day in the neighborhood," Delgado said.

Kevin smiled. In the three short months since he had been paired to fly with Delgado, Kevin had already grown to like the short and slim East L.A. native, who at twenty-five years of age had already seen more than any man's fair share of death in the streets of that volatile section of Los Angeles. Still, Delgado, like most naval aviators and flight officers, had managed to keep a sense of humor that Kevin considered necessary while flying a multimillion-dollar aircraft in hostile territory. That attitude helped Kevin endure the sorties he had flown patrolling the waters of the Gulf, as well as the skies over Kuwait and northern Saudi Arabia, and Iraqi airspace south of the thirty-second parallel—the region called the no-fly zone. Although he had encountered no resistance, Kevin knew he should not get overconfident. He had to continue to fly under the assumption that the Iraqis were as treacherous as his superiors had described them since his arrival at the carrier six months before. The Clinton administration had ordered not only a larger naval force to protect the region from Saddam Hussein's reenergized forces, but also deployed squadrons of F-15 Eagles, F-117A Stealth fighters, AH-64 Apache helicopters, and A-10 Warthog "tank-killers," along with supporting tankers, AWACS, and rescue helicopters. In addition, the American president had sent 45,000 troops and two hundred tanks to the region, deploying them along the northern border of Kuwait and Saudi Arabia. Britain, Italy, and France also had forces in the region.

After a brief glance at the thumbs-up from the bow safety observer, and a final visual check on the fighter, the cat officer, still in a semi-crouch, thrust his torso, arm and hand toward the carrier's bow. Kevin's smile faded away as he leaned his head forward and visualized the cat operator striking the palm-size launch button.

One potato, two potato, yahoo!

The g-forces grew rapidly from the pull of the shuttle connecting his craft's nose strut to the catapult piston, which was driven by a colossal volume of highly pressurized steam stored in a tank under the flight deck. Kevin's vision momentarily narrowed. Most of his blood sank to the back of his body, and his limbs tingled from the sudden lack of circulation.

As the pressure subsided at the end of the catapult stroke, Kevin scanned his instruments, keeping rearward pressure on the control stick and slapping the gear handle up. Only then did he indulge himself in a quick backward glance at the ship. The USS *Ranger* (CV-61) already appeared small against the clear blue waters of the Gulf. The carrier's peaceful wake extended for miles.

While executing a clearing turn to the right to avoid a conflict with the *Ranger*'s air traffic, Kevin kept the nose at an eight-degree angle over the horizon and slowly watched his airspeed increase . . . 210 knots . . . 220 knots. He raised the flaps at 225 knots, adjusted throttle, and increased his angle of climb to twenty degrees.

He leveled off at ten thousand feet and a comfortable 230 knots, bringing the nose of his Tomcat twenty feet below and to the right of his flight leader, Commander DeWayne "Shadow" Lancaster, who also happened to be the Executive Officer (XO) of Kevin's squadron, Wolfpack, one of two F-14A squadrons aboard the *Ranger*.

Lancaster had been Kevin's flight instructor for most of his stay at Naval Air Station Miramar, where Kevin had learned to fly the Tomcat. Upon graduation, Kevin had been ordered to the *Ranger,* where he had learned that Lancaster had also been ordered. That had been a pleasant surprise to Kevin, who regarded Lancaster as a solid pilot, a fair instructor, and a friend. From fellow classmates at Miramar, Kevin had learned early on about Lancaster's reputation. A poor black, he had survived both the South Bronx and the Navy's rigorous aviator training to become a top-notch pilot.

Kevin shook those thoughts away and followed Lancaster's Tomcat at "max conserve" speed—230 knots during nonthreatening situations—for maximum conservation of fuel. For the next thirty minutes, the pair of Tomcats flew north. Their mission, as defined by the day's Air Tasking Order, was to fly Combat Air Patrol (CAP) twenty miles north of the battleship USS *Wisconsin* (BB-64), which, during Operation Desert Storm, had pounded Iraq with 16-inch shells and dozens of Tomahawk missiles. The *Wisconsin* had been called back to the area six months ago, when Iraq, in addition to restricting the access of a United Nations inspection team, began deployment of SA-2 and SA-3 surface-to-air missiles in the southern no-fly zone.

ATO mission plans, similar to those used during Desert Storm, were generated daily by U.S. Central Command Air Forces (CENTAF) in Riyadh. Today's ATO had arrived at the *Ranger* the night before, as usual, providing air crews and support sections the time needed to make all necessary mission preparations. But unlike the ATOs of Operation Desert Storm—which included targets, the aircraft assigned to each target, the time each plane would take off, the time to attack each target, and the ordnance to be used during the attack—the current ATOs were mostly CAPs.

Following Lancaster's lead, Kevin gently inched the control stick forward and to the left while applying left rudder to execute a coordinated dive turn. He kept his eyes trained on Lancaster's plane, which softly grazed the edge of a cloud. The *Wisconsin* loomed over the horizon. Kevin waited for Lancaster's RIO, Lieutenant Gary "Baby" Johnson, to make radio contact with the USS *Bunker Hill* (CG-52), one of two guided-missile cruisers escorting the *Wisconsin*. While flying wingman, Kevin was required to keep radio chatter outside the squadron frequency to a minimum and let the lead RIO do most of the talking.

"Red Crown, Wolfpack Two Zero Two, over," Kevin heard Baby Johnson say over the radio. Red Crown was the call sign assigned to the *Bunker Hill* that particular day by the ATO, which also dictated the call signs of all aircraft in the region, except for those flying Combat Air Patrol. For planes flying CAP, the call sign was the combination of the squadron's name and the plane's side number.

"Two Zero Two, Red Crown, go ahead."

"Two Zero Two, checking in with Two One Four," responded Johnson, confirming his mission to the cruiser and also relaying Kevin's plane's call sign.

"Zero Two," came the reply from the *Bunker Hill,* which followed the standard procedure of only using the plane's last two digits after establishing communication.

Still following Lancaster's lead, Kevin held his Tomcat at max conserve and settled into a racetrack pattern. According to the ATO, he and Lancaster would remain in the region for the next two hours.

AMAN BAKISH AIR BASE NEAR AN NAJAF, SOUTHERN IRAQ.
Day One. 0845 Local Time.

Colonel Abunnasr Manesh taxied his Mikoyan-Gurevich-23, NATO code name "Flogger," air superiority fighter, out of the camouflaged shelter and onto the single paved runway of the dusty airfield, and waited for three other MiGs from his flight unit to position themselves behind him in an inverted "V" formation. Shimmering waves of heat rose from the blistering tarmac beneath the craft.

Manesh frowned, still disappointed with the flight crew that hadn't been able to finish the repairs on his MiG-29 in time for today's mission, forcing him to fly the sluggish Flogger. In actuality, Manesh knew that the MiG-23 was not a slow plane, but compared to the modern MiG-29, the old Flogger fell short in maneuverability—a basic need for modern-day dogfight survival.

He frowned again, more disappointed in his government, which had ordered him to lead this flight in and out of the no-fly zone in defiance of U.N. resolutions. Manesh felt they should be using the high-performance fighters to stop the intruders from controlling sections of their homeland. But at least there were men like his superior, General Qazi Ali, who never hesitated to speak up when the orders from Baghdad did not make sense. The very popular General Ali was one of very few men in Iraq with enough clout to protest orders that would put Iraqi fighting men in unnecessary danger, such as the recent deployment of forces south of the thirty-second parallel, or the flight Manesh was about to begin. But insane or not, Saddam's orders were the laws of the land, and upset as he was, Manesh knew how to follow them. General Ali, however, had taken the matter a step further this time, not only protesting the senseless orders, but flying to Baghdad to discuss the matter with Saddam personally.

"Preflight check," Manesh spoke into the voice-activated microphone attached to his helmet as he stepped on the brakes and applied three-fourths throttle. A second later, Manesh could hear the intimidating sound of four Tumanskii R-29B afterburning turbofans accelerating in unison. He moved his control stick to the right and left and checked that the ailerons at the end of the swing wings responded to his commands. Satisfied, he scanned the engine gauges one last time and reduced power.

"We are the selected ones, my brothers! The blasphemous West shall not stop us from flying over our own land!"

"Inshallah!" was the unanimous response from the pilots of the other Floggers.

Colonel Manesh lowered the flaps and applied full throttle, still keeping his feet against the brake pedals. The MiG trembled under conflicting commands. His sweaty palm fought to maintain a solid grip on the control stick as he waited for a few more seconds while he eyed the short runway.

Suddenly, Manesh let go of the brakes; the craft jerked forward and sped down the runway under the scorching midmorning sun. His eyes were fixed on his airspeed indicator. *Just a few more knots . . .* he thought, inching back the control stick when the needle darted past 150 knots. The Flogger gracefully left the ground but did not climb far. As soon as Manesh was airborne, he retracted the gear and lowered the nose, almost instantly feeling the pressure of the seat against his back when the sudden loss of drag allowed the craft to reach three hundred knots in a few more seconds. Manesh kept the MiG below one hundred feet and glanced backward. The squadron would remain low and slow to avoid radar detection.

Manesh thanked Allah, certain that the true Islamic spirit was with him and his beloved Iraq, not with the barbarous Americans who had so mercilessly murdered his parents during Operation Desert Storm in an air raid on the Iraqi city of Abadan. During the first night of that dreaded war, when his government had allowed him to fight back, Manesh and several other MiG pilots had engaged the invaders by the Saudi border. In less than five minutes, the sky had filled with enemy planes. Manesh had been the only one to make it back to the aircraft shelter, buried under several feet of sand and reinforced concrete and, in theory, impenetrable. Iraq had invested billions in the construction of nearly five hundred hardened aircraft shelters. The craft were protected. At least, that was Baghdad's original assessment. A day later, when an American fighter dropped a laser-guided bomb through a shelter's ventilation shaft at Talil Air Base, destroying every fighter inside, Baghdad changed its plans and ordered MiGs to Iran.

Iran. Bastards! thought Manesh. The Iranians were responsible for killing his wife and newborn a decade before, during Iraq's eight-year-long struggle with its neighbor. The Iranians leveled his village while the Americans watched from the safety of their destroyers. Just a few of those fancy American surface-to-air missiles and the Iranians would have had to pull back. But it didn't happen that way. Manesh had found his family a day later, buried under the four feet of rubble that had been their home. He mourned them for weeks, until slowly his grief turned into hate—hate for those who had so brutally taken his family away from him. They were all guilty in his mind: the Iranians for pulling the trigger, and the Westerners for not doing anything about it. It was then that Colonel Abunnasr Manesh led the retaliatory air strike against the Iranian city of Khorramshahr, meaning "the city of greenness and happiness." Within a single month, Manesh had dropped enough explosives on the oil-rich city that his government renamed it Khuninshahr . . . "the city of blood."

With his mind still in the past, Manesh remained below one hundred feet as he flew over the Euphrates and approached the swamplands surrounding the Shatt al Arab waterway, deep in the no-fly zone.

"Wolfpack Two Zero Two, Cougar," Lieutenant Kevin Dalton heard the crew from an Airborne Warning and Control System (AWACS)—a modified Boeing 707 fitted with an overfuselage radome almost thirty feet in diameter—transmitting over the control frequency to get the Tomcats' attention. AWACS, which did not use numbers in their call signs, housed state-of-the-art computers, radars, and communication equipment to monitor and control air activity in a three-hundred-mile radius. Dividing the country into three sectors—east, central, and west—AWACS had the entire Iraqi airspace wired. Round-the-clock AWACS crews electronically interrogated every aircraft within their range. If the code in the interrogated aircraft's Identification Friendly or Foe (IFF) system didn't match any of the day's ATO-supplied codes, the craft would be tagged as hostile and its coordinates passed to the nearest Allied interceptor squadron.

"Cougar, Two Zero Two," Lieutenant Baby Johnson responded over the radio.

"Four bandits. Your vector's three four zero for one five zero, buster," the AWACS crew said, providing Lancaster and Kevin not only with the enemy's position with respect to the *Wisconsin,* but also using the term "bust-

er," which told them to intercept as fast as possible without afterburners.

"Got them!" confirmed Lieutenant Chico Delgado over the ICS.

"Phoenix selected," said Kevin, arming one of the Hughes AIM-54A Phoenix long-range air-to-air missiles his Tomcat carried under the fuselage.

"Three four zero, one fifty miles, one hundred feet at three hundred knots, headin' zero niner zero," Delgado responded, providing the bearing, range, altitude, speed, and heading (BRASH) of the enemy in precisely that order.

"Breaking four bandits heading one six zero," said Baby Johnson.

"Same," responded Delgado.

Kevin followed his lead as the pair of Tomcats accelerated to six hundred knots. Delgado had already activated the Tomcat's pulse-Doppler search and tracking radar system. The complex computer was directly in control of the four Phoenix missiles mounted on pallets under the aircraft's belly. The system was designed to simultaneously track up to twenty-four targets.

Kevin smelled Iraqi meat. He felt the adrenaline flood his system as the possibility of combat neared. He hadn't seen any real action yet, having flown only uneventful escort missions so far. The untamed pilot in Kevin longed for combat, but his logical side told him that he was still a rookie learning the ropes. With his heartbeat rocketing, Kevin followed Lancaster, adding more throttle and putting his craft into a shallow dive toward the coast. The F-14A accelerated through the sound barrier with minimal disturbance. The central air data computer, the onboard electronics system that controlled the wing's angle of sweep, automatically moved the wings aft, bringing them to the fully swept position of sixty-eight degrees as Kevin read Mach 1.2 on his control instrument panel.

"Talk to me, Chico," said Kevin over the ICS.

"Bandits now three four five, ninety miles, heading three three zero. They're turning around."

"Damn."

Leaving the waters of the Gulf behind, the F-14As streaked through clear skies at Mach 1.4 and flew an intercept vector while descending to one thousand feet. The pilots flew a toboggan letdown, which "unloaded" the aircraft and allowed it to accelerate more rapidly without increasing fuel consumption.

"Bandits now in two sections! They must have detected us on their warning gear," said Delgado as he watched the symbols on his screen abruptly change course. "One section to three three one, the other to zero one zero."

"How long before they leave the zone?" asked Kevin.

"In seconds . . . going single target track on the lead!"

The Tomcats zeroed in on the two MiGs that had turned to heading zero one zero.

Colonel Manesh's tail warning aerial went off. The alarm told him that he had at least one F-14 locked on his craft but that it had not yet fired, otherwise the Electronic Counter Measures alarms would have been blaring inside the cockpit. With his wingman glued to his right, Manesh pushed the throttles to the forward stops and the Flogger accelerated to Mach 1.1. His wingman remained with him.

Under his oxygen mask, Colonel Manesh smiled broadly as his plane crossed north of the thirty-second parallel.

"Two Zero Two, Red Crown. Knock-it-off. Repeat, knock-it-off. Approaching Waterloo Red," Kevin heard the voice from the *Bunker Hill* crackling through his headset, ordering them to turn around as they got dangerously close to the thirty-second parallel.

Kevin couldn't believe it. Just a few more seconds and he would have had them. *Damn!*

"Two Zero Two, resetting," Kevin heard Baby Johnson respond as Lancaster broke off the attack.

Following Shadow Lancaster, Kevin eased the control column to the right while executing a steep climb to six thousand feet. The Tomcats leveled off and continued on a southerly heading.

"Better luck next time," Kevin said over the intercom.

"Mierda! Someone's got a radar lock on us!" snapped Delgado.

Delgado hadn't finished speaking when alarms went off inside Kevin's cockpit.

"Dios mio! We got two Floggers at our six! The other MiGs must have turned around!"

Wh—what? Instinctively, Kevin applied full throttle and put his craft into a vertical climb.

"Dammit! All Floggers turned around. We got four bandits!" fumed Lieutenant Baby Johnson from the backseat of Lancaster's Tomcat over the squadron frequency.

Kevin started dispensing chaff in anticipation of enemy missiles. Spotting the wispy contrails of two missiles closing in fast, Kevin cut left as Lancaster continued after the first two MiGs.

"Chaff doing any good?" asked Kevin.

"You beat one! The second one's still on us!"

Kevin continued the turn, but the missile stayed on him. He threw the stick forward and pointed the nose straight down toward the desert. His airspeed shot above 450 knots. The desert sands filled his windscreen. He knew he had one last move before impact and he made it, simultaneously pumping more chaff and pulling the control stick back hard as the altimeter reading rushed below two hundred feet. With the warning gear blaring crazily, the wings—covered with vapor—automatically swung forward as speed bled off, increasing the craft's lift. But even with the loss of airspeed, over seven g's blasted against the craft's Titanium-layered air surfaces. The F-14's G sensor, detecting the monumental pressure hammering the craft and crew, rushed compressed air through the hose connected to Kevin's G suit—a pair of zippered pants with air bladders around his waist, thighs, and calves—forcing blood back up to his head to keep him from losing consciousness.

The Tomcat vibrated to the point of near disintegration under the ferocious pressure, which pounded Kevin into his ejection seat. Feeling seven times heavier than normal, and with his vision reduced to the information painted on the Heads-up Display, Kevin kept up the pull on the center stick. Slowly, the pressure subsided as Kevin silently thanked the Grumman engineers who had designed his F-14. He grinned triumphantly as the nose rose over the horizon.

The missile, lacking such maneuverability, spit out of the turn and plunged into the sand with a bright explosion.

Kevin took a deep breath as the G-suit deflated. "Where's the Floggers?"

"Tally four bogeys. Bastards turned around. Two at two o'clock, high, on Shadow. Two at our eight, high, watching us."

Finding it nearly impossible to believe that the Iraqi planes had actually turned around, sneaked up on him, and fired their missiles, Kevin turned into the threat, switching to Sidewinders, and hurtled after the MiGs while Lancaster went vertical, pumping chaff and flares.

"I'm at your seven, low, Shadow, engaged."

"Roger, I'm a little busy," responded Lancaster.

Kevin swung the control column to the left and back, positioning himself behind the MiGs threatening Lancaster, who cut a tight left turn. The Iraqis simultaneously broke formation, one to the right, the other to the left. Kevin stayed on the left one to protect his lead and smoothly advanced the throttles to military power.

"They're gonna try to sandwich us!" warned Delgado over the ICS.

"I won't give them the chance!" Kevin pushed full throttle and felt the turbofans' afterburners punching him in the back as the Tomcat gathered speed and quickly closed the gap. Kevin selected a radar mode that would yield an automatic lock. He was rewarded with a white diamond on the Heads-up Display directly in front of his line of sight, signaling a radar lock on the Flogger.

The Flogger went into a steep climbing turn after Lancaster. The MiG's burner was wide open as the craft rolled and dove, but Kevin easily stayed with it, adjusting the throttle setting while rolling his craft on its back and dropping on the MiG like a hawk. The maneuverability of his Tomcat was far superior to that of the MiG-23, whose sweep wings were not automatic—a liability in a dogfight. The MiG's white-hot tailpipe screamed for a Sidewinder. As the desert and sky swapped places, Kevin frowned under his oxygen mask. His headphones rattled with the buzzing tone of a Sidewinder infrared track. The range to the MiG, however, was only a few hundred feet.

"Damn! Too close for missiles! Switching to guns!"

Kevin put the pipper on the MiG and pulled the trigger. The General Electric 20mm multibarrel Vulcan cannon came to life. Kevin kept an eye on the digital counter painted on the HUD. The gun came with 670 rounds, but firing at a rate of one thousand rounds per minute gave him less than forty seconds of firing time. To avoid using up the ammo too fast, he squeezed off two short bursts while he adjusted the pipper on the HUD. As a river of shells ripped across the MiG's left wing, the Iraqi fighter broke its attack on Lancaster, briefly leveled off, and pulled up into a vertical corkscrew, ruining Kevin's angle.

As Lancaster went after the other MiGs, Kevin jammed the throttles to the forward stops and pulled back on the stick, trying to stay with his target. The g's hammered him once again. The G counter reached 6.8 as his G suit inflated again. With his vision tunneling, Kevin followed the Flogger up to twenty thousand feet. His index finger caressed the trigger of the Vulcan, but before he got a chance to line up the craft, the MiG rolled its wings and dropped back down. Kevin remained glued to its tail. Another turn and a climb, and he regained the angle. With the MiG's tail filling his windscreen, he fired.

The Flogger's turbofan spewed fire and smoke as the 20mm rounds penetrated the fuselage. Without power, the MiG entered a flat spin. Without an engine, Kevin knew the Iraqi pilot would not be able to recover.

"Good shootin'! His buddy's eight, low, hose away," Delgado said.

"Got him!"

Kevin saw the wingman in his rearview mirror and grinned. With the burners still wide open, Kevin put the Tomcat in a vertical oblique climbing turn, allowing Kevin to turn inside the MiG's turning circle. The MiG turned north at full speed. Once again, the monumental pressure resulted in the temporary loss of peripheral vision as Kevin sank deep into his seat. Struggling against five g's, Kevin double-checked his selection of a Sidewinder. As the radar locked, the Sidewinder seeker head slaved to the target and began its buzzing. The F-14 saddled in behind the MiG at almost a thousand feet over the desert.

"Good lock, shoot, shoot . . . oh, shit, Waterloo Red, Crackers! The bandit's Waterloo Red. Knock-it-off!" said Delgado, realizing that the MiG had just reached the thirty-second parallel.

Kevin released a Sidewinder before breaking hard right. The missile's MK36 solid-propellant rocket motor came alive, thrusting the 180-pound missile to Mach 3.

"Tracking . . . it's tracking!"

The Sidewinder's infrared tracking system homed into the sizzling-hot exhaust of the MiG-23. Kevin watched the Flogger go for a dive while it released infrared flares, but the missile was too close to be fooled. Twenty-five pounds of high explosives with preformed rods blasted the tail section of the Flogger as the canopy blew upward, followed by the pilot on a rocket-propelled ejection seat. Kevin watched a bright red parachute open to his left and pulled the throttle aft to sixty percent.

Commander Shadow Lancaster had the advantage on the remaining two MiGs, still caught below the thirty-second parallel.

"Fire one!"

The Phoenix missile disengaged itself from the pallet and remained suspended in midair a few feet under the Tomcat's belly for a second before the solid-propellant rocket kicked in and accelerated the missile toward the right Flogger. Since it was less than a mile away, the Phoenix automatically switched off from the Tomcat's pulse-Doppler system to its own active radar, homing in on the MiG at an incredible Mach 3.8. In less than five seconds, the missile's high-explosive warhead reached the Flogger.

Colonel Manesh's ECM had started beeping seconds ago. He instinctively cut sharp left. As he did so, he saw a ball of fire to his right. His wingman's craft had just disintegrated. He turned north and applied full throttle.

Manesh frowned, realizing that it had not been Allah's wish to destroy the American fighters. He crossed north of the thirty-second parallel a few seconds later.

"Two Zero Two, Red Crown. Say status," Kevin heard the voice from the *Bunker Hill* cruiser say.

"Two Zero Two, Two One Four, up and up, requesting victory break," responded Lieutenant Baby Johnson.

"Zero Two."

"Shadow, why'd you let the last MiG go?" asked Kevin on the squadron discrete frequency.

"It reached Iraqi neutral airspace before I could get him. By the way, nice job, Crackers. Two Floggers with heaters and the gun? Who'd you say was your instructor?"

Kevin smiled as he brought his Tomcat below and slightly behind and to the right of Lancaster's in order to perform a visual inspection of his leader's craft. "I learned how in the movies. You know . . . *Top Gun?"*

Kevin heard laughter over the squadron channel. "You're clean and dry, Shadow," said Kevin, finding no damage or leaks on Lancaster's F-14.

Kevin noticed Lancaster now inspecting his craft. A few moments later Lancaster said, "Crackers, you're clean and dry too."

"How about some gas?" said Kevin.

"Sounds good."

"Red Crown, Two Zero Two, vector to Texaco," said Baby Johnson.

"Zero Two, Texaco en route, vector one six zero."

"Zero Two."

* * *

Forty minutes later, after refueling from a KA-6D, an A-6 Intruder modified as a flying gas station, Lieutenant Dalton approached the *Ranger* on the upwind leg at eight hundred feet with the wings fully swept back and doing almost 550 knots. The moment the nose of his craft reached a point three hundred feet to the right of the carrier's stern, Kevin executed the first of two victory rolls, one per kill. He finished the first as he flew next to the carrier's island, and rolled out of the second by the time he flew past the *Ranger*'s bow, where he leveled off, applied the air brakes, and cut back power to bleed some airspeed.

The wings swept to the fully forward position while he turned in front of the carrier and entered the downwind leg, maintaining eight hundred feet. The *Ranger* was now to his left. He lowered flaps and gear: airspeed 132 knots. He waited until the carrier was a third of a mile behind him before making a wide one-eighty turn. Unlike airport traffic patterns, carrier patterns did not have a base leg. Kevin rolled out of the turn on final with the *Ranger*'s stern lined up with the nose of his craft.

Kevin aimed his Tomcat at the third of four specially woven and hardened arresting wires stretched across the landing area forward of the carrier's stern. He had already lowered the tailhook shortly after refueling. He pulled the throttle aft to seventy-five percent power, keeping his airspeed just under 130 knots.

"MiG Killer, call the ball," came the voice from the duty Landing Signal Officer, who usually remained silent during daylight approaches unless there was trouble or a special occasion.

"Roger," responded Kevin with a smile.

"MiG Killer, all down, clear deck. Clear deck. Quarter-mile," said the duty LSO, confirming that the Tomcat's landing gear and tailhook were down. This was also unnecessary radio chatter during daylight landings, but Kevin figured that they were probably recording the event on tape for posterity.

"Roger. Quarter-mile," he responded, playing along.

At the LSO platform, the duty LSO not only graded Kevin's approach but also had the power to signal him to wave-it-off, or abort his approach if he spotted trouble. Additionally, there were a half-dozen men either listening to the radio or relaying information to other sections of the ship. Kevin knew from his NAS Pensacola training days that he was dropping fast, but as long as he kept the lighted orange ball centered in the landing mirror of the *Ranger*'s deck edge, he was certain his approach was safe.

"Two One Four, Tomcat ball, five point six," Kevin said over the radio as he kept the Tomcat's nose aligned with the carrier's stern, also informing the LSO that he had 5,600 pounds of fuel left. Kevin's eyes shifted between the ball, the carrier's centerline, the landing area, and a quick glance at the indicated airspeed.

"Roger ball, MiG Killer," the LSO responded.

The F-14A cleared the deck by sixteen feet three seconds before Kevin slammed the craft down in a "controlled crash." As the landing gear hit the deck with the force of nearly seventy tons, Kevin threw his throttle forward to full power in case his tailhook had missed the wire. The strong hook snatched arresting wire number three. Its ends were connected to a greasy inch-and-a-half-diameter cable secured to large grooved pulley wheels, which were jerked in rotation and exploded in a cloud of oil mist as the massive arresting mechanism stopped the heavy craft, traveling at 120 knots, in under two seconds.

Kevin felt the seat's harness digging into his shoulders as the craft came to an abrupt halt a hundred feet from the forward edge of the *Ranger*'s deck. He idled the turbines at the command of the yellow-shirted director, who was running across the deck with both hands up in the air.

"OK, MiG Killer," the duty LSO said over the radio, telling Kevin that he had executed a perfect landing.

"Nice pass, Crackers. You should do this for a living," said Delgado over the ICS.

Kevin chuckled.

The springback pull of the arresting wire pulled loose of the tailhook, allowing Kevin to raise it and taxi the

F-14A to the right side of the deck, where the plane captain, wearing a brown jersey and an array of chains and hooks hanging loose off his shoulders, patiently waited to tie down "his" aircraft.

One minute later, Lancaster pulled alongside Kevin's F-14A. Kevin and Delgado climbed down the side of the fighter and jumped down to the armored deck while Lancaster raised the canopy of his jet. A couple of photographers ran to the side of Kevin's craft and began snapping photos of the aviators in full gear standing next to their machine while other pilots spray-painted two MiG silhouettes on the Tomcat's side below the cockpit.

Kevin felt good about himself. He had not only fooled two enemy missiles, but he'd managed to nail two MiGs. The long hours of training and hard work had definitely paid off. In the midst of all the excitement and back patting, Kevin heard a familiar voice.

"You people gave us one hell of a scare out there!"

Kevin and Delgado turned around and stared into the blue eyes of the F-14A Wolfpack's Commanding Officer, Commander John "Ghost" McDeere, a six-feet-two man with the broadest shoulders in the Navy. Kevin, at just under 185 pounds and five feet ten, found him thoroughly intimidating. The forty-two-year-old CO stood near the Tomcat's left stabilator with his hands on his hips. His comment had quieted down the welcoming committee.

"Ah, well, sir, they didn't leave us much of a—" Delgado began to respond.

McDeere raised his right hand in a fist, thumb extended, and pointed it to the stairs. "Beat it, Delgado. I'll see you at the debrief. Right now they're waiting for you at the CIC," he said, referring to the combat intelligence center.

"Yessir!" Delgado fled.

McDeere put his hand back on his hip and stared at Kevin. "You've got a lot to learn about rules of engagement, mister!"

The photographers and the other pilots slowly retreated.

The comment took Kevin entirely by surprise. He had expected a compliment for a job well done. Puzzled, he rubbed a hand through his thick black hair and regarded McDeere for a moment before saying, "They really didn't leave us much of a choice out there, sir."

"We'll see. I just spoke with the CAG, and he wants to see us immediately. I gotta tell you, he's pissed, and with good reason." CAG, an acronym used decades before for Commander Air Group, was used in the modern-day Navy to refer to the Carrier Air Wing Commander, the officer in charge of all aircraft, crew, and operations aboard the carrier.

"Who's pissed off, Ghost?" Lancaster asked as he approached them, holding his helmet in his right hand and motioning his RIO to follow Delgado. As Executive Officer, or second in command of the squadron, Lancaster reported to McDeere.

Lancaster was as large as McDeere, but that's where any similarity ended. The color of their skin was as different as their personalities. McDeere, a borderline albino with thinning blond hair, a million freckles, and thick eyebrows, knew only how to go by the book, the book, and nothing but the book. He followed his orders blindly, never questioned authority, and despised those who did. He was a model officer and a top-notch aviator, but in Kevin's mind he could also be one royal pain in the ass at times. Lancaster, on the other hand, not only was coal-black, but his explosive youth had taught him to take life a bit easier. His lined face complemented the traces of gray in his otherwise black hair, which lately seemed to be losing ground to a growing forehead. Like McDeere, Lancaster also realized that there was a book to be followed, but he also knew that the book was written by humans, and humans always made mistakes, particularly those employed in the armed forces.

"The CAG's pissed off," responded McDeere, rubbing the back of his neck while briefly closing his eyes. "I'm afraid you two set him off."

"You think I can take a leak before we go see good ol' Brassballs?"

The comment brought a smile to Kevin's lips.

"Don't get smart, Shadow," McDeere fired back. "If the CAG ever hears you calling him that, the only thing you'll be flying till you retire are C-130s out of Okinawa filled with sushi." He turned his attention to Kevin. "At this moment I don't see any reason for smiles. In case you haven't been keeping up with current events, you *failed* to follow rules of engagement."

"Oh, c'mon, Ghost," Lancaster said. "Cut Crackers some slack, would ya? We had knocked it off and were headin' south when they doubled back on us."

"Well, let's head over to see the CAG. And I suggest you two watch your mouth and play it cool while we're in there."

Kevin still couldn't figure out what had gone wrong. All he did was defend himself against the MiGs. He pressed McDeere for an answer. "But, sir, I don't see what in the world I—"

McDeere raised an eyebrow while slowly shaking his head. "You're about to find out, Crackers. Now let's go. The CAG's waiting." McDeere turned around and followed Lancaster down the stairs. Kevin exhaled, shook his head, and went after them.

Two minutes later, the door almost snapped off of its hinges when the *Ranger*'s Carrier Air Wing Commander, Captain Vince "Brassballs" Cutter slammed it after Kevin, Lancaster, and McDeere walked into his relatively spacious quarters. Kevin and Lancaster had not even had the chance to stop at the dressing room to remove their flight gear. Both wore their olive-drab flying suits and gear vests, a mass of zippered pockets housing their survival equipment. The long tubes for the G suit connection hung at their sides. Their hair was soaking wet from perspiration, which continued to drip down the deep red marks left on their faces by the oxygen masks.

Kevin studied Cutter, a slightly overweight fifty-one-year-old who had gone completely bald two decades before. The captain had started his career in the Navy during the Vietnam War as a pilot in the venerable A-6 Intruder. Rumor was that he had single-handedly taken care of a half-dozen Vietcong after being shot down inside enemy territory and had carried his unconscious navigator/bombardier on his shoulders for almost five miles before he had called in to be evacuated. Later on, when asked why he simply hadn't requested a helicopter at the crash site, Cutter had responded that the site had been too exposed, and he had wanted to make sure he had lost any trailing VC before endangering the lives of the rescue crew. Looking at him now, Kevin doubted the overweight CAG could endure a two-minute walk through dense jungle, much less carry someone on his shoulders.

The trio snapped to attention as the CAG approached them. "At ease, Ghost. Step aside, please."

"Yes, sir." McDeere moved to the side of the room.

Oh, shit, thought Kevin, remaining perfectly still, his eyes focused on the painting of a clipper behind Cutter's desk. He'd seen a second painting to the right of the room, where the CAG also kept a small table filled with framed photos, newspaper articles, and medals. *Here comes the wrath of Brassballs.*

"Just what in the fuck did you two idiots think you were doing?"

"Sir, with all due—"

"Oh, spare me the bullshit, Shadow!"

"Ahem . . . sir? May I say some—" Kevin began.

"If you know what's good for you, mister, you better keep your mouth shut and pray to remain airborne." Cutter looked at Lancaster, veins in his head standing out. "Jesus Christ, Shadow! I've known you for years! How could you let your wingman do something so damned stupid and violate Iraqi airspace north of the thirty-second?"

"It may have been pretty close, but those bastards fired two missiles at us, for crying out loud, sir! We had no choice. What were we supposed to do? Fly by and give them the bird while they fired at us? We blew their asses right out of the sky!"

"Watch your mouth, Shadow! Don't you forget who in the fuck you're talking to!" Cutter's face was now inches away from Lancaster's.

Lancaster inhaled deeply and dropped his voice a couple of decibels. Cutter took a step back.

"No disrespect intended, CAG. We had broken off pursuit and were headed south when we were jumped. We were in a defensive role and reacted to their attack. Two MiGs attacked Lieutenant Dalton. One fired two missiles at him. He not only protected a multimillion-dollar plane with his flying, but he destroyed the two MiG-23s using a single Sidewinder and the guns, again acting totally in self-defense. I also had to evade two of their missiles before going in pursuit of the other two MiGs. After seeing the way they'd attacked us, I made a judgment call. I do hope you noticed that I didn't go after that last MiG when it disengaged and left the zone."

"That's the only reason why you're still wearing those wings, Shadow." Cutter shifted his gaze to Kevin, who remained at attention next to Lancaster. "Two MiGs, eh?"

"Yes, sir."

"How long have you been out of flight school?"

"One year, sir." Kevin's eyes slowly gravitated toward Cutter, who burned him with his stare. Kevin's attention went back to the painting.

"One year out of the RAG, ah?" Cutter continued while pacing back and forth in front of Kevin. The RAG, or Replacement Air Group, is the final phase of a Navy pilot's training, where pilots specialize in a certain type of plane. "Well, let me tell you something. A year ain't shit, son! You're too damned green to start making your own decisions in the air! You're a rookie, dammit! Nothing but a fucking RAG grad with an inflated ego because you just downed two MiGs!"

"But, sir, those MiGs—"

"Listen, Crackers. If you think you're so smart, then answer this. After you destroyed the first MiG and had saddled in on the second one, how far was it from leaving the zone?"

Kevin realized Cutter was trapping him, but there wasn't anything he could do, especially since he didn't remember the exact location where he'd shot down the second MiG. "Sir, we were a little busy. I don't seem to recall which . . ." He trailed off as Delgado's words came back to him: *Approaching Waterloo Red! Knock-it-off! Waterloo Red!*

"In that case, let me refresh your memory. According to the AWACS and the cruiser's coverage of the incident, that second MiG was already north of the thirty-second, get it? The pilot was already out of our legal boundaries for engagement, but you were too fucking busy trying to blow him away to realize that! When that MiG left the zone, you weren't supposed to go after it and kill it with a Sidewinder! You were supposed to fly back to your leader! And worst of all, your own RIO told you you were approaching fucking Waterloo Red, dammit!"

Kevin was blushing, finally realizing his mistake. All he could do was take the punishment. "Sorry, sir. I made a mistake. I was too busy trying to fight off the MiGs. I guess my RIO's words didn't register until it was too late. I should have been listening more carefully. I'm very sorry, sir."

"Sorry? You shouldn't be sorry, mister, you should be *worried* out of your mind about your future in the Navy!"

Now it was Kevin's turn to get Cutter's round face stuck in front of him. He could smell the CAG's strong aftershave. "Sir, I . . . ah, I—"

"That's all for now. You're dismissed! You too, Shadow! Get out of my face!"

"Yessir!" They turned and left the room.

"I don't think Crackers got the message, CAG," said McDeere after the two pilots left the room.

"You don't? I thought he did. He does seem a little too trigger-happy. He should have let that second MiG go, but that's typical of all newcomers. He'll be all right. Just gotta shake him a little bit to make him put things in perspective."

"I still don't think he realizes what he did wrong."

Cutter exhaled. "It's hard to knock-it-off when you're surrounded with missile trails. You tend to think of surviving, not running. I mean, who knows, Ghost? If he'd disengaged, they could have tried to run him down again. Those Iraqis are tricky bastards. He might not have survived another brace of missiles."

"He just makes me nervous . . . if you know what I mean."

"What are you saying? That I should ground him indefinitely?"

McDeere raised an eyebrow and tilted his head. "Maybe for a little while. I'm not sure yet, though. There's something about Crackers that bothers me."

"Oh, c'mon, Ghost!" Cutter said, waving a hand in the air. "You and I know that what he did was wrong, but it wasn't bad enough to deprive him of a second chance. The Navy's invested a million bucks training him. Besides, in your last report you did indicate that he was a natural."

"Well, yes. He is, but—"

"Then give him another chance. Remember, we need those young guns out there where they belong."

"You really think he got the message, CAG?"

Cutter exhaled and nodded. "Yes, yes. He got it all right."

"Very well. I'll talk to him later, after he gets a chance to think about it for a while."

"Good. That's all. You're dismissed."

McDeere reached for the door.

"Ghost?"

"Yes, CAG?"

"Two MiGs, eh?"

"Yep."

"Damn. The kid's good."

McDeere didn't respond as he left, closing the door behind him.

Cursing himself for having overlooked the location on that second MiG, Lieutenant Kevin Dalton paced back and forth in the tiny ten-by-twelve-foot stateroom he shared with Chico Delgado. Identical modular storage units occupied the right and left sides of the room, where Kevin and Delgado kept all personal belongings in the multiple drawers, footlockers, and cabinets. Each unit sported a fold-down desktop with a built-in fluorescent lamp. A small stainless steel sink under a mirror, whose metal frame was painted pale green, stood next to one of the modular units. A nineteen-inch Sony TV stood next to the other. Along the back side of the room were steel bunks, also painted pale green, with thin mattresses and gray woolen blankets. Kevin occupied the bottom bunk and Delgado the top one, which only gave the East L.A. native just over three feet of clearance from a ceiling threaded with pipes, wires, hoses, and ventilating ducts. All that furniture left them little space to move around.

He drove a fist into his hand and went back in his mind through the entire episode for the fourth time, realizing that he would have fired the Sidewinder even if Delgado's warning had come a few seconds earlier. The adrenaline had clouded his senses. He had been focused on only one thing: killing that MiG. He could still see it in his mind every time he closed his eyes. For that tiny fraction of time in Kevin's life, putting a Sidewinder through the MiG's tailpipe had been all that mattered. No warnings, no threats, no other inputs would have changed the outcome during those last few seconds before he'd fired. Kevin then recalled how stupidly he had asked Lancaster why he hadn't destroyed the second MiG.

Damn! Kevin thought, reaching the conclusion that air combat experience meant not only the ability to fly a Tomcat and shoot down enemy planes, but the wisdom to make rational split-second decisions while flying at twice the speed of sound.

"The CAG ripped you a new asshole, didn't he, Crackers?"

Kevin turned around and found Delgado standing by the entrance. The sleeves of his flight suit were rolled up to his elbows, revealing a tattoo of a white bulldog's head with a patch over one eye on Delgado's left forearm. It seemed out of place with his RIO's otherwise clean-cut appearance. The Hispanic lieutenant had a long, thin face, which went well with the rest of his slim yet muscular body. Nearly four inches shorter than Kevin, Delgado gave the impression of someone who had been a marathon runner and then put on ten pounds of muscle by working out. But what had caught Kevin's attention the first time they met, aside from the odd-looking tattoo on his forearm, were Delgado's black eyes, which showed an intensity absent in most people Kevin knew. At the same time, the eyes were somewhat melancholy, like those belonging to someone who had seen more than his share of violence. Violence Kevin knew did not come from Delgado's four-year-old career in the Navy.

"How do you know he chewed me out?"

"Are you kiddin' me, man? You got a sad puppy-dog look all over your face."

"He says I screwed up this morning."

"What do you think?"

"I'm afraid he's right."

"I bet you he nailed you for blowin' away that second MiG, didn't he?"

"Yep. And you warned me about it when I had the chance to stop."

"I know I did, but I wasn't sure if you actually heard me. You know, with the dogfight and all."

"I heard, but I didn't listen. I was too busy trying to blow him away. How come you didn't mention it afterward?"

"Dunno. Guess I got carried away, too. After all, the bastards tried to nail us first. Besides, this was the first time that we got close enough to an Iraqi to engage. They're always hidin' from us."

"Well, the harm's already done. We'll see what happens next." Kevin sat down on his bed and stared at his reflection on the glass of a framed eight-by-ten autographed photo of the Blue Angels, the Navy's aerobatics team, hanging on the wall next to his bed. Kevin gazed into his own brown eyes, the ends of which turned downward, giving a somber look to his otherwise baby face. But today he saw more than just sadness in his eyes. Kevin saw fear. "Dammit!" he said, giving voice to his frustration. He had never tolerated personal failure very well.

"I wouldn't worry about it too much, man."

"I hope everyone forgets about this."

"I surely hope that *you* don't forget about this incident, Mr. Dalton."

Kevin and Delgado snapped to attention as Commander John McDeere appeared in the doorway.

"At ease, gentlemen. Looks like the CAG's in a good mood, and he'll cut you some slack. Personally, I wouldn't mind grounding you for a few weeks to let you think about what you did out there, but we're short of pilots. So, there you go. You're still flying."

"Thank you, sir."

The freckles on McDeere's face moved as his face hardened. He stared at Kevin with his ice-cold blue eyes. "No, Crackers. Don't fucking thank me. But *do* think about what you did, because the next time you might not be so lucky; you could get your ass shot right out of the sky. If you ever break a rule like this again and survive, you may be out of the Navy and at the mercy of international law. You got me, mister?"

"Yessir!"

"Good." McDeere began to leave, hesitated, and then looked at Kevin once more. His voice was low and hoarse. "I'm gonna be watching you, Crackers, and if you breathe the wrong way I'm gonna squash you like a roach. Next time the president himself won't be able to help you. When you look bad, my squadron looks bad, and when that happens, *I* look bad. I'll be damned if I'm gonna let you do that. Next time, you better listen to every fucking word your RIO's telling you. You follow me?"

Kevin remained silent for a few seconds as he struggled to absorb the sting of McDeere's comments.

"Are you deaf, Lieutenant? I said, do you understand?"

With his jaw clenched, Kevin managed to mutter a low but audible "I understand, sir."

"Good!" With that McDeere turned and left the room.

"Fuck me," Delgado murmured after he'd made sure McDeere was a fair distance away. "I think the bastard's got it in for you, man. Bummer."

Kevin sat back down on his bunk and shook his head.

"Dammit! This sucks. I'm at the complete mercy of that son of a bitch."

"Go easy on yourself, Crackers."

Kevin lifted his head. The voice wasn't Delgado's but Lancaster's.

"Hello, sir," he said rising to face his executive officer. "I hope I didn't get you into too much trouble today."

Lancaster stood by the entryway. He smiled. "Nah, the Ghost's just under a lot of pressure these days."

"But, sir, we didn't—"

"I know that, and the CAG knows that too, but he also thinks you overreacted. You should have let that second MiG go, Crackers. That was your mistake . . . but this was your first time and you have limited experience. Those two factors are probably what saved your ass from being suspended or grounded indefinitely. The CAG—unlike our beloved squadron commanding officer—is a fair man. He just gave you another shot. The message here's be careful."

"That's a lot easier said once you're on the ground and have plenty of time to fully analyze an air battle, sir, but there's not much time to react when you're dodging missiles and chasing MiGs. I mean, one moment of hesitation and—"

Lancaster laughed. "Crackers, Crackers, you always take things to the other extreme. I know what goes on up there. I was there, remember? I'm just telling you the same thing I've been telling you since the day I taught you how to climb inside an F-14 cockpit: you need to learn from your mistakes. Next time you go up there, I bet you a hundred bucks you'll keep an eye on your position and listen to your RIO, even when pulling maximum gee in the ugliest of dogfights."

"You got that right, sir."

"All you have to do is use your best judgment. Think about what kind of role you have and play it accordingly. I could have shot down that second MiG easy. I had him locked up, but he was already north of the zone, so I let him go. Believe me when I tell you I had to force myself to let him go, but rules are rules. Do you get my point?"

"Guess so, sir."

"And don't think about Ghost. He's just worried about you staining his perfect record. Besides, the guy's probably just pissed that he hasn't had a chance to mix it up himself yet. And to tell you the truth, I think he's sore that we did."

Kevin's black eyebrows dropped a bit. "You mean he's mad with us because it wasn't him out there today?"

Lancaster's teeth shone bright against his skin as he grinned. "Could be. You've got a lot to learn. See, the fastest way to move up in the Navy's by doing extraordinary things—good things, of course—that have a lot of visibility. Being a hero is on top of the list of things you can do to quickly promote yourself. Flying a nice, quiet CAP isn't. So, don't worry about McDeere. Really, the hell with him."

"But he's still in charge of—"

"Look, I've been around for a while, and I've seen more than my share of McDeeres out there. They come and go, but good pilots always get ahead. The bastard also had a chat with me, where he unloaded just like he did with you. Ignore him. You just keep on doing what you do best and he won't be able to touch you. I'm living proof of that."

Kevin breathed deeply and slowly nodded at Lancaster's reassuring words. "Thank you, sir. That helps."

"Now," Lancaster continued, his square face turning serious, "that doesn't mean that you should push your luck. If I were you, I would keep a low profile for a couple of months until this thing fades away."

"You can count on that."

Lancaster checked his watch. "Well, if you gentlemen will excuse me, I've got work to do," he said before he continued down the long hall.

"I guess you're gonna be all right, Crackers," said Delgado, rubbing his stomach in obvious discomfort.

"Hope so . . . say, why are you holding your belly?"

"Dunno, man. I think the chicken I had for lunch didn't go down too well. It's probably a delayed reaction from all this excitement." Delgado reached down and unzipped a compartment on the right leg of his flight suit and removed a plastic bag. Kevin noticed it was filled with a white powder.

"What's that?"

"It's a *curatodo,* man."

"A what?"

"A *curatodo* . . . a cure-all type medicine. My grand-mother gave it to me before I left home."

"What's in it?"

"Heck, who knows? All I know's that a tablespoon of this in warm water will handle most headaches and stomach pains."

"Hmm . . . sounds like something they oughta give to all pilots before and after missions."

"Nope. You gotta be careful with this stuff. One tablespoon once in a while and your aches will go bye-bye. More than that, and you'll get a severe case of the shits."

Kevin laughed and headed for the door.

"Where you goin'?"

"Outside. I need some fresh air."

Five minutes later, Lieutenant Kevin Dalton stepped up to Vulture's Row on the carrier's island and gazed down at the relatively peaceful flight deck. He watched more than sixty men completing a Foreign Object Damage walkdown, a flight deck ritual performed a few times each day to ensure that there were no loose objects on the deck that could be sucked in by a jet engine's air intake. Kevin knew that could result in disaster. The men performing the FOD cleared the deck while pilots headed for their fighters.

He shifted his gaze west, toward Saudi Arabia, barely visible in the hazy late-afternoon sky. The Forrestal-class *Ranger,* displacing nearly 78,000 tons, steamed along a parallel course with the Saudi coastline. In spite of Cutter's negative remarks—and McDeere's threats—today had been a victory for the pilot in Kevin. All the years of training and hard work had been put to the ultimate test for three brief minutes. Kevin knew he had the talent to be a pilot from the day his flying instructor had allowed him to solo a single-engine Cessna 172 Skyhawk on his sixteenth birthday in his hometown of Melbourne, Florida. His progress and enthusiasm continued, and a year later, after acing his private pilot's written exam, Kevin successfully passed his practical exam and fulfilled the first of a long string of dreams.

His father, a chemical engineer, wanted Kevin to pursue a similar engineering degree, something that did not appeal to Kevin. After repeated arguments with his father and a couple of marginal college semesters taking courses he loathed, Kevin decided to leave home and try his luck in the Navy. As a college dropout, the Navy did not consider him serious enough to pilot a multimillion-dollar craft and gave him a choice: finish college and then join the officer's training course, or start as an enlisted man, put in the time, and *then* apply for the chance to become a pilot, and hope his application was taken seriously. Kevin, not a gambler by nature, decided to finish college first. Refusing to let his father continue to run his life, Kevin attended the Florida Institute of Technology, working nights and going to school during the day, until he obtained a degree in aeronautical engineering three years after he had walked out of the Navy's recruitment office. Three months later, he arrived at Pensacola Naval Air Station, nicknamed the Cradle of Naval Aviation, where he started his basic officer training. Here, in addition to surviving the Navy's version of boot camp, Candidate Kevin Dalton also endured the Aviation Physiology Training unit, where he went through decompression chamber sessions, spatial disorientation training, simulated aircraft ejection exercises, and learned how to survive ejections over water and land. Upon graduation, Ensign Kevin Dalton started his formal flight training in a T-34C, a two-seat turbo-prop-powered trainer. From there he moved up to the Rockwell T-2 Buckeye, a general-purpose jet trainer. In the T-2 Kevin learned all there was to be known about carrier operations, from taking off to landing on a carrier's deck. After he had mastered the essentials of naval aviation, Kevin moved to the McDonnell Douglas TA-4J Skyhawk for the remainder of his "advanced flight training."

With 280 hours of flight time, Kevin headed for the RAG, which in his case meant an assignment to F-14 pilot training at NAS Miramar in San Diego, California, where, under Lancaster's guidance, he flew an additional one hundred hours and quickly rose to become first in his class. Kevin never flew slow if he could fly fast. He never made a shallow turn if he could cut a tight one, even at the expense of pulling maximum g. His degree in aeronautics gave him a better understanding of aircraft specifications. He knew that aircraft manufacturers only published a conservative version of their specs, allowing themselves some margin for safety. He used that knowledge to "safely" push his machine beyond the envelope to achieve his goals. This attitude earned him his nickname during his early days with the Navy. However, Kevin learned the hard way that top-notch flying is not all that was required to be the best. During a simulated air combat in his last week of training at Miramar, Kevin made the mistake of leaving his flight leader to pursue a bandit and got shot down. He couldn't make up the below average grade on the flight and was awarded second place during graduation. That setback seemed negligible when compared to being grounded today.

To Kevin, life was a constant challenge, a never-ending string of obstacles he felt compelled to overcome in order to truly succeed in life. *But obstacles come in different shapes and forms,* thought Kevin as a fully loaded F-14A taxied to cat one. The trick, he reasoned, was to figure out which obstacles really mattered and go after them with uncompromising resolve, setting short-term goals which, strung with one another, would eventually enable him to conquer that long-term goal which was the obstacle itself. So far he considered himself lucky for having been able to achieve all his dreams.

Kevin watched a green-shirted "hookman" run forward in a crouch and kneel beside the F-14A, where he engaged the nose tow—a bar protruding from the Tomcat's nosewheel—to the catapult shuttle. The hookman then looked over to the edge of the flight deck, where the cat operator was holding up his right index finger. *Ready on the cat.* The catapult officer, a yellowvest standing in front of the Tomcat, held up his hands in fists. *Brakes on.* Then the yellowvest gave the hand signal. *Brakes off and full power!* The hookman ran clear of the F-14A as the cat officer issued a few more hand signals to the pilot before snapping to attention and saluting. Finally the cat officer gracefully sank and touched the deck before stretching his right arm toward the *Ranger's* bow.

The blazing sun slowly disappeared over the horizon, transforming the vivid orange-stained sky into one of lesser hues. Kevin watched the heat waves from the Tomcat roaring off the carrier's deck. The scorching blast of its Pratt & Whitney turbofans crashed against the saltwater-cooled jet blast deflector as the cat officer solemnly waved at the departing jet. Kevin Dalton was proud to be a part of the Navy.

■ 2 ■

CORRIDORS OF POWER

Political power grows out of the barrel of a gun.
—Mao Tse-Tung

THE WHITE HOUSE.
Day One. 0830 Local Time.

President Bill Clinton sat on his high-backed leather chair behind his wooden desk just in front of the Armorlite bulletproof windows facing the White House lawn. The chair, internally layered with sheets of Kevlar, provided the president with additional protection against bullets a terrorist might fire through the Armorlite glass.

Across from his desk, beyond the presidential seal embroidered on the light blue carpet in the center of the oval-shaped room, were two cream-colored sofas facing each other. The director of Central Intelligence, the secretary of state, the defense secretary, and Air Force General Kenneth Draper, whom Clinton had named undersecretary for Middle Eastern affairs, quietly sat, waiting for the president to speak. The president, intelligent blue eyes narrowed and shiny, lips tightly pursed, read the President's Daily Brief, a top-secret intelligence document prepared by the CIA, containing briefs of the latest activities home and abroad.

Pinching the bottom of his chin, President Clinton finished the section on the Middle East situation, briefly nodded to himself, and got up. The others in the room also stood up, but the president waved them to sit back down while he walked to one of the tall windows next to the Stars and Stripes behind his desk.

A stiff wind blew dark clouds over the nation's capital, quickly turning a clear sky into one as black as night. Flashes of lightning streaked across the billowing clouds. Mist and drizzle gave way to heavy rain crashing down on the morning traffic on Pennsylvania Avenue.

Hands behind his back, President Clinton watched the storm gather strength. The rain pounded on the thick glass. Branches of nearby trees swirled at the mercy of the wind. Secret Service men in overcoats ran for cover.

Strong storm.

The president, dressed in a chalk-striped dark suit, breathed in deeply through his mouth, slowly exhaling through his nostrils. A storm was definitely gathering strength in the Middle East again. The storm of Saddam Hussein.

The president briefly closed his eyes. The situation was getting out of control in Iraq. His current policy of flexing some muscles by sending in troops and heavy hardware to show Saddam that the Clinton administration would not put up with Iraq's noncompliance of U.N. Security Council resolutions didn't seem adequate anymore. The CIA had indisputable proof that Saddam was on the verge of assembling nuclear weapons, which probably was the reason why the Iraqi leader continued to prevent U.N. inspectors from doing their job. According to the briefings and the dozens of meetings the Commander in Chief had had with his top advisors in the past two weeks, the Iraqi president had obtained Russian nuclear technology and components. The president felt that perhaps Saddam's latest actions—ordering MiGs into the no-fly zone—had an ulterior motive than just to directly annoy him. *Does he have them assembled already? Is Saddam trying to provoke an American attack so that he can respond with his nukes?*

And to make matters worse, the recent terrorist bombing in the underground parking garage beneath the World Trade Center twin towers, in the heart of New York City, had sent a clear message to President Clinton: *Beware, America, you are not isolated from the rest of the world.* The president shivered at the thought of someone like Saddam in possession of nuclear weapons, which the Iraqi leader could use not only to blast half the Middle East off the map but could also secrete one into the United States.

The president, eyes half-shut, looked at his right hand, the one he had used to shake President John F. Kennedy's hand in 1963, and he made a tight fist with it. Just like Khrushchev during the Cuban Missile Crisis, Saddam Hussein understood only one language. *Only one.*

Turning around and walking to the front of his desk, where he leaned against it and placed both hands on its smooth surface, the president silently probed his top advisors, starting with his secretary of state.

The gray-haired veteran diplomat, wearing a dark blue suit, crossed his legs and raised his heavy brows, regarding the president with filmy eyes. Deep creases of decision folded in the secretary's face as he said, "Mr. President, Saddam Hussein plays by the same rules used by any other dictator still in power in that region. Some scholars call them the rules of Hamma."

The secretary paused while Clinton crossed his arms and stared off in the distance. In 1982, Syrian President Hafez al-Assad ordered the destruction of Hamma, a city located 120 miles northwest of Damascus, and believed to be the headquarters of the Muslim Brotherhood, a Muslim fundamentalist organization hostile to the government of Assad. The Brotherhood was accused by Assad of car bombings and other terrorist attacks, including plots to overthrow his government. The Syrian president decided to show everyone what happens to those who dared defy his rule. In the first week of February 1982, Soviet-made T-64 tanks, helicopters, and artillery units leveled Hamma's Muslim neighborhoods, bringing down buildings and burying anyone in the way. An army of bulldozers and steamrollers finished up the job, leveling the rubble. The death toll reached the tens of thousands.

President Clinton gazed into the secretary's eyes once again.

"Saddam Hussein is some piece of work, Mr. President. He has survived because he follows this basic rule when dealing with his enemies. He is not only brutal but smart. He has no friends, only enemies and agents. He has set up several intelligence agencies within his government to spy on each other, on the army, the air force, and even on his own Republican Guard. Saddam is very dangerous because he is an extremist who knows where to stop. He usually knows exactly how much he can get away with and always stops short. He knows when to reach out and when to hunker down. He doesn't care if he loses half a million soldiers as long as he remains in control. He loves to defy us because we are a superpower, and in doing so he *becomes* a superpower in the eyes of the Arab world, for only a superpower can defy another and survive to tell the story. And right now he feels on top of the world because he has outlasted the leaders of the countries that attacked him during Desert Storm."

President Clinton said, "And your recommendation?"

The secretary crossed his legs before turning his gaze back to the president and saying, "Sir, if Saddam is indeed assembling nukes, and if he is successful, we will have a serious problem on our hands, not only abroad, but also at home. Remember that a tactical nuclear weapon—the twelve-kiloton class that fits inside the tip of a 155mm artillery shell—can be easily stored in the trunk of just about any midsize car. My recommendation is to spare no expense to find the location where he is assembling the nukes. No level of diplomacy or economic sanctions is going to work here, Mr. President. We must use every possible means at our disposal to find them . . ."

"Without telegraphing our intentions," finished the president. The secretary nodded.

The president turned to his defense secretary. "What's the situation over there?"

The defense secretary, a former House Armed Services chairman, was a large man with a round face, a large creased forehead extending well past the hairline of his youth, and thinning white hair. Rearranging his glasses, he locked eyes with the president. "We had the incident yesterday, when our guys nailed three MiGs that had ventured south of the thirty-second. Aside from that, all other air missions have been uneventful. Our AWACS have picked up nothing besides those MiGs. Looks like Saddam has the rest of his air force hunkered down. His army, however, appears to be getting restless."

Clinton reached behind him and snagged the President's Daily Briefing, waving it at the defense secretary. "This ground activity . . . these Iraqi troop deployments south of the thirty-second parallel. Exactly what are we facing here?"

His defense secretary turned to the director of Central Intelligence, Craig Kettler, a tall and fairly overweight man with a full head of unkempt gray hair, a double chin, and skin coarse and pitted from a case of bad acne during his youth. "That information is only two hours old," replied the fifty-year-old director. "The last KH-11 pass over southern Iraq showed elements of Saddam's Republican Guard slowly moving south of the thirty-second parallel. At this rate, they will reach the border with Kuwait and Saudi Arabia in four days."

"How many?"

"About sixty thousand men and four hundred tanks."

Clinton shook his head. Saddam had not gotten the message from the last bombing several months ago, when two hundred planes from the United States, Britain, and France attacked Talil Air Base, and SAM positions in Amara and Basra.

Then again, the president reflected, *Saddam didn't get the message from Operation Desert Storm, either.* According to diplomatic sources in Baghdad, the air strikes that followed the 1991 Gulf War—and the war itself—had actually helped Saddam politically, by showing his own people that even a coalition of all the nations of the world couldn't oust Saddam from power.

The president turned toward his defense secretary. "What is your take on Iraq's latest move?"

The defense secretary pushed the glasses up the bridge of his nose with an index finger. He turned his eyes, sunk in purple sockets and bloodshot with fatigue, toward the president. "I think he is trying to draw us back in, sir."

Clinton grimaced. "And what is your suggested response?"

"I recommend a strong response, Mr. President. By that I mean a *very* strong air strike using not just F-117s and F-111s, but also B-52 bombers, sir. Let's take out most of his advancing troops, several power stations, refineries, air fields, and radar installations. Let's do something more than just damage a few planes and SAM installations. Saddam laughed at our last strike several months back, sir. It did nothing to damage him strategically. I feel this time around we need to send Saddam a clear message that this administration will not tolerate any violations of the U.N. resolutions, and that there will be more punishment coming if he doesn't behave. It's the only language he understands, sir."

"I object to that, Mr. Secretary," cut in General Kenneth Draper.

"And why is that, General?" the defense secretary asked.

At forty-nine years of age, General Kenneth Draper— he preferred people to address him as general and not as undersecretary—had a pink-and-white face, thick backswept silver hair, thin lips curving down at the ends, and a pair of light gray eyes, which stared back at the defense secretary with matching intensity. Waving a hand in the air while leaning forward on the sofa, Draper said:

"I object to such an air strike for two important reasons. First, an air strike will only serve to improve Saddam's popularity at home. At this point in the game, I hesitate on using air strikes as a weapon to punish Saddam simply because air strikes have not really worked that well in the past. Saddam always finds a way to turn them around . . . you know, use them as a propaganda tool by showing pictures of dead women and children allegedly killed by our bombs. Even after the strongest of poundings during Desert Storm, Saddam always managed to pull his country back together again.

"My second reason is actually far more important than the first, for it concerns the possibility that Saddam has already assembled his nukes, and he is simply waiting for the opportunity to use them. Maybe he is trying to provoke us, to draw us in and then drop a warhead on our troops." Draper paused for a few seconds to let his words sink in. He finished with, "Those, Mr. Secretary, are my two reasons why we should not order an air strike on Iraq at this time."

The room fell silent. Draper leaned back, drumming a finger on the arm of the sofa. President Clinton crossed his arms, dropped his gaze, and stared at the presidential seal through half-closed eyes. Draper was right on the ball. Without knowing how close Saddam was from completing the assembly of the weapons, without even knowing where he was assembling them, Clinton had to play very, *very* cautiously, or risk nuclear retaliation.

The president turned to the director of the CIA. "Who do we have over there looking into the whereabouts of these weapons?"

The CIA director cleared his throat. "His name is Robert Bourdeaux, sir. He's our top senior operations officer on the Covert Action Staff. Since Operation Desert Storm he has recruited a number of agents inside Iraq, including a few Kurdish guerrillas, with whom he trades small arms for information. He also worked for our satellite imagery division for a number of years. A well-rounded and seasoned officer."

"I'm assuming that you also have your best people in Langley working on this?" the president asked.

"Yes, Mr. President," responded the director.

Clinton nodded. "Very well, gentlemen. I want hourly reports on the whereabouts of these Iraqi deployments south of the thirty-second. In the meantime, put our troops on full alert, but don't mobilize anyone from their current posts. I want our infantry to continue with their ground exercises. I want Air Force and Navy planes to continue flying their patrol missions, but I want to take a more conservative approach in regards to rules of engagement. If an Iraqi MiG violates the no-fly zone, I want him *escorted* back north, not shot down without warning—unless he poses an imminent threat to us or our allies. I want our boys to fire only if fired upon."

The president slowly scanned the faces of all present. "Keep in mind the big picture here. At this moment, we don't want to do anything that might trigger a nuclear response from Saddam until we know exactly where he stands on the assembly of the weapons."

With that, the president pressed a button on his desk, and a few seconds later two poker-faced Secret Service men, wearing discrete earphones attached to wires that coiled into their dark suits, entered the room and escorted the group out.

President Bill Clinton walked behind his desk but didn't sit down. Tight fists pressed against the polished wooden surface of his desk, the president peered at the eight-by-ten framed photo of Hillary and Chelsea. He could not let Saddam get away with this game anymore, especially with the possibility of nuclear weapons brought onto the field. Weapons which had definitely promoted Saddam Hussein from being a mere pain in the butt to a major menace.

Clinton hated the Iraqi president for dictating the terms of this round, forcing him to react to Saddam's moves. *But what choice do I have?*

The president knew it was well within his power to order an air strike, even a large one, and blast half of the Iraqi troops moving south. *But what if that's exactly what he wants me to do? What if Saddam is just looking for an excuse to nuke half the Middle East?*

No. Clinton couldn't do that. Saddam might be able to sacrifice thousands of troops in the flick of an eye, but President Bill Clinton had a much larger responsibility to his people, to his soldiers, than just sending them into a battle they couldn't win. He had to find out the real status of Saddam's weaponry. Attacking before knowing that would be completely irresponsible.

BAGHDAD, IRAQ.
Day One. 1800 Local Time.

While shooting a propaganda film, Iraqi President Saddam Hussein stood in the middle of the reception hall surrounded by his closest generals and bodyguards. Wearing a new light brown uniform and black beret for the camera crew to his near left, and with his Russian Makarov secured inside a shiny black leather holster attached to the belt of his uniform, the Iraqi leader held out his right arm slightly in front of him as one of dozens of officers of his Republican Guard and Air Force, as well as delegates from Russia and China, and a number of bankers, black market arms dealers, and oil businessmen lined up at the other end of the long hall, walked toward him. The approaching major's clicking steps on the brown marble floors echoed hollowly in the large room, decorated with fifteen-foot-tall portraits of Saddam. Iraqi flags hung from the cathedral ceiling.

A general standing to Saddam's right whispered the name of the young officer, and Saddam, giving the major a smile while shaking his hand, said warmly, "May Allah be with you, Major Fahim Said."

The young major's eyes filled. "And with you, O Great One."

Saddam's smile remained frozen even after the major did an about-face and headed down the other side of the hall.

Next came a Syrian banker Saddam had dealt with personally on a number of occasions, most recently during the months that followed the war of 1991. The tall, thin banking executive with salt-and-pepper hair, thin mustache, and deep-green eyes had secretly provided the Iraqi president with an enormous line of credit to help finance the extensive repairs needed to restore electricity and water services throughout cities in central Iraq.

"It is good to see your beautiful country smiling again."

Saddam, his smile a bit broader now, gazed deeply into the eyes of the banker. *This man understands the needs of my people.* "And much of it is due to your help, my friend," Saddam responded, vigorously pumping the banker's hand. "The will of Allah shall be done in the end, and I am His instrument of justice."

"May I live to see the day when the great Satan and all its allies pay for what they did to this land!"

"And you shall, my friend. And you shall."

Taking in a lungful of air, the banker nodded before turning around and walking away, to be replaced by another friend, a retired Ukrainian colonel now living in Jordan. The general standing next to Saddam waved over a short, thin man wearing a pair of silver-framed glasses and a tan suit, who had been sitting behind the video crew. He was one of Saddam's personal translators.

"It is good to see you again, Colonel Yakolev. Were the arrangements I've made for you adequate?" Saddam asked. Colonel Andrei Yakolev had played a key role in the secret transfer of Russian nuclear technology to Iraq. In return, Saddam had given the colonel the equivalent of two million American dollars plus a new life in Jordan.

The translator spoke in Russian to Colonel Yakolev and, nodding, the Ukrainian colonel said something to the translator while his eyes remained level with Saddam's.

The translator then turned to the Iraqi president and said, "Great One, the colonel is grateful for your generosity. Everything is as you had promised."

After another glance into Saddam's eyes, the colonel left, and a young officer replaced him. The general whispered a name and gave Saddam a small white box. The Iraqi president took the box in his hands and said, "Lieutenant Zahur Khazanni, your efforts to crush the Kurdish rebellion in the northern region have been commendable. Your commander informs me that you have shown great courage and valor against the enemy, and he has recommended you to receive the Republican League of Honor award."

While gazing deeply into the wide black eyes of the nervous young lieutenant, Saddam Hussein removed a small purple medal from the box and pinned it on the officer's left shirt pocket.

"May Allah and the spirit of Islam guide you, Lieutenant Khazanni!"

"*Inshallah,* Great One!" responded the officer before turning around and walking away.

Another officer approached him. This time, the general didn't need to whisper a name to Saddam, whose face suddenly became rigid. The recently promoted general walking in his direction was Qazi Ali, a rising star in the Air Force for his recent victories against Kurdish rebels, and to Saddam's fury, a mild critic of Saddam's latest deployment south of the thirty-second parallel. He had also criticized the recent order to violate the no-fly zone, which had just resulted in three downed MiGs.

Saddam's stern face quickly softened. General Ali, a short man in his late forties, with a large defiant mouth, heavy nose, and brown eyes behind rimless glasses came to attention in front of the Iraqi president and shook his hand. A neatly trimmed mustache moved as General Ali gave Saddam a broad grin. "Greetings, Great One."

Saddam returned the smile and said in a low, hoarse voice, "*Sabah al-kair,* General. I have heard your comments on the latest deployment of forces south." ·

Ali pushed out his thick lips while Saddam regarded him quizzically. With his bulging brown eyes showing a glint of fear, General Ali tried to remain calm. "Great One, I fear that our latest deployment of forces might lead to major losses at a time when we are still rebuilding our army."

Saddam nodded. "I see. Perhaps we should discuss this matter in private. I am most interested in listening to your opinion."

Ali's eyes brightened at the comment. "I will be honored, Great One."

Without another word, and with the rest of the crowd gathered at the reception hall looking on, Saddam turned around, followed by his staff and General Ali. The camera crew stopped filming as the group walked up to a set of large wooden double doors on the right side of the reception hall. An armed soldier standing guard opened it, letting through only Saddam and General Ali.

Once inside, Saddam pulled out his sidearm, cocked it, and leveled it at the shocked general, who took a few steps back. "I beg your forgiveness, oh, Great One. I never meant any harm with my remarks. I was just concerned about our troops."

Saddam lowered the Makarov and studied the general with faint distaste before pointing to a nearby chair. General Ali sat down as ordered and nervously crossed his legs.

"Who is your leader, General Ali?"

Rubbing his hands, Ali kept shifting his weight on the chair, crossing and uncrossing his legs. "You are, of course, my president." he responded. His chin trembling.

"That is right, General. I *am* the Supreme One. I am the Great One. And do you know why I have remained in power for so long?"

Dropping his gaze to the marble floor, Ali slowly shook his head.

"Because it is the will of Allah that I remain in power to lead my people to greatness. But there are many evils who will try to prevent me from accomplishing my holy work. And evils are not only the Americans, general. There are also Iraqi evils, like those who oppose my mandates. It is my duty to eliminate such evils for the greater cause."

Without another word, Saddam Hussein trained the Makarov on General Ali, who remained still, his narrowed eyes on Saddam's. The Iraqi leader cocked the weapon and fired once. The report seemed amplified inside the small room. The bullet crashed through Ali's glasses, striking him in the right eye, exploding through the back of his cranium in a cloud of bloody debris, and shoving him back against the chair.

While Ali's left arm and leg shook for a few seconds,

Saddam slowly holstered the weapon, wondering if the American president was man enough to do the same with an insubordinate officer. Somehow he doubted it. President Clinton was soft and predictable. Saddam could feel it. American presidents, especially one who not only had not been in any war but had refused to go to the Vietnam War for fear of getting hurt, could not pose a serious threat to him. The evil George Bush was different, Saddam reflected. The former president had been an insane man who did not know his limitations, but Allah's justice had prevailed in the end. Saddam was still in power, while Bush had been voted out of power by his own people.

President Bill Clinton. Saddam managed a thin smile. The photogenic president was too much of a humanitarian to stomach the death of his own men. For the same reason he had dodged the Vietnam draft, Clinton would most likely back down if confronted with enough force. Saddam could feel it in his bones, and that feeling made him smile, because now more than ever he felt he could really be a powerful force against American imperialism —not only in this region of the world, but also in their own United States.

The bomb that rocked the World Trade Center would be mere fireworks when compared to the weapons of mass destruction Saddam Hussein envisioned smuggling into the United States. *But not just yet,* he reflected while holstering the Makarov. The Iraqi leader would complete his plan to assemble the missiles first. Later on, he would get his scientists to construct two additional nuclear warheads, which he would then sneak into New York City and Washington, D.C.

Soon, Mr. Clinton. Soon my weapons of mass destruction will be assembled, and then you will know the meaning of the word horror. You will experience what your predecessor made me experience during Operation Desert Storm.

As the dead body of General Ali stared back at Saddam with one eye, the Iraqi president approached him, spat on him, and murmured, "Your death will serve as an example to those who think about challenging my command."

With that, Saddam Hussein turned around and walked back into the reception hall, whispering to the guard by the door to get someone to come and clean the mess inside. He still had a long list of guests wanting to pay their respects. The camera crew resumed filming a smiling Saddam Hussein.

■ 3 ■

KURDS

There the Greeks spent a happy night, with plenty to eat, talking about the struggle now past. For they had been seven days passing through the country of the Kurds, fighting all the time, and they had suffered worse things at the hands of the Kurds than all the King of Persia, and his general, Tissaphernes, could do to them.

—Anabasis of Xenophon (400 B.C.)

SOUTHERN IRAQ.
Day One. 1900 Local Time.

Firmly clutching a weathered AK-47 assault rifle, Ishmael Mohammed Barzani moved swiftly under a crystalline moonless night in Eastern Mesopotamia, all the while being sure to blend his sounds with those of the desert. Stopping his quiet advance, he warily scanned the sand dunes in front of him and listened carefully before moving ahead once again.

The short, tight jacket Ishmael wore was drenched with sweat, just like his baggy trousers. Perspiration rolled down from his soaked black hair and into his eyes, stinging them. He blinked several times and tried to readjust his vision as the last of the day's heat left what had been scorching sands hours ago. Ishmael felt a cool, refreshing breeze swirling down from the high plains of the Zagros Mountains behind him and thanked Allah for allowing him this simple pleasure.

A jolt of pain from his rotten teeth and diseased gums caused him to grimace before he shivered it away. He continued moving through the night, keeping the weapon ready at all times. His teeth had begun decaying a few years before, when the Iranian dentist that used to visit his village once a year was arrested by the Iraqis and hanged on espionage charges. Since then he had steadily lost several teeth. The remaining ones, many of them blackened, should just as well fall out, he decided. Eating anything solid had grown to be a very painful experience. Lucky for him, his slim body didn't need much nourishment to function. He didn't need much sleep, either. Ishmael could walk for days with little food or water. He had to. He was a Kurd, and that alone meant a hard life. His face, however, did not show the harsh life he had endured. Ishmael was a handsome man, with a thin mustache, tanned face, and a pair of intelligent, sunken, brown eyes.

Ishmael was a Kurdish guerrilla, but more than that, he was a Barzani: Allah's last true warrior, he reflected. Ishmael was a direct decedent of Mullah Mustafa Barzani, the leader who had inspired the nine-year Kurdish Revolt that started in 1943. The Mullah and his tribe of warring Barzanis, feared and hated by other Kurdish tribes, had established the short-lived but glorious Kurdish Republic of Mahabad. Ishmael still remembered with great detail his father's stories of how the Soviets had withdrawn from Persia and allowed the Persian Army to march against the young Kurdish nation, killing many of its citizens and forcing the rest to retreat to the mountains. Fifteen years later, still under the leadership of Mullah Barzani, the Kurds had organized an armed resistance against Iraqi rule. After a decade of fighting, Iraq's Baath party had attempted to pacify the rebellious Kurds in 1971 with an offer for autonomy, but the agreement didn't hold. During the mid-seventies, the Kurds had resumed their fighting, this time backed by the Shah of Iran, who had simply been using them as a bargaining chip against Saddam Hussein in order to get Iraq to agree to share sovereignty of the Shatt al-Arab waterway, which provided access to the Persian Gulf. Without Iran's backing, Saddam had crushed the rebels and forced them back into the mountains. Years later, after Operation Desert Storm, the Kurdish brotherhood had tried to overthrow the ruthless dictator, but again, the forces of Saddam had squashed the rebels in days. That had been a great defeat for the Kurds, but not powerful enough to destroy the Kurdish spirit of independence. It had been only one of several times when Kurdish hopes for a homeland had ended in disaster, the reason Kurdish guerrillas called themselves *peshmerga*—those who face death. Slowly, the exiled tribes joined forces and began fighting once more.

The Mullah was Ishmael's inspiration. *Peshmerga* was his way of life.

Another bolt of pain made him close his eyes for a moment. Another molar had become loose. Ishmael moved it with his tongue at the price of yet another sharp jolt. *I will have to pull it out before eating again,* Ishmael thought as he heard Abdul's footsteps to his right. Abdul Mozakhu was a large Iranian-born Kurd, who this night alone had silently killed two men with his bare hands. They weren't men, Ishmael noted, they were the blasphemous enemy belonging to the same government who had so brutally dropped mustard gas over Ishmael's village three years ago, killing the last of his relatives. That blow had been a large one for Ishmael, when he had lost his younger brother Jasseer to the blistering gas, but an even larger and more scarring loss had occurred five years before, when the same government forces had dropped lethal cyanide gas on his hometown of Halabja, near the Iranian border. His wife Raniya and their two daughters had perished there. He and most of the village men had gone to the Dilaya River region in search of fish and dates and were spared from the hell that lasted but a single minute. Ishmael's only consolation had been that they all had died in their sleep; none had suffered except for the living. That, he reasoned, was why Allah had put him and everyone else on this earth: to test one's character and to prove one's worthiness to enter that sacred kingdom beyond this world. In his own mind, Ishmael had proven he was worthy of Allah's kingdom time and time again. Tonight he prepared himself to prove it once more.

He reached over and placed his hands on Abdul's massive shoulders and looked into the green eyes of someone that could have easily been his enemy, had it not been for the fact that a Kurd was a Kurd, and not an Iraqi, Iranian, or Turk. The Kurdish brotherhood, whose number amounted to several million, were members of different tribes which inhabited the sprawling mountainous territory encompassed by the Black Sea, the Caspian Sea, the Persian Gulf, and the Mediterranean. They were united by a common culture and language, a Persian-derivative tongue. The name *Kurd* had been given to them by the conquering and evangelizing Arabs in the seventh century, who had tried to convert the tribes to Islam but had soon realized their mistake and had left the Kurds alone in the mountains. With time, new armies would arrive and try to either conquer or eliminate the Kurds once and for all, and again the Kurds would manage to survive and continue their long struggle for independence: a struggle which had brought them closer together than any other group in this volatile region of the globe.

"You look troubled, *Isha,*" Abdul said.

"Not troubled but concerned, my brother. There is not much time before they arrive," Ishmael responded, accidentally moving the loose tooth with his tongue as he spoke. He tensed from the pain.

"We have great warriors among us. You mustn't worry." Abdul turned around and faced two dozen battle-hardened Kurdish guerrillas. "Look at them. They are indeed Allah's Army!"

Nodding his head, ignoring the pain, Ishmael lifted his left hand up in the air and made a fist. Instantly, the well-trained rebels spread to both sides of him and lay on the cool sand, weapons ready, facing the ten-foot-tall chain-link fence of the well-camouflaged ammunition, food, and medicine distribution center for government forces in the area.

It appeared deserted, save for a few floodlights, the monotone humming of a gasoline-powered electric generator, and a lonely guard on the far right side of the fence next to the only gate into the small complex.

Ishmael looked at Abdul one last time, dropped to a crouch, and slowly moved forward, silently closing the two-hundred-foot gap between himself and the sentry. Ishmael had expected to find the complex underguarded. Most of the government soldiers assigned to this base had been deployed to the northern city of Mandali a few hours ago, where rumors of a rebellion at the region's oil wells had alarmed the government. Ishmael smiled, again grateful that Allah had given him the intelligence to contrive such diversion. The Mullah would have been proud of him. Soon after the soldiers had left, Ishmael and his group arrived in their stolen Rover four-by-fours, which they'd parked behind sand dunes a few hundred meters back.

He now crawled over the sandy terrain next to the fence, slowly closing in on the guard, who had just lit a cigarette. Ishmael could dimly see the face of a boy not older than his younger brother. The smile on Ishmael's face faded away when memories flashed in front of his eyes of the blistered corpse of what had once been Jasseer, brought to him three days after the attack. *Jasseer.* He clenched his teeth in anger, and a flash of pain raced across his teeth and into his temples, bringing him back to the present.

The guard brought one hand up, took another draw on the cigarette, then replaced his slim hand on the barrel of a shiny RPK Russian-made light submachine gun. Its long thirty-round magazine, Ishmael observed, curved under the weapon in the same manner as the magazine clip did on the AK-47 slung across his back. But tonight he would not use the Kalashnikov. Ishmael reached down into his waist sash and removed a ten-inch stainless steel knife he had taken from an Iraqi officer Abdul had killed a year ago. He placed the blade sideways in his mouth, careful to press on it only with his dry lips. He continued crawling forward.

The young guard, Ishmael noted, had his back against the fence, obviously expecting intruders to approach from the field surrounding the complex. But that assumption would cost him his life on this cool, windy night. For that assumption to work, there should have been guards all around the perimeter, not just on one side.

Inch after agonizing inch, Ishmael soundlessly got to within six feet of the sentry, still smoking peacefully and looking up at the stars. With the lightning speed of a desert sandstorm, Ishmael clutched the blade's wooden handle, recoiled, and lunged. The sentry began to turn around when the blade entered his throat at an angle, cutting through the larynx. Oblivious to the expulsion of air and blood, and using muscles toughened by two decades of fighting, Ishmael drove the knife up through the jaw and into the guard's brain.

The young man's dying eyes stared at him, probably not understanding why he had to die so young. They remained there for eternal seconds, eyes locked, the guard's hands grasping Ishmael's as his warm blood ran down Ishmael's hand and forearm. Ishmael retrieved his blade when he saw no life left in those brown eyes.

"May Allah be merciful to you," he whispered as he dragged the body down the side of the fence and hid it behind a low sand dune, out of sight from anyone inside the complex.

While he cleaned off the blood from the knife and his own hand, Ishmael looked back at Abdul and pointed to the young soldier. Abdul nodded and signaled a young rebel to come with him to the fence. The two raced across the front of the perimeter and reached Ishmael's position in less than a minute. Ishmael stared at the young boy's bright eyes and placed both hands on his shoulders.

"Jasseer, I renamed you after my lost brother the same day your parents were killed. That day you swore revenge against those who had killed them, and I believed you. It was that internal fire that compelled me to let you join our holy crusade. Tonight is your night to leave childhood memories behind and become a man." Ishmael pointed to the young dead soldier and then toward the complex's gate.

Jasseer's eyes showed understanding and determination to obey his leader's orders. Without another word,

Abdul helped him get undressed as Ishmael removed the uniform from the dead soldier.

A minute later, Jasseer stepped away from them and casually walked toward the gate holding the fifteen-pound weapon just as Ishmael had shown him—right hand across the front with his index finger fixed around the trigger and left hand under the base of the light barrel.

Ishmael saw Jasseer reach the gate and try to open it, but it was locked from the inside. The young man squeezed his hands through the openings of the chain-link fence, but could not reach the bolt. Confused, he looked back at Ishmael and Abdul for advice.

Ishmael motioned him to crawl over the fence. Jasseer slung the weapon across his back and pulled himself up the small fence. Using the RPK to pull down the single string of barbed wire on top, Jasseer quietly went over and down the other side, where he reached for the bolt and pulled it, unlocking the sliding gate.

Ishmael and Abdul ran to him when they saw the small boy struggling to slide the heavy gate. They were thirty feet from him when Ishmael watched in helpless horror as three bullets erupted in a cloud from Jasseer's chest, propelling him out of the complex through the opening in the gate. There had been no sounds, expect for the brief spit of gunfire from the center of the complex.

"Allahu Akhbar!" Ishmael screamed at the top of his lungs as he slid the Kalashnikov to his chest, trained it on the guard he now could see standing fifty feet away, and unloaded a few rounds. Abdul did the same. Suddenly, the guerrillas emerged from their hiding places and raced toward the complex, keeping their array of weapons in front of them, but without firing a single round. Ishmael had given them strict orders not to fire unless they had a target. Next to water, ammunition was their most precious commodity.

Gunfire broke out from the other two buildings, but was quickly ended by a Kurdish shower of mixed-caliber fire impacting the thin sheet metal walls of the small buildings. The episode lasted fifteen seconds.

Silence.

Ishmael slowly walked toward Jasseer, who was still quietly moving his lips as he stared up at the stars. Abdul leaned down to pick him up, but Ishmael stopped him.

"Leave him, he is talking to Allah."

Abdul stood next to Ishmael, and they joined Jasseer in his final prayers until the young man's lips ceased to move. Then Ishmael leaned down and closed his eyes.

They turned around and joined the others already inside the complex, which consisted of a large warehouse-like building in the center and two smaller buildings, probably the guard's quarters, on either side. Ishmael's seasoned fighters had taken control of the complex with minimum resistance. He walked to the large gate of the central building, where Abdul was already hard at work trying to break the lock. He watched his large Iranian brother fire twice into the locking mechanism. Then, using only one hand, he slid the heavy door to the side, exposing the spacious interior.

Ishmael entered first, followed by Abdul and the others. Inside the large but poorly lit room were boxes of supplies on pallets, stacked five meters high, covering most of the available floor space and leaving barely enough room for the three yellow forklifts parked by the entrance. Large red signs on the boxes indicated their contents: medical supplies, ammunition, RPG shoulder-launched antitank weapons, AK-47s, even American plastic explosives. Ishmael had raided similar posts before, and although the mix of weaponry satisfied most of his band's needs, Ishmael seldom got his hands on the one weapon the Kurds really needed to defend themselves against Iraqi helicopters: shoulder-launched surface-to-air missiles.

"My brothers! Allah has been generous today! Let's take what we need and offer the rest to him!" Ishmael called.

While the men filled their sacks with supplies and others ran to get the Rovers, Ishmael, curious, walked to the far right section of the warehouse by a large table with a neon lamp hanging over it. He saw a large map of the southern regions with several symbols drawn on it. His eyes opened wide when he looked to the edge of the map and read the legend.

"Abdul!"

The large Iranian, who was lifting ammunition crates from a stockpile and bringing them outside, where several men were opening them and distributing magazine clips, turned his head when he heard his name called by his leader.

"What is the matter?" He approached the dimly lit corner of the building.

"Look, my brother! Allah has just shown us the way to stop the terror in our villages!"

Abdul read the words next to the symbols on the corner of the map, then shifted his gaze to Ishmael.

"The American?"

"Yes, my brother. We must show this to our American friend at the border. He will help us get the missiles that we need to fight the helicopters."

They quickly collected the map and any other documents they could lay their hands on. Then, when all the men had loaded the Rovers, Abdul lifted the heavy fuel barrel he had found next to the electric generator and emptied its contents on the rest of the ammunition crates. After everyone left the complex, he set it ablaze.

AMAN BAKISH AIR BASE NEAR AN NAJAF, SOUTHERN IRAQ.
Day One. 2030 Local Time.

As he walked around the concrete blast wall in front of the entrance to the large bunker, Colonel Abunnasr Manesh felt nauseated by the news of General Qazi Ali's death. Saddam himself had shot him in the face for questioning his orders. *Insanity!* General Ali had nothing but the best intentions toward his men and had no interest in military or political advancements. He was an officer for whom his men always came first; but Saddam had put a bullet through his head for speaking his feelings.

Disgusted with his leader, Manesh reached the entrance of the bunker. The two-foot-thick sliding steel door was opened a bit to let personnel in and out. He walked inside the shelter and approached two technicians working on the left Tumanskii turbofan of his beloved MiG-29 Fulcrum. The multirole attack fighter, utterly different from any previous MiG, stood in the middle of the large hangar, next to several MiG-23s. Its red, white, and black striped flag on each of the two canted vertical tails indicated that this MiG belonged to the Iraqi Air Force. The green stripes on the wing and nose indicated that it belonged to Manesh. The badge of the Mikoyan Gurevich design bureau was displayed on the sophisticated intake of both engines; a stylized wing with the acronym MiG in Cyrillic script. Manesh had thought about having the Soviet manufacturer's symbol removed, but decided against it. The Soviets should be proud of their creation.

"I would not have lost three MiG-23s this morning if my plane had been ready!"

The younger of the two technicians turned around and looked up into Manesh's brown eyes. He was about five inches shorter than Manesh's six feet. "I'm sorry, my colonel, but the engine had to be replaced. The spare parts from Baghdad did not arrive in time. We have been working without rest for twenty—"

"How long before it's ready?" Manesh asked, cutting off the mechanic's excuses.

The young man looked at the other mechanic, who was tightening a clamp on a hose over the single pressure refueling point in the port main undercarriage bay. They mumbled a few sentences back and forth. Finally, the young technician faced Manesh.

"Five more hours to complete all the checks."

Manesh looked at his watch. It was almost nine o'clock. "I'll be back at sunrise. That's almost nine hours from now." He walked away from the hangar and toward the runway on the other side of the blast wall. The base's living quarters and underground fuel tanks were on the opposite side of the runway from the concrete shelter, a simple but effective safety measure.

Before going around the blast wall, Manesh stared back at his MiG-29 through the small opening on the sliding door. It had always amazed him how the Soviets had managed to devise its unusual camouflage scheme, which seemed to change color slightly under different conditions, going from a sharp greenish hue at dawn and dusk to a mild bluish gray during the middle of the day.

With a final glance at the MiG, convinced that his plane would be airborne in just a few hours, Manesh walked into the base's living quarters—a camouflaged concrete building without air-conditioning. Not that having a cooling unit in his quarters had mattered since Kurdish rebels had knocked out the electricity three weeks before, forcing Manesh to rely on diesel-powered generators to provide electricity for the hangar and the communications bunker. Candles provided lighting for the rest of the base.

Pushing open a brown metallic door, Manesh walked inside the building. A short, narrow corridor ended in another door leading back outside. A single candle burned on a plastic dish on the floor of the corridor. Its dim light cast a flickering yellowish glow on the bare brick walls. There were three rooms on either side. Manesh's was the first on the right. It was also the only one with a private sink. He leaned down and grabbed the dish with the candle, then straightened and went inside his room.

The air felt thick. Manesh opened a window behind the bed. He set the dish on the wooden stand and walked to the sink, where he turned the knob of a single faucet on the side of a rusted basin. He was rewarded with a trickle of precious water, which he caught and splattered on his face. The Kurdish rebels had also sabotaged the main water pipes. Repair crews were still working to restore them. Tonight Allah had been merciful and spared a handful of water.

Breathing deeply and placing both hands on the sink, he raised his gaze and stared at the wrinkles around his brown eyes in the cracked mirror over the sink. Years of living in the desert had taken a toll on Manesh's forty-year-old body. The full cheeks of his youth now sagged down the sides of his face, making his once oval face look bottom-heavy. His full lips, as dry and coarse as the rest of his skin, made his face seem more off balance. With a receding hairline and a long, prominent nose, Manesh was not a handsome man by any means, but that didn't matter to the Iraqi colonel. He had stopped caring about the way he looked the day he dug his wife and newborn child out from under the rubble that had been his home during the war with Iran. From that day on, whatever love Manesh had ever felt turned into hatred. Hatred toward the Iranians for pulling the trigger and the Americans for not doing anything about it. After that day, he stopped caring about himself. He became aggressive in his flying, without concern for how close he came to death while pushing MiGs to the outer envelope of their design. He had nothing to lose. Nothing. The loss of his family had liberated him from all fear. There was nothing the enemy could take away from him that he hadn't already lost, except for his life. *And that,* Manesh thought as he walked to his bed, *would most certainly be a blessing.*

The colonel's thoughts returned to General Qazi Ali, one of the few friends he had left. Most had died during the war of 1991, and the rest, amazingly enough, had been killed by his own government for one reason or another.

Something has to give, reflected Manesh as he closed his eyes. *We simply can't continue living like this. Something has to give.*

He fell asleep in seconds.

USS *RANGER*. EIGHTY MILES NORTH OF BAHRAIN, PERSIAN GULF. Day One. 2100 Local Time.

The air inside the large hangar deck was hazy with engine fumes, making the fluorescent lights on the other side of the six-hundred-foot-long room almost invisible. Lieutenant Chico Delgado tried to make his way out of the crowded place, his ears ringing from the loud noise. Tomcats, Intruders, Prowlers, and Vikings filled the cavernous room as mechanics ran down checklists, performed diagnostics, and replaced damaged components.

Delgado struggled to hold his breath until he reached the exit but failed. He took a deep breath and wondered how his airplane mechanic friends could endure the constant smell of engine oil and other fumes that saturated the air in spite of the powerful ventilation system. He frowned. This had not been the first time that he'd come down to the hangar to visit his friends from the old *barrio* back in East L.A., yet for some reason tonight Delgado felt nauseated by the odors.

With his eyes half closed, he bumped into a mechanic. The smell of grease and the mechanic's rancid breath almost made Delgado vomit. The mechanic, a large, middle-aged man with his shirtsleeves rolled up to his elbows, displaying massive forearms decorated in tattoos, stared at Chico. Delgado politely apologized and continued his quest for the exit. He spotted the dim red light over the stairs leading to the upper deck and headed toward it, hoping to control his stomach until he got outside.

Delgado came out in the open and was welcomed by the night's cool, soothing breeze. He inhaled and exhaled several times, trying to expel every smoke particle out of his lungs before heading for the ship's medical facility. Something was definitely wrong with him. He gazed at the large island on the carrier's deck and then looked down toward the bow. He saw no planes on the catapults and a long row of men walking from the bow. *FOD walkdown.*

As he stood next to the nose of an A-6 Intruder with its wings folded up, Delgado's stomach muscles contracted, forcing food and bile into his throat. He clenched his teeth and managed to send the fetid mixture back down to his upset stomach. He knew he would not be able to block it again. He raced to the edge of the large flight deck, under the Intruder's exhaust, and unloaded his dinner over the side. Kneeling on the deck, he continued gagging for several minutes.

He slowly got up and inhaled the fresh night air several

times while leaning against one of the Intruder's rear landing struts, trying to pull himself back together again, but failed. The pain intensified; he fell on his side holding his stomach. Delgado heard noises and felt someone lifting him off the flight deck. Then everything went dark.

■ 4 ■

REVELATIONS

And you shall know the truth, and the truth shall make you free.
—John 8:32

Inside a six-by-six-foot cell, a young Iraqi officer named Syed Faisel stared at an unconscious fellow officer, also caged like an animal, across the narrow hall. He appeared to be at least forty, Syed reflected, estimating his age not on the way the colonel looked at that very moment, but the way he had looked a few hours ago, before Mossad officers took him away for an interrogation session. They had returned him only minutes ago, and now the coppery smell of blood from the colonel's bleeding face filled Syed's nostrils. He wasn't exactly sure what to say to such a brave man, who would endure so much pain to defend secrets of national security from the Israelis.

Syed frowned as he inspected the interior of the large room for the thousandth time: four red brick walls with two white doors. The ceiling, made of concrete, stood just a foot over his cage. He sighed, silently cursing himself for having been so stupid. Five months ago, he had been part of a secret escort mission aboard the

Omanian tanker *Kilf* in the Mediterranean, returning home from the Soviet port of Novorossiysk in the Black Sea. At the time, the large ship had been anchored three miles off the coast of Beirut, Lebanon, where Syed and the rest of the Iraqi escort team had transferred a number of small crates to a fishing boat and taken them ashore. After loading the cargo onto trucks in order to smuggle it through Syria and into Iraq, the team had parked the trucks inside a warehouse in East Beirut. Syed's commanding officer then sent him and another soldier back to the port to signal the fishing boat that the cargo was safe. On their way back, they had seen a very attractive woman standing on the side of the road next to a car with the hood up. She waved at them. They stopped and got out. She wore a black miniskirt and silk blouse. Syed and the other soldier approached her and she told them she was on her way to a party and her car had just quit running. She rubbed her fingers through her long, black hair and winked at them, asking if they would be kind enough to take her there. Syed noticed her hardened dark nipples pressed against her silk blouse. Since they didn't have to report back for another two hours, Syed had agreed.

Syed drove a fist into his palm as he vividly recalled how they had driven the woman to a house on the outskirts of the city. He had suspected something when the house they approached was dark, but she assured him that her girlfriends had probably stepped out for a little while. Then, when he had least expected it, several spotlights turned on him and the other soldier, and the woman had pulled out a gun from under her miniskirt and aimed it at them, saying that they were now her prisoners. Syed's friend had tried to resist, and she had shot him in the face. They tied and blindfolded Syed, put him on the back of a truck, and took him to a ship. He spent two months by himself inside a dark room, his only contact the silent guard who had brought him food and drink twice a day. From there his captors had taken him to their headquarters, where Syed found out he had been abducted by the Mossad. The woman was one of their agents.

Syed noticed the other officer open his eyes.

"Sabah al-kair," Syed said to the colonel, trying to cheer him up, but the colonel did not look up, remaining hunched over in his cage, holding his stomach.

"What did those blasphemous pigs do to you, sir?"

"Hmm . . . bastards! If I could only get my hands on . . . ahh, my ribs . . . on her, I would crush her neck with my hands."

Syed removed his uniform shirt and tossed it to the colonel, just a few feet away.

"Here, sir. Use it to wipe off the blood on your face." He saw the officer pick up the shirt and gently rub his face and neck with it.

"Your generosity is commendable, Lieutenant . . ."

"Faisel, sir," Syed responded, seeing the colonel squint to make out the remnants of what once had been the sewn name over the left pocket of Syed's long-sleeved army shirt.

"Why isn't your name—"

"I tore it off right before I was captured, sir. Those blasphemous pigs will never be able to get any information out of me, not even my name."

"Lieutenant Faisel, if we get out of this alive, I will personally see that you move to the rank of captain."

"That is very generous of you, sir."

"How did these pigs capture you?"

"It is an embarrassment, sir."

"I have heard many strange tales, Lieutenant. You mustn't worry. Go ahead. It is all right."

Syed cleared his throat and told him everything up to the point when they had brought him to his cell. The colonel did not interrupt him, letting him narrate the entire incident.

"So you know Khalela?"

Syed narrowed his eyes. "Well . . . yes, how do you . . ."

"I just spent the last few hours with her. She is the one who disfigured me. I tell you, Lieutenant, in all my years in the service I have never seen someone so beautiful and sadistic."

"Well, she tricked me in Beirut."

As Syed finished saying that, Khalela Yishaid, a senior Mossad operative, casually strode into the room, her tight-fitting dark olive fatigues revealing her well-proportioned curves. Both men stared at her.

"Have you changed your mind, Colonel?" she asked with a trace of sarcasm.

"Burn in hell, sadistic whore!" the colonel snapped back.

Syed remained silent, simply staring at Khalela. She was slightly tall, but definitely beautiful. Her light olive skin seemed radiant, even under the harsh light. The impressive high cheekbones, crowned with a pair of light green eyes . . . *Damn! No wonder I fell for it,* he reflected. Syed had not seen her since his arrival at the Mossad headquarters a few months back.

"I shall return, Colonel. We will talk then." She turned to Syed. "And you should not get so jealous, Lieutenant. Your turn comes next."

Syed looked back at the colonel's broken face and didn't respond. She strode out of the room as casually as she had stepped in. Syed breathed easier.

"I would not worry about it, Lieutenant. I don't believe she meant it."

"Well, after what she did to you, sir . . ."

"I will survive."

"Excuse my manners, Colonel, but I never did ask your name."

"Colonel Fassid Jassan, Third Tank Division, Western Iraq."

"An honor to meet you, sir."

"The honor is mine, Lieutenant. I do hope that the cargo made it to Iraq."

Syed looked around the large room, then spoke quietly. "It better, sir. You see, part of our secret cargo was conventional military equipment—rifles, ammunition, and spare parts. I know this because we had to inspect the cargo before loading it onto the trucks."

"And?"

"There were several unmarked boxes."

"Hmm . . . any idea of their contents?"

Syed spoke quietly with the colonel for a few moments. When he finished, the colonel's eyes were wide open.

"For the love of Allah! Do you realize what you are saying?"

"Yes, sir, and I would die rather than tell these pigs about it. Our government is finally about to become a major world power."

"Listen to me, Lieutenant. We must maintain secrecy. Only Allah knows how they would react if they knew about this."

"They shall get nothing from me, sir."

"Good. Now tell me, how long ago did you say they kidnapped you?"

"About five months ago, sir."

"Was the cargo headed for Baghdad?"

"No, sir. The orders were that once we reached Iraq we would take our cargo to a dairy products factory."

"A milk factory? Where?"

"South of An Najaf."

"Is Allahbad the place you're talking about?" asked Colonel Jassan with surprise, referring to one of the largest dairy products factories in Iraq that had survived the bombing of the 1991 Gulf War.

"Yes, sir. That is the one."

"That means by this time they must be assembling the first prototypes! Lieutenant, do you realize the implications of having such weapons?"

"Yes, colonel. The West will finally see that Iraq is a nation to be reckoned with!"

"Fi aman Allah!"

"You better count on more than Allah's protection to get you through this one," said Khalela, storming into the room accompanied by three large guards.

Neither of the two responded.

"Bring the colonel in for another session," she commanded her three guards. They unlocked the cage and dragged Jassan back out.

"Hazzan sayidan, Colonel!" shouted Syed, clutching his hands around the heavy steel bars.

"He will need more than just good luck to survive. Remember, I shall be back for you next."

Syed closed his eyes as they slammed the door behind them.

Colonel Jassan, in reality Hassin Abaraka, Mossad chief of Middle East operations, removed the plastic makeup from his face as Khalela handed him a wet towel.

"Did he talk?"

"Khalela, if I wasn't married I would give you a kiss right now! Your plan was brilliant! He told me everything. Hurry now, let's call for a general meeting. We mustn't waste any time! You must leave immediately!"

"Leave? Where? What did he tell you?" Khalela asked her superior.

"You won't believe your ears."

USS *RANGER*. EIGHTY MILES NORTH OF BAHRAIN, PERSIAN GULF. Day One. 2230 Local Time.

Lieutenant Kevin Dalton walked through a maze of compartments, each about thirty feet in length, oval-shaped hatches in the bulkheads connecting them. The hatches were identical in size and in perfect alignment. Kevin went down a flight of stairs, turned right, and continued for a hundred more feet until reaching his quarters, located between the top of the carrier's colossal hangars and the bottom side of the armored flight deck. He couldn't wait to tell Delgado the good news: they'd been assigned to fly together the following afternoon.

"Hey, Chico, guess what hap—May I help you?" he asked the medical officer looking inside his bunkmate's locker.

Lieutenant Chico Delgado did not feel great, but he definitely felt better than he had several hours before when some sailors had found him on the flight deck during the FOD walkdown. They had brought him to the carrier's medical facility, which resembled a small hospital, with a fully loaded operating room and intensive care unit. It had taken the doctor on duty less than five minutes to diagnose a severe case of food poisoning. After several laxatives and a stomach pump job that left Delgado swearing he would never eat again, the doctor had ordered him to rest for forty-eight hours before flying again.

Delgado stared at the ghostly pale, skinny orderly on the other side of the long room. The orderly lifted his head and regarded Delgado with his sunken, bloodshot eyes before going back to a paperback.

Delgado exhaled and flipped through a month-old issue of *Approach,* the naval aviation safety review magazine, without really reading anything. He couldn't concentrate in a place that felt, looked, and smelled like a hospital. He hated being here, and to make matters worse, the orderly looked like a mortician. Delgado would have already been out of here if he hadn't felt so bad.

Frowning and silently cursing his bad luck, he rubbed his hand over his bulldog tattoo. His mind drifted back to the foul-smelling, tattooed mechanic down in the maintenance deck. Those tattoos reminded him of the days when he was growing up in a *barrio* in East Los Angeles. Delgado smiled, remembering the old lady that lived down the street from his parents' house.

She had a friendly bulldog named Ernie. Delgado and his friends called him Pug. Delgado had grown attached to Pug. His owner let him out when Delgado and his friends were playing ball on the street, and Pug would fetch sticks and balls.

One day, members from a gang had come to his street while Delgado and his friends were playing with Pug. The gang members started to tease Pug, and the dog had bitten one of them. The other members then pulled out knives and stabbed the dog in front of Delgado. His friends, scared of the gang members, hadn't done anything about the dog yelping and bleeding in the street. Without thinking, an infuriated Delgado had shot across the street and kicked one of gang members in the groin. The others jumped him. Two put a knife in him and then the whole gang ran away. Delgado had been taken to the hospital with a cut in his leg and left forearm and was released the following morning. Pug had died that night. Delgado's parents had been upset at him for not cooperating with the police, for telling them nothing. They didn't understand the rules of the street. Anyone who cooperated with the police wound up dead or missing, or something terrible happened to their homes. *The law of the* barrio. *Unwritten but strictly enforced.*

A month later, after the doctors had pulled the stitches out of his arm and leg, Delgado had done something his entire family thought extremely stupid. Still upset about Pug, he had grabbed an old photo of the dog and gotten a tattoo. The scar on his forearm went across Pug's forehead.

He glanced across the room and caught the morbid orderly staring at him. *What's your problem anyway, dude?* Delgado thought. *Get a life, man! Go up on the deck and catch some rays. You're giving me the fucking creeps!*

Delgado heard footsteps. He lifted his head, relieved to see Kevin.

"I thought you guys from south of the border could eat and drink just about anything." Kevin grinned.

Delgado forced a smile. Kevin was one of few pilots Delgado truly liked. Kevin didn't have that arrogance that seemed to prevail among fighter pilots. "Not very funny, Crackers. You ever gotten your stomach pumped?"

"Nope."

"I tell you, man, I'd been stabbed a few times durin' the days back in the old *barrio,* but what that doctor did to me was worse."

"I talked to some medical officer. He says you'll be out of here in a couple of days." Kevin pulled up a chair next to the bed. "I guess that white stuff you drank didn't work, eh?"

Delgado saw a trace of amusement in Kevin's brown eyes.

"This must have been one of those few cases. I'm tellin' you, the shit's great."

Kevin smiled.

Delgado's long face became serious. "Say, *hermano,* the flight surgeon says I can't fly for a couple of days."

Kevin nodded. "Yep. You don't look in any shape to pull gees."

"No shit. I feel like hell."

Kevin checked his watch. "Well, gotta go get some sleep. Briefing's at eleven sharp. Be back to check on you tomorrow after the flight."

"Yeah, you do that, man. This place gives me the creeps, and that pale dude over there looks like he's ready to pull out the shovel and bury me."

Kevin smiled broadly while shaking his head. "See ya."

SALMAN ASAD AIR BASE, SAUDI ARABIA. NEAR IRAQI BORDER.
Day Two. 1020 Local Time.

In the dark, dry interior of the weathered tent, Ishmael Barzani could not make out the face of his American friend's companion, who had quietly sat in the corner sipping coffee throughout the entire debriefing. A single gas lamp hanging in the corner of the room provided all the illumination. Aside from the table and the few chairs scattered around, Ishmael saw no other furniture inside the tent.

He sat near the entrance, next to Abdul. The American sat across the table wearing a white short-sleeved shirt and dark pants. He was a tall man, slightly on the heavy side, but not by much. His black hair fell over his forehead, partially covering a pair of eyebrows as thick as his full lips. Ishmael didn't know his real name, but that didn't matter to him or his band. They referred to the American as the *Ba'i,* or merchant. All that really mattered to the Kurdish rebel were the British-made shoulder-launched Javelin missiles neatly arranged behind the *Ba'i.*

"I'll take it you wish to make a trade, my friend?"

Ishmael, the only one in the guerrilla group who spoke English—courtesy of some British missionaries he'd known for a number of years almost a decade before—

nodded slightly. The missionaries had not only taught Ishmael English but also geography and math—enough for the intelligent Kurd to teach his own people after the Iraqi government had expelled the missionaries for espionage.

Ishmael looked at Abdul Mozakhu sitting next to him and then pointed to the American *Ba'i*. Abdul pulled out a small sack and handed it to Ishmael, who in turn looked at the American, pulled out the documents and the map, unfolded a section of the map—enough for the *Ba'i* to raise an eyebrow—and pointed at the missiles. "These are very important papers," Ishmael said in a low voice, careful not to touch his loose tooth with his tongue. He still had not found the time to pull it out.

The American leaned back on his chair. "Very well, if they are of any importance to our troops, we might be able to reach an agreement."

Ishmael nodded. The American *Ba'i* was always fair, as long as they brought something to bargain with. This time, he tossed the documents and the map across the table. The American grabbed them, inspected them briefly, and then lifted his head in obvious surprise.

"Damn! Where in the hell did you guys get a hold of something like this?"

Ishmael smiled, proud that Allah had given him the wisdom to correctly assess the strategic value of the documents. "That is our secret, *Ba'i*."

The American frowned slightly, then extended his right hand across the table. "All right, Ishmael, it seems that we will be able to help each other once more."

Ishmael, already aware of this Western custom, responded by also extending his hand and pumping the American's. He gave Ishmael a thin smile, revealing two rows of glistening white teeth. As another bolt of pain streaked across his diseased molars, the Kurd couldn't help but feel jealous of the American. In a way, Ishmael wished he could bargain for some dental care at the American base. He felt certain that it wouldn't take long for an American doctor and his expensive equipment to fix Ishmael's problems, but the Barzani in him could never allow that. Such public acknowledgment of his misfortune would be unbecoming to a Kurdish leader.

After his men had carried the powerful Javelins outside and loaded them up into their Rover desert vehicles, Ishmael turned around and stared at the American *Ba'i,* standing by the canvas entrance of the large tent. "Thank you, *Ba'i.*"

"No, thank *you,* Ishmael. This information will be very helpful to us. Listen, these are very complex weapons to use effectively. Would you like us to give you or any of your men some training?"

"Not necessary, *Ba'i,* training will come." He smiled and waved as the four-vehicle caravan sped away.

"Those weapons won't do them any good without proper training, Bob. How are they going to use them?" asked Colonel Peter Halston, U.S. Air Force, from the corner of the room.

Robert Bourdeaux, senior officer from the Cover Action staff within the Directory of Operations of the CIA, regarded Halston for a few seconds. "Ishmael hinted that their training will come. I'm not sure what he meant by that."

"You think their maps are really worth that much?" Halston approached Bourdeaux and leaned over the table.

"Well, look here and tell me what you think." Bourdeaux finished unfolding the large map on the dimly lit table inside the desert-camouflage tent. Unlike Bourdeaux, who measured almost six feet tall and weighed nearly two hundred pounds—twenty pounds too many, in Bourdeaux's opinion—Halston was just a couple of inches shorter, in awesome physical shape, and always had a perfect tan.

Bourdeaux didn't have a tan; he hadn't had one since leaving the Air Force a decade before to go back to school to pursue a doctorate in Middle Eastern Affairs. He had landed a job instantly at the CIA upon graduation, where it didn't take him long to work himself up to his current position as one of the best operations officers the agency had to offer. His ability to recruit agents inside Iraq, like the Kurd Ishmael, and his objectivity and common sense in analyzing data and problems—in addition to his thorough knowledge of the Middle East—were the reasons he had been posted here, where the action was. As an operations officer and satellite imaging expert temporarily reporting directly to the director of Central Intelligence back in Langley, Bourdeaux knew the importance of being here. Under normal circumstances, Bourdeaux would report to the deputy director for operations, who reported to the deputy director of Central Intelligence, who in turn reported to the director of the CIA, but given the recent findings in the European Division about Saddam Hussein acquiring nuclear weapons components, the CIA director had broken the chain of command and had sent Bourdeaux to the region under orders to report directly to him.

Bourdeaux liked Halston, who had a full plate of responsibilities these days. Not only was Halston responsible for interfacing with the CIA, he also happened to be the base commanding officer's right-hand man. Halston was responsible for Combat Search and Rescue (CSAR) teams, and he had recently inherited the job of managing a full staff of majors and captains overlooking dozens of technicians handling the mind-numbing communications of the base with other bases, with U.S. Central Command Air Forces (CENTAF) back in Riyadh, and with the AWACS controlling fighters in the southern no-fly zone.

But Bourdeaux didn't like Halston only because of the colonel's amazing ability to handle many tasks at once. Their friendship went back to their Air Force years, before Bourdeaux had left to pursue other interests. Although they'd been best of friends in the service, they had seldom heard from one another after Bourdeaux left the Air Force. They both had chosen very demanding careers, Halston had gotten married, and between his job and his wife, Bourdeaux just about lost touch with his old Air Force buddy. A few years later, Bourdeaux had received a call in the middle of the night from a mourning Halston—his wife had been killed in an auto accident. Bourdeaux had wasted no time in going to his friend's side. Years later, Bourdeaux finally realized what a small world it was when he had arrived at the desert air base and found Halston as his liaison.

"See this, Pete?" Bourdeaux pointed to a red pencil line connecting the port of Umm Qasr in the Persian Gulf to a large red circle encompassing almost five hundred square miles of land centered around An Najaf, in south-central Iraq.

"Yeah, what about it?"

"This is the destination of a cargo unloaded at Umm Qasr."

"Cargo? What cargo?"

Running a finger over the Arabic writing of the document Ishmael had given him along with the map, Bourdeaux said, "The cargo of thirty Russian-made SS-11 rocket boosters."

"Wh—what? SS-11s? Why in the hell . . . Jesus! Does that mean what I think it means?"

The CIA officer nodded grimly. "I'm afraid so. We've had our suspicions about the Iraqis assembling a larger rocket to use in conjunction with their nuclear weapons program, and this map is the first solid piece of evidence that they're doing just that."

"Well, that might be true, but five hundred square miles is a lot of space. Those boosters could be anywhere."

Bourdeaux nodded. Included in the circle were four chemical plants, two large dairy products factories, one large oil refinery, five air bases, and several large cities, including Baghdad, Karbala, Falluja, Salman Pak, and Al Kut.

"Has anything been picked up from satellite photos?" Halston asked.

"Ah . . . no. We have several KH-11 orbital passes each day. Nothing's been picked up on the satellite's high-resolution camera, though I'm not that surprised."

Halston tilted his head and studied Bourdeaux for a moment. "What makes you say that?"

"Well, you see, we're talking about boosters only, not

entire SS-11 missiles. I think the boosters are somewhere in the neighborhood of eight to ten feet long, right?" Bourdeaux waited for Halston to acknowledge before continuing. "I'm sure that if the Iraqis didn't want us to know about them, they might have had them dismantled prior to shipment." Bourdeaux walked to the gas lamp hanging in the corner and turned the knob to maximum intensity. "Did our bombers hit these plants during Desert Storm?"

"Ah, yes and no," responded Halston as he leaned over the map once more and inspected it closer. "We hit all four chemical factories repeatedly. We also blasted their refinery and a number of power plants around Baghdad and other cities, but we never touched the dairy products factories. They're still considered civilian structures at CENTAF. They provide food for a lot of women and children. Dairy products are a big part of their diet. During Desert Storm, CENTAF decided to leave those two factories alone. They had no military significance, but there would have been bad political repercussions if we'd hit them without proper motive, if you catch my drift."

"Exactly how far away is the center of the circle—An Najaf—from us?"

"Ah . . . let's see," Halston said, looking at the map. "It looks like it's a little over two hundred miles from where Iraq, Kuwait, and Saudi Arabia intersect."

"Don't we have a large deployment of tanks further west of there?" Bourdeaux pointed to a location a hundred miles west of the intersection, where allied forces ran war exercises in preparation for a second ground war, if it ever came to that.

"Yes, that's correct. Those men are about one hundred seventy miles away from An Najaf."

"Isn't that within the range of the Scud B?" Bourdeaux asked.

"Well, the Scud's range is somewhere between one hundred and two hundred miles, depending on the type of warhead used. But the Iraqis have modified them to improve their range, and renamed them the 'Al Hussein' missile."

"What's its range?" asked Bourdeaux while rubbing a hand through his thinning brown hair.

Halston stared in the distance for a second or two. "Okay, to start with, keep in mind that the Al Hussein, just like the Scud B from which it was developed, is a very inaccurate missile that the Iraqis have used in the past against densely populated areas only. Our estimate's that they modified it to achieve a range of roughly three hundred fifty miles. The changes they made, though, were very crude. The Scud's a solid-propellant missile. The Iraqis simply strapped liquid-propellant rockets to the sides. In doing so, they increased the range but lost reliability—part of the reason why some of them fell apart in midair during Desert Storm. Also, their accuracy wasn't improved much."

"But with that range, they could get lucky and hit some of our installations in Saudi Arabia—assuming they fire them from within this red circle."

"Yes, they could, but I wouldn't worry about it much. You've seen how inaccurate their missiles have been. The Scud in its present form is nothing but a terrorist weapon. It has no strategic purpose from a military standpoint. But based on the Kurds' information, I think the Iraqis might be working on a next generation Scud, one that uses liquid-propellant technology reliably."

Bourdeaux rubbed his chin as Halston sat back on his chair and continued his dissertation on the Iraqi missiles. Fifteen minutes later, Halston left for the communications tent.

Robert Bourdeaux felt the stinging pain behind his eyes and in the back of his neck returning. He'd developed chronic headaches during college. His family doctor had told him it was due to a combination of excessive reading, too much stress, a poor diet, and lack of sleep. At the time, Bourdeaux was trying to get his bachelor's and master's degrees in five years instead of the regular six. Averaging twenty-one credit-hours per semester, Bourdeaux didn't have any time left for himself. That's when his parents put the brakes on him and forced him to take a semester off. Bourdeaux argued that he would fall behind in his career, but after his parents insisted,

Bourdeaux agreed, finally realizing he was on the verge of burnout. In time, the chronic headaches subsided, but they never went away completely, always returning whenever he allowed too much stress in his life, or if he began cutting back his sleeping hours or ate poorly. He reached into his pocket and pulled out the ever-present pack of extra-strength Tylenol caplets. In his line of work he couldn't afford to operate without them.

As he popped three in his mouth—two just didn't quite do the job anymore—Bourdeaux recalled the information Halston had just told him about the rumors floating around Air Force Intelligence about Iraqis working on an even longer range missile. Something they called the "Al Ahar" missile. It was supposed to be another Scud B-based missile, but with far longer range than any of its predecessors. Halston felt that was the reason for the new boosters. If Halston's military analysts had done their homework right, the consensus was that Iraq could be in the process of developing a tactical missile with a range in excess of one thousand miles and a much more accurate guidance system.

Bourdeaux's square face hardened and slowly turned blood-red as he clenched his teeth and pressed his full lips into a tight frown. *How? How in the hell did we allow those maniacs access to the damned technology to build weapons!* He was aware of the implications of such a missile. It would give the Iraqis the capability of striking targets anywhere from Greece down to the Gulf of Oman. Most of the oil installations in the region would be within their reach. And if they combined the accuracy of such a missile with the massive destruction of a nuclear warhead . . . *Jesus, what a nightmare!*

Bourdeaux rubbed the two-day-old stubble on his chin, then turned his head when he heard the thundering roar of the main rotors of two Apache helicopters accelerating to takeoff RPM a hundred yards away at the edge of the paved runway. The large dark gray beasts, with an array of mixed weapons under their fixed wings, left the ground under the powerful thrust generated by two large turbofans, creating a cloud of dust that ap-

peared to engulf them, until they reappeared and accelerated toward the west.

He shook his head, disappointed that their satellites
would not be able to pick up much of the activity.
Satellites were great for noticing deployment of troops,
tanks, and aircraft, but the disassembled rockets were
not that big. Satellites would not be able to pick them out
until it was too late. In addition, the Iraqis probably
would camouflage them, well aware of satellite capability.

Bourdeaux knew he had to do something about it
immediately. He had the feeling that given their limited
resources the Iraqis were probably assembling the rockets at one place. The United States had to strike while all
the rockets were grouped in one location. After assembly
the Iraqis would be able to scatter them across the
country in mobile-launcher units, making it extremely
difficult—if not impossible—for the United States to
find them.

He was about to go over the information on the map
again when the base's sirens came to life.

Damn!

Bourdeaux raced toward the communications tent but
stopped halfway. Halston was already running out of it.

"What is going on? Another drill?"

"No drill. Three Scuds! All headed for King Khalid
Military City. We're gonna try to intercept them as they
fly overhead." Halston ran toward the MSQ-104 Patriot
control station, mounted on an M-818 tractor, located a
few hundred feet from the communications tent. King
Khalid Military City was one of the largest air bases in
Saudi Arabia. The U.S. Air Force still kept a large
number of planes and pilots stationed there. "Radar
shows the missiles to be fifty miles away. We'll intercept
in a few minutes."

Bourdeaux started breathing heavily as he struggled to
keep up with Halston's pace. Iraq had not fired a single
Scud since the end of the Gulf War . . . could those
missiles actually be . . . *Oh, Jesus!*

"Pete . . . those missiles could be nuclear!"

Halston came to a screeching halt.

"Fuck! I never thought about—"

"I hope to God they're just Scuds, but . . ."

Halston nodded. "No shit. I hope so, too." He began to run again. "Well, that still doesn't change the way we're gonna blast them."

Bourdeaux ran after him. Halston reached the back of the control station and knocked twice. The phased-array radar—the key element in the Patriot system—stood less than fifty feet in front of the control station. Consisting of more than five thousand radar antenna elements, the radar system was capable of detecting and tracking one hundred targets at a time. Two hundred feet beyond the radar was a row of eight M-901 launcher stations, each housing four missiles.

The rear door swung open, and they stepped inside the murky room and closed the door behind them.

"How does it look?" Halston asked a black sergeant manning the control station.

"No problem. System's in automatic. We got 'em tracked," the sergeant responded without looking away from the screen.

Halston turned to Bourdeaux. "The phase-array radar found them and is waiting for the right time to launch."

Bourdeaux nodded.

"There isn't much that's going to happen in here," Halston said. "Let's go back outside."

Bourdeaux followed him out, and the two of them stood next to the portable generator that powered the entire system.

Bourdeaux spotted a sudden bright flash coming from one of the launchers. He snapped his head in the direction of the launcher and watched the Thiokol TX-486 single-thrust solid rocket motor propel the 2200-pound missile through the rubbery membrane that sealed the launch tube and into a bright sky, accelerating it to Mach 3 in seconds. There were five more flashes. Five more Patriots.

His eyes quickly scanned the sky for a sign of the incoming Scuds.

"Over there, Bob," said Halston. "See it?"

Bourdeaux could see the contrail of two Patriots closing in on something. . . . *Wait, there it is!*

Two bright flashes in the sky were followed by an even larger flash.

"That's a kill," said Halston. Bourdeaux nodded and shifted his gaze toward the second set of Patriots closing in on another Scud: two flashes as the Patriots' high-explosive warheads were detonated by proximity fuses. The resulting cloud of shrapnel engulfed the incoming Scud, creating the third flash that Bourdeaux saw a few seconds before his ears registered the blast. By that time, the third Scud had also been destroyed.

In the distance, roughly twenty miles away and five thousand feet high, Bourdeaux saw three clouds of smoking debris, each spaced about two miles from the others, slowly fall down to earth. Holding his breath, he waited. Most nuclear warheads were fitted with an altimeter fuse, which detonated the warhead after it descended below a certain altitude.

Bourdeaux smiled when the debris disappeared below the horizon and nothing else happened. That meant that the missiles were either regular Scuds, or the Patriots had taken out the nuclear warheads and not just the booster sections of the missiles. That was the reason for firing two Patriots per Scud. The first few Scuds that had gotten through the missile defenses back in 1991 were actually struck by Patriots but not fully destroyed. In one case, a Patriot struck the tail of an incoming Scud, leaving the warhead intact. Two Patriots per Scud doubled the chances of the antimissile missile system. It had earned the respect of the same military analysts that originally considered it a costly boondoggle. The Patriot system had experienced several setbacks and cost overruns during development, mostly because the air-defense system was pushing the limits of state-of-the-art technology, but after the initial problems had been solved, the Patriot system worked exactly as designed.

Bourdeaux scanned the horizon one final time. The Patriot's kill ratio was miraculous.

THE WHITE HOUSE.
Day Two. 0530 Local Time.

Sitting behind his desk, President Bill Clinton read his daily briefing in the presence of his CIA director, defense secretary, and the undersecretary of Middle Eastern Affairs, General Kenneth Draper. His secretary of state was in Geneva talking with Iraqi Foreign Minister Tariq Aziz in a last-ditch effort to settle the problem through diplomacy, but Clinton knew the trip was academic. As it had been prior to the Gulf War of 1991, nothing would be accomplished. The onsite CIA officer Bourdeaux, however, had come up with a piece of highly revealing data. The Iraqis had acquired thirty SS-11 boosters, and they were hiding them somewhere in south-central Iraq.

President Clinton, wearing a pair of khaki slacks, a white Polo shirt, and white tennis shoes, stood, checked his watch, walked around the desk, then sat on a chair close to the cream sofas. Legs crossed, hands resting on the arms of the wooden chair, and blue analytical eyes half-closed, the president said to Kettler, "How soon before you can narrow down the exact spot where they're hiding the boosters?"

The CIA director rubbed a hand through his unkempt hair and thought for a few moments. "Now we look for abnormal patterns, Mr. President."

Clinton tilted his head. "Abnormal patterns?"

"Yes, sir. We have satellite image archives that go back three decades, and because of the Gulf War of 1991, we have collected a very detailed picture of how much traffic to expect at certain factories during specific times of the day in the region. We know the traffic patterns of all roads in Iraq during the day and night. We also know the types and sizes of vehicles associated with each plant and road. Now we start looking for anomalies in those patterns, out-of-the-ordinary events that might lead us to the spot where the Iraqis are assembling those nukes. Although this might sound a bit far-reaching, it is a very exact science, just like during the Cuban Missile Crisis, when the CIA was in the business of counting Soviet missiles entering Cuba. Even though the missiles were crated and often covered with canvas during shipment, we could tell which kind of missile it was based on the length, shape, and width of the crates. Our situation is a bit different since we're not dealing with fully assembled missiles, but the principle is the same.

"The bottom line here, sir, is that the CIA has images on anyone who does anything on this planet that's exposed to the sky. You put those images in the hands of expert analysts, and you got yourself mounds of information."

"And then again, you might not get *mounds* of information," added Kenneth Draper to the obvious annoyance of the CIA director. Draper ignored Kettler's burning stare and continued, his eyes on President Clinton. "Although I agree with Mr. Kettler that satellite imagery does a lot of good for intelligence gathering, I strongly believe that it is *not* an exact science, Mr. President. The problem with this approach is that the data could be misleading, making you believe that an increase in traffic at a specific location, or the usage of larger or different sized vehicles at that location means you have found your boosters, while in reality it could be due to an entirely different reason, sending you on a wild-goose chase. Yes, you can take pictures of everything that is going on, but you can't get inside the heads of the people that you're taking pictures of, and actions can be very deceiving at times. Also, don't forget that the Iraqis are no fools. They know we're watching them. They could have changed the traffic pattern of one location as a diversion while moving the boosters to another using normal traffic patterns."

"That's a possibility," countered CIA Director Kettler, "but we're fully versed on the art of camouflage, decoys, and deception. In its history, the CIA has succeeded time and again at filtering out decoys to find the real data."

"When?" Draper asked.

"That's classified. You don't need to know."

"That's enough, gentlemen," the president said as

Kettler and Draper exchanged stern glances.

Theories. Possibilities. Clinton sighed, closing his eyes. He had to be sure of the location before launching an air strike. The recent Scud attack had telegraphed Saddam's position clearly: he was trying to provoke U.S. action in the region to which, Clinton feared, the Iraqi leader would retaliate with nuclear weapons.

Shaking his head, Clinton decided he could not risk an air strike at this moment. Doing so could result in devastating consequences.

Jaws clenched, his eyes burning a hole into the carpet, the president drove a fist into his palm, muttering, "If I only knew where they were."

▪ 5 ▪

⸳CAPs

"Our strategy to go after this army is very, very simple. First, we're going to cut it off, and then we're going to kill it."

—General Colin Powell
(during Operation Desert Storm)

USS _RANGER_. EIGHTY MILES NORTH OF BAHRAIN, PERSIAN GULF.
Day Two. 1130 Local Time.

Lieutenant Kevin Dalton braced himself against the g-forces pressing him into his ejection seat as the Tomcat accelerated down the carrier's short deck from zero to 140 knots in less than three seconds. Kevin climbed quickly to ten thousand feet and joined Lancaster to fly yet another CAP mission for the USS _Wisconsin_.

"Head to three three zero and station bears three six zero for ninety," Kevin's new RIO, Lieutenant Jeffrey "Soup" Campbell, a twenty-year-old native of Oklahoma City, said over the ICS, giving Kevin a courtesy bearing and heading. In reality, since Kevin was flying wing for Lancaster, he really didn't need to know their heading. As wing, Kevin merely had to follow Lancaster.

"Rog," responded Kevin. This was the first time that he had been teamed up with Campbell.

The fighters continued on a northerly course under a cloudy afternoon sky.

AMAN BAKISH AIR BASE NEAR AN NAJAF, SOUTHERN IRAQ.
Day Two. 1215 Local Time.

Colonel Abunnasr Manesh strode into the airplane shelter and approached the red cockpit ladder of his MiG-29 Fulcrum. He stopped briefly to zipper up the G suit he wore over his flight suit and to double-check the green visor of his helmet. Three older MiG-21s stood behind the Fulcrum—all the fighters remaining from his twenty-plane air wing. The other three aircraft shelters in the base were filled with four T-72 tanks, two small Gazelle scout helicopters, two Hind-D attack helicopters, a couple of supply trucks, and five jeeps.

Manesh glanced at boxes of spare parts and a ton of maintenance equipment filling the entire left side of the bunker. The blackened concrete floor—the result of countless tire marks and oil spills—contrasted harshly with the white-painted walls and ceiling, from which a maze of neon lights hung. Two huge openings at the rear led to well-disguised ventilation tubes on the surface.

"Your plane is ready, Colonel!"

Ignoring the young technician's proud announcement, Manesh stepped up the ladder, and with a graceful gymnastic maneuver, he lifted his legs over the side and positioned himself inside the cockpit. Once more, his superiors were asking him to fly a mission into the no-fly zone. This time, Manesh would make the flight count. "Has the first team been advised?"

"Yes, sir. They will leave in five minutes."

"Perfect!"

Manesh started the Tumanskii turbofans and lowered the hinged canopy. He scanned the conventional, all-analog instrument panel, mentally going through the pre-taxi checklist, very similar to that of the older MiG-23. As he finished this initial and critical check, Manesh plugged the plastic hose from his G suit into a receptacle under the instrument panel. He inched forward the side-by-side throttle controls, which were mounted on piggyback slides on the right side of the cockpit, and stepped hard on the brake pedals. The craft began to move forward and abruptly stopped. Satisfied that the brakes were operating properly, Manesh released them and the 39,000-pound craft bolted forward, leaving behind the safety of the concrete shelter.

Although all he needed to taxi the craft were minor throttle adjustments and use of the rudder pedals, which directly controlled the nosewheel, Manesh curled the fingers of his left hand around the control stick and thanked Allah and the engineers at Mikoyan-Gurevich for having designed such a long control column. It gave him excellent leverage.

Minutes later, the Fulcrum rolled off the hot tarmac at 170 knots and leveled off in flight at 150 feet above ground level.

Closely following the contours of the rugged terrain, Manesh concentrated on altitude and speed, trying to avoid radar detection by the American fighters and the ever-present AWACS. He succeeded. Five minutes later, the MiG-29 entered Iranian airspace, where he flew low and slow over the coastline, well within safety, yet close enough to monitor Allied activities in the Persian Gulf.

He checked his watch. The decoy team of MiG-21s would arrive in the area in one minute.

"Wolfpack Two Zero Two, Cougar," Kevin Dalton heard the crew from the AWACS say over the squadron frequency.

"Cougar, Two Zero Two," replied Lieutenant Baby Johnson from the backseat of Lancaster's plane.

"Three bandits. Your vector zero six zero at seventy, buster."

Kevin briefly closed his eyes as Johnson responded, *"Two Zero Two."*

"You got them, Soup?" Kevin asked.

"Flight of three, echelon, stacked left, one five zero at sixty-eight. Select Phoenix," Campbell responded, confirming radar painting of three MiGs heading southeast sixty-eight miles away in a straight line for the *Wisconsin.*

They're going after the ships! Kevin flicked his thumb on the control stick and saw an AIM-54 Phoenix selected. He felt his heartbeat increasing. The rules of engagement had been changed since yesterday by presidential order: Kevin was not allowed to fire unless the incoming MiGs fired first. *Oh, shit. Here we go again.*

"Head zero two zero to intercept," said Campbell.

"Knockers up," directed Lancaster, calling to select master arm of all weapons aboard the Tomcat. *"Rules of engagement, gentlemen!"*

The pair of Tomcats lowered their noses, dashing earthward through the sky on a near-vertical descent to five thousand feet, where they leveled off. The MiGs continued on a direct course toward the *Wisconsin,* only forty miles away.

"Sorted, Shadow," Kevin heard Soup Campbell say over the squadron frequency, indicating that he had a lock on the lead bandit.

"Burners, now," directed Lancaster. The Tomcats went into afterburners to reduce the smoke coming out of their exhausts.

Kevin strained his eyes, trying to get a visual on the enemy, who slowly appeared over the horizon as mere specks.

"Tally three ten, slightly high," said Baby Johnson as Kevin spotted three MiG-21 "Fishbeds" flying in an echelon formation at ten o'clock. His index finger caressed the firing trigger on his control stick but waited for Lancaster to make the first move. The MiGs were too close to the *Wisconsin.*

"I got all three, Shadow! They're not breaking away!" reconfirmed Campbell.

"Fox three!" ordered Lancaster, giving Kevin the order to fire.

Kevin loosed one Phoenix; Lancaster another one. Being so close to the targets, the missiles immediately switched to their own active radar seeking system.

While flying below twenty feet above the waters off the Iranian coast, Manesh saw the Americans fire on the MiG-21s. He manually inflated his G suit and armed three of his AA-11 Archer air-to-air missiles. After a brief prayer to Allah, he turned toward the Tomcats.

The huge plumes of white smoke racing toward the MiGs got the attention of the Iraqi pilots right away. Kevin knew that the Iraqis had plenty of respect for the F-14 and the Phoenix from the years of war against the Iranians and their Tomcats, as well as from the Desert Storm experience. He watched all three MiG pilots eject before the missiles struck. What bothered him was that the pilot of the third MiG ejected without having a missile on his tail. . . .

"Break left! Missiles in the air!" Kevin heard Lancaster shout as his Tomcat broke hard to the left.

What in the hell's going on? Kevin thought as he wracked his Tomcat in a hard left turn following his lead. A second later, he saw three contrails snaking toward Lancaster. *Jesus!*

Kevin watched in helpless horror as three missiles closed in on Lancaster's F-14 from the direction of Iran. The Tomcat, almost in a vertical dive, managed to fool two of the three missiles by dispensing flares before the last one impacted its left turbofan.

"Mayday, Mayday! I'm single engine, losing hydraulics on both sides!"

With the loss of one engine, the wounded Tomcat was crippled but flyable. Without hydraulics, the aircraft could not be controlled. Before Lancaster could react, the F-14 stalled and went into a spin. Kevin watched the fighter, almost as if it had been sucked in by a tornado, spiraling toward the gulf.

"Tally one Bandit. Eleven o'clock low!" said Campbell, but Kevin barely heard him. His eyes followed his leader's plane.

"Pull up, Shadow!" Kevin screamed. "Pull up, dammit!"

Using the surviving turbofan and the little that remained of hydraulics, Lancaster pulled out of the spin and managed to level off just as a MiG-29 rolled behind him.

"Fulcrum at your six!" Kevin called.

"Get him off my ass!" screamed Lancaster.

"Cavalry's coming, Shadow. I'll get him off your tail. Just a few more seconds."

Kevin got his Tomcat behind and to the right of the MiG, but Lancaster's plane went for a dive and the MiG followed, ruining Kevin's shot by placing both aircraft in the windscreen. There was no telling which target the Sidewinder would go after.

"Dammit! The angle's no good for the heaters! I'm closing in for guns. Hang on—" Kevin's words were cut short by several bursts from the MiG's six-barrel 30mm cannon. Kevin noticed the rounds ripping across the mostly aluminum skin of Lancaster's F-14A.

"Jesus Christ, Crackers. Get this asshole off my tail!"

"Hang on, Shadow." Kevin followed the two-plane caravan through a series of turns, climbs, and dives, trying to put the pipper on the MiG's tail, but every time he got an angle, the fighters changed direction. Another burst shot from the MiG's cannon. More wing debris came off Lancaster's Tomcat. Kevin's wings were at twenty degrees now, and he thumbed out his slats to stay with the MiG.

"This guy's chewing me up!"

"Hold on!"

Smoke spewed out of Lancaster's remaining turbofan. The Tomcat began to fall.

"Get the hell out of there, Shadow!" shouted Kevin.

"Two Zero Two will eject. May Day, May D—"

The squadron frequency went dead as the MiG continued to unload 30mm projectiles all over the fuselage of the dying Tomcat.

"You bastard! It was already going down!" Kevin screamed as the canopy gave under the brutal punishment and the heads of Lancaster and the RIO snapped forward. An overwhelming sense of anger filled Kevin as the F-14A spiraled down to the ocean. The MiG stayed with the doomed craft all the way down, pulling up at the last minute and barely missing the enraged flames that surged up into the sky when the fighter hit the serene waters. The craft rolled its wings in shameless victory and turned toward the Iraqi coastline with full afterburners.

Kevin gave chase. The Iraqi jet was within Sparrow range when it made a wide left turn and safely reached land.

With the determination that comes from an utter, unyielding commitment, Kevin hurled his craft into a wickedly tight left turn and felt the g's as he stressed the craft's fuselage to maintain the turn needed to intercept.

"Wolfpack Two One Four, Red Crown. Say status." Kevin heard the crew of the missile cruiser USS *Bunker Hill* call out his craft's call sign on the squadron frequency.

Kevin eyed the radio and shifted his gaze back toward the MiG. The Iraqi flew three four zero at Mach 1.8. Kevin slowly closed the range to eight nautical miles.

"Wolfpack Two One Four, your bogey is Waterloo Red. Return to base."

Kevin didn't respond.

"Dammit, Crackers! I know you're listening. Turn around now, dammit! That MiG's heading home. It's off limits! Turn back! NOW!" cried Commander John McDeere over the squadron frequency. Kevin blinked twice in surprise, not expecting to hear his commanding officer's voice on the radio. *Must have just been launched as Alert Five to backup,* thought Kevin.

The MiG was now less than three miles away. Kevin was closing. He could see its white-hot exhausts dodging the low hills by the coast. He stayed with it, trying to get a lock.

"Dammit, Crackers! If you ever want to fly again, you better turn your craft around immediately!"

Kevin felt the left console switches until he located the radio, flipping it off and on a few times before switching it off. The radio went dead.

"Jesus, Crackers! What in the heck you think you're doing? You heard Ghost. You better—" Campbell began to say.

"Soup, just watch for MiGs, would you?"

"Like fucking shit! You better turn this plane around right now!"

"No way."

"Turn around, Crackers, or I'll eject us both!"

"We're too fast—besides I know you want this guy as bad as I do! C'mon, man! That asshole just killed Shadow and Baby Johnson in cold blood in front of your eyes. Are you going to let him get away with it? I'm going after the fucker, and whether you like it or not, you're coming along! Got that?"

Campbell mumbled something in a half-apologetic tone, but Kevin wasn't listening anymore. He felt the fury from within consuming him as he blinked his watery eyes to focus them on the tiny point in the sky less than three miles away. The HUD painted a white diamond over it. Through tears, he saw the craft grow larger and larger. The solid wall of blue five hundred feet below abruptly turned brown and green as the Tomcat reached the coastal plains of Iraq.

Kevin hurtled after the MiG-29 in a tight turn, but the Fulcrum countered by going into a steep climb and turn to the left, momentarily widening the gap. Kevin stayed on him and closed. He glanced at the white diamond.

"Select heat!" noted Campbell.

"Switching . . . range?"

"Two miles and closing."

Kevin kept closing the gap as the Iraqi craft attempted to outmaneuver him. The diamond flashed. "Fox two!"

The solid-propellant rocket boosted the missile to Mach 3 and Kevin watched its river of smoke hastening toward the MiG.

With one missile locked on his tail, Colonel Abunnasr Manesh simultaneously pulled the control stick and enabled the flare dispenser by depressing a button on the control column. The craft responded by adopting a vertical climb and dispensing a cloud of hot flares. The American missile went for the decoy as he continued applying rearward pressure on the control stick to achieve an inverted loop, but the American fighter stayed with him. Manesh slammed the stick forward left and felt his body lifting from the seat and the top of his thighs pressing against the bands lying flush against the bottom of the instrument panel, the craft's leg restraint system, as negative g's piled up on his body. With his eyeballs pounding from the rising blood pressure in his head, Manesh forced a backward glance and noticed the Tomcat rolling off behind him and closing. Manesh estimated the American fighter was now within cannon firing range as both craft sped toward the ground at one and a half times the speed of sound.

When Lieutenant Kevin Dalton estimated that the runaway MiG had entered the range of his Vulcan cannon, he switched to guns and lined up the craft on the pipper of the HUD, but the moment he released the first burst of 20mm fire, the MiG cut sharp left, ruining his angle.

Cursing inside his oxygen mask, Kevin swung the control stick left and followed it. Halfway through the turn, the MiG inverted and switched directions before dropping to treetop level and heading back for the beach. Kevin remained with him but could not get an angle on the agile Fulcrum. The maneuverability of the MiG was remarkable.

Kevin watched the MiG's air brakes pop up. He reacted just in time, cutting back throttles and engaging the F-14's air brake. His Tomcat nearly rammed into the MiG as Kevin watched his airspeed drop to 195 knots. With the wings in the fully forward position, Kevin saddled his Tomcat directly behind the Fulcrum.

"There . . . got ya!" Kevin screamed as he finally lined up the MiG and let go a second burst. The MiG turned right at the last possible moment before continuing on a parallel course with the shoreline, a few feet over the sandy beach.

Manesh smiled and laughed out loud when he spotted the hundreds of birds gathered on the beach, eating fish trapped from the last high tide. He had the American fighter exactly where he wanted it. He flipped the manual override switch of the computer that automatically controlled the doors to the huge main engine air inlets, and closed them. As the main doors closed, the system automatically opened a row of alternative inlet apertures above each wing, designed to prevent foreign-object damage during takeoff and landings. He cut back throttles and his airspeed dropped below 170 knots.

Suddenly, a cloud of birds left the sand as the roaring jets approached. Manesh maintained the same course as a bloody mass of bones and feathers covered his windscreen, but that didn't matter. Not a single winged animal could fit through the narrow slots of the secondary air intake of the two Tumanskii turbofans. The MiG emerged through the cloud with some leading edge damage, but otherwise in one piece. Manesh pulled back the control stick, added power, and rose to three hundred feet before making a steep right turn. The American craft remained inside the bloody cloud.

"Engine stall! Engine Stall!" screamed Lieutenant Campbell as dozens of birds were sucked into the main air inlets of the F-14.

Kevin Dalton saw the two bright amber stall lights winking and managed to pull the jet up in time to prevent total damage to one of the two engines. Alarms blared while the control panel suddenly filled with warning lights.

"Lost the starboard engine!" shouted Campbell.

Kevin applied full throttle, but was disappointed at the sluggishness of his craft with only one turbofan providing the thrust, even in full afterburner. He accelerated into the no-fly zone, dominated by the Allies, hoping the MiG would not dare follow him.

"We're spiked! The MiG's got us locked! He's gonna fire!"

Kevin spotted hills to his left and darted toward them in an attempt to lose the MiG, aware that he didn't stand a chance over the ocean, where he could not hide.

Forcing the wounded Tomcat into a tight turn, he flew in between two hills and continued inland, trying to coax every last knot out of his crippled jet. The MiG was within machine gun range, but did not fire. As Kevin flew deeper inside Iraq, the MiG closed in for the kill.

Soup Campbell switched frequency to Guard, the UHF emergency channel monitored by most Allied forces. "May Day! May Day! This is Wolfpack Two One Four. We're single engine with a MiG at our six!"

Kevin turned his head. The MiG was too close. *What are you waiting for, asshole?*

Kevin threw his craft in a set of alternating right and left turns combined with climbs, but the MiG-29 easily stayed with him.

As the ocean disappeared behind the low hills, the MiG opened fire. Kevin jammed the stick forward and forced his wounded jet to hug the rugged terrain.

"This is Wolfpack Two One Four. We're in trouble. Repeat. We're in trouble. Request immediate assistance, over."

"Two One Four, this is Gypsy One Oh, U.S. Air Force. You're sixty miles away. I'll be there in two minutes."

"Two minutes? This thing'll be over in seconds!"

"Hang in there, One Four."

The MiG managed to position itself behind the Tomcat once more and opened fire. This time Kevin was trapped. A river of bullets blasted across the left wing. Bits and pieces of the wing's aluminum skin washed away in the slipstream.

Kevin cut left and went into a shallow climb to get out of the way of the MiG's cannon, but due to the Tomcat's sluggishness, the MiG reacquired in seconds and fired again.

"Jesus! Mayday, Mayday. This is Wolfpack—"

Kevin heard a loud blast as several 30mm rounds pierced the back of the canopy.

With the image of Lancaster's falling F-14 still vivid in his mind, Kevin glanced at the artificial horizon to verify if he was within the ejection envelope. His angles of bank and pitch were within the sixty-degree maximum, but he still had a 350-knot indicated airspeed instead of the maximum recommended of 250 knots. *Too bad.* He pulled the ejection handles.

The entire world appeared to catch fire around him as the canopy blew up and back 0.3 seconds after he'd pulled on the handle, clearing the way as the two Martin-Baker ejection seats were shot upward by the rocket booster under each seat. The booster under

Kevin's seat—a solid-propellant shaped charge—gave him an initial high level boost for 0.15 seconds to get him out of the plane, followed by a sustained low level boost for an additional 0.85 seconds to get him away from the Tomcat. The moment the ejection seat left the plane, the URT-33 Automatic Guard System—an emergency radio integrated with the ejection seat—kicked in, broadcasting an emergency signal.

Kevin closed his eyes and bellowed into his mask as twelve g's nearly crushed his shoulders and the windblast pressed him against the back of the seat while he hurtled higher and higher. He blinked in astonishment as the earth and sky changed positions over and over. Then the pressure was gone, along with the initial windblast, replaced by a peaceful breeze that appeared to caress him as his mind fiddled at the edge of unconsciousness. He was free-falling, and it gave him a peaceful feeling of isolation.

A sudden jerk told him that the parachute had safely deployed. It was the last conscious input before his thoughts faded away and everything went black.

Ishmael Barzani and Abdul Mozakhu turned their heads away from their weapons instructor when they heard the cannon fire followed by a loud bang in the sky. All three raced for the rustic windows of their safe house outside the town of Ash Shinafiyah by the shores of the Euphrates River.

"What was that?" asked Abdul, puzzled.

"I think it was a bomb of some sort," responded Ishmael.

"That was not a bomb," corrected their instructor. "That was an airplane."

All three stared at the burning dirty gray cloud hanging in midair. From its center, two bright objects shot up in a parabolic curve, trailing narrow white streaks. The objects, which by now Ishmael had assumed were pilots ejecting from a fighter, started to fall at their apex. White parachutes opening indicated that the pilots, if still alive, would make it safely to ground as the craft's charred remains plummeted to earth.

"Enemy pilots!" Abdul shouted. "Allah has given us enemy pilots! Hurry, *Isha!* We must get to them before the search party finds them."

"Those are not Iraqi pilots," noted the instructor.

Abdul looked back at his teacher. "What . . . how do you . . . ?"

"The parachute. It's not red. The Iraqi government uses mostly Russian planes; remember our training last month?"

Both Kurds looked at one another before nodding in agreement.

"Who do you think they are?" asked Ishmael, pointing at the white parachutes gently swirling down to earth.

"I believe those are Allied pilots, most likely American."

"American?" Ishmael glanced at Abdul and grinned widely, which stretched his gums, sending a bolt of pain across his face. Ignoring it, Ishmael stared into Abdul's green eyes as the trainer looked on. The *Ba'i* would no doubt be very grateful if they delivered him two strayed pilots. It would probably mean more of the sophisticated Javelins, and perhaps even some Stingers.

"We must rescue them, Abdul."

"Yes, *Isha.*"

They turned to the instructor, who was holding one of the Javelin shoulder-launched surface-to-air missiles Ishmael had received the day before.

"Would you help us, Khalela?"

The Mossad operative, who had arrived just a few hours before, hesitated at first, but then slowly agreed.

"This is Sandy Five Five. Do you copy, over?"

Nothing.

"This is Sandy Five Five. Do you copy, over?"

For the past few minutes, the pilot of an A-10 Warthog, Colonel Jake Leary, U.S. Air Force, had been unsuccessfully trying to contact the Navy jet. An F-15 had managed to make contact just before the Tomcat went off the air, and it had requested cover for the downed pilots. Leary had left his flight of A-10s engaging in a war exercise in Kuwait after picking up the F-14's beacon on Guard at about the same time that the F-15's pilot had requested cover. Leary had rushed to the site to cover the downed pilots until a combat search-and-rescue (CSAR) helicopter could arrive. His call sign, "Sandy," followed the tradition of CSAR-trained pilots flying propeller-driven ground-attack planes in Vietnam.

The early morning sun filtered through the armored canopy, forcing Leary to lower the green visor over his flying helmet as he readjusted power to obtain maximum speed. The quiet noise from the two General Electric high-bypass turbofans increased as the craft accelerated to 400 knots.

Leary sat in what was called an "armored bathtub" of thick titanium, resistant to all but the heaviest caliber guns. The two large turbofans in the rear of the craft were heavily armored, quiet, and had relatively cool exhausts, which made the A-10 hard to lock onto with heat-seeking SAMs. The craft's long wings provided the necessary lift during slow flights and fast turns. It also served as the platform for a warload of over twelve thousand pounds.

Nudging the stick forward while cutting back throttle, he descended to one thousand feet and approached the crash site. *Whoever did this got the hell out of here mighty fast,* he thought as he banked his plane thirty degrees to the right to search for any parachutes.

Leary smiled when he spotted them, roughly two miles apart. He couldn't see anyone moving. *Maybe they're hurt,* he thought, while praying that the rescue chopper would get here before the Iraqis did. He checked his fuel situation and frowned. He updated the coordinates to the rescue team before heading for the refueling tanker track just south of the border.

Fifteen minutes later, Leary approached a Boeing KC-135 Stratotanker from the stern, at 300 knots. The boom was lowered from the tail of the tanker as Leary closed in. When he was less than sixty feet from the craft, he flipped the refueling switch. The cover of the air-to-air refueling receptacle slid back between the cockpit and the nose of the craft, over the 30mm gun.

With the boom swirling softly under the tanker, at the

end of the sixty-foot hose, Leary brought his A-10 to within five feet of the boom and waited to snag it. He knew that the trick to this maneuver was to get close enough to the boom and wait to get it aligned with the receptacle, before closing in fast and latching on. A slow approach for the last few feet would result in the boom being pushed away by the air displaced by the nose of the Warthog.

As the boom swirled in his direction, Leary inched the throttles forward to grab it. He made contact and began refueling. A few minutes later, he backed away from the tanker, closed the cover over the receptacle, and headed back toward Wolfpack Two One Four.

AMAN BAKISH AIR BASE NEAR AN NAJAF, SOUTHERN IRAQ.
Day Two. 1345 Local Time.

Maintaining full afterburners and remaining less than fifty feet above ground, Manesh had managed to avoid Allied fighters in the area. He now brought his MiG-29 to a full stop inside the bunker as the ground crew approached the craft, whose leading edges had been severely damaged by the birds. The moment the hinged canopy pivoted up, Manesh removed his helmet and scratched his face and head. He had not been able to shower in over two weeks, and he itched all over.

"Is the search party on its way as ordered?"

"Yes, Colonel. The two Gazelles are on the way."

"When did they leave?"

"Ten minutes ago, sir."

"Did they take the soldiers and the missiles along?"

"Yes, sir. They should be close to the crash site by now."

"Good," Manesh said, aware that the F-14 had gone down roughly thirty miles south of the airfield, well within the no-fly zone.

"Fix my MiG immediately!"

"But Colonel, we might not have the spares necessa—"

"I don't care if you need to get them from Baghdad!

Get my fighter fixed right away!" Without waiting for a response, Manesh headed for the communications bunker across the hot tarmac. The American pilots would be a phenomenal trophy for his government, but Manesh needed to get there first and capture them before the Americans tried to rescue them. He also needed to inform Baghdad of the aerial victory.

The bright, scorching sun shown through his closed eyelids as Lieutenant Kevin Dalton drifted painfully back into consciousness. His limbs, tangled with the nylon lines of his parachute and still aching from the pounding g's, were not the only parts of his body in pain. His head felt like it was about to burst from the worst headache Kevin had had in his entire life. The pounding of veins against his temples was unbearable. With his eyes closed, he fumbled with a zipper on his flight suit and pulled out a pair of dark sunglasses. His elbows stung. He looked down at his arms and noticed that the sleeves of his flight suit were ripped below the elbows, probably a result of his rolling on the ground during his parachute landing. He grabbed the Gerber hunting knife strapped to his right leg and cut off the shreds, leaving his tanned forearms exposed. He checked the rest of his body, and except for a bloody patch on his flight suit above the left knee, again probably due to the fall, he found no other damage, beyond general soreness due to the ejection. He knew that adrenaline was lessening the effects of the windblast and the spinal compression resulting from being shot out of the Tomcat like a bullet. In another hour, he would be really hurting.

His mind was in turmoil, trying to cope with the reality that he had been shot down after disobeying McDeere's direct order to break off the pursuit. Kevin lowered his gaze and shook his head, very much aware of what that meant. For one thing, he reflected, his negligence to comply with that order had caused the loss of a thirty-million-dollar plane. That charge alone would be enough to keep him from flying for the rest of his days.

Even with the sunglasses on, Kevin blinked several

times, trying to bring the cluster of trees in front of him into focus as he got to his feet and unstrapped the belts of his parachute. He could see the burning wreck in the distance, estimating it to be a few thousand feet away. The black smoke swirling up to the heavens marked the crash site for everyone.

Kevin unstrapped his seat survival kit, the removable section of the ejection seat that he had automatically attached himself to when strapping in. It had remained with him through ejection and parachute landing. He then removed his torso harness, unzipped his G suit, collected the parachute, and dragged them to the trees, where he used his helmet to dig out an area under the thick underbrush. He buried it all, including the helmet.

Kevin reached inside the seat survival kit and disabled the URT-33 beacon. This he did for two important reasons. First, the system broadcast an emergency signal at 243.0 MHz, the Guard emergency frequency, which not only was being monitored by Allied forces but also by Iraqi forces. Second, the URT-33 signal would cancel transmissions from Kevin's Motorola PRC-90 hand-held radio, which also operated on the Guard frequency as a beacon—like the URT-33—or as a two-way radio.

He reached for the PRC-90, wishing he had been issued the newer PRC-112 which, unlike the old model, could be encrypted to jump frequencies to prevent unwanted listeners from monitoring Allied radio conversations. Unfortunately, there just weren't enough PRC-112s to go around, and the *Ranger* got stuck with the old PRC-90s.

He flipped the radio on, set it to Talk—two-way communications—and tried to reach Campbell for about thirty seconds. He got no response. Kevin had no idea if Campbell was alive or not. He couldn't remember much after the ejection. He scanned the surroundings but could see no sign of Campbell or his parachute. Kevin sighed, switched off the radio, and strapped it back into a pouch of the gear vest he wore over his flight suit. During survival training, he'd been told to conserve batteries and only use the beacon for a few seconds every hour or so while moving away from the crash site. He'd also been told to switch to Talk only after getting a visual on the rescue team.

He briefly inspected his survival kit, an assortment of essentials: a basic first-aid kit, a dozen aspirins (he quickly swallowed three), flares, signaling mirrors, lip balm, sunscreen, and a compass, among other items. Strapped to his belt was a slim, plastic canteen holding eleven ounces of drinking water. Kevin opened a zipper on the gear vest and inspected the plastic pouch holding another eleven ounces of water. Twenty-two ounces of water would have ranked Kevin in the lower twenty-five percent of the informal competition among aviators to see who could carry more water in his flight gear. Kevin knew pilots who carried up to a hundred ounces of water. Wishing now he were one of those pilots, Kevin drank a few ounces from the plastic canteen.

Evaluating his current situation, he decided that his first priority should be to move away from the crash site. An enemy search team could be on its way, especially since that MiG pilot had seen them eject. The problem with moving too far away from his current position, Kevin reasoned, was that he would also make it difficult for his people to find him, although they could still locate him by homing in on the PRC-90's beacon. Depending totally on his radio, however, was risky; rescue teams knew it was possible for the enemy to get ahold of a downed pilot's radio to draw some choppers in for an ambush. The Air Tasking Orders provided some level of protection by issuing new call signs every day, but Kevin knew that those call signs could also be monitored by the Iraqis listening to Guard. Kevin didn't see any other choice, though. He had to play it cautious and assume the enemy would come looking for him first. The last thing he needed to add to his list of problems was an extended vacation in Saddam Hussein's Baghdad Baltimore, with daily tortures on the house. Or worse yet, to get paraded in chains around Baghdad.

On the practical side, Kevin decided to remain close to the river he had spotted a mile or two east of his position, feeling certain that for the next few days water would be his most precious commodity.

The sound of helicopters broke his train of thought. *Choppers? So soon?*

Clutching the stainless steel handle of the slim Smith & Wesson Model 39 he had just removed from a Velcro-secured pouch of his gear vest, Kevin hid in the trees. He wasn't sure who would get to him first and—

He saw them: two helicopters flying in formation roughly fifty feet above the ground. They made their approach from the northeast. That alone told Kevin they were most likely unfriendly, since he expected a rescue team to come in from the south. He switched his radio back to Talk and left the Guard channel open. Static. No one was trying to communicate with him.

The helicopters made a wide circle over what was left of Wolfpack Two One Four before briefly landing, dropping a search party about a half mile away from Kevin, and heading back out the same way they had come in. The soldiers disappeared behind a cluster of trees almost as fast as the choppers got out of sight. Kevin went through his options again. Should he try to make a run for it to put some distance between the wreck and himself? Or should he stick around? A rescue party could very likely be on its way, he reasoned, remembering the craft he had managed to make contact with before the MiG had shot him down. Its pilot no doubt had marked his coordinates and passed them to some rescue unit standing by at the border. In addition, the URT-33 had broadcast his position to everyone from the moment he had ejected until he had finally shut it off.

Kevin decided to move to another cluster of trees a few hundred yards east. Five minutes later, he heard a jet in the distance. He searched for it and smiled when he recognized the shape. *An A-10!* Kevin brought the radio to his lips.

"Sandy, this is Wolfpack Two One Four Alpha," Colonel Jake Leary heard the F-14 pilot say, telling him not only the plane's call sign, but also that he was the pilot of the

craft. Had it been the RIO, the downed American would have finished the call sign with Bravo, instead of Alpha.

"One Four, Sandy Five Five. You hot?"

"Affirmative, Sandy. There are some unfriendlies roughly two thousand feet northwest of my fix."

"Five Five."

Leary advanced the throttles of the Warthog and climbed to a thousand feet to scan the . . . *there!* He had them. Leary spotted a group of five or six men hiding in the sparse underbrush near a small cluster of trees precisely where the F-14 pilot said they would be. He put the A-10 in a dive and watched his speed indicator climb to 500 knots. He switched to guns.

Lieutenant Ali Umesh lay behind the rest of his team in the overgrowth next to the trees. He was one of the few officers in his division who had received training on the Soviet-made SA-7b "Grail" shoulder-launched SAM. Umesh, however, preferred the more reliable Stinger, for which he had been comprehensively trained by the CIA during the Iraq-Iran war. Next to him, Umesh had two Grails waiting for an American helicopter.

Suddenly, out of nowhere, an American fighter dropped on them, and a second later the deafening noise of its cannon ripped across the desert. Fortunately, Umesh was the closest one to the trees and was able to reach cover while hauling both Grails. The rounds reached his position.

Colonel Leary unloaded almost one hundred depleted uranium 30mm rounds on the Iraqis. The projectiles created a cloud of dust and sand where the soldiers had been a fraction of a second before. He stopped firing, climbed to five thousand feet, and circled the area to survey the damage.

Umesh silently prayed to Allah for the strength to endure the agonizing pain of a severed foot. In spite of his quick reaction, a round had amputated his right foot exactly at the ankle. Struggling to remain calm, the Iraqi lieutenant tore off the shirt of his uniform and tied it firmly around the wound to keep his blood from gushing out. His finger came in direct contact with broken bones and torn cartilage. The smell of burnt flesh filled his nostrils. He fought the impulse to vomit; he was a soldier in battle and had to remain focused. Unlike his fellow soldiers, who had been pureed into a mass of human refuse, Umesh had managed to survive the jet's initial attack, and there was a chance that its pilot might think that he had cleared the way for a rescue helicopter.

Umesh clenched his teeth and crawled to the edge of the trees, where he saw the American jet circling overhead. With his eyes filling from the excruciating pain, he kneeled down, reached for an SA-7b, set it over his right shoulder, and aimed it. He trained it on the circling jet but did not try to acquire a fix. The Grail was not designed to take on a jet. It was neither fast enough nor had the range to endure a long chase.

Umesh endured the pain and waited for Allah to deliver him an American helicopter. A minute later, his prayers were answered.

With the desert sand just twenty feet below his helicopter's landing gear, Captain Patrick W. Heersen, U.S. Air Force, flew almost by instinct, right hand on the cyclic—or center stick—and left hand on the collective lever of the HH-60G Pave Hawk helicopter, a special variant of the Sikorsky Black Hawk configured for combat search and rescue. His copilot, Lieutenant Geraldo Parra, kept a close eye for any sign of Iraqis on the ground as the 25,000-pound chopper hugged the desert floor while cruising at 185 knots.

In the rear of the craft, in addition to two airmen manning the M-60 machine guns on both opened side doors, Heersen's crew consisted of two pararescue-men, better known as PJs (Parachute Jumpers), who were specially trained for this type of mission. Cover for this run would be provided by an A-10, which had just finished sanitizing the area.

"There, sir. See it?" said Parra over the intercom.

Heersen noticed a trail of black smoke in the distance. "Got it!" He swung the cyclic in the direction of the F-14 wreck. The moment he had the chopper's nose lined up with the crash site, he added back pressure to the cyclic and lowered the collective with gentle, controlled movements to slow down the helicopter while maintaining altitude. It took two seconds for the large Sikorsky helicopter to respond to Heersen's commands. The craft decelerated to 100 knots.

"Sandy, Sundance Four Oh, over," said Heersen over his radio.

"Four Oh, Sandy. All is clear. Go in and pick up our boy. I'll keep circling."

"Roger, Sandy." Heersen pushed the manual frequency scan button on the cyclic's handle to Guard Talk, and spoke on his voice-activated headset.

"Sundance Four Oh."

"Hello, Four Oh. This is Wolfpack Two One Four Alpha, and I read you loud and clear."

"Pop some smoke, One Four."

"Roger."

A half minute later, Heersen turned the craft in the direction of red smoke filtering through a cluster of trees a half mile away.

Umesh aimed the optical sighting and tracking device of his SA-7b missile on the right turboshaft exhaust of the large American helicopter. The craft was less than one thousand feet away heading toward a cloud of red smoke near a cluster of trees. He activated the infrared missile seeker. With the target so close, the missile lock indicator light went on almost instantly.

Umesh squeezed the trigger.

The launcher jerked back as the twenty-one-pound missile thrust forward, accelerating to the speed of sound.

"We've been hit! We've been hit! Losing turbine pressure. We're going down!" Heersen heard Parra scream over the intercom as he scanned the array of warning lights and instinctively lowered the collective all the way down to disengage the turbine from the main rotor and enter an autorotation. The large chopper began a slow descent as the main rotor's momentum provided enough downward draft to cushion the fall.

Umesh already had the wounded craft centered in the optical sights of his second SA-7b. As he heard the jets of the American fighter getting louder, he achieved missile lock on the left exhaust and fired. The missile streaked across the sky toward the crippled helicopter. Umesh heard the thundering cannon of the American fighter, and an instant later he felt his chest burst open before all went dark.

The second missile found its target, striking the Pave Hawk's main rotor casing. The giant rotor, still turning, separated from the fuselage. The Pave Hawk plummeted toward the ground twenty feet below, but the chopper never made it to the ground in one piece. The rotor struck the helicopter's center fuselage with such speed that the Kevlar over Nomex material of the rotor blades sliced through the Pave Hawk's center fuselage, cutting into the integral fuel tanks. The resulting explosion engulfed the craft.

Lieutenant Kevin Dalton stared in sheer disbelief at the burning helicopter. The Iraqis had used him as bait. They had played him beautifully. *Jesus Christ! This can't be really happening to me!* he thought as his emotional side momentarily took over, but the soldier in him quickly regained control.

Priorities, Kevin. First, he had to get out of that area. He simply had to distance himself from the wreck to avoid capture.

"Wolfpack Two One Four, Sandy, over."

Kevin brought the radio to his lips. "Jesus, Sandy! Bastards used me as bait."

"Get away from this place, One Four. Get off the air and come back on in a few hours. We'll try again at dusk."

"Roger, Sandy."

"Hang in there, One Four. We'll pull you out. I can cover you for another twenty minutes before I need to refuel."

"One Four out."

Kevin switched off the PRC-90. Guided by a small compass—also a part of his survival gear—he moved southeast, past the cluster of trees and across the vegetation-rich lands surrounding the Euphrates. He estimated reaching the river in a couple of hours, assuming the Iraqis didn't find him first.

USS *RANGER*. ARABIAN SEA, NEAR THE GULF OF OMAN.
Day Two. 1530 Local Time.

Enduring the pain in his stomach, Lieutenant Delgado left the medical bay and walked past the mess area under a latticework of pipes and wires. He reached a ladder and went up one level, where he found more pipes on the ceiling and walls, along with firefighting hoses and numerous unidentified buttons and knobs. He reached the next large steel door on the adequately lit corridor. Each watertight door, spaced thirty or so feet apart, Delgado knew, had been designed to isolate sections of the ship from flooding. Nearly three thousand separate compartments could be individually sealed to prevent the ship from sinking during battle.

Slowly going up one more level, he reached McDeere's quarters. The door was closed. He knocked twice but got no response. Cursing the orderly who had told him that his squadron's commanding officer was in his quarters, Delgado began to turn around when McDeere's rough voice crackled from the other side of the door.

"Yeah?"

"Sir?"

"Yeah? Who's that?"

"Lieutenant Delgado, sir. I've just heard the news about the crash."

The door opened. Delgado glanced past the albino officer and noticed the typewriter on his desk next to several handwritten pages. McDeere's room was as big as

Delgado's, but the commander didn't have to share it with anyone.

McDeere exhaled. "We lost two F-14s. From what we can tell, Shadow's plane exploded upon impacting the waters off the coast of Kuwait. Crackers disobeyed my direct order to get his ass back in here and was also shot down, somewhere over Iraq."

"Dios mio! Any survivors, sir?"

"Not at this point. We got a couple of helicopters searching the area where Shadow's plane went down."

"What about Crackers, sir?"

"Our forces at the border are handling it. No news yet."

"What does that mean, sir?"

McDeere rubbed his eyes before raising his right eyebrow. The freckles on his pale face appeared to come alive. "Chico, that means *exactly* what it means. There's no news yet! If he's still alive, he'll be facing a court-martial for insubordination of the highest degree. I haven't decided what to do about Soup. That's if either of the two's still alive."

Delgado was caught off guard by McDeere's comments and remained silent for a few moments, debating whether or not he should back off and let the brass deal with this problem.

"Are the CSAR guys gonna try for a rescue, sir?"

McDeere frowned. "Listen, Chico. I think I understand that Crackers was your friend, but the reason why he got shot down was sheer negligence. I should have suspended him when I had the chance. Now it's too late for that, and I have not one but two downed jets and four missing aviators in my sack. Dammit!" After driving a fist into his palm, McDeere breathed deeply a few times before speaking again. "I expect you to act like the professional you are and leave all rescue matters to our guys in Saudi. Believe me, I would love to get Crackers back here so that I can personally tattoo the soles of my shoes on his ass, but it's out of my hands. You'll resume flying as soon as you feel up to it. In the meantime, relax and get some rest. The way you're holding your stomach sure looks like you could use a break."

McDeere turned and went back to his work. Delgado quietly left.

THE WHITE HOUSE.
Day Two. 0750 Local Time.

Wearing a YMCA light gray sweatshirt, matching jogging pants, white tennis shoes, and a University of Arkansas baseball cap, President Bill Clinton returned from his morning jog, holding a McDonald's paper cup filled with steaming coffee in his right hand. As he walked up the steps leading to a White House side entrance, he saw Chelsea coming out, books in her left hand. His daughter wore her gray school uniform, dark shoes, her long hair put up in a bun. She gave him a playful smile.

"Hello, darling," he said, meeting her halfway up the steps, where Chelsea threw her arms around the Commander in Chief and gave him a kiss on the left cheek. "Hi, Dad," she said, eyes glistening at him.

"Off to school, I presume—" The president stopped in mid-sentence when he spotted his defense secretary, dressed in a light brown suit, jumping out of a black limousine and walking fast in his direction.

"I'm afraid we have a situation, Mr. President," the secretary said, breathing hard as he reached the bottom of the steps.

With Chelsea standing by his side, the president took a sip of coffee. He turned to Chelsea and kissed her forehead. "Have a great day, babe."

"You too, Dad." Chelsea continued down the steps and disappeared inside another limo.

"Yes?" the president said to the defense secretary in a somewhat annoyed voice. Clinton cherished the little time he spent with his family.

"The Iraqis just downed two F-14s, sir."

"How?" was all the president said, and for the next few minutes the secretary gave him all the details—including a report on how Iraq had actually set up a trap for the Americans, using old MiG-21s as decoys—as they walked inside the White House and toward the Oval Office, where the president slowly paced back and forth in front of his desk. He could just picture Saddam Hussein at that very moment, boasting of how his superior Air Force had downed two of the famous American Tomcats. Two pilots had apparently died in the Persian Gulf, the other two were missing. A CSAR effort was underway. No news on that just yet.

What angered the president more than anything was the fact that he couldn't retaliate. He even wondered if Saddam Hussein would try to use a nuke on someone in response for the three MiG-21s the F-14s got before they too were shot down—assuming the Iraqi leader already had any nuclear weapons assembled.

With his defense secretary sitting on one of the sofas, President Clinton stopped in front of a window behind his desk and stared at the trees for a long time. He had lost the initiative in this conflict and was simply reacting to Saddam's moves, refusing to retaliate for fear of a nuclear response. He desperately needed to find the location of the nukes and the boosters to switch to an offensive game.

In the short term, he had the downed Tomcats to deal with. The fact that the crew of one of the F-14s had been shot down after disobeying an order to turn back bothered him somewhat, but Clinton refused to pass judgment on that right away. Clinton felt it was inappropriate—actually, downright unfair—to judge the actions of a pilot who had just seen his leader shot out of the sky by an Iraqi MiG, especially after the trap the Iraqis had set up for the two Navy fighters.

With his sight lost in the cumulus clouds dotting the sky over Washington, President Clinton's thoughts turned to the downed American pilots and their families.

SOUTHERN IRAQ.
Day Two. 1600 Local Time.

Lieutenant Kevin Dalton spotted the white parachute in between two clusters of trees almost two miles from the crash site. After circling the area to make sure it wasn't a trap, he walked toward the parachute and reached it a few minutes later. Kevin froze. Campbell was still strapped to the ejection seat, face down. The bullet hole in the back of his helmet told Kevin all he needed to know.

Oh, God. What have I done? A wave of guilt engulfed him. Seeing his RIO, his responsibility, dead because of Kevin's own negligence was more than he could emotionally handle.

Kevin turned Campbell over and felt bile rushing up his throat when he realized that Campbell's face—along with a chunk of the visor—was gone. All that remained was a mess of hair, flesh, and bones supported by a blood-stained neck.

He pulled away in horror. "Oh, God! Oh, Sweet Jesus!"

Kevin couldn't control the convulsion and leaned over to vomit. He dropped to his hands and knees and breathed deeply, struggling to regain control of his heaving body. He waited a few minutes until he managed to relax somewhat.

Forcing his mind to ignore the sight, Kevin got up and broke both the URT-33 beacon and Campbell's PRC-90 radio—after removing the batteries. He took Campbell's automatic, two eight-shot spare clips, his water bottle, and the survival kit, no longer of any use to the naval officer Kevin had helped kill.

Without looking back once, Kevin continued moving southeast.

BAGHDAD.
Day Two. 1620 Local Time.

Inside a dark wood-paneled rectangular room in one of his dozen luxurious underground bunkers in Baghdad, President Saddam Hussein smoked a cigar while going through his daily reports from the field. Although his eyes burned, his mouth felt dry, and his stomach was nauseated from lack of sleep, the Iraqi leader couldn't be more pleased. His bluff was working on the soft American president, who still had not retaliated for the Scud attacks, the downed fighters, or the troops moving south. And the latest field reports showed that an American rescue helicopter had also been destroyed, killing even more of their soldiers. The fact that some of his own men and equipment were also lost in the process was insignificant. Unlike the weak American president, who Saddam knew could not stomach the loss of even one of his fighting men, the Iraqi leader was prepared to lose tens of thousands, as long as he could get revenge for the unmerciful massacres of 1991.

After drafting a one-page memo congratulating Air Force Colonel Abunnasr Manesh for his brilliant plan, and promoting him to the rank of general, the Iraqi leader got up from the head of the long conference table and walked to a huge map of the Middle East on the right side of the room. Through the smoke rising from his cigar, the Iraqi leader's bloodshot eyes traveled from Baghdad to a red X marking a spot thirty miles south of An Najaf, the location of the Allahbad Processing Complex.

Soon, Saddam Hussein thought, licking his dry lips, looking at the red X, and then at Tel Aviv, Riyadh, and Kuwait City with half-shut eyes. Slowly, his gaze gravitated to a map of the world on the opposite wall, found North America, and zeroed in on the East Coast states. *New York City and Washington, D.C.* The places where Saddam would soon send secret envoys carrying very special cargoes.

The corners of Saddam's thick black mustache rose a bit as a smile flashed across his lined face. Images of American civilians being rescued after the bombing in New York brought a small wave of satisfaction to his mind, but it in no way compared to the tidal wave of joy the Iraqi president would experience when the first nuclear detonation on American soil incinerated a million imperialists in the blink of an eye.

Soon, Mr. Clinton, the Mother of All Battles shall commence.

NON-CONVENTIONAL WARFARE

Should the Americans become embroiled, we will make them swim in their own blood, God willing.

—Saddam Hussein

ALLAHBAD PROCESSING COMPLEX, SOUTH OF AN NAJAF, IRAQ.
Day Two. 1630 Local Time.

A single ten-foot-tall chain-link fence surrounded the complex. At a glance, it looked as if it had been built almost as a mere formality, just something to outline the outer limits of the dairy products facility. But a closer look revealed that this was no ordinary fence. Thick electric cables, carrying one thousand volts, were connected to the top of the fence at a dozen places around the perimeter. Inside the electric walls, over one hundred Iraqi soldiers, with enough weaponry to stop a small army, were hidden throughout the complex in underground bunkers or camouflaged buildings. Along both sides of the huge warehouse at the front of the complex were a half dozen shelters housing Soviet-made ZSU-23-4 Shilka antiaircraft artillery systems. At each corner of the square complex, inside the perimeter, were well-camouflaged batteries of Soviet-made SA-6 Gainful surface-to-air missiles. A single gate at the front of the complex allowed access to the otherwise electrically sealed facility.

Under a bright mid-afternoon sun, Major Mohammed Hassoud stormed down the narrow walkway connecting the living quarters of the complex's security forces to the large warehouse at the front of the facility. His strides were long and confident as he approached the chief scientist, Dr. Radsul Sakkar, who stood on the opposite end of the paved walkway. The doctor appeared nervous. Beads of sweat accumulated on his upper lip and bald head.

"My staff is getting very worried about the recent incidents with the Americans, Major. They are all wondering if we might be under attack soon."

"Allahbad is not a military target, Doctor. As far as the world is concerned, this place only makes dairy products. The Allies won't dare touch it. You can tell your staff that we are not in any danger," responded Hassoud in his deep authoritative voice.

A thick beard covered most of Hassoud's face. With a full head of coal-black hair almost meeting his thick eyebrows, all that one could really see of the major's face was a scarred nose and his eyes.

There was, however, a very good reason why the major kept so much hair on his face, even during the hottest months of the year. Nearly fifteen years before, during the short period of time when Iran had backed the Kurds' struggle for independence, Hassoud had fought the rebels south of Sulaymaniyah, a city twenty miles west of the border with Iran. Using shoulder-launched RPGs, the Kurds had ambushed Hassoud's tank platoon. Most of his men died during the heavy gunfight, which only lasted a minute. Hassoud, however, was captured alive. Instead of killing him, though, the Kurds tied him down to the ground and slowly carved his skin with their knives. Hassoud passed out from the pain after the first few minutes, and when he woke up, he found himself covered with bandages at a hospital in Baghdad. Another patrol had surprised the Kurds before they were finished with Hassoud.

A month later, when the bandages were removed, Hassoud vomited at the sight of his own face, disfigured beyond his own recognition—as was most of his body.

Due to his rank, his government allowed him to receive some level of plastic surgery, but even that didn't help much. The Kurds had done too thorough a job on him. From that day on, Hassoud swore revenge on all Kurds, a personal vendetta against the tribe of savages that had marked him for life.

"Why don't you tell them yourself, Major?" Sakkar asked. "After all, I'm sure your word of assurance that all is well will be better welcomed than mine."

Hassoud momentarily looked away. The last thing he needed was to give a lecture to a bunch of nervous scientists with half-inch-thick glasses. Then again, they were developing the ultimate weapon for his country, and that was what really mattered. Besides, in the six months that he had been in charge of the complex's security, he had never been allowed inside the underground facility. His orders were limited to the proper maintenance of the well-camouflaged antiaircraft equipment and conducting regular evacuation drills. He decided this was an opportunity to actually see what it was he was defending. "Of course, Doctor. I'll be delighted to assure your staff that we're safe."

"Thank you, Major."

Hassoud, who did not have the slightest idea how the scientists were going about modifying the Russian rocket boosters they had received recently, led the way into the gigantic warehouse, where technicians and workers unloaded the contents of trucks making deliveries for the complex.

Elevators, mused Hassoud as they walked across the concrete floor to the other side of the building and approached the huge brown doors of the service elevator that led underground. The major pressed the call button. That was one of the few things built at Allahbad which were not properly thought out beforehand. Not because it was unreliable—the large elevator had never failed from the first day it went into operation—but because the warehouse was a one-story building. An elevator would have looked more natural on the west section of the plant, where the complex was three stories high.

The bell rang and the door opened. Hassoud made a

gesture for Sakkar to go in first. Once inside, Hassoud glanced at the floor numbers starting at level zero all the way down to minus five. He pressed level minus two.

Twenty seconds later and fifty feet below the desert sands, the doors slid to the side, revealing a cavernous, two-acre room.

Inside, over one hundred men and women in white suits moved about carrying notepads or pushing equipment carts. The area, separated from Hassoud and Sakkar by an immense glass wall, was divided into thirty stations, each with its own staff and equipment to support the required missile modifications.

Major Hassoud stepped across the stark-white floor and reached the control station, where a technician handed each man a white suit, rubber gloves, and boots made out of a special material. In addition, each had to wear a headpiece that covered their hair, mouth, and nose, with an opening for the eyes. Over that they slid hoods with a clear section at eye level. After each man was properly dressed, the technician pressed a button on his control panel and a glass door opened.

Hassoud turned around. "Doctor, is this supposed to protect me? I thought that the suit had to be totally sealed."

Sakkar laughed. "There is no danger in there, Major, unless something goes wrong. Do you see those red lights over the sirens on the back wall?"

"Yes. What about them?"

"If they go off, it means that there has been a leak from somewhere. These suits will temporarily protect your body from exposure until you can get out of the room, which is one hundred percent sealed." He looked at Hassoud and pointed to the door. "After you, Major."

Hassoud went into the small compartment, followed by Sakkar. As the door closed behind them, air jets started loosening dirt particles off their nearly clean suits and they were sucked out by a huge air extractor overhead. As Sakkar explained, the extractor was connected to one of two huge ventilation tunnels that ran on either side of the facility from the lowest level up to the surface, where they were heavily camouflaged to prevent detection from the skies. The cleaning procedure lasted a minute. The air quality inside the small compartment was brought up to the same class-one-thousand environment as that inside the large working area which, the doctor explained, meant there were a maximum of one thousand particles of dirt for every one million particles of air—a necessity for the delicate operations underway. To put things in perspective, the doctor further explained that a regular room contained somewhere in the neighborhood of 75,000 particles of dirt for every one million particles of air.

They walked to the center of the large "clean room," as the scientists called it. Sakkar addressed the group.

"May I have your attention, please? Ladies and gentlemen, please!"

All discussions quieted down as the scientific community recognized Hassoud's deep voice.

"I just want you to be assured that our facility has never been in any danger of attack, nor will it ever be. It is very wisely disguised, and the fact that not a single bomb has been dropped here indicates our enemies still think Allahbad is nothing but a milk factory. In the extremely rare event that a stray bomb or missile hits the plant above, let me remind you of the dozens of feet of reinforced concrete that isolates us from the outside world. I'll be surprised if any of you even hears a bomb go off. So please, don't worry about external threats—that's my job. Yours is to continue as you were. Thank you for your attention."

"Everyone back to work," commanded Sakkar.

Conversation went up a few decibels and people began to move around the area again.

"How are we progressing, Doctor?" Hassoud asked as he glanced over at station number thirteen to his right where a technician worked next to the four-feet-tall hollow nose section of a missile. Next to it, on the table, was a large steel ball and a long cylindrical steel piece, whose grooved end appeared large enough to fit the round opening on top of the ball.

"Is that . . . the . . ."

"Yes, Major, you are looking at what will soon be a

twenty-kiloton nuclear warhead, with equivalent destructive power to the ones the American imperialists used against Japan at the end of World War II."

"It doesn't look like much," responded Hassoud. "How does it work?" The moment he said that, Hassoud noticed the doctor's face brightening up. It was obvious to him that Sakkar truly enjoyed his work.

"Well, our weapon will be quite primitive when compared to the Americans' arsenal, but it will be just as effective for the job it is intended to do. It works on the principle of atomic fission, meaning the splitting of an atom, which produces the heat and radiation characteristic of an atomic explosion. There are two ways of achieving enough energy to split an atom. Our method is called the implosion type. Let me explain. See this large steel ball?" Sakkar pointed to the ball that Hassoud had already spotted next to the hollow nosecap.

"Yes."

"Well, this ball is hollow. The inside wall is lined with a common explosive that surrounds one of the plutonium spheres that arrived a few months ago. The basic idea is to use the blast from the explosive to compress the plutonium in the center, therefore triggering a nuclear chain reaction."

"That doesn't sound too difficult, Doctor. If that's all it takes to generate a nuclear explosion, I'm surprised other countries have not developed it yet."

"Actually, it's a lot more complicated than that. You need to have the exact amount of plutonium in the center, called the critical mass. Without it, it won't matter how much you compress the plutonium with conventional explosives; it won't trigger the necessary self-sustained chain reaction. Also, say somehow you figure out your critical mass. You still need a way of compressing it. You can't just pack explosives around it and trigger them. The explosives must burn perfectly concentrically toward the center to achieve the desired compression of the plutonium. In addition, there are hundreds of other complications, but those are the two main obstacles that prevent more nations from getting the bomb."

Hassoud and Sakkar walked around the area for a few more minutes as the doctor proudly explained other phases of their operation, including loading the armed weapon inside the hollow head and missile deployment. To prevent accidental explosions, the warheads would be automatically armed after the missile reached an altitude of ten thousand feet.

Sakkar also mentioned that each warhead was enclosed in a steel casing to prevent its destruction if an American missile intercepted it. This had been a design directive from Baghdad after the 1991 Gulf War experience, when Patriot missiles would strike only the booster section of a Scud, but the resulting explosion would also destroy the warhead. In order for a Patriot to truly destroy the new missile, it would have to score a direct hit on the cone section, cracking the steel enclosure and destroying the warhead inside. Otherwise, the warhead would simply fall back to earth, detonating at an altitude of five hundred feet, when an altimeter fuse would trigger the chain reaction of the plutonium core.

Hassoud noticed a number of tables packed with hardware off to the far left side of the room. Unlike the main stations with numbers from one to thirty, these smaller tables were labeled with letters, starting with "A," all the way to "L."

"What is on those tables over there, Doctor? Spare parts?" the major asked.

Sakkar said, "Those are the components for weapons we plan to assemble for the second phase of our nuclear project."

Hassoud tilted his head. "Second phase? Are we building more missiles?"

"No," the scientist responded. "No more missiles, just more bombs."

"As backup?"

Sakkar shook his head. "No. Those bombs will leave the complex after assembly and will be delivered to Baghdad."

"Baghdad? Why?"

"To be smuggled out of the country."

"Smuggled? Where are they going?"

"New York City and Washington, D.C."

Hassoud gazed into the scientist's eyes and smiled broadly.

With that, both men headed for the single door leading to the cleaning room. After handing the clean room gear to the waiting technician, they headed for the elevator.

SALMAN ASAD AIR BASE, SAUDI ARABIA. NEAR IRAQI BORDER.
Day Two. 1700 Local Time.

"Colonel Halston? Colonel Halston?"

Robert Bourdeaux shifted his gaze from a set of satellite photos spread across the desk of Peter Halston to the young airman, who stormed inside the colonel's private tent. Halston also looked in the private's direction.

"Yes, what's the matter?"

"Sir, we lost the Pave Hawk we sent out to rescue the downed F-14 pilots."

Halston pinched the bridge of his nose. "Damn! How in the hell did that happen?"

"Looks like it got nailed by a handheld SAM, sir. We were monitoring their communications with one of the pilots on the ground, and then all hell broke loose for a few seconds before their radio went dead."

"Who was supposed to cover them?"

The private shifted his weight. "An A-10, sir. It supposedly sanitized the area before the chopper went in, but somehow the A-10 guy missed somebody. The Iraqis fired two SAMs at the chopper. Two hits."

Halston pounded a fist on the desk and shook his head. "Dammit! Do we know if there were any survivors?"

"Not likely, sir. The A-10 flew over the area and couldn't get any response."

"Well, have the backup rescue team standing by."

Bourdeaux watched Halston pace back and forth inside the tent.

"I can't believe this," said Halston. "I just can't fucking believe it. Shit!" He headed out of the tent.

"Where you going?"

"I'll be right back."

Meal hours for dinner had just begun at the base's mess area—a huge desert-camouflage tent that could hold almost one hundred soldiers at once. A cafeteria-style line with trays and utensils covered one entire side of the rectangular room. An array of tables, three wide by almost twenty deep, were mostly empty at such an early hour. Most everyone ate at around 1830, when the sun went down.

Pave Hawk helicopter pilot Captain Amanda Green, U.S. Air Force, quietly sat by herself in a corner, fiddling with her meal. She hated greasy food and felt so nauseated at the smell of hamburgers and fries that she wound up pushing the tray away. The action got the attention of a sergeant sitting three tables down.

"Don't want your hot chow, Captain?"

"Ah, no, Sergeant."

"In that case, you don't mind if I . . . ?"

"Help yourself." She passed over the entire food tray, save for the carton of milk, to the triple-striper who could not have been older than twenty-five.

"Thank you, Captain."

"You're welcome," she casually responded as she noticed several newcomers entering the mess area and looking in her direction while talking among themselves.

She ignored them and simply stared out the ventilation holes on the canvas wall to her left. That kind of attention didn't bother her anymore. She had grown used to being treated like that for years by both commanding officers and fellow pilots. *And all because I don't carry that silly burden between my legs,* reflected Amanda as the new GIs waved at her. She continued to ignore them, smiling internally because it was obvious to her that they hadn't yet recognized the rank patches on her shoulders. In reality, she was used to living and working among men from the days when she had been the only girl in a family of five. She'd also been the youngest. From an early age, she had had to put up with her brothers' jokes and put-downs until she had slowly gained their solemn respect, which to this day had never ceased. Her father had been different, though. A helicopter pilot himself during Vietnam, he'd felt very proud that his daughter had chosen to follow in his footsteps, unlike her "tough" brothers, who chose the safer, but boring, civilian life.

Her physical appearance was another factor that had made it harder for her to succeed as an Air Force helicopter test pilot. Her prominent features, hard to hide in the desert-camouflaged, tight-fitting fatigues, revealed a slim yet well-proportioned body, which on many occasions had been the cause of animalistic responses from the troops, especially from those who didn't know her reputation as a pilot. Although federal law prevented women from piloting aircraft in combat, as a test pilot Amanda was able to log enough hours on the Pave Hawk to qualify as a pilot for SAR outside Iraq. She had successfully piloted her craft on several non-combat missions in Saudi Arabia, ranging from rescuing downed pilots, who had safely made it out of Iraq before bailing out, to evacuating injured personnel from all sorts of accidents. Even though Amanda knew she was contributing to the overall war effort, the soldier in her demanded combat.

The laughter died down when one of the new GIs walked by her and spotted the bars on her feminine, narrow shoulders. Amanda noticed Colonel Peter Halston's well-built figure entering the tent, briefly scanning the tables until his gaze met hers. He started walking in her direction but stopped at another table, where Captain Orlando Delaney, U.S. Army, a top-notch Apache helicopter pilot, sat by himself eating his meal.

Amanda had liked the good-looking Halston from the first day that she had arrived at the base a couple of months back. Although there was a chemistry between them that had turned into an instant friendship, the relationship had stagnated after the first month for a few reasons. First, as Saddam Hussein grew restless, the colonel's responsibilities had grown to the point that he now barely had time to handle the multiple duties the base commander had assigned to him, much less have any time left for her. Second, Amanda had always noticed Halston quickly distancing himself the moment they became too comfortable with each other's company. Amanda felt it had to do with Halston's late wife, who Halston had clearly loved. And third, Halston was Amanda's superior; a personal relationship between them was not advisable.

Amanda noticed Halston shaking hands with Captain Delaney before approaching her table and sitting down.

"Morning, Pete."

"Hello, Amanda. How are things?"

"Like usual," she responded, rolling her eyes.

Halston looked two tables down at the GIs and understood. "I'm gonna have a word with them." Halston began to get up.

Amanda motioned him to sit down. "Please, Pete, don't. It'll only make things worse for me. Now tell me, how can I help you?"

Halston glanced at the GIs, exhaled, and sat back down. That was another reason she felt so attracted to Halston. The colonel had always been very professional, never once making the slightest remark about her being a female pilot. Peter Halston was a decent man, a good soldier, and a friend. She only wished they could go one step further.

"Did you hear about the Pave Hawk crash?"

Amanda shook her head. Halston told her the story.

"Oh, Jesus. And Captain Heersen? I knew him well. This is terrible. Anything I can do?"

"Well, I just got Delaney's help for CSAR. Next time we get a call, I want to have him in his Apache covering the rescue craft in addition to the Sandies."

"Anything *I* can do?" she repeated.

"Ah . . . well, you know the rules about women in combat. I think you're doing a fine job where—"

"Right. Three days ago I had to pick up a couple of grunts in the middle of desert ten miles south of here because the idiots ran out of gas. That was really *some* mission." She shook her head and lowered her gaze. Her fingers toyed with the carton of milk.

"C'mon, Amanda."

"Just remember, Pete, if you need me to go inside Iraq, I'll be in and out before anyone notices," she responded.

Halston closed his eyes for a few moments. "Look, after today I'm down to two Pave Hawks and four pilots, one of whom is in the hospital with early pneumonia. I've got a request into CENTAF for another two pilots, but in the meantime, if we get in a crunch, maybe I'll let you go in as a copilot . . . maybe."

"I can do it," she responded firmly.

Halston nodded once and got up. "All right, Amanda. I hope I don't regret this."

"You won't. But don't rush off. How have you been? I don't think we've talked in two weeks."

Halston slowly sat back down. "All right, I guess. I think this job's getting to me. Iraq's latest flights into the zone, troop deployments, and Scud attacks have kept me quite busy. Don't even have time to breathe."

Amanda gave him a smile. "Somehow I think you'll be able to pull through."

"Well, I sure hope so."

"I sure miss your company," she said, taking advantage of the opportunity to probe a bit farther.

Their eyes locked for a few seconds before Halston looked away.

"Ah, yeah. . . . Listen, I really gotta run. I'm up to my eyeballs." He got up.

"See you around, Colonel," she said, raising her right eyebrow. The message was clear.

Halston gave her a slight nod before turning around and walking away.

Colonel Peter Halston. What is it with you?

Amanda opened her carton of milk and took a sip.

THE WHITE HOUSE.
Day Two. 0920 Local Time.

Leaning back against the edge of his desk, President Clinton felt a knot form in his stomach as his defense secretary gave him the bad news about the downed Pave Hawk. The death toll was up to eight, not counting the two pilots who ejected over Iraq. Scanning the Oval Office, the president's gaze shifted from his defense secretary to Undersecretary Kenneth Draper, finally zeroing in on the director of the CIA, Craig Kettler.

Still wearing his jogging suit, the president said, "Craig, how many people do you have actively working on the images gathered by our KH-11s over the region?"

Kettler tilted his head, arranging his pock-marked face into the tired gravity of his portrait at the entrance of the CIA headquarters. The group that analyzed and interpreted satellite images was the National Photographic Interpretation Center (NPIC), a component of the CIA's Directorate of Science and Technology. Located not in Langley but next to the Washington Navy Yard at First and M streets in downtown Washington, D.C., the NPIC headquarters consisted of three buildings covering two city blocks. With three shifts and two thousand employees, the NPIC was responsible for all aspects of satellite surveillance, from cleaning distortions made by the satellites' imaging sensors and atmospheric effects, to providing strategic and tactical intelligence reports to all departments of the U.S. government. It was the NPIC that told President Kennedy about the missiles in Cuba and President Reagan about the terrorist training camps in Libya. It was the NPIC that helped the CIA predict the 1967 Arab-Israeli war, the Soviet invasion of Afghanistan, and the Iraqi invasion of Kuwait. It was within the NPIC's charter to locate marijuana and cocaine fields, track the movement of warships, measure the extent of forest fires, and ensure that the old Soviet Union complied with arms limitation agreements during the Cold War years.

"Mr. President," Kettler said, "the NPIC is a very large organization with a very large task. Out of two thousand employees, I currently have almost one hundred working exclusively on this. That's three times the regular size of the team covering the Mid—"

"That is *not* what I asked you," the president interrupted. "I know that you use an army of computer experts to receive the digital images and clean them up before passing them on to the workstations of the actual analysts. My question is, *after* the images are processed and enhanced, how many of your NPIC analysts are actively combing through the hundreds of images collected by the satellites every ninety minutes?"

Kettler shifted his weight uncomfortably on the cream sofa before saying, "About thirty, sir."

The president briefly closed his eyes. "This is the most critical event of the moment, Craig. I want you to put as many operations on hold as feasibly possible and divert those resources to this region, starting this minute."

"I'll take care of that right away, Mr. President."

"Thank you, Craig." Clinton checked his watch. "Ken."

General Kenneth Draper looked at the president. "Yes, sir?"

"I want you to hop on a plane—preferably an Air Force jet—and get over to Riyadh right away. I want you to stay close to General Marshall and also keep close contact with the CIA director, with his man Bourdeaux, and also with this office. You're an expert in the area. Please give me a close assessment of the situation as you see it after you arrive, and from then on, I'll expect at least daily reports," the president said, referring to three-star General Roy Marshall, currently commanding CENTAF in Riyadh. "Of course, you can always call me directly in an emergency."

"Yes, Mr. President."

"Well, if you'll now excuse me, gentlemen, I think I'm going to take a quick shower."

Everyone stood up and left the room in single file.

SOUTHERN IRAQ.
Day Two. 1720 Local Time.

After refueling, the two Aerospatiale Gazelle utility helicopters closely followed the vegetation-rich flatlands surrounding the Euphrates, each under the power of a single turboshaft, which enabled the Iraqi craft to carry two pods of Matra 68mm rockets and two 7.62mm machine guns.

The two choppers hovered over the slow flowing waters of the ancient river and then continued downstream, one over each bank. Inside, two spotters scanned the shores with binoculars in a last-minute attempt to find the American pilots before sundown.

Lieutenant Kevin Dalton heard the steady *whop whop* of the helicopters approaching and hid behind a cluster of trees two hundred feet from the river, surprised that the Iraqis were able to pin down his position so quickly. He had fast-walked nonstop for a few hours, putting what he guessed were at least five miles between himself and the crash site. Now that the adrenaline had left his system, Kevin felt sore all over.

He removed his sunglasses, wiped the sweat off his forehead, then wiped the glasses against the right shoulder of his flight suit, and put them back on. He frowned as he felt the two small empty canteens strapped to the belt of his suit. The plastic water pouch was also empty. Although he had forced himself to space out water breaks during his short but exhausting journey, it had only taken him two hours to drink it all. Feeling the beginnings of blisters on his dry lips, Kevin rubbed on more lip balm before slowly moving to the other side of his small forest blanket, where he watched the choppers continue down the river. It took all his self-control to stop himself from running to the river and immersing his entire body in the cool, refreshing water, but the professional soldier in him told him that the choppers were still too close. If they turned around while he was in the open between the river and the trees, they would most likely spot him.

Cursing the helicopter pilots for taking too long to move downstream, and feeling light-headed from exposure to the sun, Kevin sat down and leaned his head against the thin trunk of a tree. He closed his eyes and tried to put things in perspective, but soon realized— again—that there was no perspective. He was doomed if captured, and he was doomed if he managed to get away. It was a choice between Iraqi prison or military prison.

Neither looked attractive to him at the very least. *But that,* he thought, *is the price I have to pay for playing John Wayne . . . and Campbell, and the crew of the rescue Pave Hawk . . . shit.* Guilt engulfed him, taking him down the avenue of truth he had tried to avoid since the crash hours ago: his stupidity had caused death to so many others. *I might just as well have pulled the trigger myself,* Kevin concluded. He knew their blood was on his hands. The Navy . . . McDeere would see to it that Kevin paid dearly for disobeying a direct order. *Jesus, what have I done?*

Reflecting on the futility of his own situation, Kevin did not realize that the loud noise he had heard belonged to the helicopters coming back and not to the last few seconds of a dogfight his mind played over and over again, tormenting him with Campbell's final words before everything around them exploded:

"Ar-rajul!"

Kevin's attention snapped back to the present, but it was too late. The helicopters were back, and because he had moved to the edge of the cluster of trees, he was now in plain view. A soldier, wearing camouflage fatigues and crouched by the small open door behind the pilot's seat of the Gazelle helicopter, pointed at him from only two hundred feet away. He noticed the other helicopter coming around. They were going to sandwich him.

Clutching the Smith & Wesson Model 39, he raced for a larger section of forest over one thousand feet away. He had only taken a few steps when the second helicopter appeared in front of him. Its side-mounted machine gun pods were trained in his direction. The craft hung there in midair. The pilot appeared immobile behind the control stick.

Kevin understood their message: Move and you're dead. He complied as the second helicopter moved toward him from the side and started to descend.

Khalela Yishaid had watched the entire episode from the large section of forest the American pilot had been running toward. She looked at Ishmael Barzani.

"Are you sure, Ishmael? There could be reprisals against your people for this."

"No more damage than what's already been done."

"Very well," she responded as she picked up one of the two Javelin launcher units Abdul Mozakhu had carried on his shoulders.

Khalela clipped one of the missile/canister combinations that Ishmael had strapped on his back onto the launcher unit. She lifted the assembled unit, rested the canister section on her right shoulder, and centered the closest helicopter on the monocular sight.

"You're absolutely certain you want to do this, right?"

"Inshallah, Khalela! If Allah wills it."

With sweat running down her forehead and neck, soaking the white cotton T-shirt she wore underneath the buttoned-down desert-camouflage fatigues, Khalela realigned the target on the crosshairs of the Javelin's sights and fired.

The two-stage solid propellant rocket motor came to life, thrusting the twenty-six-pound missile to Mach 1.8. She kept the helicopter centered in her sight as the semiautomatic line-of-sight command guidance system sent the necessary control commands to the missile. The Javelin's control surfaces responded to the launcher unit's radio command by moving in the desired direction.

Lieutenant Kevin Dalton was the only one that noticed the flash preceding the trail of smoke moving directly toward the helicopter in front of him. Instinctively, he dropped to the ground and rolled away from the craft and toward the small cluster of trees. His elbows, back, and knees stung with every roll. The sunglasses flew to the side. Through the ear-numbing rotor noise, Kevin heard the chopper's machine guns vomiting rounds. The earth seemed to explode around him as 7.62mm rounds showered the area where he had been a fraction of a second before. A burning pain in his left leg was followed by a shock wave from the blast as the missile's warhead struck the craft under the main rotor shaft, instantly severing it. The three thirty-four-foot-long blades tried to continue their trajectory, but without a pivot point, they rotated out of control and darted through the air over Kevin's head at astounding speed, disintegrating as they crashed on the other side of the cluster of trees. The craft's turbofan spun itself into burnout without the counter-load from the rotors.

Hiding behind some trees, Kevin cringed as he watched the craft plummet to the ground, exploding on impact. The blast threw him back against the trees. Disoriented from the powerful blow, Kevin crawled around the trees in an effort to escape the flames that consumed the fallen craft and its occupants. Only then did he realize he had been shot in the leg. Blood flowed from a wound a couple of inches below the knee, staining the leg of his flight suit. Feeling light-headed, he pulled a handkerchief from a side pocket and tied it slightly above the wound to slow down the blood loss. Through the smoke, he saw the second helicopter circle the first before heading for the spot at the edge of the clearing where the missile had come from. He struggled to remain conscious, but the combination of the stress from the ejection, the arduous journey, and the gunshot were enough to throw him once again into the void as the blurry shape of the helicopter disappeared behind a wall of flames.

Khalela already had the second helicopter centered in the sight of the launcher unit to which she had just clipped a second missile-canister combination. The craft approached her a few feet above the ground with its machine guns ready to fire. Khalela's finger was fixed on the weapon's trigger when the helicopter's guns came to life.

She fired.

As the missile, fitted with flares, left the launcher, a sensor in the launcher's arming unit detected the flares and automatically commanded the four-foot-long missile to keep to the center of Khalela's field of view.

Ignoring the muzzle flashes from the chopper's guns,

Khalela maintained her position. She focused her concentration on keeping the helicopter's cabin centered within the crosshairs of the launcher's sights. Bullets grazed the branches over her position, forcing Ishmael and Abdul to drop to the ground.

Suddenly, a stray 7.62mm bullet impacted the steel base of the launcher unit and ricocheted upward. The blow was strong enough to push Khalela back a few feet and point the launcher unit up. The missile, receiving new instructions from the line-of-sight guidance system, also darted upward, entirely missing the incoming craft.

Khalela threw the weapon to the side, dropped to the ground, and rolled to the left. As she did so, she reached for her 9mm Beretta. Briefly stopping twenty feet away from her previous position, she spotted Ishmael and Abdul signaling her to go around the other side. She understood, and getting to her feet, she raced along the side of the tree line, which curved out and around the helicopter. She could barely see Ishmael's slim figure on the other side of the half-moon-shaped clearing. She reached a position directly perpendicular to the path of the craft, which had stopped firing and hung, menacing, by the edge of the clearing, about a hundred feet from where Khalela stood with her weapon cocked and aimed.

The slow rattle of Ishmael's AK-47 rifle from the other side gave the signal. Khalela rushed forward as the helicopter, barely five feet off the ground, rotated toward the source of gunfire and away from her. Her rugged boots dug into the sandy terrain as she closed the gap while the machine guns blasted a blanket of rounds in a thundering, earth-trembling display of force. She reached the tail rotor and ducked under to the other side.

As the craft shook under the recoil of the powerful weapons, Khalela brought her weapon up and fired the Beretta through the open rear door and into the faces of two startled soldiers sitting in the back. The pilot, still concentrating on the edge of the clearing, while maintaining the craft in a near-perfect hover, did not hear the two shots.

Khalela backed away several feet, kneeled down, and

trained the pistol on the front Plexiglas cover of the stationary craft. She fired into it three times. The bullets pierced through and struck the pilot, who snapped forward and over the cyclic. The Gazelle responded by moving forward.

Khalela's long hair swayed in the wind as she raced across the clearing and back toward the protective blanket of the forest. She knew she had only a few seconds before the craft crashed, and she used them to the fullest, kicking as hard as she could against the soft terrain. Her strides were long and powerful. Her eyes focused solely on the approaching trees. The blast came, and the shock wave propelled her forward almost ten feet. Landing sideways on the ground, she glanced back at the blazing orange ball of flames by the tree line, dangerously near the Kurdish guerrillas.

Ishmael Barzani felt as close to Allah as he had ever been. The helicopter's forward momentum was barely stopped by several large trees next to the clearing, isolating Abdul and him from the flames that engulfed the doomed craft.

"Allah is truly with us today, my friend!" he said triumphantly, gazing into Abdul's green eyes.

The large rebel, still shaking from the close call, got to his feet and wiped the sand off his clothes. "That was too close, *Isha*. We risked much just to save the American."

"The American will be useful to us, Abdul. The *Ba'i* will be most generous when we bring the pilot to him."

The two Kurdish rebels walked around the wreck and into the clearing, where Khalela was already waiting for them. They approached the American pilot.

An hour later, back in the Kurdish hideout, Khalela Yişhaid finished cleaning the unconscious pilot's leg wound using the first-aid kits the pilot had carried with him, along with his other survival gear. She still couldn't believe she was doing this, but Ishmael had felt very strongly about keeping him alive.

Sitting on the edge of the bed, Khalela removed the

pilot's dogtags and studied them. *Lieutenant Kevin Dalton*. She placed them in a pocket of her fatigues and stared at the sunburned face of the stranger. Khalela brought a hand up to his face and gently pushed up an eyelid: brown eyes. *Well, Lieutenant Dalton, looks like you got lucky today.*

Khalela's gaze left the American's face and refocused out the small window above the bed. She stared at the early evening stars, inhaled deeply, and ran a hand through her long hair. The stars always brought back memories; brought back the pain. She remembered gazing at them countless times during countless nights with her older sister Suleima long ago. *Decades ago.*

Khalela stared at the stars, but in her mind she saw only the past.

She was seven then, and could still remember the blasts that sliced through the silent classroom like a knife, forcing Khalela to dive under her desk, pressing her little hands against her ears. Khalela had prayed to God that the sounds would go away, but they were soon joined by mortar fire from the hills surrounding her village. The Arabs by the border were coming again. Khalela's older sister had come from another classroom, grabbed her by the collar and dragged her out of the building. They broke into a run toward the village a few thousand feet away. When they reached it, several Arabs soldiers were already there. She saw them while hiding behind the only wall left of her house. The soldiers, dressed in olive-green fatigues and armed with automatic weapons, walked over dozens of corpses searching for survivors, firing salvo after salvo into the heads of the few who had lived through the initial mortar massacre. And then she saw the twisted shape of her mother lying next to her father, their eyes wide open and faces contorted.

Khalela had gagged, then started to sob. A soldier turned his head and saw them. Before Khalela could react, Suleima pushed her back and motioned Khalela to hide. The older sister broke into a run. Khalela tried to stop her, but she was gone before she could react. She didn't go after Suleima, but remained behind the wall. The shouts came, followed by cries and more laughter. When Khalela had looked again, she saw the Arabs tearing off Suleima's dress while making a circle around her. One forced Suleima down. Khalela had closed her eyes and curled up behind the wall, flanked by broken cinder blocks, wood, and other debris. She had listened to her sister's cries, listened to her pleas as the Arabs took turns.

Khalela had lost track of time. It could have been minutes or hours. She had remained still long after the cries and the laughter subsided. Long after two shots fired in rapid succession put an end to Suleima's cries. Long after the Arabs swept over her village, her family, her sister Suleima . . . her life.

Drenched in sweat, Khalela jumped when she felt a hand on her right shoulder. Startled she got up and spun around.

"Are you all right?" asked the giant Abdul, arching his thick black eyebrows into triangles.

Khalela briefly closed her eyes and wiped off her cheeks with her sleeve. "Ye—yes, I'm fine."

"Ishmael wants to know if the American will survive."

She nodded. The Kurd turned and left.

Khalela Yishaid gave the stars a final glance, silently apologizing to her dead sister. She knew she was responsible. From that day on, the flashback had always come back. Always reminded her that she had sinned, had caused pain to the person that she had loved most dearly in this world. . . . *But I didn't mean to make so much noise, Suleima. I didn't. It just happened. It just . . . please forgive me . . . please!*

Khalela inhaled deeply and silently left the room.

· 7 ·

MILITARY INTELLIGENCE

Military Intelligence—a contradiction in terms.
—Oswald Garrison Villard

AMAN BAKISH AIR BASE NEAR AN NAJAF, SOUTHERN IRAQ.
Day Two. 1920 Local Time.

Newly promoted General Abunnasr Manesh paced back
and forth behind Fassan Tabriz, a young communications specialist operating the portable gear stationed
inside the only air-conditioned bunker on the base, a
necessity for all the state-of-the-art radio equipment.
What could have gone wrong? Manesh asked himself.
The first part of the mission had gone perfectly. He had
successfully destroyed an American rescue helicopter.
His government had indeed been correct about the way
the American government felt toward their fighting men;
they hated to see one of them die or taken prisoner and
were willing to risk the lives of many more just to save
one. *Incredible.*

Manesh chewed his lower lip in thought. The search-
and-rescue mission was supposed to have been a fairly
simple one: a stunned pilot shot down, over hostile
desert, miles away from friendly lines. But somehow
they had lost contact with the two helicopters almost two
hours ago.

Manesh left the bunker and was welcomed by a cool breeze. He glanced at the early evening stars as he rolled up the sleeves of his khaki long-sleeved shirt and walked toward the sleeping quarters. He went in and opened the first door on his left.

The inside was dark and the air heavy. Five men slept there, all pilots. One of them raised his head and recognized him.

"Istaigaza!" the young pilot shouted to wake up the others as he came to attention. Within seconds, the rest of the men had leaped out of their cots and stood motionless in their underwear.

"At ease, my brothers. I am very glad to see that you are using one of Allah's best weapons: rest. A clear mind is the best weapon against the enemy!"

"Inshallah!" all responded in unison.

He paused briefly to look into their fierce eyes. There was not an ounce of doubt in them. They were indeed Allah's Army. "The American pilot is still at large. I need a pilot and a gunner first thing tomorrow morning!"

Manesh smiled when all five pilots stepped forward in unison. Now more than ever he needed the support of his people to keep him alive and well. The promotion to general came with plenty of strings attached. With General Qazi Ali dead, Manesh now reported directly to Saddam Hussein, who had very little tolerance for mistakes.

SALMAN ASAD AIR BASE, SAUDI ARABIA. NEAR IRAQI BORDER.
Day Two. 1930 Local Time.

Colonel Peter Halston's head snapped up when Robert Bourdeaux stormed into his tent carrying a set of photographs. The CIA officer walked straight to the desk and spread them across the wooden surface, under the soft white light of a single bulb dangling from the canvas ceiling at the end of an electric cord.

"What do you have there, Bob?" asked Halston from his cot in the corner of the tent.

"A gift from the CIA. Some interesting shots taken by one of our KH-11s about an hour ago."

Halston rose from his seat and joined Bourdeaux, already hunched over the large black-and-white photographs.

"Here he is," Bourdeaux said, his finger pointing to a spot on one of the photos.

"Who?"

"One of the downed pilots. It has to be him."

"Huh?" Halston mumbled, looking at the photo for a few moments before saying, "Okay. You got my attention. Tell me about it."

Bourdeaux cleared his throat. "These are a set of photographs taken within a period of three minutes about five miles east of where the F-14 went down. This one," he said, pulling out a photo from the bottom of the stack, "is the first one of the series. It shows two Iraqi helicopters, probably searching for our pilots, next to the Euphrates. Here, take a closer look."

Halston leaned forward until his tanned face was within inches of the photo. He recognized the shapes of the craft: dark circular silhouettes against the white sand and light-colored water. "All right, I'm with you."

Bourdeaux pulled a second photo in the sequence. "This one was taken a minute or so later. Can you find the choppers?"

Halston's eyes searched the shores of the river to no avail. He could not find them and looked to Bourdeaux.

"See this?" Bourdeaux pointed to a small, dark, oval shape next to the river. "Here's one and here's the other."

"Oh, I see . . . they're surrounding this cluster of trees."

"Exactly," said Bourdeaux. "Both choppers are facing a relatively small cluster of trees next to the river as if they found something or someone."

"Who? Our boys?"

"Yep. That's what I think. See this small shadow next to the trees. It moved from where it was on the first photo." He pulled it back out and put them side by side.

"I'll be damned! Did *you* figure this out?"

"Nope. Our analysts at the NPIC did. They actually used high-resolution graphics terminals to zoom in and clean up the frames before sending me digitized copies over the computer link."

"Amazing. How did you know to take photos of that particular area?"

"Actually, you can thank our president for this one. The word from Langley's that by executive order a number of operations have been put on hold and the resources diverted to work on this."

"Incredible, but that's only one shadow," Halston said pointing at the photo. "If you're right in your assumption, that means that the pilots either got separated after ejecting, or one of them is . . ."

"Yep. That's what I'm afraid of."

"All right, so what happened after that?"

"This is when it gets better."

Ten minutes later, Halston walked to the small entry to his tent and stared at the short row of Apache helicopters lined up on the far side of the tarmac. He now knew they had to pull the pilot out of there fast. *The Iraqis are not going to be very pleased when they find two of their helicopters destroyed. What if the helicopters managed to radio for help? How long before they react?* Halston asked himself, quickly realizing that another Iraqi search party was a possibility. The Iraqis would do just about anything to get their hands on downed American pilots for propaganda purposes.

A grim look crossed Halston's face. The thought of leaving a pilot in the hands of those savages was not a pleasant one. He turned around, walked by Bourdeaux and stared at the KH-11 frames once more. The evidence was all there. The shots showed the entire incident up to the point where the second helicopter was destroyed. The smoke from the fire made the rest of the photographs too blurry for proper interpretation. As his eyes scanned the images, Halston wondered who had actually destroyed the craft. There were no Allied fighters in the area at the time. Bourdeaux believed the Kurds were responsible. *That's a good possibility. Now the real*

*question is, where did the pilot go? Where did the Kurds—
if indeed they're involved—take him? Without a beacon,
it's impossible to locate him.*

Halston sighed and continued staring at the pictures.

SOUTHERN IRAQ.
Day Two. 2000 Local Time.

For Lieutenant Kevin Dalton, it was the second journey
back into consciousness in the same day. This time,
though, he opened his eyes in comfortable shadows; it
was already dark outside. He clenched his teeth in
agonizing pain when he tried to move his left leg, and
settled for just shifting his gaze to inspect the rustic
interior of the room, not knowing whether he was in
friendly or hostile hands.

When he felt certain there was no other person in the
room with him, he painfully sat up and stared at the
bandage over most of the lower section of his left leg
right above the ankle, also noticing he only wore his
underpants. He spotted the opened first-aid kits from his
and Campbell's survival kits by the foot of the bed.

He remembered how close he had come to the shower
of fire from the cannons of that helicopter. That was
right before the blast . . . the pressure . . . the heat.
Everything after that seemed too cloudy for him to
remember. The blurry shape of the second helicopter
was the last image he had registered before blacking out.

His thoughts were abruptly interrupted when a large
man with massive shoulders entered the room carrying
two wooden bowls. Kevin sat up against the wall in
defiance at the sight of the menacing-looking Arab. Both
men stared at one another for several seconds until the
Arab extended both hands and smiled.

"Akala . . . shariba," the Arab said.

Kevin shrugged and gave him a puzzled look.

"To eat . . . to drink."

Kevin inspected the contents of the bowls. One had
dates, the second . . . *water!*

Startling the Arab, Kevin reached for the bowl on the
right and brought it to his face, gulping it down in

seconds. When he lowered the bowl, he noticed a second person standing by the door.

"I guess you have met Abdul, Lieutenant Dalton."

Kevin was startled. The statement had come from an extremely attractive, tall woman wearing a set of tight-fitting fatigues. Her long black hair went well with her light olive skin. The top of her fatigues was unbuttoned down to the middle of her chest, exposing the white T-shirt she wore underneath.

"How do you know my—" He stopped when he saw his own dogtags hanging off her left hand. "How did I get here?"

"We spotted you after you ejected. We have been following you since."

"The helicopters . . . were you the one . . . ?"

"It was us." She approached him. Kevin noticed her tight leg muscles pumping against the camouflage cloth with every step. She sat on the edge of the bed. Kevin looked at himself and reached for the blanket, half-embarrassed.

"Don't worry about that, Lieutenant. I'm a soldier, too."

Kevin blushed and briefly lowered his gaze before staring into the most beautiful light green eyes he had ever seen. They crowned her high cheekbones.

"I think I should be grateful, then. You saved my life."

"I doubt that very seriously."

"But you said that you destroyed the helicopter."

"Yes."

"Well, that means . . ."

The woman drew her lips into a tight smile. "I doubt they would have killed you . . . Kevin?"

Kevin nodded. She continued.

"I think they would most likely have used you as a propaganda weapon."

"Who are you?"

"Who I am is not important at this moment. You are in the hands of Kurdish guerrillas—but do not worry, they are our allies."

Kevin's gaze became more calculating. *"Our* allies? Are you part of the . . ."

"Coalition? No, I am not. You are going to have to trust me for now. I am a friend."

Kevin exhaled. "May I at least know your name?"

She smiled once more. "Khalela."

"A very intriguing name. Tell me, what's going to happen to me now?"

"That is out of my hands. For now you must rest, if you want that wound to heal. You are lucky the round barely grazed your leg. It could have been a lot worse."

"I need to get in contact with—"

"In time. Right now, my Kurdish friends and I are in the middle of an important discovery. I'm afraid you are just going to have to come with us."

"A discovery . . . what are you talking about? What discovery?"

"I cannot discuss that now. Again, you are going to have to trust me. After we are finished with our work, we will take you back across to your people. I promise."

"Look, where is my radio? All I have to do is enable the beacon and—"

"I'm afraid that will not be possible for now."

"Why not?"

"Because this location is a secret. Bringing rescue helicopters will draw unwanted attention to this place. Perhaps tomorrow, when we are in the open."

Kevin leaned his head back against the wall and frowned. "That's just as well . . . shit."

"Excuse me?"

"Ah, don't worry about it. Just a personal problem."

Kevin watched Khalela's eyebrows dropping a bit. She was obviously studying him, trying to figure him out. "Personal? You mean you have a family waiting for you?"

"No, no. I wish that was it."

"Then? I mean, if you feel like talking about it."

"I disobeyed a direct order not to engage with that MiG."

"Oh? I thought that was your job. You are a pilot, correct?"

"It's more complicated than that. The MiG bastard

mercilessly shot down one of ours, and machine-gunned the pilot and RIO as they were trying to eject. I was trying to get even, but in the process I violated our rules of engagement. I was ordered to turn back, but instead . . . well, damn."

"That was terrible of the MiG pilot to do. What kind of MiG was it?"

"MiG-29. Very fast and maneuverable."

"What kind of plane were you in?"

"F-14."

Her eyes rolled in obvious disappointment. "I do not want to sound too critical, but it seems to me that you were on even terms as far as airplanes were concerned."

"Thanks a lot! That kind of comment's exactly what I need right now."

"Calm down. It was not an insult. I am just interested in knowing how a MiG-29 was able to shoot down two F-14s."

"He sneaked in on us flying very low. By the time my leader spotted him it was too late. In my case, the bastard tricked me by forcing me to fly into a cloud of birds. I lost an engine. From then on, I was a sitting duck. He wasted no time in shooting me down with his cannon."

Khalela tilted her head. "I am very sorry to hear that. Perhaps next time . . ."

"There won't be a next time."

She looked at him briefly and got up. "We will talk more later. For now you should rest. You will need all your strength tomorrow."

"Where are we going?"

"North." She turned around and started walking out.

"Khalela?"

"Yes?"

"Thanks."

She smiled, and her eyebrows—a bit full for a woman —rose a trifle. "You are welcome." She turned and left the room.

Kevin sighed, wondering who Khalela really was. She seemed to be familiar to some degree with Soviet and American fighter planes. Was she in the military? If so, which country's military? She denied being part of the coalition, and she seemed too civilized to belong to the Kurds. *So, where's she from? And what about this important discovery north of here? Is that the only reason she's here? Damn!*

Frustrated, Kevin frowned and reached for the bowl filled with dates.

"How did it go?" asked Ishmael Barzani.

"You really want to take him with us?" Khalela Yishaid asked.

"Pilot Dalton will be very valuable later on. Keeping him next to me is the only way I can make sure he stays alive long enough to bring him to the *Ba'i*. Today you showed us what those weapons are capable of doing. Remember, Khalela. The Kurdish struggle continues just as it has for many generations. We must take advantage of every opportunity to get our hands on new weapons. The American *Ba'i* will be most generous when we bring him pilot Dalton."

"I have my doubts about Dalton being able to endure the trip. He needs plenty of rest to fully recover from that wound."

"Allah's will prevails. If we are meant to get those weapons, then He will keep pilot Dalton alive."

SALMAN ASAD AIR BASE, SAUDI ARABIA. NEAR IRAQI BORDER. Day Two. 2030 Local Time.

Robert Bourdeaux sat across from Colonel Peter Halston at a narrow table in the deserted mess tent. Meal hours were finished and only a single soldier worked on the far side of the portable cafeteria-style line, doing something unidentifiable with a large wrench. Bourdeaux shifted his gaze back to Halston, who showed signs of severe exhaustion. The job was really taking a toll on the colonel's athletic body, and this new conflict was only in its initial stages.

For the last thirty minutes, they had gone over the latest set of KH-11 images, which showed an increase in activity at one of the two dairy products factories within the five hundred square miles outlined on Ishmael's map. A place called Allahbad Chemical Complex. At Bourdeaux's insistence, Halston had gone back to the communications tent and retrieved the images from previous KH-11 passes, which reconfirmed Bourdeaux's fears. The processing complex did not have as many supply and delivery trucks parked beside the large warehouse as it had several hours back. They were additions. *Why? A sudden demand for more dairy products?* Bourdeaux asked himself as his hands flipped through several eleven-by-fourteen frames.

Bourdeaux's eyes drifted away from the photos, past Halston, and trained them on one of the Apaches parked outside the mess tent. *Additional trucks at Allahbad. . . . What does that mean?* The number of trucks had nearly doubled in less than twelve hours. Also, now that they had taken a closer look at Allahbad, Bourdeaux noticed a number of small shelters spread out at the perimeter of the complex. He had noticed something else: several pairs of thick power lines connected to the top of the fence at various points around the perimeter and quite a few guards patrolling the area. *So much protection for just a milk factory?* He also observed that only a few trucks parked there appeared to be tankers, the rest looked like regular trucks with canvas-covered long beds.

After inspecting the images, Bourdeaux had immediately contacted the NPIC, requesting close-up shots of not only Allahbad, but also of the second dairy products factory within the area of interest. Thirty minutes later, he had them, and the analyst in him smiled when he saw that the other milk factory a hundred miles away, near Baghdad, had mostly tanker trucks regularly flowing in and out of the complex, which was also not fenced-in or patrolled like Allahbad. In fact, the close-up KH-11 images had shown people lined up on one side of the complex, presumably getting their dairy products directly from the plant. The buildings were similar in size and shape to Allahbad, with the exception of a gigantic warehouse in the front. The complex near Baghdad had what looked like a distribution center—a rectangular-shaped building—in the front. One side of the building was used by the tanker trucks and some regular trucks to load up the dairy products. The line of people went into the other side of the building, which looked roughly a twentieth the size of the enormous warehouse at Allahbad.

Bourdeaux shifted his gaze back to Halston, who now stood by the windows next to the table. *Something is definitely strange about this place.*

"I gotta strong hunch here, Pete. I've been around for a while at the CIA and have seen my share of well-camouflaged sites. The Soviets used to try to deceive our satellites all the time in the old days. The Cubans and the Chinese are also good at it. I think the Iraqis are covering something very important here. Something they don't want us—or anyone else—to know about. Normally, I would hesitate to jump to any conclusions, but based on the fact that we *know* they're trying to assemble nukes, plus the info I got from Ishmael . . . well, I think Allahbad is our place. Otherwise, why the tight security? Why the electric fence? Why so many guards? And where are the lines of people? Where are the tankers carrying milk out of the place? And why all those trucks?"

Halston rubbed his eyes. "Shit. You got a point there."

"Pete, I need you to get me a C-12 and a pilot. I'm going on a quick trip tonight."

Halston tilted his head. "Trip? Where to?"

"Riyadh."

"You're going to see Marshall?" asked Halston.

"Yep. I'll make some calls and have my people in Riyadh set it up immediately," Bourdeaux said. "I'll need all the documents we have on Allahbad and nearby air defenses ready as soon as possible."

"No problem."

"Thanks." Bourdeaux headed for the communications tent. It was going to be a long night.

SOUTHERN IRAQ.
Day Two. 2200 Local Time.

Lieutenant Kevin Dalton woke up with another headache, mixed with cold sweats. A delayed reaction, he decided, to the antibiotics Abdul had given him a couple of hours earlier. Now he wished he hadn't taken them. The risk of infection was very minimal thanks to the careful bandaging Khalela had applied, something she had done while he was sleeping, according to Abdul. *Abdul—there's some big son of a gun,* he mused, staring at the large frame of the Iranian-born guerrilla hunched back on a chair against the wall, snoring peacefully. In Abdul's hands was a wooden cup filled with a clear liquid Abdul had called *'araq.* He had given Kevin a taste of it earlier. Kevin wasn't a regular drinker but could tolerate several beers or a few stiff drinks, but that *'araq,* made from dates . . . *now that's some potent shit.*

As big as the giant Kurdish rebel was, Kevin had already decided he had a soft heart when it came to friends. Kevin had noticed that Abdul made it a personal commitment to see there was nothing that his new American friend needed.

Communicating through gestures and a few English words Abdul had picked up from Ishmael, the band's leader, Kevin had learned about some of the atrocities Ishmael's family, as well as the families of other members of the group, had been exposed to. When Kevin pointed at Abdul, the large Kurd had indicated that he was one of the lucky ones. Most of his family lived in the eastern provinces of Iran, far away from all the madness. He did indicate that he had a sister living nearby. Kevin was shocked by the stories he heard. *Chemical assassinations of entire villages? Jesus Christ! What kind of enemy are we fighting?* He gazed at three Javelin missiles leaning against the back wall. *And those weapons? How in the hell did they get them? Black market?*

Abdul had opened a small window over Kevin's bed, through which he now admired a full moon, bashfully hiding behind a cloud under a blanket of bright stars.

The peaceful sight seemed to soothe away the chaos in his mind and body.

Kevin frowned, realizing that he needed to relieve himself, something he hadn't done in a couple of hours. He thought about getting Abdul to carry him outside again, but chose against it, not wishing to disturb the peaceful sleep of the Iranian giant. Instead, Kevin decided to test the strength of his leg as well as Khalela's bandage job.

He sat up and moved his good leg to the edge of the bed. Then slowly, he slid his left leg to the side and clenched his teeth in anticipation of the pain he had become used to since that afternoon. There was none. Actually there was some discomfort, but nothing compared to the agonizing pain five hours ago. His head, however, would not stop its pounding. The aspirins he'd taken before falling asleep had not done the job.

Puzzled at how he had managed to recover so quickly, Kevin decided to stand up on one leg. As he did so, he felt the blood rush toward his wound. His lower leg began to throb, but it was still manageable pain. He grabbed the stick Abdul had given him and used it to support part of his weight.

Confident that he was capable of moving without help, Kevin threw a blanket over his shoulder—it was cold outside—and slowly walked across the room. He reached the small living room and then the outside door, which he pushed open.

He filled his lungs with the cold night air and briefly scanned the horizon before walking to the side of the house and relieving himself.

When he was finished, he walked back to the front and was startled to see Khalela with a weapon leveled at him. She wore a white, short-sleeved T-shirt tucked inside the pants of her fatigues. Kevin couldn't help but notice that she wore no bra; her dark nipples pressed against the thin cotton fabric. She looked terrific in the moonlight. At night her eyes didn't look quite as green, but somewhere in between green and blue.

"That was not a wise thing to do, Kevin. I could easily have killed you."

Khalela holstered the weapon and inspected him. Kevin felt embarrassed again, walking around in his underpants. "Looks like that leg is healing faster than I thought. You should thank Abdul and—"

"I know it was you. Abdul told me all about the great doctoring job you did with the stuff in the first-aid kits. Is that just another one of your many talents?"

Khalela laughed. "Do you always ask so many questions?"

"Sometimes." Kevin walked closer, mesmerized by the natural beauty of her face, so radiant and full of life. Her perfect teeth glistened in the dark. Her lips appeared moist despite the desert's daily dryness. Kevin wondered how she managed that. It didn't take but a day in the desert for his face and lips to get sunburned, even with the sunscreen and lip balm.

"Where are you from, Khalela?"

The smile quickly vanished from her face. "I thought we had decided to leave that line of questioning for now."

"Sorry, I was just curious. You have an accent that I can't really place. It's not Arab, it's—"

"Sorry. As they say in America, no deal."

"What can you tell me about yourself?" Kevin noticed she shifted her weight back and forth, obviously uncomfortable with his questioning.

"What is it that you want to know?"

"Well, for one thing, what's your relationship with the guerrillas?"

She relaxed a bit after hearing the question. "I help them with their problems."

"Are you the one who provided them with those Javelin missiles?"

She shook her head slowly. "You ask too many questions."

"Since I'm going to be under your protection, it's only fair to ask a few questions about the people who are protecting me."

"As I said, you ask too many questions."

"Well, you don't belong to the Kurds and you claim you're not an American, yet you speak fluent English and seem to be familiar with MiGs and American fighters. That could mean you're either with the military or . . . perhaps with some intelligence network. Which is it?"

"It is getting late."

"Can't blame me for trying. Let me ask you a question that you might be able to answer. When do we leave?" He checked his watch. It was two in the morning.

"At about five o'clock. You had better get some sleep. You will need it."

With that, she turned around and went back in. Kevin was in his bed in seconds, once again wondering who Khalela was. He had noticed a slight flicker in her eyes when he'd mentioned "intelligence network." Was she CIA? Kevin shook his head. No, unless she had been lying when she'd told him she was not American. Kevin remembered her saying that the Kurds were "our allies." Our allies? Kevin knew that in this part of the world, the United States' true allies were few: the British, the Germans, and sometimes the French and Israelis. Actually, Britain was the only true ally. The French were too unpredictable and could turn their backs on the United States at any time. The Germans were good at providing large amounts of cash but no manpower. The Israelis . . . Because of their proximity to Iraq, the Israelis had an active interest in making sure Iraq remained on a leash. Besides that, the United States stood pretty much alone. The other members of the coalition force supported the United States out of necessity; the Saudis because they wanted United States protection from Iraq. The Russians had too many domestic problems to do more than offer moral support.

She had to be either British, French, or Israeli. No other origin made sense. As far as intelligence networks went, the British Secret Service and the Mossad ranked up there with the CIA and the KGB. French intelligence was not significant enough to really matter. *British or Israeli? Mossad, maybe?* he wondered.

Kevin slowly fell asleep.

Ishmael Barzani held a piece of bread in his hand. The unleavened barley bread was made in large, thin, pliable discs that made it easy for Ishmael to use as a spoon to scoop up the goat cheese from the wooden bowl next to him. He sat by a ravine one hundred feet away. He had seen pilot Dalton come outside to relieve himself. He then watched Khalela talking to him for a few minutes before both went back in. His eyes gravitated to the three guards he had posted next to the half dozen four-by-four vehicles parked behind the house. It was a quiet night.

He focused his attention on the piece of bread covered with white goat cheese and knew that it would be painful, but he had no choice. Once in a while he did have to eat to continue fighting. Putting the small piece of bread in his mouth, Ishmael bit into it slowly, testing the ground before applying more pressure. Using his tongue, he pushed the piece of bread toward his back teeth and closed his eyes as a piercing pain made him shiver the moment he attempted to chew with the right side of his mouth. He eased back on the pressure and the throbbing subsided. Another bolt of pain caused him to inhale deeply as he tried chewing with his left side. With the coppery taste of his own blood from his diseased gums, Ishmael kept the piece of bread on his tongue and waited until it became soggy from blood and saliva before swallowing it. He did the same with a dozen more chunks of bread and goat cheese.

He finished and then stared at the stars. The distant stars, he thought as he eased himself against a large rock and took a sip from a cup filled with 'araq, which burned his gums but somehow felt good. 'Araq was the best way to stay warm in the cold desert nights, Ishmael reflected as he wiped his thin mustache clean of the potent drink. He remembered a period in his life when he didn't need to drink 'araq to keep warm at night. Ishmael remembered his nights with Raniya, his young wife.

A few tears slowly flowed from Ishmael's sunken eyes and made their way down his tanned face as he remembered the first time he'd seen her in a small village north of Halabjah. She had been getting water from the well in the center of the village. Ishmael had just arrived with his guerrilla group after two weeks of heavy fighting with the Iranians at the border. His group had taken many casualties. Ishmael himself had a bullet wound in his right forearm.

Ishmael drank more *'araq* and rubbed a hand over the two-inch scar on his arm. He remembered when the women by the well saw them and instantly ran to them, then brought them to the local school, where the wounded were tended. Raniya took care of Ishmael. She cleaned his wound and kept a fresh bandage on it for the next few days. Ishmael learned that Raniya's father was a *Shi'ah,* the town's spiritual leader, a man respected for his religious learning. In a matter of days, Ishmael had fallen in love with Raniya and decided to approach her father and ask for her hand. This he did right away, only to find out from the *Shi'ah* that Raniya's hand was already promised to her first cousin, a local tough, a *shaqawah.* Although hated by most, as Raniya's first cousin the *shaqawah* traditionally had the right to marry her. Ishmael's first thought had been to take Raniya away with him, but he quickly discarded the idea. In tribal custom, runaway marriages were not accepted and often led to death. A broken-hearted Ishmael was pacing back and forth in the center of the small village when he heard someone calling his name. He turned around and to his surprise saw the *shaqawah* walking toward him with a knife in his right hand. Ishmael could only guess he'd somehow heard about his feelings toward Raniya. He had known a fight to the death would take place. It was customary. It was the only way for the *shaqawah* to protect his honor. It was the Kurdish way.

Ishmael leaned forward and took another sip as he recalled the short yet bloody fight. The *shaqawah* was no match for Ishmael's skills, as he quickly learned after attacking Ishmael with the knife. Ishmael easily blocked it and kicked him in the rear, sending him flying into the shallow pond next to the well. The *shaqawah* landed head first, then bolted up and looked at Ishmael in surprise, obviously realizing his mistake. He had already committed himself to fight to the death when he knew he could not win. The *shaqawah* looked at Ishmael and then at all the villagers. Raniya stood there next to her father.

The options for the *shaqawah* were clear: death or dishonor. He chose the former and lunged. This time Ishmael pulled out his own knife, blocked the *shaqawah's* amateurish attack, and sliced his throat. The following week Ishmael had married the young Raniya, barely seventeen at the time.

Raniya . . .

Ishmael Barzani continued sipping *'araq* and staring at the stars. His gums burned. His teeth ached.

150 MILES NORTHWEST OF RIYADH, SAUDI ARABIA.
Day Two. 2300 Local Time.

"You feeling all right, pal?" asked the officer sitting to the left of Robert Bourdeaux in the back of the Beech C-12A, one of the many military utility transport aircraft providing courier service to Allied forces in Saudi Arabia and Kuwait.

Bourdeaux didn't answer. His head had not reacted well to the change in pressure after the plane had taken off fifteen minutes ago. Now, with the aircraft experiencing some unexpected turbulence, Bourdeaux kept his eyes closed and massaged his temples. His stomach was not handling the choppy flight all that well, either, something that surprised Bourdeaux. He seldom got nauseated. On the other hand, since his arrival in the region he had fallen for the deadly combination of poor diet, lack of sleep, and excessive stress that always messed up his body.

"Say, buddy, you okay?" asked the officer, a trace of concern in his voice.

"I'll survive."

"You don't sound too convincin' to me."

"Let's just say . . . that I have felt better before, all right? My body doesn't handle . . . changes in pressure all that well."

"Whatever you say. Name's Lieutenant Colonel Richard Kramer, but my friends call me Longhorn."

"Bourdeaux . . . Robert Bourdeaux." He pressed both hands against his stomach. His nausea slowly grew out of control.

"Well, nice to meet you, Bob—you go by Bob, right? . . . oh, shit! Grab one of 'em bags to your right if you feel like pukin'! No offense, buddy, but I don't feel like smellin' your barf all the way to Riyadh."

Bourdeaux fumbled with the airsick bag, opened it, and stared into its shiny plastic lining. Nothing, just a dry heave. He sat up, but kept the open bag in his hands. Now his headache kicked into high gear. *Jesus Christ!*

"Are you a pilot?" Bourdeaux forced himself to ask, trying to get his mind off his head and stomach.

"Yep, but not tonight. My damned state-of-the-art jet had some problems last night during an exercise and I had to make an emergency landing at your base. Can't say I was too happy about that, but at least I made it in one piece."

"Sorry to hear that, Colonel. So why are you going to Riyadh?"

"Just a quick trip to visit a buddy of mine. Gotta be back at the base before sunrise, though. Mechanics are fixin' my bird at seven sharp and I wanna be there." Kramer checked his watch. "Well, looks like twenty more minutes to go before we get there."

"Great. I can't wait to step on solid ground."

"You're a landlubber, aren't ya?"

"Excuse me?"

"Ah, forget it."

"Say, Colonel?"

"Yeah?"

"Where were you stationed before this conflict?" Bourdeaux asked to try to get his mind off his misery.

"With the 37th Tactical Fighter Wing at Tonopah, in Nevada, and before that I served in Desert Storm."

Bourdeaux was impressed. "The 37th? That's near Nellis Air Force Base. Isn't that where the Air Force keeps the stealth fighters?"

"You got it. And your lookin' at the cream of the stealth fighter pilots in the whole damned Air Force. Too bad mine malfunctioned last night."

"How long have you been flying the F-117A?"

"Hmm . . . for about five years. Flew one of the first

ones that came off the production line at Lockheed."

"Where are they keeping you guys and your fancy toys these days?"

"Same place we kept them during Desert Storm. The whole squadron—except for my bird—is at Khamis Mushait air base, a place in the mountains of southwestern Saudi, but no one's allowed in there unless they got a good reason. Say, where are you from, partna?"

"Born and raised in D.C. I guess I shouldn't even ask where *you're* from."

"Waco, Texas! Where else? The place where you can find the best damned barbecue in the world. Once you try 'em ol' beef ribs there, you'll never wanna eat barbecue anywhere else again."

That was the final straw. Bourdeaux could not control his stomach any longer and, bending over, he vomited.

"Oh, shit! Sorry 'bout that! Guess silly me didn't think what I was sayin'."

Bourdeaux didn't respond. He couldn't even if he wanted to. His body was purging itself of all unwanted substances. He inhaled deeply several times and finally managed to raise his head. "Damn!"

"Go easy on yourself. It happens to everybody for the first few times until your stomach gets stronger."

With tears rolling down his face, and a pounding headache, Bourdeaux felt a second convulsion coming and placed his mouth on the bag again. *Damned job!* he thought as he stared at his own shoes.

SALMAN ASAD AIR BASE, SAUDI ARABIA. NEAR IRAQI BORDER.
Day Two. 2320 Local Time.

Colonel Peter Halston remembered the music and the smell of fresh flowers. He remembered Elaine's white dress, too. The small church was packed. Her family on one side. His on the other. Halston saw his friends in the rear signaling him to skip town while he still could. He saw his mother crying with joy. But most of all, he remembered Elaine's face. Remembered her eyes finding his through the veil. Her lips moving softly as she spoke the vows she intended to keep for a lifetime . . . however short. He was back by her side. Back in her life. Back in a perfect world that slowly unraveled itself to the young couple and showed the promise of a good life. Then something changed. The lights inside the church dimmed. The people slowly left the pews and made a line in the center of the church. One by one they approached him. The smiles were gone. The flowers remained, but the music had changed. And the people . . . his mother, dressed in black, stood by his side. His friends, somber looks painted across their faces, made their way up the aisle to briefly and weakly shake his hand while mumbling something Peter Halston could not understand. Then they were gone. All of them. He was alone . . . alone with the coffin, her coffin. He saw it being lowered into the ground. Saw the single rose in his hands slowly falling on top to soon be covered by the same dirt that drowned his love, his hope, his life. Peter Halston fought against the memory, but he failed. He saw the curve on the road. Spotted the oncoming truck's headlights. Felt the steering wheel under his hands quiver the moment he drove onto the shoulder to avoid the head-on collision. But the tree . . . he couldn't avoid the tree. The sound of the impact rang in his ears long after all motion ceased. Long after his safety belt cut into his chest as it absorbed the same forward momentum that propelled Elaine through the windshield, like a rocket, colliding against the wide trunk, and bouncing back onto the hood. Her disfigured face crushed against the windshield. Her dead eyes stared at him . . . her eyes . . . her eyes . . .

Peter Halston sat up in bed and inhaled deeply. *Jesus Christ. When will this end?* After six years, he could still remember it as if it had only happened yesterday.

He shook his head and checked his watch. He knew it would take some time before he could go back to sleep. His heartbeat was up and he felt adrenaline knotting his stomach. He jumped out of his cot, put on a set of clean fatigues, and walked outside his tent.

The base seemed unusually quiet. The fighters were all secured on the ramp. He strolled down the tarmac and admired a Pave Hawk tied down near the edge of the ramp. He gazed up and was rewarded by a crystalline cosmos. Sitting down under the nose of the helicopter, Halston gazed into the distance. At night in the desert, without a moon, it was difficult to tell where the earth and sky met. The only reference point was the imaginary line where the stars stopped. Other than that, the desert looked like a huge black hole with no beginning and no end.

A black hole. "Sounds like the story of my life," he murmured.

"I didn't know you liked to talk to yourself, Pete."

Startled, Halston turned around, only to find a smiling Amanda Green with her arms crossed, standing underneath the Pave Hawk's tail rotor.

"I guess you can't sleep either, huh?" she said, walking toward him.

"Nope."

"May I?"

Halston patted the ground next to him with his right hand. She sat down and hugged her knees.

"This is so peaceful," he said. "Pretty hard to believe that there's been so much killing out there."

"I know, and the way it looks, there's probably gonna be more blood and death if those Iraqis don't stop their senseless tactics," she said.

"For us it's death. For the people at home it's almost like watching a G-rated movie. Ever since the start of Desert Storm, every time we attack Iraq everything seems sanitized."

"You can thank CNN for that," she said, running a hand through her short brown hair. "My father fought in Vietnam. He was a helicopter pilot, too. After the war, he came home and used to spend hours at night simply watching the stars, just like this. I used to sit out with him and he would talk about what he saw over there. Funny. He hardly ever discussed the war with anybody else, but he would talk very freely during those nights. These wars, like Desert Storm and what is going on now, are very different from the war he fought in, very detached from reality—at least on our side. No big emphasis on body counts. No specifics. Everything shown on TV's sanitized, cleaned. Makes you wonder."

"Anyone else in your family in the military besides you and your father?"

She shook her head. "Nope. None of my four brothers liked the service. My father was proud when he found out I decided to become a helicopter pilot. I think he felt as if I was the only one following his footsteps."

Halston smiled. He felt very comfortable in the company of Amanda Green.

"Does he still fly?"

"He lost his job as a commercial helicopter pilot after he failed to pass the eye exam on his physical last year. His vision is tunneling, and it can't be corrected. My mother and he live off his military pension, which ain't much. I try to help them with what I can. My brothers do the same."

"I didn't know that. I'm truly sorry. You and your father close?"

She inhaled deeply. "Yep. Very. I'm still his little girl."

"What about your mother?"

"We get along, but things were never the same after I joined up. Unlike my father, she's kind of old-fashioned when it comes to women and their role in society. She never worked a day in her life. With Dad I really get along, though. I miss him."

"You get letters often?"

"Yes, but it's not the same. I miss him. I miss his voice. I guess that comes with the job."

"You can call, you know."

"Yes, but it's too expensive. We can't afford it."

Halston's eyes inched toward her and studied the profile of her face: a somewhat pointy nose, small lips, and small round chin framed by short brown hair that just barely covered the back of her neck.

"You ever worry about what tomorrow might bring? After all, we might go into another war with these people," he asked her.

"I'm doing what my father did in Vietnam: take it one day at a time."

Halston smiled and gazed into her brown eyes. She smiled back and lowered her gaze after a few moments. "What are we doing?" she asked.

"Nothing yet," responded Halston. "But this could get complicated. I'm your superior."

"Yes, I know," she said.

"I'd hate to see this affect your career. You're a terrific pilot."

They remained quiet for several minutes before heading back to their tents. Halston got in bed and stared at the canvas ceiling of his small tent. As long as Amanda was under his command, a personal relationship was inappropriate, but on the other hand, Elaine had left an immense vacuum in him. To this day he still felt incomplete, alone, without a true purpose. Yes, the Air Force gave him a sense of accomplishment that no personal relationship could, but there was more to life than firing Patriots and filling out forms. He wasn't a loner by nature. He needed someone to share his life with. Colonel Peter Halston, U.S. Air Force, realized that he needed the company of a woman in his life again, and that woman could very well be Amanda Green. She fit right into his ideal of what a woman should be—except she was under his command.

But did he really want to get close to someone here? With another war maybe around the corner? Elaine's death had nearly crushed him. It had taken him years to fully return to a normal life, and even then the nightmares still haunted him. Could he really survive a second disaster like that one in his life?

The bombardment of questions slowly faded away and Halston fell asleep.

THE WHITE HOUSE.
Day Two. 1630 Local Time.

Sitting behind his desk, President Bill Clinton did not interrupt CIA Director Craig Kettler as he related the latest analysis by Robert Bourdeaux of the strange differences between the two dairy products factories. Listening intently, the president understood why the director had sent someone like Bourdeaux over there. The man had a sixth sense when it came to intelligence work. Although it didn't take long for the army of analysts at the NPIC to find an anomaly in the traffic to and from the Allahbad complex, it took a man like Bourdeaux to add another dimension of value to the satellite images by comparing Allahbad to another dairy factory and trying to find explanations for the differences.

Allahbad Chemical Complex. Was it for real? Or was Saddam playing games, trying to make the Americans look in the wrong place while the Iraqi leader maneuvered himself into an even stronger position? The Republican Guard group was only forty-eight hours from reaching the border with Kuwait and Saudi Arabia, and Clinton had already placed all Allied forces in the region on full alert. All he had to do was give the order and his bombers would smoke the advancing Iraqis in a few hours. But he couldn't. Not yet.

Kettler finished his pitch by stating that Bourdeaux had requested a meeting in Riyadh with General Marshall.

Clinton nodded. "I like that. Be sure that Draper attends this meeting. Afterward, I want to have a conference call with both Draper and Marshall."

"Yes, Mr. President."

For the first time in days, President Clinton saw a ray of hope, at least as far as the complex was concerned. He still felt troubled about the fate of the two pilots missing in action. He silently prayed for their well-being.

■ 8 ■

COMMANDERS

A president's hardest task is not to do what is right but to know what is right.

— Lyndon B. Johnson

Robert Bourdeaux was growing tired of the murky interior of the rectangular room where he had been ushered after arriving at CENTAF, nicknamed the Black Hole. After walking down a flight of stairs to the cellar installation, where General Roy Marshall and his staff controlled the skies over the region, Bourdeaux quickly understood the reason for the nickname. The place was gloomy and depressing. It seemed hard to believe that from this place the Allies' supreme air commander conducted all the briefings and meetings required to issue Air Tasking Orders.

Although his stomach problems had faded away the moment they landed in Riyadh, the pounding headache had not left. Bourdeaux sat impatiently, not only because he had been ignored for the past two hours since his arrival there, but also because the three-extra-strength Tylenols he had taken twenty minutes ago refused to kick in.

Aside from the corkboard, where Bourdeaux had

already pinned a few KH-11 photos, along with the map he'd gotten from the Kurd Ishmael, the only other furniture in the room was an old metallic table and three folding chairs on each side. A tripod stood at one end of the table. A brown door was at the other.

The door swung open. Bourdeaux stood up, but slowly exhaled when he recognized the same captain who had shown him to the room an hour before.

"Well?" Bourdeaux said, his voice beginning to show an edge. "I thought my people arranged this."

"They did, Mr. Bourdeaux," responded the captain, a short and somewhat plump, middle-aged man with a shiny forehead and a pointy nose. "The general has been tied up in meetings, but he'll be with you shortly, along with some members of his staff. So that you know, sir, it's been a very long day for the general, and he's tired and cranky. Get right down to your business as quickly as possible, and be brief and to the point. The general will appreciate that."

"Thanks for the tip."

The captain left the room.

Ten minutes later, the door swung open again. Bourdeaux, sitting on the edge of the table by the tripod, watched four men in desert fatigues enter the room. He recognized General Marshall from newspaper pictures and from watching CNN. He was the only three-star general in the group. The other three sported only one star. Marshall grabbed a chair from the right side of the table and moved it to the head. With his back against the door, the general slowly sat down while measuring Bourdeaux with his stare.

What impressed Bourdeaux the most was Marshall's penetrating gaze. Wearing a standard military crew cut, Marshall was a man of dark complexion, dark brown eyes, and black hair. A receding hairline gave him a square wall of forehead underlined with thin eyebrows drooping at the ends. A prominent nose hung over a pair of wiry lips blending into a strong chin, which gave him a kind of rugged geniality. *The general's been around the block plenty of times,* decided Bourdeaux. His face definitely showed it. Marshall was all business.

"Good evening, gentlemen," Bourdeaux said.

"Good evening, Mr. Bourdeaux," Marshall responded with a slight nod. The members of his staff remained quiet. "These are Generals Tom Kleiner and Hutch Potter. They are two of my top advisors. With me is also General Kenneth Draper, the undersecretary for Middle Eastern Affairs. Gentlemen, the director of the CIA called me two hours ago requesting that I meet with Mr. Bourdeaux in regards to critical information on the development of nuclear weapons inside Iraq."

Kleiner and Potter sat to Marshall's right, Draper to his left. Aside from Marshall, the only other person in the room Bourdeaux recognized was Draper, a silver-haired opportunist. General Kenneth J. Draper had pretty strong ties not only within the Clinton administration and the upper ranks of the U.S. Armed Forces, but also within the intelligence community in general. He came from a very wealthy family in Washington D.C., and he knew a lot of high-ranking politicians. The rumor around Langley was that Draper had quickly moved up the ladder by making allegiances of convenience with certain factions of the Armed Forces and Congress, which included helping politicians with timely and substantial campaign contributions. Draper would quickly switch sides when the opportunity for a promotion presented itself. The Silver Rat, as Draper was commonly known among some circles in the intelligence community, would not hesitate to ruin anyone's career if the action helped augment his own. Draper was always considered a politician wearing a uniform, and oddly enough, he finally became one when President Clinton named him undersecretary. As a matter of fact, there were those at Langley who believed the only reason Draper went into the military was to use the service as a launchpad for his political career. For all those reasons, Bourdeaux was not all that surprised to see Draper sitting here. Fortunately for Bourdeaux, Draper did not know him, which gave Bourdeaux an edge.

Praying that the Tylenols would soon come into play, Bourdeaux began. "Pleasure to meet you, gentlemen, and thanks for meeting me here on such short notice. I'll be brief and to the point." Bourdeaux walked up to the corkboard. "Gentlemen, I'm a senior CIA officer currently posted with the 47th Tactical Fighter Wing at Salman Asad. Part of my job's to gather intelligence from agents I've recruited inside Iraq. I'm also chartered with the task of organizing and analyzing the data I get, reviewing satellite imagery collected by the National Photographic Interpretation Center, and generating recommendations and options for probable courses of action based on my interpretation of that data. At exactly nine hundred hours local time yesterday, I met with a group of Kurdish guerrillas, who, in the process of raiding an Iraqi command post, came across this map. . . ." Bourdeaux continued with his speech for ten more minutes, covering everything Halston and he had gathered from the map, documents, and satellite photos, including the discrepancies between the two milk factories. The moment he finished, General Draper raised his hand.

"Yes, General?" Bourdeaux asked him.

"Mr. Bourdeaux, your data appears to be solid. The director of Central Intelligence and the president himself also appear to share that opinion. You seem to have covered all the angles."

Bourdeaux pushed his bottom lip forward a bit, studying Draper while the hammering inside his head intensified. *What in the heck's wrong with those Tylenols?* Bourdeaux could sense that Draper was about to start one of his classic maneuvers to make himself look good in front of Marshall while stomping on Bourdeaux. He decided to play it cool. "Thank you, Mr. Undersecretary."

"I'd rather you address me as General Draper, Mr. Bourdeaux. I believe I've earned that rank."

Right. "Of, course, *General.*"

"Like I just said, Mr. Bourdeaux," Draper repeated, waving a hand up in the air, "you appeared to have covered all the angles . . . except for one."

Bourdeaux waited a few seconds while Draper regarded him. Before Bourdeaux could say anything, Marshall opened his arms, palms facing up.

"General Draper? You mind telling us what it is that Mr. Bourdeaux's missed?"

Draper grinned at Bourdeaux. "The president's making a lot of decisions based on the information that you have gathered, Mr. Bourdeaux. Do *you* feel comfortable with the data the Kurds gave to you? Have you cross-checked it with other sources?"

"Give him more credit. These CIA guys always have multiple sources. I'm sure that he's already cross-checked it," interjected Marshall. "Isn't that right, Mr. Bourdeaux?"

The headache was out of control. Bourdeaux forced himself to ignore it. Marshall's eyes, as well as everyone else's, were on him. They waited for a response. How could he answer? *No, General, we didn't exactly confirm it with other sources, because guess what? Saddam has already killed most of my other agents inside Iraq, but I've got one helluva hunch that this is for real.* Bourdeaux knew that such response would have him removed from his current post and returned to Langley, where his days would most likely be numbered for embarrassing the Agency in front of someone of the caliber and authority of General Roy Marshall. Draper was playing with him, checking the tightness of his story. Nevertheless, Bourdeaux was not about to let Draper—liked by President Clinton or not—take him down the drain. He defiantly stared back at Draper, cleared his throat, and began.

"We have cross-checked this information in several ways, gentlemen," Bourdeaux started, struggling to formulate an answer good enough to shut Draper up. "First, let me start with a known fact, and that's the strong relationship that I have developed with the Kurdish guerrillas since—"

"Ahem . . . Mr. Bourdeaux," said Draper in a soft voice. "Isn't there a chance they are double agents? Iraqi soldiers dressed as Kurds, maybe?"

"Let him finish," Marshall said, before Bourdeaux got a chance to respond.

"Yessir." Draper pressed his lips together and leaned back against the metallic chair.

Bourdeaux ignored Draper's stare and forced himself to appear relaxed. "Like I was saying, gentlemen, in the past, the relationship that I have developed with the Kurds has provided me—and in turn you—with accurate strategic information on numbers of tanks, aircraft, and troop deployments, all confirmed through satellite passes. We have no reason to believe that this new information's any different in accuracy from previous data.

"In addition, we have confirmed an increased level of activity at Allahbad, where I believe the Iraqis are engaged in something more important than just processing milk. Given the tight security of the complex, the electric fence, the shelters I believe to be camouflaged antiaircraft installations, and the drastic differences between Allahbad and the other milk factory near Baghdad, I fear that we might be looking at the place where the rockets are being assembled. I admit that it is a somewhat reaching statement, but given all the data, at this point my recommendation's that we don't take any chances. I propose a nighttime stealth recon mission to get a closer look. If the recon flight confirms my suspicions, I would like to recommend an air strike on the complex."

"Incredible," said Draper, getting up and walking to the corkboard. His face was a few inches from the photos. After a few moments, Draper turned to Marshall. "This is a civilian facility, general. It makes baby formula, not weapons, or electricity, or . . . anything else that can substantially help the Iraqi military. An attack on this plant could give the Iraqis ammunition for a propaganda war. For all we know, the Iraqi government probably has the place packed with civilians. They're probably *praying* we attack it so that they can show the world the United States is not interested in restoring peace in the region, but in the destruction of the people of Iraq. I'm sorry, sir. I strongly disagree with Mr. Bourdeaux."

Marshall nodded, got up, and walked to the corkboard. Bourdeaux and Draper stepped aside. Marshall remained there for a few moments, hands behind his back, chin up, eyes inspecting the satellite photos. Bourdeaux knew he was pondering, thinking, playing out different scenarios in that brilliant mind of his.

"I see your point, Mr. Bourdeaux. The difference between the two factories is indeed significant," Marshall said as he turned around and faced his selected staff. "Any of you have any more questions for Mr. Bourdeaux?" He waited but got no response. "All right, then. Mr. Bourdeaux?"

"Yes, General?"

"Damned good briefing! I need you to get back over there right away. We'll get on the horn with the president and will let you know of our decision soon. In the meantime, keep on collecting as much information about that factory as you can. We might have more questions for you by the time you get back. Thank you for your help."

"Thank you for your time, General Marshall, gentlemen." With that, Bourdeaux placed the map and satellite photos back in his briefcase and left the room.

SALMAN ASAD AIR BASE, SAUDI ARABIA. NEAR IRAQI BORDER. Day Three. 0900 Local Time.

The pilot's door sprang open, revealing the cramped interior of the Apache gunship. After completing the preflight inspection of the exterior of the helicopter, Captain Orlando Delaney crawled inside, pulled the door down and locked it. He saw his copilot/gunner, Lieutenant Steve Rizzo approach the craft from the left-hand side, where the gunner's door was situated. Rizzo nodded and crawled up the built-in steps near the nose. He turned and pulled on the door handle, crawled in, and settled himself directly in front and slightly below Delaney's seat. He also closed his door.

Delaney reached for the left control console and flipped the electrical power switch to battery mode. The avionics quickly powered up. He fixed his gaze on the vertical scale instruments in front and to the right on the main console. There were two fuel gauges: one for each of the crash-resistant fuel cells located in the fuselage. Each cell was capable of holding a maximum of one hundred seventy gallons, or one thousand pounds of fuel. He followed the needles up to the top of the scale. He adjusted the throttle settings on the side-by-side throttle controls below the electrical power switch. Satisfied, he finished the preflight checklist and pushed down the square red button next to the dual throttle controls. The main rotor began to turn in response to the 125-horsepower engine starter located on the right engine nacelle in the aft equipment bay. The dual General Electric turbines kicked into life. Delaney watched the rotor RPM increase in response to his throttle controls.

All the information he immediately needed was shown in the video display unit, a seven-inch-square CRT display located directly in front of him at eye level. The display was surrounded by backup analog instrumentation. His Apache was ready for business.

Delaney smiled. He loved his job, and he loved the Army, where a soldier was a soldier, where promotions were tied to one's merit and not to the color of one's skin.

As a black growing up in Willoma, Mississippi, a town somewhere between Jackson, the capital, and Memphis, Tennessee, the skinny Delaney had seen enough rednecks and had been called nigger more times than he had hairs on his head. Delaney hated rednecks with an overwhelming passion. He despised them for what they said and what they stood for. Delaney and his three brothers had always been harassed at the racially integrated high school in downtown Willoma. For his parents, the fact all four of their boys were attending a high school that only a few years before had been kept strictly white was an honor. Their kids had a shot at getting a decent education. For the Delaney boys, it had been nothing but living hell for the first year: from finding ropes and white sheets inside their lockers, to constant threats and harassment by the rednecks, to the dangerous encounter with white-robed Klansmen one summer night long ago, when a half dozen hooded racists surprised a nineteen-year-old Delaney while he was celebrating with his girlfriend in his father's truck off a side road a mile outside Willoma. Delaney had just been accepted to attend college in Florida, courtesy of the Army ROTC program. To this day, Delaney could vividly recall the way his girlfriend's face had been instantly painted with terror. Her flared nostrils, wide-open eyes, and quivering lips showed that she was well aware of the fate black women faced if caught in the middle of the night by the Klan. The thought of a brutal gang rape followed by a hanging sent her into panic. With the hooded men banging on his truck's locked doors, Delaney pulled out the Smith & Wesson .38 Special his father always kept in the glove compartment and prayed that he didn't have to use it. The men began to throw rocks at the vehicle, cracking the windshield and side windows. A rock blasted through the driver's side window with a loud bang, and Delaney was bathed in broken glass. Another rock struck him in the shoulder. A hand reached in to unlock the door. He knew what would happen next. With the curses from the Klansmen mixed with his girlfriend's hair-curling shrieks, Orlando Delaney cocked the .38 Special and fired twice. One man fell back holding his chest. The others ran away as the police arrived and arrested the young Delaney for murder. Two months later, he was acquitted for reasons of self-defense in one of the most controversial cases in Mississippi. But Delaney, fully aware that in Willoma whites dispensed justice for blacks by two different avenues, left town the same day he was acquitted. He knew there had to be a better life waiting for him outside Mississippi. Orlando Delaney found it in the Army.

Captain Amanda Green, sitting in the copilot's seat of an HH-60G Pave Hawk helicopter, twisted the motorcycle-style, front-end grip of the collective lever by an extra half turn, increasing rotor RPM to eighty-five percent maximum power to compensate for the hot, thin air lifting off the already sizzling runway. When she had achieved the desired rotation, she pulled up the front end of the hinged collective with her left hand and gently applied forward pressure to the cyclic with her right. The Pave Hawk helicopter responded by gently lifting off the soft tarmac. Amanda applied additional right rudder to compensate for the rotor torque-induced rotation on the fuselage.

The Pave Hawk remained in a perfect hover five feet from the ground as Amanda waited for the second Pave Hawk rescue helicopter and for Captain Orlando Delaney's Apache to leave the ground. An F-15C from the 58th Tactical Fighter Squadron had picked up a beacon on Guard several miles north of the spot where the F-14 had gone down the day before. Although no two-way radio contact had been made with the downed pilot, the beacon had been enough for Halston to activate a second CSAR effort.

Captain Orlando Delaney joined the first Pave Hawk in a hover while waiting for the second one to reach take-off RPM.

"Navigation systems check," confirmed Rizzo, sitting in front of and below Delaney in the dual cockpit.

"Weapons check?"

"Weapons ready."

"All right. Tango Seven Niner and Tango Six Five, Dragonfly Niner Two."

"Niner Two, Tango Six. Airborne and turning to zero one zero."

In Tango Six Five, Amanda Green watched the second Pave Hawk take off and head north after the Apache. She applied additional forward pressure on the cyclic and the heavy craft responded by accelerating to 100 knots, keeping her craft below twenty feet, as briefed.

"Keep your eyes open," the Pave Hawk's pilot, Major Steve Poole, told her over the intercom as the three-craft caravan closely followed the flat terrain, leaving behind a cloud of sand.

"Roger."

"ETA?" asked Poole.

"Thirty minutes."

She smiled, grateful that Poole was letting her fly the helo. Keeping it less than fifty feet away from the other rescue chopper was almost second nature to her, especially when flying the Pave Hawk, a craft she had learned to appreciate after training for many years on the older and lighter Bell Model 212. She particularly liked the way the craft, as large as it was, responded to her commands. She understood why the engineers at Sikorsky were so proud of the Pave Hawk. The 15,000-pound craft was a long ways from the smaller Bell she had trained on a decade ago. To this day, Amanda still vividly remembered her first helicopter flying lesson. It had happened a few weeks after she had earned her private pilot's license in a single-engine airplane. The first thing her instructor had told her was to forget everything she had learned about flying airplanes. *The helicopter is an entirely different animal,* she recalled him saying. She also remembered how stubbornly she had refused to accept the change at first, finally giving in after a few failed lessons when she had repeatedly lost control of the rotorcraft and would have crashed had it not been for the instructor and the dual controls of the small trainer. Now she was in total control, no instructor to save her from disaster, no passing or failing grade, just survival or death. Amanda felt the adrenaline rush knotting her stomach as the possibility of combat neared. This is what she had wished for, and here it finally was. The real thing.

As the caravan crossed into Iraq, Amanda prayed to do it right.

"Dragonfly Niner Two, Cougar," Delaney heard the voice from the AWACS crew.

"Cougar, Niner Two," responded Delaney.

"Bogey. One five zero at two zero miles. One thirty knots."

"Niner Two."

Delaney didn't like this. A single unidentified craft, probably a propeller plane or maybe a helicopter, had been picked up by the AWACS near the same area where they were headed. Delaney frowned. He did not believe in coincidences, and the fact that an enemy craft was heading in the same direction bothered him. "Keep your eyes open," he told his gunner over the intercom.

"Yes, sir."

The young Iraqi pilot sitting behind the gunner in the dual cockpit of the Soviet-made Hind-D combat helicopter swung the cyclic forward and left, throwing the 24,000-pound craft into a steep diving turn. When his altimeter shot past one thousand feet, he gently applied rear pressure and adjusted rudder and throttle, keeping his craft leveled off at a comfortable 140 knots.

The small village was directly below, exactly where Colonel Manesh had told him it would be, standing peacefully next to a wide stream. There were hundreds of these villages around the country. What made this one special was its proximity—only three miles away—to the place where the two search and rescue helicopters had been destroyed.

The village consisted of several brick and stone houses along with a few tents, and a water well that fed a large circular pond in the clearing in the middle of the village.

The Hind circled the village near treetop level and finally landed in the large clearing next to the water well. As soon as the gear touched the ground, eight soldiers bolted out of the craft, carrying a diesel-powered generator and a roll of thick cable.

The last man out gave a clear signal to the pilot, who increased throttle, lifted the collective, and applied forward cyclic pressure. The Hind climbed enough to clear the rooftops and hid safely in between two stone houses.

"Dragonfly Niner Two, Cougar. Bogey's gone."

"Cougar, Niner Two. Gone?" asked Delaney.

"Affirmative. Disappeared from radar. Exercise extreme caution."

"Niner Two."

Delaney sighed, aware of what that meant. The helicopter had probably landed somewhere and was hiding, or maybe it was flying low.

"Captain, I just picked up a beacon on Guard," he heard Rizzo say.

Delaney switched frequencies to Guard and tried to communicate with the Tomcat's pilot. "This is Dragonfly Niner Two."

No response.

"This is Dragonfly Niner Two, over."

Nothing.

Amanda kept watch and listened to Delaney on Guard while Poole flew. She did not like the smell of their situation. There was the possibility that the crew, in order to save batteries, didn't have their radio switched to Talk, which was standard procedure until they got a visual on the CSAR team. On the other hand, that radio could be in the hands of Iraqis waiting to ambush another American rescue helicopter. The disappearing blip certainly told her the latter possibility was more realistic than the first. She would have objected about continuing had it not been for the CIA satellite coverage of the destruction of two Iraqi helicopters and the subsequent rescue of one of the downed pilots by what the man from the CIA had claimed to be Kurdish guerrillas. Even then, she still didn't like her situation. Not knowing the exact location of the enemy was worse than having to face them head-on. *At least that way things are even,* she reflected. *Both sides have equal time to react. But when the enemy is hiding, all bets are off.*

"Tangos, Dragonfly Niner Two."

"Come in, Niner Two," responded Amanda.

"Possible bandit helo hiding on the ground ten miles away. Do a three-sixty and remain behind me."

"Rog."

Amanda watched Poole lower the collective and drop the craft by another ten feet; thin branches grazed the landing gear. She could see the second Pave Hawk's light brown underside four hundred feet in front of them.

The distinctive sound of helicopter rotors could be heard in the distance as Ishmael Barzani reached the top of the hill overlooking the small village where they usually stopped to eat and sleep. Most of the villagers were Kurdish sympathizers and had always been generous and supportive of Ishmael's holy crusade. The helicopter, which he recognized as the kind used to drop gas on villages, had landed in a clearing between two houses. Through his field binoculars, Ishmael could see the craft's rotor still moving fast.

"See anything, *Isha?*" asked Abdul as he reached the edge.

"Just the helicopter we heard a few minutes ago. See it?" Ishmael pointed to a spot about five hundred feet away.

"Yes, I see it."

"What is that helicopter doing there?" asked Khalela as she too reached the top and positioned herself on the other side of Ishmael.

"Causing pain to our people," Ishmael responded in a sad tone.

"Our spotter in the village just reported three helicopters approaching, sir," said the Hind's gunner.

The Iraqi pilot increased throttle to remove most of the weight from the landing gear, but not enough to take off, although he could do it at a moment's notice.

The pilot applied right rudder and the craft responded by rotating and facing that direction. Then, moving the cyclic aft and increasing collective by a dash, he managed to lift the nosewheel off the ground while still keeping the rear wheels on the arid soil. "Cannon status?"

"Cannon enabled."

Captain Amanda Green spotted the small village straight ahead at twelve o'clock. Poole continued at treetop level behind and slightly below the second Pave Hawk, following the Apache in front. Throwing the cyclic forward as he darted past a small hill overlooking the village, Poole managed to remain close to the rolling hill as it smoothly leveled off at the bottom.

Dust swirled up as the craft reached a dry patch of grass a few thousand feet before the village.

"See anything?" Poole asked, warily scanning the sides of the valley. It was deserted.

"No. Whatever it was is gone," she responded.

Orlando Delaney surveyed the surroundings while the rustic stone houses by the edge of the village accelerated toward them. He was prepared to add throttle and increase collective aft pressure to clear the red roofs when he saw something up ahead and to his left. He wasn't exactly sure what it was at first. *A reflection? A metallic object reflecting the sun's early light? Could it be the—*

Highly polished instincts took over when several muzzle flashes confirmed his suspicion. Delaney applied full throttle and pulled back the cyclic, struggling to get out of range of the guns before crossing in front of the large helicopter hiding between two houses. The Pave Hawk directly behind him was not so lucky. Flying right behind him, the large rescue craft—lacking the maneuverability of the Apache—could not break away before the four-barrel cannon of what Delaney had now confirmed as a Hind-D gunship helicopter unleashed a shower of rounds across the underside of the rescue craft. A trail of black debris marked the path of destruction along the Pave Hawk's fuselage. The rescue craft went out of control, vibrating as bullets struck the carefully balanced turboshaft.

"Engine failure! Seven Niner going down!"

While Poole got their Pave Hawk out of range of the guns, Amanda watched in horror as bullets ripped across the fuselage of the other rescue chopper. She couldn't do anything for them. The helicopter had taken a direct hit at short range. The Pave Hawk went into an autorotation after turbine failure. Amanda watched as the pilot fought to get the wounded craft—still taking hits and now streaming smoke—clear of any houses before attempting a crash landing, which he nearly made, had it not been for what Amanda knew had to be a round hitting a fuel cell.

* * *

Delaney saw the Pave Hawk explode in a ball of orange flames that briefly reached up into the sky. From behind the smoke, he watched the Hind-D take off and circle around and behind his craft as he tried to bank left, out of the way.

"He's trying to get behind us!" shouted Lieutenant Steve Rizzo.

"Tango Six get out of here!"

"Six Five!"

"Infrared suppresser activated!"

"Cougar, Dragonfly Niner Two. We're engaged with a Hind!"

"Niner Two, Cougar. Say status."

"Niner Six destroyed. Have a Hind on my tail!"

"A flight of F-16s will be there in five minutes, over."

"Rog. Five minutes!"

Thanking Allah for giving him his first kill, the young Iraqi pilot activated the infrared seeker of the SA-7 Grail missile stored under the left stub-wing—a jury-rigged attempt to give the Hind-D air-to-air combat capability by using the popular shoulder-launched missile. The pilot activated the optical sighting system built into his helmet and trained it on the Apache. The missile's infrared tracking device went into operation, trying to lock onto the American helicopter's dual exhausts, but nothing happened; the seeker didn't respond, the missile lock indicator didn't light. Puzzled, he switched to guns, applied full throttle, and pushed the cyclic forward, rushing after the zigzagging enemy craft.

Orlando Delaney swung the cyclic in every direction. The craft trembled under the powerful thrust of two turboshafts fitted with an infrared suppresser system that broke up the hot gas plume from the engine's exhausts and reduced its temperature below the lock-on threshold of infrared detection systems. In seconds he reached the opposite hill and shot up, while fighting the hammering g's, trying to reach the top before the Hind got a firing angle.

With his right hand gripping the cyclic and index finger fixed around the firing button, Delaney jammed the right rudder pedal against the armored floor. The Apache's tail swung 180 degrees. He faced the incoming Hind.

The young Iraqi pilot was caught with his finger off the trigger when the American craft suddenly pivoted in midair and the cannon mounted in the turret below the nose came alive. He instinctively raised the collective, applied full throttle, and flung the cyclic left, missing the river of 30mm shells that barely grazed his heavily armored underside.

"Niner Two, Cougar. Three bogeys. Three three five at fifteen miles. One hundred fifty knots," the AWACS warned.

"Niner Two," responded Delaney. Now there were three more enemy craft approaching. He frowned. He had almost gotten the Hind but had missed the shot. Hastily, he now descended on the opposite side of the hill. The Hind was out of sight. He went around the hill and reappeared on the other side, expecting to see the Iraqi chopper, but it wasn't there.

"I don't know about you, Captain, but the shit's just about to hit the fan, and with four against one, we are the shit. Those F-16s are still four minutes away. Suggest we get the hell out of here while we can."

Rizzo was right; it was not going to be an even match. It would be more like suicide to try and take on four craft alone. There was no other way but to leave . . . defeated.

Still angry for having missed his one shot and failing to achieve retribution for either of the Pave Hawks—yesterday's and today's—Captain Orlando Delaney turned the Apache around and sped away after the surviving rescue helo. As the trail of smoke from the fallen rescue helicopter disappeared in the distance, Delaney, convinced he had not done his job well, silently apologized to the Pave Hawk's six dead crew members.

* * *

"Sweet Jesus!" exclaimed Lieutenant Kevin Dalton. The Apache grazed over their heads while they hid under sparse clusters of trees to avoid detection during the dogfight—a precaution Khalela had insisted on taking. "That was one of ours! And so was the one that went down."

"They were probably looking for you, Kevin."

"I know . . . dammit!" Guilt overwhelmed him as he quietly watched the smoke swirling up from the destroyed craft.

He felt Khalela's hand on his shoulder. "It was not your fault, you know."

Kevin didn't respond. He couldn't help but feel responsible, and reaching down for the PRC-90 strapped to his soiled gear vest, he switched it off.

"What did you do that for?" asked Khalela. Her long hair was pulled back and tied in a short bun. The change made her high cheekbones more pronounced.

"I should have never turned it back on. I'll either make it out of here on my own or I'll die trying. I won't have half the Allied forces looking for me simply because I couldn't control myself and got shot down. It's my mistake; I'll accept the consequences."

The Hind was soon joined by three others, deploying a total of nearly thirty soldiers in the village. Using binoculars Abdul had given him, Kevin was able to see the soldiers throwing large camouflage canopies over the helicopters to hide them from coalition fighters, before spreading around the small village in groups of two or three. Several approached houses, peeping through the windows and then going around and kicking in doors.

Kevin closed his eyes when he heard female screams soon after the soldiers went inside. He looked at Khalela. "We can't let those bastards—"

"This is nothing new, pilot Dalton," interrupted Ishmael Barzani, staring into Kevin's eyes with his penetrating gaze. "The raping and looting of our villages has been going on for years. The pain . . . we must endure the pain, for the end is near, Allah's kingdom will be true for all those who are suffering in that village right now."

"Do you know those villagers?" asked Kevin, mesmerized by Ishmael's response.

"I grew up in these regions. I know a great deal of people. Sometimes I think that is my curse. Hardly a day goes by that Allah does not take away a friend."

"It's just not fair," responded Kevin. "Those soldiers down there must be dealt with!"

Ishmael grinned, showing his rotten teeth and blackened gums to Kevin. "Oh, you do not really think we are going to let them get away with such brutality, do you?" He looked at Abdul and mumbled something.

Abdul rubbed the back of his thumb across his neck and smiled. *"Qatala,"* he said simply, and pointed toward the helicopters.

Kevin nodded. He didn't understand the exact meaning of the word Abdul had just said, but he knew the meaning of the Kurd's body language. He gazed into his new friend's eyes and saw in them deep, uncompromising resolve.

Ishmael led the single-file formation of rebels down the winding path that descended lazily toward the left side of the valley. Khalela was right behind him, closely followed by Abdul, who had one arm around Kevin's back. The two walked side by side. Kevin felt the throbbing in his leg return as he applied pressure on it, and he was grateful that Abdul supported part of his weight, making the pain somewhat bearable. The bandage that Khalela had given him, although moist from perspiration, still held firmly in place. Kevin glanced down at it. Khalela had cut off that leg of his flight suit at the knee, exposing his skinned knee to the hot sun. Kevin thought it might be better that way, since his other knee—also skinned—kept sticking to the inside of his flight suit every time he stopped moving for too long. That only added to his list of problems. His back and hips felt as if someone had hammered them against each other. In reality, that was exactly what had happened during his ejection.

Slowly moving along ravines on the side of the hill to avoid being spotted, the group reached the flat land of the valley, where Ishmael stopped and brought his right hand up in a fist.

Kevin looked behind him and watched how the battle-hardened guerrillas spread out to the sides and easily blended with the surroundings. Kevin and Abdul remained several feet behind Khalela and Ishmael.

Through his binoculars, Kevin spotted four soldiers drinking water from the stream that separated the village from him. Kevin noticed that they did not carry automatic weapons, and their fatigues looked more like . . . *flight suits?* The Iraqis remained there for several moments before walking back to two Hinds parked several feet behind them. The camouflaged canopies hung from the stationary rotors.

Kevin put down the binoculars and smiled.

"Those four out there are pilots," he whispered in a voice loud enough for Khalela and Ishmael to turn their heads.

"That's what I think, too," responded Khalela, following it up with a few Arabic sentences.

Ishmael pointed to his left and then moved his hand toward the village. He signaled to his men on his right in the same way. Instantly, Kevin watched the guerrillas crawl on their bellies and start moving toward the slow-flowing waters of the stream.

"Shouldn't we wait for nightfall? Those guys might spot them."

Khalela turned around and smiled. "Good observation, but not for desert warfare."

"Uh?"

"See the sun?"

"Yeah, it's behind—"

"That's right. With the sun behind us, the glare reflecting off the sand will make anybody in the village look the other way."

"I see." Kevin watched the Kurds stalk. The rebels covered the distance in a few minutes, then one by one they swam across the water, holding their weapons over their heads, and quickly dropped back to ground when they reached the opposite shore.

Kevin rotated the adjusting wheel in between the

binocular lenses and focused on the young face of one of the pilots casually standing in front of a helicopter. The others were out of sight on the other side of the Hind, probably seeking refuge from the already scorching beams of the late-morning sun. The young pilot had his eyes closed and face lifted, as if enjoying the warmth.

Kevin's pulse went up, and he felt his stomach knotting when he spotted a Kurd on the far right, slowly crawling toward the pilot. His approach was a calculated one, noted Kevin, as he watched the guerrilla move forward slowly on his knees and elbows, the AK-47 tightly held in front. Kevin grimaced, imagining how painful it must be to crawl over the hot sand. The Kurd stopped and tilted his head in every direction, then moved forward once again. Slowly, foot after agonizing foot, the guerrilla made it to just behind the tail rotor of the Hind.

Kevin stopped breathing when the Kurd, after carefully glancing at the other side of the Hind, raised to a crouch, slung the Kalashnikov across his back, and pulled a blade out of his boot. With only a few feet separating them, the Kurd recoiled and lunged. The soldier turned his head as the knife cut him across the throat.

Wondering how the Kurd had managed to kill and drag the body away without making enough noise for the other soldiers to hear him, Kevin watched in utter astonishment as three other Kurds emerged from behind the Hinds, each dragging his own victim.

"How in the hell . . . ?" he began to say, lowering the binoculars.

Ishmael looked at him and grinned, showing his rotten teeth again. "We are Allah's warriors, pilot Dalton. He watches over us."

Kevin looked at Khalela, who simply raised her left eyebrow and pressed her binoculars against her eyes. Kevin did the same and spotted a signal from one of the four Kurds below them.

Ishmael moved forward. They followed him.

Kevin, still being helped by Abdul, motioned Khalela to come closer. "Are they really going to take on all those armed soldiers?"

She drew her lips into a tight smile. "You have not seen anything yet. We are on the—"

Kevin snapped his head toward the village at the horrifying shriek of a man. So did everyone else. Kevin felt a cold chill propagating up his spine. He had heard people scream in pain during a car accident, but this wasn't even remotely close. Everyone picked up speed, moving toward the village. *That was a man in total agony. But from what? What in the world could inflict so much pain on a human being that I heard him several hundred feet away?* Kevin struggled to keep up as Abdul began to mumble something Kevin was certain were obscenities and curses against the Iraqi soldiers.

They reached the stream, which was deeper than he'd anticipated. The water quickly rose over his shoulders as he kept his weapon above his head. The PRC-90 was waterproof. Although they were in a hurry to get to the other side, Kevin couldn't help but enjoy a brief second of pleasure as the cool water caressed his multiple bruises. The throbbing from his leg also seemed to subside as he waded next to Abdul.

They reached the other side and positioned themselves behind the Hind. Ishmael looked at the group and motioned them to surround the village. Half the Kurds went in one direction and the rest followed Ishmael, who was already moving to the back of one of the houses.

As he wiped the water off his face, Kevin jumped at the loud sound of a second shriek. This one had come from a woman, but the intensity was the same. The terror in her voice made Kevin quicken his pace, almost catching up with Ishmael.

Kevin walked on his own, the pain from his leg momentarily suppressed by the rush of adrenaline. He pressed his soaked back hard against the wall of a house and was instantly reminded of the bruises he'd gotten while rolling away from the Iraqi helicopter the day before.

Abdul reached for the rifle slung across his back and brought it out. Kevin flipped the safety lever mounted on the slide of his Model 39. He glanced at Khalela, who also had her pistol cocked and ready. Kevin couldn't help but notice how the wet white T-shirt that she wore underneath the buttoned-down fatigues stuck to her breasts. Hard black nipples pressed firmly against the soaked fabric.

Khalela moved toward the back door, closely followed by Ishmael, Abdul, and Kevin. She pushed it open. The four went quietly through the open doorway and into the back room, where they could hear mumbles and cries coming from one of two rooms on either side of the short corridor. Ishmael positioned himself against one side with Abdul, Khalela, and Kevin on the other.

Kevin watched Khalela position her body sideways to the door, then in one swift move, she lifted and kicked her right foot at the center of the door. The heel landed hard. The door gave, and she dropped to the ground and rolled inside. He followed her and heard Abdul crashing against the second door.

The room was empty. Khalela turned around and raced for the second room. He ran after her but froze at the entrance.

The bloody, bullet-riddled bodies of an older man and a woman lay on the right side of the room. Kevin shifted his gaze to the soldier kneeling next to Abdul. The pants of his uniform were down at his ankles; his contorted face was accompanied by cries as he begged for his life. Kevin felt some sympathy for him, but that quickly faded away and was replaced with anger when he spotted the bruised, half-naked body of a girl. *Sweet Jesus!* he thought as Khalela rushed past Ishmael and kneeled next to her, covering her with a blanket from the bed. *What kind of an animal could do . . . ?* Kevin's eyes locked with the girl's, who could not have been older than fifteen. An immense sense of compassion filled him when the young girl, tears rolling down her cheeks, crawled over to the old couple, whom by now Kevin had guessed were her parents. Khalela stayed with her. All of a sudden the bruises and cuts on his body seemed insignificant.

Kevin felt his anger spiraling out of control. The

overwhelming sight of such brutality threw him into a rage that took control of his body. He shifted his gaze back and forth between the begging soldier and the now quiet girl resting her head on Khalela's shoulder.

With the unbending resolve to avenge an unforgivable crime, Kevin tucked the Smith & Wesson Model 39 in the Velcro-secured pouch on the side of his soaked flight suit and slowly walked toward Abdul. He reached for the knife tucked in the Kurd's waist sash. His eyes never left Abdul's as he curled the fingers of his right hand around the wooden handle. Kevin noticed his hand wasn't shaking, an observation that surprised him. He stepped behind the kneeling soldier, grabbed a clump of hair, and pulled the head back.

The girl looked at him once more. Her gaze melted with Kevin's as in one swift move he brought the knife down and across the soldier's neck, severing the larynx. Oblivious to the jerks of the soldier and the sickening expulsion of bloody foam, Kevin held the soldier's head back until the man went limp. He then let him crash headfirst against the rocky floor.

Ishmael stared at Kevin with respect. Abdul looked at him in surprise. It was obvious to Kevin that neither of them had expected him to have reacted like that.

A third shriek made the girl press her hands against her ears while Ishmael and Abdul raced to the front of the house where, joined by Kevin, the trio found the source.

Kevin saw that most of the villagers were lined up on the left side of the clearing in the middle of the village. Out of a high-voltage electric generator, a thick pair of cables snaked into the adjacent knee-deep pond. Three bodies floated face down in its electrified waters while two soldiers dragged a kicking and screaming woman toward it.

A soldier wearing a slightly different uniform than the rest—probably their leader, reflected Kevin—stood next to the pond. The woman was thrown at his feet. The officer slowly leaned down and gently helped her up. Words were exchanged.

Kevin looked at Ishmael. The Kurd's hardened expression mixed with a dash of guilt conveyed all the explanation Kevin needed. The villagers were being interrogated about Ishmael and his guerrilla band.

A few moments later, the leader slapped the woman across the face and, grabbing her by the shoulders, he shook her to no avail. The woman did not respond.

Showing signs of obvious frustration, the leader picked her small frame off the ground and threw her into the pond; she landed on her side.

Her first and final shriek pierced Kevin to his soul. He watched through tears as amused Iraqi soldiers, using long poles, mercilessly pushed the young woman back into the water after she had managed to roll to the edge, until there was no movement left, no life, no sound . . . except for the small ripples lazily slapping the cracked and weathered concrete edges of the pond.

Kevin breathed deeply and gazed into Ishmael's eyes, which held nothing but hatred and torment. Quietly sobbing, Abdul's hands covered his face.

"No more," Ishmael said with fierce conviction. The unyielding determination of the Kurdish leader's voice fueled Kevin's internal fire.

"That's right, my friend, no more," Kevin responded. They helped up Abdul who, still sobbing, mumbled a single word. Ishmael and Kevin got closer. .

"Uktun . . . uktun . . ."

Kevin watched Ishmael freeze for a moment before placing both hands on the Iranian-born Kurd. *"Hasstha?"*

Abdul nodded.

Ishmael continued in Arabic for several moments before helping his larger comrade to his feet. Abdul regained his composure and slowly walked to the back of the house.

Puzzled, Kevin was about to ask Ishmael what had happened when the Kurdish leader motioned him to follow. He complied and pulled out the Model 39 once more. They passed the room where Khalela was still comforting the young girl and went out the back, where he saw seven more dead soldiers piled against the back wall. Blood dripped down their bodies from their slit throats.

"There are only fifteen left in the clearing," Ishmael said to him. "We will surprise them!" Without another word, Ishmael stepped up on several empty oil barrels and crawled on the roof. Abdul followed him and then helped Kevin up.

From the top, Kevin noticed that most of the rebels were already strategically positioned on the roofs of houses surrounding the clearing with their automatic weapons pointed at the Iraqi perpetrators. Two soldiers were dragging the next victim to the pond: a young boy. Kevin looked at Ishmael, who nodded, and after briefly scanning the rooftops, he inhaled and screamed at the top of his lungs:

"Fi aman Allah!"

A torrential blanket of mixed-caliber rounds swept across the clearing, stopping mere feet from where the villagers huddled against one another. Fourteen soldiers dropped instantly under the deadly accurate fire from Ishmael's sharpshooters. Kevin noticed that three villagers stood up and grabbed the last soldier as he tried to run away. Then he saw something he had only heard about. As the gunfire subsided, the women approached the trapped soldier. Each picked up a stone. The soldier must have known what was going to happen to him because he began to spit and curse.

Through his binoculars, Kevin watched how the soldier was nearly stoned to death, saved only by Ishmael's men, who raced across the clearing and ordered the villagers off.

Minutes later, the Kurdish band stood by the edge of the pond. The village was quiet, save for the continuous hum of the electric generator. The bruised but proud Iraqi soldier was next to them. A light breeze swirled Khalela's hair and brushed it against Kevin, who now held the raped girl's hand.

Kevin watched Ishmael's stern gaze fight an equally unyielding stare from the soldier. Ishmael motioned him to step into the pond. The soldier hesitated at first, but with a self-dignity and pride that Kevin had never seen, the soldier nodded his head, looked around him, and finally jumped in. He screamed and rolled around in the waters until he too floated silently, alongside his victims.

When it was over, Kevin closed his eyes and turned his head.

"Are you all right?"

He turned to Khalela's dazzling eyes and felt comforted by them; there was a welcoming warmth about them that drew him in. He wasn't sure why he felt so attracted to this beautiful stranger. He sighed. "Yeah, I'm fine. Perhaps a little too much excitement for one day."

"Yes, we should all rest soon."

The humming stopped; the generator was disconnected. Abdul waded into the pond and lifted the body of the young woman they had seen killed minutes ago.

"Khalela?"

"Yes?"

"Back in the house . . . while you were in the other room . . ."

"Yes?"

"We watched that young woman die. Abdul began to sob, and at the sight mumbled the word *uktun*. What does it mean?"

Khalela closed her eyes for a second before looking back at Kevin. He saw a tinge of sadness in her light green eyes. "Kevin, that woman was his sister."

Kevin's eyes filled once more as he watched his Iranian friend climb out of the water with his head buried against his sister's body. He carried her to the side of the clearing and was soon joined by the women, who kneeled in front of her and raised their arms to the sky.

"Jesus Christ! What kind of world is this?"

"A world very different from where you come from, pilot Dalton," was the reply from behind.

"I'm sorry about Abdul's sister, Ishmael," Kevin said, turning around.

"We live in a world of sorrow. Earth is a test of

worthiness before acceptance to Allah's kingdom. We all must do what we have to in order to get there. You fly jets for your government, I fight against mine. Neither of us is right in the eyes of many, but as long as we are right in the eyes of Allah, then our place in paradise is secured. Allah will see to that. Do not worry if your enemy does you wrong today. Allah will make it right in the end. There is an old Arab proverb: 'Have patience and the body of your enemy will be carried past your door.' Have patience, pilot Dalton. Allah's justice will prevail, even if it takes a lifetime. After all, a lifetime is what we all have to prove ourselves worthy to enter Allah's kingdom."

Kevin was caught off guard, not knowing how to reply to those words, especially coming from someone who had just ordered another man to jump to his death. But then he realized that this was a war, and for the Kurds, a holy war. They were not fighting for oil wells or money; the Kurdish guerrillas had been fighting for centuries to simply live in peace.

"You're right," responded Kevin, staring into Ishmael's dark face. "We all must do what we have to do."

Ishmael nodded and turned to his men. Kevin and Khalela walked back to the house as two women came and took the young girl away.

They walked in silence. Khalela spoke first.

"Kevin?"

"Yes?"

"What you did in the house . . ."

"You mean . . ."

"Yes."

Kevin frowned, and as they reached the front porch of one of the stone houses, he sat down on a rustic wooden bench in the shade. She sat next to him. "I can't say I'm very proud of what I did, but at the time it felt right. I didn't kill a man today, at least not a man as defined in my book. That was a beast, probably the product of a deranged government, but nevertheless a beast. All I did was help the world by removing him. In the Navy, they told us not to take military matters personally. A dogfight was supposed to be just a dogfight, period. Our military code of honor called for professional behavior and courtesy at all times on the battlefield. All of that changed after the other day's air battle. I wasn't fighting against a professional pilot but against another beast. That butcher not only shot down my flight leader, but kept his cannons blasting on the plane as it plummeted toward the ocean! What was I supposed to do? Obey an order to knock-it-off from someone hundreds of miles away who had no knowledge of what really happened up there? No, Khalela, I couldn't allow that Iraqi bastard to fly off and get away with that murder, just like I didn't let that beast get away with raping that girl. It just ain't right!"

Khalela stared at him and put a hand on his shoulder. "I'm sorry I upset you," she started, in a voice filled with understanding. "You did what you felt was right; you followed your heart and that's all that matters. I have seen only a handful of men do what you did today, and I tell you, it may seem easy for observers to see someone else kill a person in cold blood, but when it's you pulling the trigger or plunging the knife, it's a whole different story."

"You mean, you too have—"

"Like you, I also had no choice. I live in a small border town in Israel and—"

"I knew it! I knew you were Israeli. You're Mossad, aren't you?" interrupted Kevin.

Khalela obviously realized what she had just said, and blushed. Probably upset at her unprofessionalism, decided Kevin. Somehow things had gotten a little too personal, and it was obvious that her feelings had momentarily clouded her senses. Kevin noticed that she recovered quickly. "Yes, I am Israeli."

"Why the big secret? I mean, we're allies."

"You are right, we are allies and we should help each other."

Kevin leaned back against the wall and briefly inspected his leg. One side of the bandage was stained red. "The pain is coming back."

"It is going to hurt tonight. You have been putting too much pressure on it. You had better stay off it for the rest of the day."

"You're the doctor," he responded in an amused tone that drew a smile from Khalela. "Khalela . . . that's a unique name. Does it mean something?"

Once again, Kevin noticed how she closed herself off, as if refusing to let her true feelings show. *Why, Khalela?* he silently asked as he stared into her mirror-brilliant eyes. Khalela sighed and turned to look at him. "It means 'beloved.'"

Kevin gave her a soft smile. "Nice, very nice. Your parents gave you a name as beautiful as—"

"I do not have any family!" she interrupted, getting up and turning around.

Kevin exhaled and shook his head. "Look, I didn't—"

"I know. I think I had better go and check with Ishmael and the others. We need to move those helicopters before the Iraqis realize what has happened, or they will level this place." Without turning back around, she started to walk away.

"You shouldn't be afraid to let some people into your life, Khalela. We're not all bad."

She stopped momentarily, and then continued walking toward the Kurdish band assembled by the pond.

BAGHDAD.
Day Three. 1000 Local Time.

Sitting in the back of a Mercedes limousine on the way to a propaganda live TV filming, Saddam Hussein, cigar in hand, listened to the voice of General Manesh on the car's speakerphone system. A Hind had managed to destroy another American rescue helicopter, and its pilot had also scared off two other American helicopters, one of them an Apache.

The Iraqi leader leaned back on the soft leather seat and smiled broadly. This was simply too good to be true. Allah was indeed being merciful to him.

His smile, however, quickly vanished when Manesh mentioned that he had lost contact with that Hind.

Actually, with three additional Hinds he had sent into the area loaded with troops to interrogate the villagers on the whereabouts of a band of Kurdish guerrillas believed to have rescued the American pilot. Saddam encouraged Manesh to find the Hinds and the pilots.

Without waiting for a reply, Saddam hung up, took another draw from his cigar, and slowly exhaled the smoke. The lost Hinds really didn't matter much to him in comparison to the downed American craft. Things were definitely going his way this time around.

THE WHITE HOUSE.
Day Three. 0230 Local Time.

It took a few seconds after waking up for President Bill Clinton to realize that the phone was ringing and that he had fallen asleep while reading in bed. One of several reports still lay scattered on his lap. Checking his watch, he realized it had only been an hour since his phone conversation with Generals Marshall and Draper, when the president decided to proceed with a recon mission over Allahbad.

First Lady Hillary Rodham Clinton, her face buried in a pillow, mumbled something incoherent and rolled to her side of the bed.

Rubbing a hand over his face, the president reached for the phone. "Yes?"

"I apologize for disturbing you at this hour, Mr. President, but I think you better turn on CNN. Saddam's about to put on a show," said the voice of an aide.

"Ah, yes, yes . . . all right. Thanks."

With all trace of sleep rapidly vanishing from his mind and body, the president quickly hung up and snagged the remote control next to the phone.

The TV came on. Hillary quickly sat up in bed.

"What are you doing?" she asked while rubbing her eyes. The president detected an edge in her voice.

The Commander in Chief briefly turned to the First Lady, who, wearing a light pink gown, covered a yawn with a long white hand.

"Sorry, honey. Saddam's just—"

The president stopped talking when the image of Saddam Hussein, dressed in one of his classic brown uniforms, walked next to a long table backed against a white wall and pointed to items recovered from the wrecks of the F-14 and one of two downed rescue helicopters. The camera panned from a confident Saddam to blackened flight helmets, boots, side panels with USAF markings, and even an ejection seat and a parachute. The Iraqi president picked up a number of watches, rings, sunglasses, and dogtags, and he said that all these men had died useless deaths. He said that their blood was on President Clinton's hands for sending them there.

Then the camera returned to Saddam, zooming in on the Iraqi leader's face until it filled the entire screen. Narrowed brown eyes burning with hatred, lips tightly pursed, nostrils inflating with every breath, Saddam Hussein remained quiet for several seconds before he began to speak in Arabic. A commentator's voice came on, translating the words.

"Mr. President Bill Clinton. You may be stronger than me, but I shall not obey you. If you dare to attack me in force, I will make another movie like this, except that behind me there will be a mountain of American helmets and guns." Saddam Hussein stopped talking and gazed at the world.

Feeling Hillary's hand on his shoulder, President Clinton breathed deeply and defiantly stared back at the Iraqi leader until the image was replaced by the CNN anchor. He flipped the TV off and set the remote control back on the nightstand.

Hillary stared at him, her face somber in the soft light, blond hair falling gently over her shoulders. She didn't have to say anything. After all these years, the president could read her face like a book.

He put a hand over hers, giving it a soft lingering pressure. In return, Hillary gave him an oblique glance and nodded.

President Bill Clinton shifted his gaze back to the blank TV screen.

■ 9 ■

EXPECTATIONS

SALMAN ASAD AIR BASE, SAUDI ARABIA. NEAR IRAQI BORDER.
Day Three. 1045 Local Time.

Drenched in sweat, his head still pounding from a combination of exhaustion and a turbulent flight, Robert Bourdeaux slowly strolled into the communications tent and looked quietly about the room until he found Peter Halston. The colonel, standing behind a radar operator, waved him over. It amazed Bourdeaux how well Halston looked today compared to the night before. Halston approached him.

"Damn, Bob. You look like shit."

Bourdeaux's eyebrows rose. "Well, it sure looks like someone got a decent night's sleep around here."

The tanned colonel smiled broadly. "I feel like a million bucks . . . although I did wake up for a couple of hours at midnight. Still, got my eight hours."

"Yeah, well, after the night I had, I can use a good chunk of that million dollars."

"All right, so you had a bad flight," Halston said, his face suddenly turning serious. "Now, tell me how things went at the Black Hole."

Bourdeaux tilted his head. "I think it went quite well. General Marshall seemed impressed with the information from my Kurdish friends and with my analysis of the satellite data. I also found out that all the stuff I'm finding's going to the president himself."

Halston's eyes opened wide. "No shit?"

"Nope. I'm hoping that the president sees the data in the same way we do."

"So, what was the outcome?"

"The general said that he was going to call the president, and that someone would get back to me on this. With that I was dismissed to get back here as soon as possible."

"I guess that's better than nothing, although I hope we can do something right away."

"Has any new information arrived from satellite surveillance?"

"You got some new shots from the NPIC on the link. Here." Halston snagged a large manila envelope from corner of the table and extracted two dozen prints.

Bourdeaux sighed, regarding the photographs with a contemptuous glance. "I guess I can always catch some sleep later."

The two of them settled down to go over the frames.

Under a partly cloudy sky, Captain Amanda Green walked away from the decelerating rotor of the Pave Hawk helicopter and headed for the communications tent, where she knew a full debriefing would take place before she could rest. *The debriefing isn't going to be fun,* she reflected as she approached one of the few air-conditioned tents on the base.

Inside she was welcomed by a rush of cool air that seemed to soothe away the glistening sweat covering her face, neck, and exposed forearms below the rolled-up sleeves of her flight suit. Her short brown hair, soaked and flattened against her head, gave the impression that she had just walked out of the shower.

She saw Orlando Delaney already talking to Colonel Halston and the CIA man at the end of the long, narrow tent, past the row of radio operators. Halston saw her and gestured her over.

Halston sat across from the CIA man at the dark green table at the back of the tent under the yellowish overheads. Delaney, who was sitting next to Halston, got up as she approached. She noticed a number of satellite photos spread over the table.

"Hello, Captain," Halston said without getting up. "Please, have a seat. Captain Delaney, anything else you wish to add?"

The skinny native of Mississippi slowly shook his head. "Nope. I think that about wraps it up."

"All right. I might have to ask you a few more questions later."

"No problem, sir." With that, Delaney turned around and left.

Amanda looked at Halston, who pointed to a chair directly across from the CIA man. "Hello, Colonel," she responded, following Halston's lead in keeping it formal when addressing one another in the presence of others.

"Captain, this is Robert Bourdeaux, senior analyst, CIA. Bob, this is Captain Amanda Green."

"Captain."

"Mr. Bourdeaux." Amanda studied the tall and slightly overweight man wearing a wrinkled white shirt. Bourdeaux had black hair that needed combing and a pair of bloodshot brown eyes, that, she soon realized, were also studying her.

Halston raised a hand, palm up. "What happened out there, Captain?"

Amanda leaned against the wooden back of her chair. She rubbed her fingers through her soaked hair and wiped the cool sweat from her cheeks. "In a nutshell, an Iraqi Hind-D ambushed us, sir. AWACS had it on radar for a few minutes, but then it descended and hid. We had a general idea of where it would be, but before we realized it, it fired on the other Pave Hawk. Captain Delaney managed to get out of the way in time. We were flying a few hundred feet behind the first rescue helo and also got out of the way. After it went down, Delaney ordered us out of the area, and he engaged in a short dogfight with the Hind without casualties on either side, but retreated after AWACS reported three more enemy craft."

"Any sight of the F-14's crew?"

"No, sir. It all happened very quickly—from the time we spotted the village to the time we left was less than a minute. For all I know, they could have watched the entire thing from the ground."

"Did you try to make radio contact with Lieutenant Dalton?"

"The major tried before the attack but got no response. All we had was a beacon."

"What about after the fight, did you try to contact them on your way out?"

"Well, their radio went dead."

"What? You mean . . ."

"Their beacon went off the air, sir."

"Was it because you were too far away?"

"Well, there's no way of knowing that, sir. The signal simply disappeared. It could mean that we got out of range, or perhaps that the radio was turned off, or maybe even destroyed."

"Damn! Who knows when we'll be able to get another fix on their position. All right. Where is Major Poole?"

Amanda glanced toward the tent's entrance. "He should be here any second, sir. He was right behind me."

Halston looked at Bourdeaux. "What do you think, Bob?"

"I'm not a soldier, but it seems as if Captain Delaney did as good as anyone could have under the circumstances. Maybe we weren't fully prepared for that rescue mission. Perhaps we should have sent more hardware along."

Halston sat back on his chair. "What a fucking mess. The Iraqis are already using this stuff for their propaganda war."

Halston stood up and then caught himself staring into Amanda's brown eyes for a few more seconds than he intended. There was a deep sadness in her gaze. He couldn't help feeling sorry for her. He could tell that somehow she felt partly responsible for the way things had gone today, but in reality it wasn't anybody's fault. It was CSAR, and CSAR was an unpredictable beast. He wanted to reach out and tell her that it would be all right, but the professional in him wouldn't allow such an emotional display. She was a soldier and he her superior. Period. "Anything else you want to add, Captain?"

Amanda lowered her gaze, put both hands on her small waist, and exhaled. "Ah . . . no, sir. I think that's it."

"That will be all for now. You're dismissed."

Amanda made eye contact with Halston once more before saying, "Yes, sir."

After she left, a somber Halston noticed Bourdeaux grinning at him.

"What? What?" Halston said defensively.

"Little Peter, I think you're being a bad boy."

Halston's face went through a few shades of red. "It showed? Damn!"

Bourdeaux smiled. "It's all among friends, Pete, but if you care to hear my opinion, I'd say that you're playing with fire."

"Nothing's happened yet, man," Halston responded while looking around the tent to make sure nobody could listen. "Really. We're just friends."

"That's how it all starts. On the positive side, though, I'm glad you've finally decided to move forward in that field."

"Listen, I don't want you to get the wrong impression here. Nothing. I mean, *nothing* has happened, and I have serious doubts about anything happening at all. There's a serious conflict of interest here. We can't have it both ways you know."

Bourdeaux shrugged. "Where there is a will . . ."

Halston nodded.

"Listen," Bourdeaux continued. "Strictly as a friend, my advice to you is that if you're serious about her, then figure a way to work around it. Get her out of CSAR.

. . . Hell, you figure it out. I don't know much about her, but on the surface she appears to be one serious lady. I hate to bring up the past, but you of all people should know just how difficult it is to get ahold of one. Remember, this conflict will be over one day, and unless you die in it, you'll be around afterward for many, *many* years. Whether you spend those years with or without her is something that will be decided based on how you act today. So, get your priorities straight, ol' buddy. Anyway, enough of the speech. You're an adult. I'm gonna get some sleep before I pass out." With that, Bourdeaux got up and left the tent.

USS *RANGER***. EIGHTY MILES NORTH OF BAHRAIN, PERSIAN GULF. Day Three. 1130 Local Time.**

Lieutenant Chico Delgado approached the technicians working on an F-14A Tomcat in the rear of the hangar. These were his friends from the barrio and even though they weren't officers, Delgado had always mingled with them. Although the bars on his shoulders placed him in a different class, in his heart he knew he was one of them: a barrio survivor.

"Heard anything about Crackers?" asked one of them.

"Nope. The CO's keepin' a tight lip about the whole situation. He says that our forces in Saudi are in charge of the rescue operation. I say it's a bunch of bullshit not to keep us informed."

"You got that right, man. I can't believe your CO's acting that way. Makes you fucking wonder, doesn't it?"

"Yep. Sure does."

Delgado remained there for ten more minutes before heading back to his quarters. He looked back at the streamlined Tomcat his friends were working on before walking away, fully convinced that regardless of the competition, behind him stood the best damned fighter plane in the world.

AMAN BAKISH AIR BASE NEAR AN NAJAF, SOUTHERN IRAQ.
Day Three. 1145 Local Time.

General Abunnasr Manesh stormed out of the communications bunker and into a strong mid-afternoon sun. Squinting and cursing, he walked toward the concrete shelter, where his green-striped MiG stood fueled and ready to go, except for the last of the bird debris which a ground crew member was scraping off the armored windscreen. All of the leading edges had been repaired.

The conversation with his president had not gone well at all, and to make matters worse, Fassan Tabriz, his radio operator, had been unsuccessful in trying to make contact with the Hinds. *What in the name of Allah is going on?* Manesh thought. *First we lose two Gazelles and now four Hinds? Something is very wrong here.* Fassan had also warned him about an increased level of Allied fighter activity in the no-fly zone—at least as much as Fassan's radar could detect after the American's powerful jamming systems significantly degraded the Russian-made radar's capability. It didn't matter any longer to Manesh. He was not about to wait inside a bunker. Manesh knew he was good, and at the controls of the powerful MiG-29, he considered himself better than everyone else, including the American pilots. Besides, if things ever got bad, as long as he remained close enough to the air base, he could quickly land and taxi his craft into the shelter.

"Do that later!" he told the ground crew member. "I need to go on a reconnaissance mission immediately."

Without responding, the technician slid down the side ladder and raced under the plane to remove the wheel chocks and missile covers, while Manesh slipped on his helmet and crawled inside the cockpit.

Both Tumanskii turbofans kicked the MiG-29 forward in response to Manesh's controlled push of the side-by-side throttles to his left. He mentally went through the pre-taxi checklist. *A mere formality at this point,* he reflected as the 39,000-pound plane cruised out of the bunker and through the heat wave lifting off the broiling tarmac.

Manesh lowered the canopy and activated the communications radio by depressing a button on the control stick.

"Fassan, Manesh here, have you established contact with the Hinds?"

"No, General. I shall continue trying."

"What are the coordinates of their last transmission?"

"Thirty-three degrees fifty minutes north, forty-five degrees east, sir."

Manesh taxied to the end of the runway and checked the heavily weathered windsock to his right. It lay flat against the pole; Manesh would have to use afterburners during takeoff to compensate for the loss of head wind and the hot, thinner air.

Pressing both feet against the pedals, he applied full throttle and felt the afterburners' kick. He released the brakes and the craft bolted forward, accelerating over the runway and achieving rollout speed fifteen seconds later. Manesh lifted the flaps and gear, and maintained 400 knots at fifty feet while flying the intercept vector.

Ishmael Barzani and seven other Kurds were busy pushing the last of the Hinds down the river, which although not deep enough to cover the entire craft, appeared to run quickly enough to drag the craft downstream, away from the village. Ishmael also knew that a mile downstream the narrow river flowed straight into the deeper and much wider Euphrates.

Ishmael frowned. The job of pushing would have gone much faster if Abdul had been helping them, but the large Kurd continued to mourn his sister's murder back in the village. Ishmael had known Abdul for a long time but had never seen his friend cry. Then again, he reflected, Abdul had never lost a loved one before.

Those thoughts quickly faded away when Ishmael sank into the knee-deep mud along the shore of the river. The helicopter's gear also sank under the colossal weight of the craft and weapons.

"Just a few more feet, my brothers. Allah will give us the strength!" he shouted, encouraging his men in their difficult task.

Manesh leveled off at twenty thousand feet to scan the area for the missing helicopters. He knew that flying so high would result in his detection by the Americans, but he had no choice. He had to find out what had happened to the Hinds. "Repeat coordinates, over."

"Thirty-three degrees fifty minutes north, forty-five degrees east, sir. Do you have a visual?"

"I do not have shit in view yet and I have been circling the area for two minutes!" cursed Manesh. "I can't hang around at this altitude for much longer. The Americans probably already have me on their radar."

The MiG started a circular descent. *Nothing,* he thought as his eyes continued to scan the village and surrounding river—

What in the name of Allah?

He wasn't sure what it was, but Manesh decided it definitely did not belong there. He had spotted an odd reflection on the river. He leveled off at fifteen thousand feet and kept the craft in a turn, trying to decipher what had caught his attention. The river reflected the sun's beams in nonuniform patterns. But what caught his eye wasn't the natural reflection of the water's surface but a superimposed reflection that did not change as it moved downstream. It was not shaped like a boat; boats usually show up as dark surfaces over the light and bright river. *No,* Manesh told himself, *this is definitely not shaped like a boat but like . . . a cross?*

Confusion and curiosity took over as he threw the stick forward while still turning left, forcing his craft on a steep descent. He noticed there were three other cross shapes flowing downstream. Then he realized they were not crosses but . . . *helicopter rotors!*

Ishmael was the first to notice the silvery shape against the blue sky, accelerating toward them as they gave the last Hind a final push.

"Race for cover my brothers!"

Several looked in his direction but quickly glanced the other way as the sound from the MiG finally reached them. Ishmael watched in horror as his men, some up to their waists in mud, struggled to reach cover. Ishmael dug both hands in the reddish mud trying to thrust his body forward while pulling his feet off the bottom of the river.

For General Manesh the revelation had come slowly at first but had then flooded into his mind as he came to the painful conclusion that his pilots and craft had become the victims of . . . *Damned savages!* He silently cursed as he dropped to treetop level to avoid surface-to-air missiles and activated the six-barrel cannon in the left wing root. Through the HUD he zeroed in on several Kurds by the shore and squeezed the trigger.

Khalela jumped to her feet when she heard the cannon fire and was about to run outside when Kevin stopped her.

"What are you doing?" she screamed as she tried to pull free.

Kevin put a hand to her chin and forced her face toward the back window. "Look!"

The Iraqi MiG completed a low pass over the Kurds by the shore. Several men were bent over, wounded, half of their bodies still stuck in the mud. The rest, Ishmael included, continued their struggle to pull free and race for the village.

"The Javelins! Where are they?" shouted Kevin.

"They will not do any good against that! All we would do is draw attention to ourselves."

"We've got to try something!" he persisted. "Where are they?"

Khalela grabbed his hand and they raced out the front door and into havoc. Men, women, and children ran screaming in every direction. Mothers held their infant sons tightly while younger men helped the old, sick, or handicapped. Most knew what would happen to them if captured, especially after what the Kurds had done to the Iraqi soldiers. Stories of blistering gas were common knowledge among everyone in the region.

"Pilot Dalton!"

Kevin snapped his head to the left. It was Abdul. "Wait, Khalela!"

The large Kurd raced toward them carrying the Javelins. Kevin grabbed one launcher and missile canister. Khalela did the same and the three raced to the edge of town facing the river.

"See it?" Kevin scanned the sky but could not see the MiG.

"No," responded Khalela.

"Damn! How do you work one of these things?" he asked her as he fumbled with the launcher unit.

"Here, look. Snap the canister on the back of the aiming unit like this." Kevin watched as Khalela's hands moved purposely for a few seconds, clipping the missile/canister combination onto the back of the green-painted launcher. He did the same.

"Got it. What now?"

"Okay, listen, this is not an infrared-seeking missile. After you fire it, you must guide it to the target."

"Are you kidding me? Do you know how fast that MiG's flying?"

"That is what I was trying to tell you when you told me that we had to try something!"

Kevin backed down. "All right, all right. What's next?"

"Bring the assembled unit up and rest it on your right shoulder, aim and fire."

"Just like that?"

"Yes, simple, isn't it? The only thing you must remember is to keep the target centered in your sight. The rest is auto—"

Kevin scanned the sky and saw the plane high on the horizon to the north. "Visual! Got a visual on the bastard!"

"Got it," Khalela said, lifting her unit and resting it on her right shoulder.

"It's coming around for another pass." Kevin watched Ishmael and three other Kurds finally make it out of the mud and race across the dusty field separating the village from the river. The MiG was in a final dive. Kevin could see the vapor streams coming off the widely flared leading-edge root extensions as the Fulcrum approached swiftly at about a hundred feet. Kevin knew the pilot would sweep over and unload a few hundred rounds without worrying much about ground fire or SAMs. The idea was to get in and out of the ground troop's field of view in two or three seconds using a combination of high speed and terrain-hugging flying. However, to an observer up on the sidelines, like himself and Khalela, the MiG would be exposed and fragile for a few more seconds, because—fast or not—the Iraqi fighter would have to cruise right in front of them. Perhaps, long enough to give a Javelin time to reach it. At the very least, the Javelin would draw the pilot's immediate attention away from the Kurds.

The MiG appeared to be doing what he expected. As the craft zoomed closer, Kevin's eyes opened wide in surprise and anger. "That MiG! It's got green stripes across the nose and wings! That's the bastard who shot me down!"

Khalela turned her head.

"Don't look at me!" he snapped. "Shoot the bastard down, and watch out. He's likely to go vertical when he sees the incoming missile!"

Barely acknowledging his advice, she activated the aiming unit and trained it on the MiG.

"Clear!"

She pressed the trigger.

General Manesh was about to unload another few hundred rounds on the savages when he noticed a bright flash to his left followed by a river of smoke coming directly at him.

What?

Instinctively, he broke his run and activated the chaff and flare dispenser directly from his control stick as he pulled up and pushed full power. The afterburning jerk propelled him vertically. He glanced back to see if the missile had gone for the chaff. The missile was still on him and closing.

Kevin saw that Khalela had listened to his advice and had anticipated the MiG's move. She had kept her left hand under the forward section of the launcher, allowing her to lift it up and follow the MiG's evasive maneuver. He frowned as the Soviet-made craft hurtled higher and higher. From the size of the missile and amount of rocket propellant left, Kevin estimated that the accuracy of the weapon would decrease rapidly at that altitude.

"Watch it," Kevin said. "The bastard can't go straight up forever. He's gonna do a dive and turn, or maybe an inverted dive at the top. Stay with him."

The MiG changed from vertical climb to an inverted loop and turn. Kevin saw Khalela try to force the Javelin to mimic the fancy maneuver, but the control signals sent via radio link to the Javelin's control surfaces were not strong enough as both craft and missile shot past fifteen thousand feet. He watched the missile run aimlessly for a few more seconds before it plummeted back to earth. Kevin knew what would come next and readied his own missile.

General Abunnasr Manesh was furious. The rebels had the nerve to fire one of their token missiles at his superior aircraft. He completed the loop and accelerated back down toward the source of the missile. He was certain it had come from one of the houses by the edge of town near the river.

He cursed himself for not being fully prepared for a ground battle. All his missiles were air-to-air. Again, he would have to resort to his cannon. He rolled out of the dive and threw the throttle forward.

Kevin had the incoming MiG in his sight as the muzzle flashes became clearly distinguishable against the jet's grayish color. He pressed the trigger and felt the powerful jerk as the twenty-six-pound missile left the red-hot launcher unit and accelerated to Mach 1.8. The first

30mm rounds from the MiG's cannon showered the area to his left, but Kevin knew that the firing would not last. The MiG would have to pull away.

Manesh barely had time to pull up and turn hard left to avoid a head-on collision with the incoming missile. To his surprise, it also did not go for the chaff he dispensed but turned with him and slowly closed in. Consecutive right and left evasive turns did not make any difference; the missile kept on closing. Manesh put his craft into another steep climb, outrunning the weapon, which ran out of propellant and fell to the earth.

Khalela jerked Kevin's arm and pulled him to the side. "There's no use. Let's go!"

Kevin threw the launcher unit to the ground and looked for Abdul, but he was gone. Kevin knew she was right. Their only chance of downing that MiG had been during their first, and maybe second, trial. The pilot in him knew that the MiG's pilot was probably well aware of their little game and would be coming around in seconds.

"Where is Abdul?"

"I don't know and we don't have time to find out. The MiG's turning around. We're out of missiles!"

Kevin raced after her back into the village. By this time, the clearing was deserted.

"Where's everybody?"

"Pilot Dalton! Over here, pilot Dalton!"

It was Abdul. Kevin turned around but did not see anyone in the clearing. "Khalela, pilot Dalton!"

"Shit, do you see him, Khalela?"

"No . . . wait, yes, yes! Over there!"

Kevin squinted and spotted his Iranian friend crazily waving his hands by the side of the clearing, fifty-some feet away from the edge of the circular pond. Half his body was inside a hole in the ground.

"What the—"

"Let's go, Kevin. Move!" She raced toward Abdul.

Kevin tried to catch up with Khalela but couldn't. The agonizing pain from his wounded leg hampered him as he kicked his legs to go faster and faster. The wind swirled his black hair as he heard the MiG's afterburners. He didn't have to look. The MiG was making its third pass. This time there were not going to be any missiles to delay its cannons. Kevin knew exactly what that pilot was going to do.

"Don't look back. Run, run!" Khalela screamed from the hole.

With the sound of jet engines ringing in his ears, Kevin called upon the last of his strength to propel his body as fast as his aching legs allowed him. All other thoughts were thrust aside as he focused entirely on making it into the—

The MiG's cannons came alive with a blistering inferno of 30mm fire that created a cloud of dust around him. Kevin knew those were the same cannons that killed Lancaster, Campbell, and Johnson. The same cannons that had killed those brave Kurds by the shoreline. With the unbending determination that comes from repeatedly defying and defeating death, Lieutenant Kevin Dalton reached into his soul and tapped the overwhelming desire to stay alive, if for nothing other than the sole purpose of seeking revenge against the murderous MiG. Boldly ignoring the cloud of hell that surrounded him, Kevin swiftly covered the last few feet and dove headfirst into the hole, bringing Khalela down with him. Abdul quickly reached up and pulled down a heavy steel door.

Inside the murky tunnel, disoriented, Kevin tried to readjust his vision, still feeling threatened by the turmoil on the surface. He jumped when several rounds struck the steel door, creating an ear-piercing high-pitched sound that made everybody in the large cave hold their hands to their ears. Children screamed and panic set in. Kevin heard Ishmael's voice shouting over everyone else's until the villagers slowly quieted down.

In the midst of all the chaos, still unable to see an inch from his face, Kevin felt the soft yet powerful embrace of Khalela.

"It is going to be all right, Kevin. You made it, you made it," she whispered from behind.

Kevin didn't respond. He leaned back and quietly

rested the back of his head against her shoulder. It felt warm, cozy, and welcoming. Closing his eyes and breathing deeply, Kevin slowly let it all go. The burning pain, the supersonic nightmares, the terror of facing death . . . until it all faded away. It felt as if Khalela's body absorbed everything, draining the smothering pain and pulling him away from the harsh reality that engulfed him. Slowly, Kevin Dalton left the agony behind and peacefully surrendered his whole self to the soothing comfort of her nearness.

SALMAN ASAD AIR BASE, SAUDI ARABIA. NEAR IRAQI BORDER.
Day Three. 1230 Local Time.

Colonel Peter Halston despised the bureaucratic drudgery that absorbed so much of his time. Bent over a pile of paperwork, he worked under the light of a single bulb. He looked up from his work when someone pulled open the canvas entrance flap of his tent.

"Pete?"

Halston recognized Amanda Green's voice as she came inside. There was a somber look on her face.

"Yes, Amanda?"

She closed the canvas flap and approached his desk. "Listen, Pete, I think perhaps we should put this whole friendship thing off for some time. It's not that I'm worried about what others might say. I'm confident in my abilities as a pilot. It's just that . . . ." She stopped and lowered her gaze.

Halston sat back and sighed. "You're afraid of getting involved, aren't you? Afraid of getting close to someone during this conflict?"

She nodded.

Halston got up and walked around the desk. "Well, join the club, Captain Amanda Green. I'm not just afraid. I'm scared shitless of getting involved with you and losing you the same way I lost Elaine. It took me years—*years*—to get over her, and I still have the damned nightmares to deal with. Do you think I really want to go through it again? No way. But what choice do I have? What choice does any of us have? What's the alternative? A lonely life? We have to take certain risks in this life, and that's just one of them. Think about it. Think about it very carefully and then make up your mind. A friend told me today that this conflict would be over one day, and then what? Back to our lonely lives? We have a chance, Amanda, you and I. And I'm willing to give it a try."

Before Halston had a chance to react, Amanda rushed into his arms. Halston felt her powerful embrace, smelled her soft perfume. Their lips met and they kissed intensely, seemingly for minutes, before slowly pulling away just enough to gaze into each other's eyes.

"I think we're going to be all right, Captain," he said, smiling.

"I think so too, Colonel," she responded, rubbing a finger over his lips, brushing off her lipstick. "I really think so, too."

FOLLOWING ORDERS

Theirs not to reason why,
Theirs but to do and die.
—Alfred, Lord Tennyson

SALMAN ASAD AIR BASE, SAUDI ARABIA. NEAR IRAQI BORDER.
Day Three. 1245 Local Time.

The inside of the communications tent seemed particularly loud this day. A dozen operators, sitting behind communication panels, remained in constant touch with the AWACS flying overhead. Operators reached for knobs, switches, and buttons while their eyes gazed into CRTs and displays. All performed their duties almost automatically, each caught up in his or her own little world of electronics.

Robert Bourdeaux watched their hands move purposefully over control panels, flipping and switching as information browsed across color displays. Some talked into the mouthpieces attached to their headsets. Others watched screens and multiple displays under the overhead neon lights, which cast a stark-white glow on the glossy dark green surface of the metallic table where Bourdeaux sat.

A light breeze, unusual for the region, blew across the base. Staring at the camouflage pattern of the canvas wall to his right, which moved softly to the rhythm of the wind, Bourdeaux felt his headache coming back. Halston had just been handed a two-paragraph note from General Roy Marshall. Bourdeaux crumpled up the computer printout and threw it to the side, startling Halston. Bourdeaux then quickly reached for his bottle of Tylenol and took two. He got up and drove a fist into his palm. *Dammit! That stupid Draper!* he silently cursed, sitting back down and grabbing the edge of the table with both hands. *He sure knows how to piss me off!*

Bourdeaux stared at his friend. The note said that they now had presidential sanction to proceed with the recon mission, to be followed by a possible bomb raid if the information collected during the mission came back positive. That wasn't what bothered Bourdeaux. The hidden strings attached to the sanction were why he now had a pounding migraine. His mind drifted back to General Kenneth Draper. The president had appointed the undersecretary of Middle Eastern Affairs to oversee the operation.

Oversee? Bullshit. Bourdeaux frowned as he finally understood Draper's game. Although Bourdeaux had been successful in fending Draper off, what good did it actually do? he asked himself, realizing that when Draper had seen everyone else—especially the president and General Marshall—agreeing with Bourdeaux's idea, the one-star general had probably shifted gears and made everyone believe he was just making sure all the bases had been covered by the CIA officer. Bourdeaux slowly nodded, deciding that was most likely the way it happened after he'd left CENTAF. Draper was now hooked up with the idea and would try to rob all the press—and therefore all the glory—from those who'd actually conceived and implemented the plan, which Draper had already baptized Operation Desert Star. *Politics.* Working at the CIA, Bourdeaux could smell a two-faced politician, and Draper stunk.

"But, Bob," Colonel Halston said, "why is he coming here? All air operations are coordinated through CENTAF. It's standard procedure."

"And it will be," responded Bourdeaux. "But in this

case—given the sensitivity of the operation—I think
Draper convinced someone, maybe even the president
himself, that it would be important to keep a closer eye
on it, just in case our information turns out to be
incorrect. Draper must have used his influence to get
assigned here as someone who can pull the plug at the
first indication that Allahbad's nothing but a milk factory."

"Why can't that someone be you?"

"Well, this is when politics get in the way. I'm sure
Marshall believes that I, or one of the high-ranking
officers at this base, can make the right call. My guess
why Draper's heading this way is that the slimy general's
probably pulling strings at the White House. I bet you
Draper sees this as a way to get some press."

"Damn. So, what's our next move?" Halston asked in
a low voice.

Bourdeaux's hands tingled from lack of circulation.
He loosened his grip on the table.

"We pretend to play by his rules, but be on your guard
at all times. Like I said earlier, this has turned into a
political game. Some of it's new for me, too, but after
getting burned a few times at the CIA, I've learned the
basics of the trade."

"So what are we supposed to do? Blow the mission to
make Draper look bad? It seems like we're stuck.
Doomed if we succeed and doomed if we don't."

"Maybe there's a way out."

"How? You said yourself that he's supposed to be
overseeing things, which means he's in charge."

"All right, Pete, first thing we gotta do is invite one of
the TV networks to do a special on the operation. They
must sign a nondisclosure agreement first, though. We
can't let any part of this operation leak out until the right
time and after we edit their tapes, but I'll be damned if
I'm going to let that bastard take all the credit when it's
over."

Halston smiled. "I like it. I'll get the network rep in
here to take some footage as the operation progresses.
We'll beat Draper at his own game."

KHAMIS MUSHAIT AIR BASE, SOUTHWESTERN SAUDI ARABIA.
Day Three. 1300 Local Time.

After taxiing his F-117A "Black Jet" stealth fighter
directly into the hangar, Lt. Colonel Richard "Longhorn" Kramer climbed down the four-segment ladder
that snaked its way up the left side of the plane. Tired
and cranky from flying all night, Kramer headed for his
barracks. The noon sun stung his eyes. He reached for his
Ray-Bans and put them on as he scanned the mountains
surrounding the isolated base. Nicknamed Tonopah
East, the air base had been reserved, for the second time,
for a squadron of the 37th Tactical Fighter Wing, up-
rooted to Saudi Arabia from its once-secret base at
Tonopah Test Range, Nevada.

Longhorn Kramer eyed two mechanics working on a
helicopter just outside the hangar. Both turned in his
direction and waved. He smiled and waved back. The
forty-five-year-old colonel loved Saudi Arabia's dry
weather, which was not much different from Waco,
Texas, where Kramer had spent most of his youth.
Except for the mountains, he decided. There were no
mountains in Central Texas. Hills, yes, but never mountains.

Kramer was a large man, almost six foot three and a
hefty 235 pounds, most of it solid muscle. His square
face ended in an equally square jaw. A thick but well-
kept mustache partially covered a pair of full lips. The
mustache had at one point blended into a closely
trimmed beard, but all that remained were a pair of
unfashionably-long sideburns, marginally violating Air
Force regulations. His fair skin, always a bit sunburned,
went well with his full head of light brown hair. Kramer
was a cowboy in the true sense of the word. He had
grown up on a ranch in central Texas, learned how to ride
a horse at six and how to tame one at thirteen. From
branding cows and sheep to readying bulls and horses for
rodeos, Kramer did it all on his family's ranch ten miles
east of Waco, a city 120 miles south of Dallas. As one of
seven boys—no girls—Longhorn Kramer learned the

oldest trade of the West from his father and older brothers and passed it on to his younger brothers. Blue jeans were passed down from the oldest to the youngest in his family. The brothers had their duties and responsibilities around the ranch, which was enough to give the Kramer boys plenty to do when not in school, since the ranch surpassed ten thousand head of cattle and half that many sheep. Longhorn Kramer loved the challenging and dirty, yet pure and simple, ranch work. It was fulfilling, old-fashioned, and invigorating. Sometimes, he felt that he loved the challenge more than the work itself. Each untamed horse was different than the one before. Each lasso throw to catch and brand a cow was never the same. Each weekend wild turkey shooting under a blazing sunrise told Longhorn Kramer that this was the way life was meant to be lived, in a corner of the world where deals were still closed based on a man's good word and a handshake.

Yes, the young Kramer loved his ranch life, until the challenge slowly faded away. The ranch duties that seemed to satisfy his other brothers just didn't do it for him any longer. That was the day Longhorn Kramer decided to look for another avenue to fill the ever-growing need for challenge. That was the day he found the Air Force. Overnight he learned everything he could about aviation and grew to love fighter planes more than he did the Kramer way of life. And so he made the break. One day he announced his plans at the family's breakfast table—breakfast was *the* meal of the day—shocking all of them. Richard "Longhorn" Kramer broke a century-long family tradition and joined the Air Force.

In spite of the heat, Kramer reached into a pocket of his flight suit and pulled out a pack of Marlboro Golds. His eelskin-covered lighter, a gift from his father—also a heavy smoker—matched his boots. The freedom of being able to wear cowboy boots instead of regulation boots was one of the privileges Kramer enjoyed most. A privilege he'd earned not only because of his rank, but also because Kramer was one of a handful of pilots who were qualified to fly the Black Jets into combat. Kramer had initially proven his skills during Operation Just Cause in Panama, where he'd led his squadron of F-117As into enemy territory and back out before the Panamanians had realized what hit them. During Desert Storm, he'd shown his skills time and time again by flying a record forty-three sorties with a near-perfect ninety-five percent kill ratio. Longhorn Kramer had put just about each of his Paveway II laser-guided bombs dead on target.

He took a last draw before going into his barracks. Pulling off his boots, he snuggled his large frame in the thin mattress and closed his eyes under the peaceful humming of the air-conditioning unit.

Kramer felt something sticking him in the back. He reached behind him and felt an envelope. He pulled it out and briefly glanced at it before opening it.

"You've got to be fuckin' kiddin' me!" he shouted after reading the short paragraph. He bolted up, put his boots back on and raced out of his barracks and into a bright sun he'd thought he would not see again until the following day.

"What in the hell's goin' on, boss? This thing for real?" Kramer asked his commanding officer, General Jeff Towers, slapping his new mission orders on the large glass-covered wooden desk.

"Relax, Longhorn, you seem a little tense. Did you have a bad trip?"

"No, boss. Trip was fine, but just got in a couple of minutes ago and thought I wasn't supposed to go back out for another twenty-four hours. I'm in no shape to fly'n F-117 right now. I spent all night in Riyadh checking in on one of my men at the hospital, all morning making sure those mechanics didn't screw up my jet, and three hours getting back here. Before that I flew nonstop exercises for six days. I'm on the edge, sir. I need a small break here. I can't go flying at 1900 this evening. That means a briefing at 1700. Four hours of sleep's not gonna cut it." Kramer watched his commanding officer grab the single sheet of paper and then check his watch. Towers' face showed the mileage of his fifty-three years. The lanky general had more wrinkles than hairs on his head.

"You realize how important this mission is?"

"Yep. Exactly why I wanna make sure I'm well-rested. Don't wanna fuck it up. 'Member flight trainin'? Th' accidents?" Kramer pulled out his Marlboro Golds and lighter. "You mind, sir?"

"Ah, no, no, that's fine, Longhorn. They're your lungs, not mine."

"Ya gotta die of somethin'. . . . Well? What's it gonna be, boss?" Kramer took a long draw and exhaled through his nostrils.

"Tell you what. It's still pretty early. I'll make sure nobody bothers you for the rest of the day, and I'll make some phone calls to push out the sortie to 2300 hours instead of the early evening mission we had previously planned. CENTAF's divided this mission in two stages. The first's pretty straight forward—a simple recon of the area to draw out their defenses. From there you'll head back to the same base you just came from and participate in a joint briefing with a few Navy Tomcat pilots we'll use as decoys and CAP during the second half of the mission. Anyway, I think we can cut down the briefing for the recon mission to just one hour. That'll give you . . . let's see . . . almost nine hours of sleep? I'll have your dinner delivered to your room. Fair enough?"

"Thanks, boss." Kramer knew that bringing up the past would help make his case. During the initial stages of the Lockheed F-117A stealth fighter training, all flight operations had been conducted at night for security reasons. Special precautions, such as keeping the fighters inside the hangar until thirty minutes after sunset, and performing ground operations in pitch-black conditions, were standard procedure. The problem was that their workloads, which at times involved two flights per night, were extremely high. That had resulted in pilot spatial disorientation and fatigue, which in turn was the cause of a few accidents.

"See ya." Kramer turned and headed for the door.

"Longhorn?"

"Yes, boss?" The cigarette was hanging off the side of his lip.

"Be careful."

Kramer grinned and took another draw. "You're worryin' too much, boss."

AMAN BAKISH AIR BASE NEAR AN NAJAF, SOUTHERN IRAQ.
Day Three. 1320 Local Time.

General Manesh walked away from his MiG-29. He was furious. The Kurds had obviously managed to attack while the helicopters were on the ground. He headed for the communications bunker across the runway and was welcomed by a rush of cool air as he pushed the heavy door and stepped inside the murky room. He found all but two operators sitting behind the large circular radar screens. The only noise inside the sound-insulated room was the constant humming of the air-conditioning unit.

Manesh blinked several times to readjust his vision. While he had been in the air, he had ordered tanks into the area to destroy the village. *Those savages are going to pay dearly for what they have done,* he thought as he approached Fassan Tabriz.

"Anything?"

"No, sir. Nothing out of the ordinary."

"Keep your eyes open."

"Yes, sir."

"Is this thing on?" He grabbed the microphone from a radio to the right of the operators.

"Yes, sir."

"Tune me in to the tanks that—"

"It's already tuned in to it, sir."

Manesh pressed the button on the microphone's handle.

"Red Lion Leader, Bakish Wind, do you copy?"

"We copy, Bakish Wind," responded the commander on the lead Soviet-made T-72 tank.

"Current position, over."

"Twenty miles from objective."

"ETA?"

"We are doing thirty miles per hour, sir. We will be there in forty minutes."

"Too long. Repeat, too long. The rebels will be long gone by then. What is the fastest you can go?"

"Forty miles per hour, sir, but I'm afraid the diesel engine might overheat and—"

"Do it."

"But, sir, we could—"

"Do it! Those blasphemous bastards destroyed four Hinds! Do you understand? Four attack helicopters! I want those Kurdish rebels dead!"

"Yes, sir! Accelerating to maximum speed. We will be there in . . . thirty minutes."

"Good. Call me when you get within firing range."

Fifteen minutes later the radio came alive. *"Bakish Wind, Red Lion Leader. Ten minutes from conventional shell range."*

Manesh brought the microphone to his lips. "What about self-propelled rounds?"

"The village is too small, sir. Our rocket-assisted projectiles are not that accurate. I'm afraid to over or undershoot and give them too much warning. Prefer to use conventional rounds, over."

Manesh frowned. The tank commander was right. RAPs were inherently inaccurate due to variations in the timing of firing and cutting off the motor. A second or two of error in the projectile's ignition after firing could mean the difference between hitting dead-on versus missing by a mile or two.

"How far away from chemical shell range?"

"Chemical, Bakish?"

"Are you deaf, Red Lion? How far away are you from chemical shell range?"

"Ahh . . . also about ten minutes. But, in order to use chemical weapons, we need direct approval from Baghdad."

"As far as you're concerned, Red Lion, I am all the direct approval you need! I am in charge of this section's security, and I'm giving you a direct order to use all the chemical weapons at your disposal to neutralize the village. Those Kurds are a threat to us, and the villagers sympathize with them. That makes them our enemy. Got that?"

"Yes, sir."

"Type of chemical shells?"

"Only blister agents, Bakish. Not very effective for immediate neutralization."

"Use them first anyway, and follow them up with conventional shells."

"Acknowledged. Five minutes to engage."

Manesh replaced the microphone and turned next to Fassan—a young but very bright radar technician, in Manesh's eyes.

"Has anything come through on the American channel?"

"Nothing yet, sir."

"Keep listening." Manesh shifted his gaze to the radar in front of Fassan. The sweep line lazily passed across the screen without any signal of enemy aircraft anywhere in a twenty-five-mile radius, at least none flying above three hundred feet. The system was capable of detecting craft as far as a hundred miles out, but the American's powerful jamming had greatly reduced the radar's range. To keep the enemy from firing one of their fancy radar-homing missiles at them, Fassan limited himself to just one or two radar sweeps every few minutes. To prevent the enemy from detecting a rhythm in the off-on radar monitoring, Manesh had ordered his subordinate to change the time lapse between sweeps and also change the duration of the sweeps.

"Bakish Wind, Red Lion Leader. Ready to commence firing. Range two thousand meters, over."

Manesh turned his head, reached over for the microphone, and brought it to his lips. "Fire!"

From the rear seat of the weathered Rover four-wheel-drive vehicle, Kevin snapped his head in the direction of the multiple blasts. He could see some flashes on the horizon.

"Iraqi tanks," explained Khalela, sitting next to him. "They sound like they are about two or three miles east of us."

Kevin thought about it for a moment as he did the math. "That's about right. You think . . ."

"Yes. They might be bombarding the village, but it shouldn't matter. All the villagers are out of there. Hopefully the shelling won't destroy everything."

"This is terrible, Khalela! What kind of government would punish one of their own vill—"

"The Iraqi government. But like I said, it won't matter much. After living under such threats for centuries, the villagers have adapted."

"*Adapted*? Adapted to what? Constant bombardment? How?"

"By living close to another village. Therefore, when one village becomes the focus of too much unwanted attention, the villagers can easily seek refuge in a nearby village. These people have learned to protect themselves."

Kevin turned his head back in the direction of the tanks as the Kurdish rebel accelerated the desert vehicle down the rugged, dusty road. He tightened his fists. "We can't just sit here and let them get away with that, Khalela. There must be something we can—"

Khalela brought both hands to his face. "Listen very carefully, for this is something that you are not used to experiencing. In the West there are laws. If you obey them, there is nothing you should worry about. If you disobey them, you go to jail, and for the most part, the punishment somehow fits the crime. But that is not the case over here. You do not have to actually do anything and you could still be punished. Don't you see? Why do you think the Kurds have been fighting for generations? In this part of the world there are no real laws. Constitutions are just pieces of paper created by temporary dictators who, after overthrowing the previous government, create their own new set of rules to satisfy their egos and lust for power. There are no elections, no real freedom, no individual rights . . . there is a true reign of terror controlled by madmen like Saddam Hussein.

Those villagers know this. They grew up knowing this, but they have hope . . . hope that one day Allah's mercy will descend upon them and liberate them from their aggressors. But until that glorious day comes, they must learn how to survive in a world like this, and what they are doing right now is exactly that—surviving."

"How? Their village—"

"There is nothing in that village except for old houses that could be rebuilt in weeks. The villagers knew that the moment we destroyed the Hinds their village was doomed. All they could hope for was to be able to make it out of there alive. In time they will come back and pick up the pieces, but for now this is the only way. Let the Iraqi government shell a few empty buildings in retaliation for the helicopters. Who cares? In all of our hearts, we have won that battle."

How? Kevin asked himself. *How can those eyes and angelic face be connected with such harsh yet true words? And what kind of a world is this, anyway?* Kevin wondered as the shelling stopped.

"Is it over?"

"Yes. Not a very big village."

Kevin stared into her mesmerizing eyes. She lowered her gaze and closed them.

"Are you all right?"

Khalela didn't respond. She simply breathed deeply for several seconds before bringing both hands to her face and rubbing her eyes.

"Khalela? Are you—"

"I'm fine," she responded, leveling her stare with his again. Kevin noticed tears in her eyes.

"Are you sure you're all right?"

"Yes. The shelling reminded me of something that happened a long time ago."

Kevin tilted his head. "You want to talk about it?"

She shook her head. He continued to look into her light green eyes, nearly losing himself in them.

"What?" she asked, a trace of curiosity dashing across her face. "Why are you looking at me like that?"

"Where are we going, Khalela? Why is the Mossad here?"

She slowly shook her head. "I thought that we had an agree—"

"That's right, we *had* an agreement, but that was before yesterday's attack. I almost got killed trying to help the Kurds. Granted, the only reason I'm alive today's because of you and the Kurds, but right now it just doesn't seem fair that I'm the only one in the group who has no knowledge of what's happening. I know more about Abdul than I know about you. And Abdul doesn't even speak English!"

Khalela turned away from him.

"Look, Khalela, I have already figured out that you're Mossad. There's no sense in trying to pretend otherwise. What I want to know is where we're headed to. I feel that my life's in as much danger as yours, and that makes us partners, and where I come from, partners share things."

She refused to look at him. Kevin reached out and softly touched her shoulder, turning her toward him. "Please?"

"Kevin, please do not make me do this. It is for your own protection. The less you know the—"

"I've heard that before, and I don't buy it. We're both in on this. I want to know where we're headed."

"All right. If you really want to know, we're headed for a place called Allahbad Processing Complex."

"What's in there?"

"On the surface it appears that they manufacture dairy products, but we have reason to believe the place is a nuclear weapons plant."

"Wh—what? Nuclear weapons?"

"Yes. Are you satisfied now?"

"Uh-uh, not yet. What are we going to do in there?"

"Look, you said that all you wanted to know was where we were headed, now I've told you—"

"You don't really expect me to just hear that and be satisfied, do you? C'mon, what are we going to do once we get there?"

"We are going to do nothing."

"What do you mean nothing? What's the purpose—"

"Observe and report. That is the purpose of my mission."

"What's it that you want to report about? That they are manufacturing nuclear weapons in there? I thought this type of reconnaissance should be done by satellite and high altitude planes. Don't you people have access—"

"That is the problem with U.S. Intelligence. Your people rely too much on satellite photographs, with little regard to the fact that the enemy *knows* about these satellites and can at times very cleverly disguise its activities by letting you see what you expect to see."

"What are you talking about? You have no idea of how sophisticated our—"

"See what I mean? You are just as blind as the rest. Have you ever wondered why the Mossad is so damned successful in all its missions? Did you ever wonder why the Israeli armed forces always seem to be a step ahead of the lot? Well, one of the reasons is because we do not just rely on what the satellites and high-altitude reconnaissance craft tell us."

"Tell me. What is it that we're going to check at that factory that our satellites couldn't pick up?"

"Do you know that Allahbad has never been bombed, not even during Desert Storm? What does that tell you?"

Kevin exhaled. "Our people still think the place is a dairy factory."

"Do you see the reason for us going there now?"

"I still get the feeling there's something else you're not telling me."

She shook her head. "Kevin, oh, Kevin, you ask far too many questions. Can't you be satisfied with what you already know?"

Kevin frowned, still suspicious. He decided to back off temporarily. "For now, Khalela, for now."

"Are all of you Americans so damned curious?"

That drew a loud laugh from Kevin, startling the Kurdish driver up front. Kevin brought both hands up in front of him, palms open and facing her. "Okay, no more job-related questions. Let's talk about you on a more personal level."

Khalela closed her eyes and sighed.

ALLAHBAD PROCESSING COMPLEX, SOUTH OF AN NAJAF, IRAQ.
Day Three. 1345 Local Time.

For Major Mohammed Hassoud this was his second trip to the underground laboratory. This time Dr. Radsul Sakkar had pressed the minus-five button on the elevator. They were going to inspect the actual rockets which, according to the sixty-year-old scientist, were due to be completed in just a few more days. Hassoud shifted his gaze to Sakkar, who rubbed his two-day-old stubble and then continued to make notes as the elevator stopped. Sakkar had invited him to accompany him on an inspection tour saying how ridiculous he found it that the head of security was not allowed to inspect the entire facility. And Sakkar had a point, Hassoud thought. It was frustrating trying to defend something he'd never seen before, but on the other hand, Hassoud admitted, the reason for such secrecy was to avoid giving out information to the enemy if they took over the facility. In the event of an attack, Hassoud, with the simple flip of a switch, could isolate the underground facility from the rest of the world by disabling the elevator and automatically sliding a thick steel plate into the elevator shaft. The underground laboratory could survive independently for weeks . . . or until help came. In the meantime, the enemy would not be able to extract any information from the surviving soldiers, even with drugs. The secret would be safe.

When the elevator's door opened, Hassoud finally realized the actual size of the underground complex. He walked behind Sakkar out of the elevator and into the colossal cylinder-shaped cave, which in Hassoud's estimation dwarfed the warhead assembly room by at least ten times.

"How in the name of Allah . . . ?"

"It is indeed impressive, ah, Major?"

"Impressive is too small a word to describe this, Doctor. This is indeed a magnificent work of engineering. How long did it take . . . ?"

Hassoud stood in utter disbelief as Sakkar told him

how it had taken almost a decade of hard labor at the cost of hundreds of lives and billions of petrodollars. The project had been kept secret by building the underground facility at the same time the processing complex behind the warehouse was built. The giant warehouse was nothing but a covered excavation site. Once workers reached a certain depth—what eventually became level minus five—the team built a concrete dome over the entire site, and from then on they continued digging underground. The entire project was invisible to anyone studying the progress of the complex's construction from the air or by satellite.

The room was much longer than it was wide. Two rows of missiles extended down the cave, one on each side, with a corridor in the middle that was wide enough to land a jetliner. Hassoud took a look around himself as they walked down the sparkling clean floors toward the first rocket on their left.

"Good afternoon, Doctor Sakkar," said a female voice coming from behind a thick fireproof suit.

"Ah, Risha! How are you?"

"Fine, Doctor, thank you," she responded, lifting the heavy hood over her head. Hassoud was captivated by intelligent blue eyes under a pair of dark, thin brows. Her slim face, with a fine nose and full lips over a pointy chin, was framed by shoulder-length light brown hair.

"Here, dear," Sakkar continued, handing her a progress report. "Please have it all filled out by the end of your shift. I'm particularly interested in the progress to correct all hydraulics leaks before deployment."

"Yes, Doctor, I will have it done with no problem, although you might want to know that my crew has completed all systems checks on number one. We will be ready for the warhead stage by tomorrow and for deployment the day after."

"Risha, I could only wish the other crews had as good a leader as you. Most of them had not even completed half of their checks as of this morning."

"Sorry to hear that, Doctor. Would you like me to assist some of them?"

"Not yet. For now concentrate on getting number one into fully operational stage. We'll talk after deployment. Thanks for the hard work. Allah's spirit truly lives in your work."

"Thank you, Doctor." She placed the hood back on and walked away from them and toward a tank with the word *Hydrazine* written across the side.

"An unusual job for such a beautiful woman, Doctor," Hassoud remarked as they approached the next station.

"She is even more beautiful up here, Major," Sakkar responded, bringing a finger to his temple. Sakkar then told him that Risha had finished first in her physics class at the Massachusetts Institute of Technology, a very highly regarded American university. Hassoud was impressed and proud. Sakkar kept on talking as they continued down the wide corridor. He learned that the crew leaders wore the white fireproof gear. The ones in yellow were also engineers but without the necessary experience to work on their own yet. They were in training.

Sakkar handed a tally sheet to the crew leader of number two, who without taking off his hood simply nodded and went back to work. They continued down the long hall. Sakkar explained to Hassoud that the workers in red were the technicians, doing the work the engineers assigned to them. Sakkar told Hassoud his only concern at first had been that since most of the technicians were from rural areas, he'd feared that word would leak out about the project. That was the driving force behind the rule prohibiting anyone from leaving the facility, even during the height of the Gulf War. Most of the men and women down at that level had not seen their relatives in years. A huge sacrifice, reflected Hassoud, realizing that at least his soldiers did get to visit their families once a month. But down there was a different world, he admitted, finally understanding the reason why not a single one of his soldiers was allowed to guard any of the underground levels. It was obvious to Hassoud that they realistically had no need for security forces. All the security they needed had already been provided through dozens of feet of reinforced concrete isolating the laboratories from the imperfect world outside. At the touch of a button, Sakkar or Hassoud could temporarily cut off the outside world, and only Sakkar could remove the steel plate when the danger was gone.

Hassoud nodded. The old doctor was right. This place had indeed been built to withstand a direct hit from a nuclear warhead.

AMAN BAKISH AIR BASE NEAR AN NAJAF, SOUTHERN IRAQ.
Day Three. 1500 Local Time.

General Abunnasr Manesh threw the microphone down on the table and cursed himself for being so slow. The entire village had been layered with blister agents, followed with conventional shells, but the tank commander reported no casualties. The place was deserted, as if the villagers had known the tanks were coming. He'd known the villagers would try to flee to nearby towns but didn't think they would do it so fast. There was no sign of them anywhere, not even on the surrounding roads. Additional tanks had blocked all roads to adjacent towns for the last few hours, but so far nothing had been reported.

"Should I request them to go to the other villages and question the people, sir?" asked Fassan.

"Ah . . . no. Tell them to come home."

"Yes, sir."

Manesh leaned back in the swivel chair, quietly staring at the dark radar screen. He frowned, disappointed that the Kurds had gotten away. If this had occurred a few months earlier, he would have ordered the tanks to blast surrounding villages until someone talked . . . or everyone was dead. But he couldn't afford that right now. His primary task was to provide defense to the processing complex several miles to the south, and those tanks were part of that defense. Manesh didn't want to spread his forces too thin. Doing that would be a formula for disaster.

"I will be in my quarters, Fassan. Call me if anything comes up."

"Yes, General."

▪ 11 ▪

BLACK JETS

The dark, angular shape silently dashed through a moonless sky at 400 knots, carefully maintaining an altitude of 25,000 feet above the desert sand. The aircraft, whose all-aluminum body was covered with platelike radar absorbent material, accelerated to a maximum speed of 600 knots with a barely audible increase in noise from the dual General Electric augmented low-bypass-ratio turbofans.

From behind the gold-laminated canopy, optimized to lower radar returns from the cockpit, Lieutenant Colonel Longhorn Kramer stared at the large central CRT display, where most of the 52,000-pound fighter's vital statistics were constantly being displayed, something that still bothered Kramer, who only felt comfortable after glancing at the analog backup instrumentation and quickly comparing their readings with those from the CRT display. Although the readings had always matched for over two thousand hours of flying time, Kramer's peace of mind came only after another successful check.

As he rapidly approached the salt marshes of south-western Iraq, Kramer increased forward pressure on the control stick to put the radar-invisible Black Jet in a gradual descent. The first phase of the destruction of Allahbad was not a bombing run but a quiet reconnais-sance pass to check for hidden antiaircraft gear, which would give the CIA story more credibility.

He checked the analog gauges again.

AMAN BAKISH AIR BASE NEAR AN NAJAF, SOUTHERN IRAQ.
Day Three. 2320 Local Time.

Shivering, General Abunnasr Manesh walked into the communications bunker, letting the warmer air caress his face and neck. For some reason, temperatures had dropped to the low forties tonight. He wasn't usually bothered by it, but tonight he just couldn't fall asleep in the cold. He could take the heat far better than cold weather.

"Cold night, General?" asked Fassan Tabriz from behind a large circular radar screen.

"The sand," Manesh replied, "releases its heat too fast." He walked to the back of the room, where two empty cots stood side by side. He lay on one of them and propped a pillow under his head.

"Care for some tea or dates, General? There's also some fresh cream, and the rest of last night's roasted lamb."

Manesh lifted his head and eyed the food on the table in the center of the room. "No, thanks. I take it that all is clear, Fassan?"

"Yes, sir. No news from this end."

"Has Baghdad called?"

"No, sir. Everything is also quiet over there."

"Good. I hope it stays that way. I'm not in the mood for trouble tonight, but do wake me if something comes up."

"Of course, sir."

Manesh closed his eyes and peacefully fell asleep.

SOUTHERN IRAQ.
Day Three. 2340 Local Time.

The night was star-filled, the air cold and dry. Crawling on his elbows, Lieutenant Kevin Dalton dragged his bruised and sunburned body to the top of a hill overlooking Allahbad Processing Complex and pressed the rubber caps of Ishmael's night-vision binoculars against his eyes. From Khalela, Kevin had learned that most of the Kurds' equipment came from raiding Iraqi supply centers and trucks. The pair of Russian-made binoculars in his hands, Kevin decided, were top-notch.

Slowly, a chain-link fence came into focus as he rotated the adjusting wheel in between the lenses. He moved the binoculars to the left and followed the fence all the way to the far end of the complex. He stopped and scanned the fence in the other direction until reaching a large sliding gate, the only entrance into the compound that he could see. So far he had counted four batteries of SAMs. *Not bad for a facility this size.*

"Pretty dark out there, Kevin."

He lowered the binoculars and turned to Khalela, who had positioned herself next to him and was already surveying the complex with her own set of binoculars.

"Yes, but there seems to be a lot of activity." He continued to pan the area. "Damn! Is that an electric fence?" Kevin noticed the thick cables connected to the top of the fence at several spots along its length.

"Yes, it is. It is going to be difficult getting in there . . . but not impossible."

"What? You mean to tell me that the plan is to actually try to get *inside?* I thought you said your mission was to observe and report."

Khalela smiled. "In all seriousness, what can you possibly observe and report from here that you cannot simply read off a satellite photograph?"

Kevin frowned. "Guess you got a point . . . but how in the hell are we going to get past the guards and the fence?"

She smiled. "Trust me." She headed back down.

"Where are you going?"

"To talk to Ishmael. I will be right back."

Kevin brought the binoculars back up to his eyes and focused on the trucks going in and out of the complex. For a few minutes, he followed the vehicles as they drove into the complex and strained to see their contents, but each truck drove into a large warehouselike building roughly four hundred feet from the gate—

What? Kevin jumped when he felt someone tapping him on the leg.

Startled, he turned around and looked up at a smiling Abdul, who was obviously amused at having scared Kevin.

"Not very funny, Abdul."

The large Kurd motioned him to come back down. Kevin crawled away from the edge and followed his Iranian friend.

As they reached the foot of the small hill, Abdul continued walking toward Ishmael and the others stalking the road to the complex. He pointed toward a small sand dune and briefly looked at Kevin. "Khalela."

Kevin looked in that direction and saw Khalela's head behind the sand dune. He approached her and was surprised to see her dressed as an Iraqi lieutenant. She was fastening her belt buckle.

"Where did you—"

"From the soldiers who attacked the village. How do I look?"

Kevin smiled. Although the uniform was a couple of sizes too large, Kevin decided that she looked great in just about anything she wore.

"Hmm? What do you think? Would I pass for an Iraqi officer?"

"A gorgeous one, yes."

She looked at him and smiled. "Thank you."

"You're welcome. Now do you mind telling me what it is that you're doing dressed like that? I didn't know the Iraqis had any female officers."

She smiled once more. "They do not. I am not planning to be seen once I get inside the perimeter. This is just in case someone spots me from far away. That is why the uniform is so loose. Trust me, I know what I am doing."

"I've heard that—"

"Pilot Dalton. Khalela. It is time!"

They turned around and saw Ishmael waving them over.

"Time for what?" Kevin asked.

"Time to go in."

"When? Now? How are you—"

"Trust me."

"Look, I'm getting tired of—"

"Please. It is better this way. This is what I do."

"In that case, I'm going in with you."

"You are crazy. That is not a good idea."

"Why? I can be of help in case—"

"Believe me. You will get us all killed. Look at yourself; look at your skin. You wouldn't last a minute in there before someone spots you. And besides, you don't speak the language. It's wiser for you to stay behind."

Kevin frowned, accepting that Khalela was right. It wouldn't take much for someone inside to figure out he didn't belong.

"But thank you for caring," she finally said before turning around and walking toward Ishmael and the other Kurds.

Kevin remained behind, confused by his feelings for her.

She turned around. "Coming?"

He nodded and caught up to her.

"Do not worry. It is going to be all right."

He took her hand and held it tight. She squeezed his in response.

They let go of each other's hands as they approached the Kurdish group. Kevin noted that Ishmael also wore an Iraqi officer's uniform.

"See you in a few hours, Kevin." She turned around and walked with Ishmael toward the road, followed by three other rebels, who were still dressed in their own clothes.

Kevin kneeled behind a small sand dune and watched them disappear around a large rock by the road. He felt a hand on his shoulder and turned around. It was Abdul again.

Kevin raised both eyebrows and frowned. The large Kurd simply nodded.

The young Iraqi lieutenant sat impatiently on the passenger seat of the supply truck headed for the complex. Bad roads and a flat tire had delayed him an hour, something he knew the officer in charge would report to his superior officer back at the port. The lieutenant was certain that he would be reprimanded when he got back. There would be no excuse in the eyes of his captain, the lieutenant knew. He should have anticipated the poor road conditions and had the tires checked before leaving the port of Al Faw by the gulf. But at the time he had decided against it for fear of wasting precious time in getting his critical cargo to its destination.

He glanced over at the old man at the wheel and decided that part of the blame rested on the incompetent driver, who did not swerve the truck in time to avoid a pothole. He frowned, perhaps he should tell his captain this, but quickly decided against it since it had also been the lieutenant's responsibility to select the driver.

He sighed, remembering how quickly he had agreed to let the old man drive the truck over younger and probably more qualified drivers from the approved pool. He had felt bad about the old man, smothered by a crowd of young hungry drivers who had pushed him aside while each begged the lieutenant to select him. The lieutenant shoved the young men to the side and grabbed the old man who, startled, immediately thanked him and Allah out loud, happy that he would now be able to buy a few hens or maybe even a goat to feed his family—*What?*

His thoughts were interrupted when he spotted what appeared to be an Iraqi officer running away from something.

"Stop!" he commanded.

The old man stepped on the brakes and nearly lost control of the truck.

"For the love of Allah, old man! Where did you learn how to drive? I said stop, not get us killed!"

The old man lowered his gaze and mumbled a few incoherent words. The lieutenant shook his head and got out. "Wait here."

He unholstered a 9mm Makarov automatic pistol and ran toward the approaching officer.

"Hold on! What is going on?"

"Kurds! They're after me! Three of them. They have automatic weapons! Call your men out of the truck, I need help!"

He stopped and stared at the well-tanned and distinguished-looking officer. There was an air of command and confidence behind the officer's brown eyes. Before the lieutenant had a chance to react, he felt a cold muzzle pressed against the back of his neck.

"One word and you're dead," said a female voice from behind. "Hand over your weapon and start moving toward the truck."

The lieutenant gave the tanned officer the Makarov, turned around, and stared into the most intriguing pair of light green eyes he'd ever seen. The woman held an AK-47. There were several rebels surrounding the truck. The old man's limp body was being dragged to the side.

"Butchers! All of you! He was just—" His words were cut short by a blade pressed against his throat.

"This is your last warning. One more word and you're dead," said the tanned soldier.

Khalela walked behind Ishmael, who held a knife to the officer's neck.

The moment they approached the truck, Ishmael pulled the lieutenant to the side and pushed him toward the rebels, one of whom drove the butt of his Kalashnikov against his face. The officer went limp.

Khalela went around the back and lifted the canvas flap hanging over the rear of the truck. She jumped in and inspected the cargo—four large steel spheres, each about six feet in diameter, were secured to the floor of the truck by chains. She recognized the words *Red-Fuming Nitric Acid* marked on the side of the two spheres to her right. The two on the left were marked *Hydrazine.*

Rocket fuel.

Her fears had been confirmed. She walked outside and explained her plan to Ishmael before crawling under the truck and tucking her slim body between the main transaxle and the truck's underside.

Ishmael walked around to the driver's side, got in, started the truck, and accelerated toward the complex.

After completing all system checks on the number one missile, under direct orders from Dr. Sakkar, Risha put on the heavy hood and walked toward her crew. The doctor, who stood in the middle of the corridor, had just finished congratulating her for being a few hours ahead of an already aggressive schedule. He now wanted her to deploy the missile so that everyone else in the room would see how fast she had completed her task. His reasoning, Risha knew, was that perhaps if they saw her missile being deployed, they would work even harder.

Her crew, on hearing her directions, ran to their preassigned places around the missile. Risha walked back and stood next to Dr. Sakkar. She removed her hood and rested it on her hip. From where she stood, she continued giving directions to her staff.

Suddenly, the colossal doors behind the missile slid open and a battery-powered cart began to slowly move over the steel tracks, deploying the rocket to its underground launchpad a mile away. The assembly area was connected to a complex array of tunnels to transport, set up, and service the rockets. Similar to the American mobile underground tactical missiles, Risha reflected. The only difference being that these missile silos had been built from below ground up to ten feet under the surface. Seconds before ignition, a shaped charge would blast upward through the last few feet of soil to open the way for the rocket.

Risha noticed that nearly all the personnel on her side of the assembly floor had stopped working and were staring at the missile, obviously not believing their eyes.

She smiled; the missile had not even disappeared behind the doors when everyone was back at work, now moving with a different intensity as if they were committed to have their own missile deployed next. It was all a matter of competition and pride, she admitted. The word would definitely get around to the other side of the assembly floor about how she had completed her assignment first. Risha smiled more broadly. She would not be surprised if some of the crews completed their assignments before dawn.

Ishmael Barzani followed the three Iraqi guards to the back of the truck, where one of them lifted the canvas flap and trained a flashlight on the spheres.

"What are the contents?" one of them asked.

"I was simply ordered to escort the shipment and deliver it along with these sealed papers," responded Ishmael.

The guard eyed the brown envelope in his hands. "What kept you? You do realize that you're over an hour late."

"I was attacked by Kurdish rebels. Under the circumstances, I'm lucky to have made it at all," he responded in an arrogant tone, realizing that he had a higher rank than any of the guards. "Any more questions, Sergeant? You do realize that now *you* are the one delaying the shipment, don't you?"

The soldier backed down. One of the soldiers waved his right hand at a guard by a booth next to the gate.

From the bottom of the truck, Khalela had held her breath during the entire conversation as her greasy arms grew numb. She had no choice but to hide. Even with a loose uniform, hair tucked under a cap, and now grease on her face, she might still be recognized as a woman from close up. Although her being there did add an element of risk to the mission, again she had no other option. As intelligent and well-educated—by Kurdish standards—as Ishmael was, in Khalela's eyes, he was still a desert rebel without the basic technical background to know what to look for. Khalela decided that she had to get firsthand information of the activities inside Allahbad. Besides, she felt certain that Ishmael would be under constant watch. She tensed as she heard Ishmael getting back in the truck. The gate slid open. The Kurd steered the truck along the dark and narrow stretch of road that connected the complex's entrance to the warehouse. Just as they had planned, Ishmael slowed down to a near-halt for a few seconds before continuing toward the large sliding door of the warehouse.

Khalela rolled away from the road, quickly got to her feet, and walked toward the side of the building, where she couldn't see any guards. She reached the side of the warehouse uneventfully and approached a parking area, where two dozen large trucks were parked side by side in two long rows over the gravel. Quietly, she walked in between the first two trucks of the row facing the back fence. She then carefully checked the clearing between the back of the trucks and the fence and jumped into the first truck. There were a number of boxes with labels in Russian. She pulled out a knife and began opening them.

Ishmael drove the truck into the brightly lighted warehouse and slowly followed another guard, who directed him to a spot next to several crates. The Kurd jumped out and was immediately approached by two guards and several men in green jumpsuits. He clenched his teeth in fear that they might realize he was an impostor. The resulting bolt of pain from his teeth made him blink just as one of the approaching officers began to open his mouth.

"It's about time, Lieutenant!" snapped one of the guards. Ishmael recognized the captain's bars on his broad shoulders.

"Sorry, Captain. I—" he started in an apologetic tone.

"Save it for your commanding officer, Lieutenant!" he fumed. "He will be informed of your incompetence. This equipment should have been here over an hour ago! Every second counts!"

Ishmael didn't respond. He grimaced and lowered his

gaze, pretending to be very apologetic—a role he played without much difficulty. The throbbing in his mouth nearly numbed his senses.

The captain continued. "There is a guest room next to the warehouse, where you will find refreshments and a toilet and sink. My guard here will escort you. I'll expect you back in no longer than one hour. In the event of an emergency, you will come back here immediately and report to me. Those are the rules. Do you understand them, Lieutenant?"

"Yes, sir."

"Very well. After that you must leave the complex at once and swear on Allah's spirit that you will not discuss what you saw here tonight with anyone else."

Ishmael watched him leave. The men in jumpsuits moved the canvas flap to the side and started unloading the tanks, wheeling them to a spot next to what appeared to be a steel sliding door. The escort tapped him on the shoulder and pointed toward the warehouse's exit. Ishmael began to walk with the guard right behind them. As they left the warehouse, a metallic noise made him turn around.

"Just keep walking, Lieutenant!" snapped the guard, but the Kurd had already seen what he now knew they didn't want visitors to see. The large metallic sliding doors revealed a compartment he recognized as an elevator. He could see the elevator operator adjusting the level of the elevator's floor with that of the warehouse.

It is true, Ishmael thought, as they left the warehouse's entrance behind. The Iraqis had gone underground with their nuclear research projects. Khalela had been right. Given the level of activity in the warehouse—not counting the tight security—he could only guess at the size of their underground facilities. It was by no means a small operation.

Kevin Dalton continued scanning the large clearing in front of the warehouse. He constantly turned the adjusting wheel between the lenses as he moved the night-vision binoculars back and forth between the chain-link fence and the warehouse, struggling to bring the greenish images into focus. The binoculars' lenses, much thicker than regular field binoculars, amplified the dim light that bounced off moving objects, producing images with lighter shades of green against a stationary, darker background. *There he is,* thought Kevin as he finally managed to bring the green face of Ishmael into focus. A few minutes earlier, he had followed Khalela from the side of the narrow road all the way to the parking lot next to the warehouse, where the Mossad operative had disappeared behind the trucks.

Kevin passed the binoculars to his larger friend and pointed at the warehouse. Abdul brought the binoculars to his eyes, nodded, then gave them back to Kevin, who continued to watch Ishmael move from the front of the warehouse to a smaller building to their right.

Risha left the supply room and headed for the warehouse. She walked slowly, peacefully admiring the blanket of stars overhead, a sight she had not seen in weeks. She was grateful to Sakkar for allowing her the simple pleasure of coming up to the surface. A reward for a job well done, she recalled Sakkar telling her after he had asked her to go to the surface and collect the shipping bills for the equipment received from Baghdad. He also had asked her to stop at the warehouse on her way back and check if the rocket fuel shipment had arrived yet. It had been due in an hour ago. She closed her eyes and breathed deeply, drawing in the night's cold air several times, trying to clear her lungs from the stagnant air down at level minus five. Although she knew that the best of air-conditioners and air purifiers were used in ventilating the underground levels, in her mind Risha still felt she was not breathing pure, natural air.

She opened her eyes and continued walking toward the warehouse's entrance. Something caught her eye. She had seen a soldier jumping out of the back of one of two dozen trucks parked on the gravel lot and quickly jumping into the back of an adjacent one. Risha saw a knife clutched in the soldier's hand.

Puzzled, she continued to walk along the side of the warehouse for a few more seconds. She noticed two uniformed men approaching. She recognized one of them.

Ishmael was standing with an Iraqi guard when a woman wearing a white jumpsuit approached them.

"Hello, Risha," said the guard.

Risha smiled.

"I have not seen you in months. How are things?"

"Everything is fine, thanks. I just came to pick up a few things for the doctor and inspect a new shipment due to arrive at any minute. I couldn't help noticing a soldier jumping in and out of supply trucks back there. Is everything all right?"

Ishmael's heart began pounding as he saw the guard's face harden.

"No one is allowed inside those trucks!" shouted the guard. "Risha, you get back to the warehouse. Lieutenant, you come with me."

Kevin Dalton saw Ishmael and the guard stop to talk to someone in a white jumpsuit. After a few seconds, the one in the jumpsuit continued toward the entrance to the warehouse, while Ishmael and the guard walked toward the—*Oh, shit. They're headed for the parking lot! Khalela, get out of there!*

Then he heard a quiet sound overhead. Kevin was not sure exactly what it was at first, but it definitely came from above. He quickly lay on his back and trained the binoculars at the sky. *That sound,* he thought. *I've heard it before somewhere.*

The sky was clear, the night moonless. Kevin continued to search but saw nothing. The sound grew slightly louder. *Jet engines,* he decided as his trained ears discerned the engine noise. There was something peculiar about the sound, almost as if it were passing through some kind of muffler or other device designed to reduce engine noise. If his ears were not playing tricks on him, his trained senses told him that the aircraft should be a few thousand feet away; it should definitely be visible with his binoculars, yet Kevin saw nothing.

Kevin rolled onto his belly and trained the binoculars back on the complex: Ishmael and the guard had already disappeared behind the trucks. *Damn!*

He cursed at himself for allowing that noise—whatever it was—to distract him. *Khalela, where in the world are you?* he thought as he frantically scanned the complex in vain.

Khalela Yishaid smiled widely when she pulled out a radiation-resistant suit from one of the boxes. In adjacent boxes she had already found hoods, gloves, and booties. *It's true,* she thought. *The Iraqis are in the nuclear business.* That, combined with the information the Kurd Ishmael had provided from the map he'd found a few days before, told Khalela everything she needed to know.

"Stay where you are!" a voice came from the rear of the truck.

Khalela froze.

"Now, slowly turn around."

She did, and to her surprise, she stared at a short, bearded guard holding an AK-47. Ishmael stood next to him, also holding a Kalashnikov in her direction. Khalela went through her options. She could easily signal the Kurd to kill the guard, but would that be the best way to play this out? What other options did she have? *Dammit!*

"Now, very slowly, set your weapon on the floor."

Khalela complied and shifted her gaze back and forth between Ishmael and the guard. Swiftly, the Kurd smashed the AK-47's butt against the side of the guard's head. The Iraqi soldier dropped.

"Lift him in here, quick," Khalela said as she approached Ishmael and helped him pull the guard's limp body inside the truck. The Kurd pulled out a knife and sliced the unconscious man's throat. Khalela looked away, wondering who was more barbaric.

"You were right, Khalela," Ishmael commented with a

wide grin. "There's an underground complex here. I saw a large service elevator in the warehouse."

Khalela stared at the Kurd and his repulsive teeth. With the warehouse being one story, the elevator could only go one way: down.

"What do we do next?" Ishmael asked.

As her mind searched for the right answer, her ears detected a faint jet engine noise in the distance.

Checking the time, Colonel Longhorn Kramer eased back his throttles to sixty percent as he approached Allahbad at five thousand feet. The infrared lenses of a KH-11 satellite were photographing the entire region at that precise moment.

He quickly checked his analog instrumentation again before putting his plane in a shallow climb and pressing the chaff-dispensing button on his control stick for what he estimated was a half second. A small door underneath the flat underside of the Black Jet slid back and released dozens of inch-long slender strips of a plastic fiber material coated with a thin metallic film. The strips had a low enough density to allow them to float in midair as Kramer's F-117A continued its southern trajectory.

Kramer pumped chaff nine more times before turning his Black Jet toward the Saudi border.

"In the name of Allah! General, General! Hurry!"

Manesh jumped up from the cot and raced to where Fassan sat, then froze when he saw the multiple targets on the radar screen.

"How many?"

"Ah . . . looks like . . . ten?"

"Yes, Fassan! Ten targets! Were you asleep?"

"No, General. They just appeared on my screen. One minute everything was quiet, then within a few seconds, the entire radar screen lit with targets!"

"Range and speed?"

"Fifty miles, speed . . . three hundred knots . . . and rapidly slowing down, sir."

"What?"

"They're down to . . . two hundred knots . . . one hundred fifty . . . sir, it doesn't make sense."

"Let's not take any chances. Warn Allahbad. Tell them there is an air strike on the way!"

Manesh raced out of the communications bunker.

Both Kevin and Abdul jumped back when the entire complex came alive. Alarms blared and dozens of doors swung open on the side of the warehouse, exposing several Russian-made self-propelled Shilka antiaircraft gun systems. He counted six of the deadly accurate Shilkas on this side of the complex alone. He could only surmise that an equal number guarded the other side. Several doors down along the same side of the complex, Kevin saw SA-6 surface-to-air missiles, which were also deployed on motorized vehicles, three missiles per self-propelled unit. Guards ran out of several buildings and approached the Shilkas and SAM antiaircraft systems. Other soldiers manned the SAM systems by the fence.

Kevin was surprised at the sense of purpose with which every soldier moved. Although there was a lot of activity, there weren't any signs of havoc, only a well-rehearsed emergency drill. In less than a minute, all personnel appeared to have reached their posts. Then just as suddenly as it had started, all the alarms went silent and the entire complex went dark.

Kevin blinked several times, trying to adjust his vision. Even with the binoculars, he still had a hard time seeing much.

Ishmael Barzani made it back to the warehouse right before the doors were closed. Inside, everyone was ordered to the large service elevator on the right side of the room. He spotted the woman in the white jumpsuit running toward the elevators. He caught up with her.

"Where . . . are we going?" Ishmael asked as they raced across the concrete floor.

"Down . . . where it is safe," Risha responded. "Don't worry, it will be all right . . . as long as we can . . . make it before . . . they block the elevator shaft."

"What are you talking about?" the Kurd asked, slowing down.

Before Risha could respond, the elevator door slid closed, disregarding the screams of dozens of workers who banged their hands against the doors.

"What is the matter now?"

"It's too late!" responded Risha.

"Too late? Too late for what?"

"The elevator shaft! It's been blocked. We're stuck up here."

"What do you mean stuck up here? What's down there?"

"The complex, the labs. It's all isolated from the outside world except for the elevator, which is automatically shut off and the shaft blocked after the alarms go off."

"So what happens next?" the Kurd asked, amazed that she would volunteer so much information to a stranger. But then again, reasoned Ishmael, he did wear the uniform of an Iraqi officer. In her eyes, he was a friend.

"We wait. We pray to Allah and wait," Risha responded.

"Is there a bomb shelter around to—"

"No. The only personnel that's usually up here are soldiers, but tonight's shipment was too big so we had to get people from level minus one to help."

This was getting better every second, Ishmael thought sarcastically. "So we are just going to sit here and wait. This seems like the ideal target for an air strike."

"We don't have a choice. The warehouse's doors are temporarily sealed once the locking mechanism engages." Risha shifted her gaze to the workers still banging their fists against the elevator doors. "See, they know we're trapped."

Ishmael sighed and sat down, resting his back against the tire of a truck. "I guess now we wait."

General Manesh applied throttle and taxied his MiG-29 out of the bunker. One minute later he was airborne.

"Talk to me, Fassan!" he shouted into the radio when he had left the runway, prompting the ground control intercept radar controller to give him a vector to the intruders.

"Ah . . . sir?"

"Yes, what is it?"

"They are gone, sir."

"They are what?"

"Gone, sir. They stopped moving altogether and slowly faded away one by one. My radar is clean, sir."

"So is mine, Fassan. What in the hell do you think happened? Decoys?"

"My only guess is chaff or some form of decoy drone, sir."

"Could be, but from where?"

"That is what has me baffled, sir. I counted ten targets and all ten slowed down to a halt and vanished just like chaff would, but there was no trace of any craft before or after that. Perhaps it was one of those American stealth fighters."

"Well, I am not taking any chances. Radio south and maintain red alert until further notice," Manesh said, referring to Allahbad. The general also felt that the Allies had just flown one or more of their stealth jets over the region. It was the only explanation that made any sense to him.

"Yes, sir!"

Kevin waited for something to happen, but after several minutes the lights in the compound came back on. Soldiers drove the antiaircraft equipment back into the building and the doors closed.

He lowered the binoculars and frowned. There was still no sign of Khalela.

"I think everything is going to be fine, Lieutenant," said the captain as he approached them. The large Iraqi glanced at Risha and motioned her to go join the other technicians gathered by the elevator doors. She complied.

"Don't tell me this was all just a drill," Ishmael said, getting up.

"No, Lieutenant. This was the real thing, but the

threat is gone for now. I don't have any more details than that."

"All right. When will I be allowed to leave?"

"As soon as the people downstairs disengage the locking mechanism. In the meantime, the technicians will continue to unload your cargo. Where is the guard that escorted you to the guest quarters?"

Ishmael forced himself to remain calm. "When the alarms began to blare, he ordered me back here. He ran the other way. I guess he's outside somewhere."

The captain thought about it for a moment before nodding and walking away.

Fifteen minutes later, Ishmael put the truck in gear and made a U-turn under the direction of a guard. The truck momentarily accelerated down the narrow road before Ishmael briefly flashed the lights off and on twice. He slowed down for a second and a figure emerged from the side of the road, jumped to the passenger side, and climbed inside. There was a three-foot-deep space in between the back of the seat and the rear wall of the truck. Khalela quickly hid there as Ishmael drove toward the gate a few hundred feet away.

"You were right, Khalela," Ishmael said in a low voice, quickly telling her what Risha had told him about the elevator shaft plate and the underground labs.

A minute later, he reached the gate. He watched one guard wave at another inside the booth. The gate slowly began to open.

It suddenly stopped.

Ishmael frowned and glanced at the guard inside the booth. He was talking on the telephone. He hung up and Ishmael immediately noticed the gate closing.

"What is the matter, *Isha?*"

He told her as he clutched the Kalashnikov. From the back, he felt Khalela placing a hand on the weapon.

"Wait. It might be nothing of importance."

"Let's just crash through the gate," he said. "My people will cover us once we're—"

"Good evening, Lieutenant."

Ishmael snapped his head to the right and stared at a very hairy officer. He was surrounded by a half dozen armed soldiers, including the captain he'd met at the warehouse.

"I'm Major Mohammed Hassoud, head of security of this complex."

"Good evening, Major. How can I be of service to you tonight?"

"Well, Lieutenant, why don't you step outside for a minute? There is something I must show you."

Ishmael felt a knot in his stomach as he pulled down on the handle and pushed the door open. His gums began to throb.

"Yes, Major?"

"See, Lieutenant, I have a minor problem and need your help to clear it up. I'm sure it's just miscommunication between the coast and us."

Silently praying to Allah, Ishmael did his best to remain calm and in control. He could not allow them to see an ounce of fear.

"What is this problem, Major?"

"Well, you were due to arrive here at a certain hour. When you didn't, I had one of my men call the coast and find out the time that you had left to see if I should send a search party after you. The response I got before the alarms went off was that Lieutenant Zahed Maustakk left with an older driver, an old man, at noon today. Now, Lieutenant, first of all, the name on your uniform says Yaiseer, and second you are alone. Now would you mind telling me what is going on and where Lieutenant Maustakk and the old man are?"

Ishmael's mind was racing. "There must be some misunderstanding, Major. You must have mistaken my truck with someone else's."

"No, I don't think I have, Lieutenant whoever-you-are. Because, you see, after everything settled down, I did a little checking with the bases around the area and asked them to track down a Lieutenant Yaiseer. And would you believe what they told me?"

Ishmael felt nauseated when he detected a touch of

sarcasm in the major's tone. "What, Major? What did they tell you?" he said, barely managing to control his voice.

"Well, they told me that Lieutenant Yaiseer was one of the officers that perished during a Kurd attack on a village south of here earlier today. Yaiseer, along with the other soldiers, were found naked in the center of the deserted village. So, you're not Zahed and you're not Yaiseer. Who in the hell are you? And how did you get that uniform?"

Ishmael lowered his gaze.

Kevin put down the binoculars in utter disbelief. First he had seen Ishmael talking to a group of soldiers by the gate. Then two soldiers jumped in the truck, and seconds later Khalela climbed down with her hands above her head. The cold reality of seeing Khalela and Ishmael captured left him speechless.

He turned to Abdul. The large Kurd frowned and slowly shook his head.

Kevin ran the tip of his right thumb across his neck and looked at Abdul for a response.

Abdul closed his eyes and nodded.

"Oh, God. . . ."

THE WHITE HOUSE.
Day Three. 1700 Local Time.

CIA Director Craig Kettler's face turned in the direction of President Bill Clinton as he explained the satellite images collected by the infrared cameras of a KH-11, which were spread over the president's desk.

"What's most interesting of all, Mr. President, is the amount of hardware defending the place, far surpassing Bourdeaux's initial estimates. I mean, this place is better guarded than anything else inside Iraq, including Baghdad."

The president silently inspected the images with half-closed eyes. To his far right, his defense secretary looked at the photos from a distance. He had already scrutinized them at the NPIC half an hour earlier and had wasted no time in giving the president his recommendation: blast the facility off the map. The CIA director had also recommended an immediate air strike.

Clinton wet his lips, laying an index finger across his chin while staring into the distance. All the information was there. All the players were in agreement as to what should be done, even his secretary of state, who was still meeting with Tariq Aziz. The Geneva talks so far had proven to be just as useless as the ones attended by former Secretary of State James Baker prior to Desert Storm.

The president reached for the side of his desk, where a white sheet of paper with the presidential seal across the top contained an executive order to carry out the attack on Allahbad. In unison, Defense and Intelligence both pulled out pens and handed them to the president, who gave them a faint smile before pulling his own pen out of his pocket and signing the order.

ALLAHBAD PROCESSING COMPLEX, SOUTH OF AN NAJAF, IRAQ.
Day Four. 0100 Local Time.

Ishmael Barzani walked into the interrogating room and immediately looked for Khalela, but all he saw was the man that called himself Major Hassoud and five guards. Ishmael noticed the major's scarred nose and cheeks surrounded by an unruly mess of hair.

"Welcome, my friend," Hassoud said in an icy tone.

Ishmael was brought up to him. His hands were tied behind his back.

"Tonight you will tell us everything we want to know."

Ishmael spat on his face.

Hassoud slowly wiped the saliva off his beard with a sleeve. "That was not a very smart thing to do, my friend . . . or what should I call you?"

Ishmael stared him in the eye with fierce conviction, but noted that Hassoud didn't flinch at his gaze. He appeared bored, as if he was doing this because he didn't have anything better to do.

"Your attitude amuses me, my friend. Guards, please?

* * *

Let us show our Kurdish friend exactly how is it that we are going to persuade him to tell us everything we want to know."

Ishmael watched in silence as a guard brought in a hen and walked with it over to a large barrel in the center of the room.

"Bring him closer. I do not want him to miss any part of the show."

A guard jammed the barrel of his pistol against Ishmael's back and pushed him forward. He noticed the crystal-clear liquid inside the barrel and thought they were going to electrocute the hen, but he could not see any wires or generator.

The hen was hung from its legs and slowly lowered over the barrel by a pulley system on the ceiling, which Ishmael estimated to be over twenty feet high.

He blinked in surprise when the relatively quiet hen went berserk and viciously flapped its wings the moment its head came in contact with the liquid, which started bubbling. It lasted maybe fifteen seconds. The liquid became blood-red.

When Hassoud lifted the hen back up, there was nothing left of its head except part of the bone structure. The rest had been dissolved away by the liquid.

"Just one of the many products we manufacture at Allahbad in addition to our line of dairy products, my friend. Believe me when I tell you that you *will* talk. One way or another, you will tell me who you are and what you are doing here. Frankly, I don't care how much pain you're willing to take before you talk. I hope a lot. It always gives me great pleasure to inflict pain on Kurdish pigs."

Hassoud brushed the hair from his forehead and Ishmael suddenly realized the reason for the major's untamed beard. Hassoud's face had been disfigured.

"Some of your Kurdish friends did this to me long ago," Hassoud said after Ishmael had gotten a good look at his forehead. "Some of you bastards slowly carved my face and the rest of my body before I was rescued by my government. I thought you might want to know that before I start working on you. Only in this case don't expect your people to come rescue you."

Ishmael closed his eyes and silently prayed to Allah to give him the strength to endure the punishment he was about to receive.

BAGHDAD.
Day Four. 0120 Local Time.

For Saddam Hussein the day had been a mixture of good and bad news. Although he had lost some helicopters, he considered that insignificant when compared to the American fighters and helicopters his own people had destroyed. Although he had been stern to General Manesh, deep inside Saddam knew the recently promoted general was carrying out his orders without question. Manesh's blazingly fast reaction when an American jet flew over Allahbad a couple of hours before had been particularly excellent.

Allahbad.
Half-naked, sitting on the edge of a king-sized bed in one of his bunkers, the Iraqi leader lit up a cigar and took a long draw, slowly exhaling through his nostrils. A Syrian woman, one of Saddam's personal whores, stirred naked, half-asleep, under the covers. The Iraqi leader patted her buttocks, and she mumbled something before turning over and going back to sleep.

Saddam smiled, but not because of the woman. He cared for her as much as he would for a stray dog. At any moment he could reach for the Makarov in the holster by his feet, blow her brains out, and then go eat a big breakfast. But he wouldn't. The tall Syrian woman could satisfy him like no one else.

The reason for his smile was that as of an hour ago, just as he'd begun to undress the whore, Iraq had become the world's newest nuclear power. At this very moment, he had the power to blow Tel Aviv off the face of the earth, but he wouldn't dare do it just yet. Not while he had only one missile ready. He would wait for the right time. In another twenty-four hours, he should be able to hit a few targets at will. In a matter of days, his country would have a total of thirty nuclear warheads, each mounted on its own booster, which could carry it up to a thousand miles away.

Then, Mr. Bill Clinton, the Middle East will be mine, and soon after that, you will experience the horror of an atomic explosion in your beloved America.

▪ 12 ▪

DIFFERENCES OF OPINION

With the early morning sun behind him, CIA officer Robert Bourdeaux walked across the warm tarmac, past the camouflage canopy shielding the F-117A fighter that had arrived the night before, and approached the Gulfstream IV taxiing to a halt on the ramp next to the mess tent. Bourdeaux watched the ground crew bring a ladder up to the VIP transport as the door was pushed open from the inside.

To Bourdeaux's surprise, the first three people who walked down the steps held a video camera and some other gear. They reached the bottom of the steps. Two moved to the side and fumbled with a few switches for a couple of seconds. The third remained by the steps. Then the one holding the camera counted from five to one with the fingers of his right hand.

Bourdeaux approached them.

The one by the steps was the reporter. Bourdeaux heard him state that they had just arrived at an American air base, where a plan was being put in place to organize an air strike against a highly strategic complex in southern Iraq.

Bourdeaux watched in total disbelief as General Kenneth Draper, wearing a perfectly starched set of desert-camouflage fatigues and a cap, slowly walked down the stairs and waved at the camera. The reporter asked him a few questions and Draper responded confidently to each one. It was obvious to Bourdeaux that the interview was well rehearsed.

Draper commented on how easy it had been for an F-117A stealth fighter to fly right over the enemy and their batteries of antiaircraft guns and missiles totally undetected, proving once more that the Black Jet was the most advanced stealth fighter in the world. He also mentioned that his presence there was that of an observer, and that the real work was being conducted by a joint CIA-Navy-Air Force command.

Draper finally approached Bourdeaux as the camera crew walked away with their gear. A half dozen men, also dressed in impeccable-looking fatigues, walked down the stairs carrying suitcases and boxes—what Bourdeaux guessed had to be the general's collection of personal items.

"Hello, Mr. Bourdeaux. How are things?"

"Fine, General. Thank you. I notice that you brought a camera crew. I had already arranged for a CNN crew to cover the event. They will arrive later on this morning."

Draper looked both ways before lowering his voice a few decibels. "Listen. Between you and me, I doubt General Marshall—or the president, for that matter—would approve of that. It's probably in your best interest to call them off. I brought along a combat camera crew approved by CENTAF to cover the event. Afterward, you and I will have full control of the editing before releasing this to the press."

"Ah . . . sure, General. No problem. I'll call them off," Bourdeaux said, staring directly into the eyes of the Silver Rat. In the first minute of his stay, Draper had already politely squashed Bourdeaux's own plan to cover the event. Bourdeaux felt a headache coming on as he tightened his fists. *This entire thing has gotten off to a bad start,* he thought. He could only hope it didn't get any worse.

"Now if you excuse me, I had a long flight and would like to freshen up. Did you get a chance to get me a tent?"

"Ah, yes, General. Right this way."

They walked in silence past the F-117A parked next to several F-15 Eagles. Bourdeaux stopped briefly while Draper glanced at the stealth fighter before continuing down the tarmac. They reached Draper's tent a moment later. Draper's staff waited by the entrance. The general pointed at one of them: a captain. Draper's face suddenly became rock hard.

"You."

"Yes, sir?"

"I need to have a private lunch for three in my tent at noon. Make it happen. Now go."

"Yessir!"

Bourdeaux blinked twice in surprise as the captain set a large footlocker on the ground, did an about-face and took off. Draper looked at Bourdeaux. The general's face became soft and pleasant again.

"I hope I don't inconvenience you by asking you to join me for lunch, Mr. Bourdeaux."

Bourdeaux couldn't believe this guy. "Sure, General. No problem."

"Great. Oh, if you could, could you bring Colonel Peter Halston along? The word I've got at CENTAF is that he's the man who really makes things happen around here. I'd like to meet him since he's going to be handling a large portion of the attack. Now, I'm beat. I need a nap. Good-bye, Mr. Bourdeaux. See you at lunch." Draper turned around and went inside, followed by his staff.

Bourdeaux stood speechlessly outside the tent. Slowly, he walked away.

THE WHITE HOUSE.
Day Four. 0030 Local Time.

Working alone inside the Oval office, President Clinton finished his daily domestic agenda and turned his attention to the latest reports on Allahbad that had arrived in the past hour.

The faxed reports from Draper and also from Bourdeaux indicated that, just as the CIA director had pointed out, the recon mission had been highly successful in showing the unusually high number of soldiers and antiaircraft equipment inside the complex.

Another report from the defense secretary and from General Roy Marshall gave last-minute details of how the operation would be carried out: a combined Navy-Air Force effort.

Clinton dropped his eyelids halfway at the remembrance of Saddam Hussein's propaganda show on TV the other night. *Now, Mr. Saddam Hussein, it's my turn.*

USS *RANGER*. EIGHTY MILES NORTH OF BAHRAIN, PERSIAN GULF.
Day Four. 0845 Local Time.

Lieutenant Chico Delgado climbed up the ladder resting against the side of his F-14A Tomcat and agilely hopped into the rear seat of the cockpit.

"Good morning, sir."

"Hello, Chico," Commander John McDeere said from the front.

Each went through his own systems checklist in silence for a few additional minutes.

"Good alignment, select missile prep," Delgado finally said over the ICS as he reached the bottom of his list.

"We're going on a tough mission here. Everything sweet back there?" McDeere snapped impatiently.

"Radar's sweet, no degrades worth mentioning and RHAW gear checks out," answered Delgado, informing his CO that the radar humming and warning gear was fully operational.

"Did you run a full built-in test?" McDeere asked

curtly, implying that Delgado hadn't performed the BIT, a test where the Tomcat's computers automatically execute an algorithm that performs a full systems check and reports any problems.

"Ah, yes, sir."

"Why don't you run it again, just to be sure."

Delgado tightened his fists. "Yes, sir!"

Good crew coordination was paramount to a successful mission, and that meant good rapport between the RIO and the pilot. McDeere had accomplished the exact opposite. As Delgado went down the checklist again, he silently cursed his CO, who by now had been promoted to the top of another list: Delgado's shit list. He resented the freckle-faced commander not only for having been so hard on Kevin but also because all the bastard cared about was his own career and how good he looked. It struck Delgado as amusing that McDeere had flown only a few sorties during the first few days of their tour, selecting missions that had the best chance of encountering MiGs. After it became evident that dogfights would not be as common as everyone had thought, due to the lack of Iraqi airborne fighters in the no-fly zone, McDeere had quietly reverted to his role as the squadron's CO, telling everyone that he had to remain aboard the carrier to cover the "big picture" of coordinating sorties. However, the moment the *Ranger* received orders from CENTAF to send a squadron of F-14s to provide escort for a special decoy bombing mission alongside the famous F-117 Black Jet, the CO had quickly nominated himself strike lead for the mission.

Damn, you're an asshole, John McDeere! Delgado thought.

Ten minutes later, the fighter hurtled off the carrier, quickly joined overhead by three others. The Tomcats turned to a northerly heading.

ALLAHBAD PROCESSING COMPLEX, SOUTH OF AN NAJAF, IRAQ.
Day Four. 1000 Local Time.

For Khalela Yishaid, the nightmare had just begun. She had not seen Ishmael Barzani since they had been taken to separate rooms the night before, and only now when she was brought into the interrogation room did she realize the brutal punishment her Kurdish friend had suffered.

She froze in horror at the sight of Ishmael, or what was left of him, hanging by the hands from the ceiling in the center of the large, square room. Half his body was immersed in a barrel filled with a dark liquid. From where she stood, she couldn't see if he was breathing or not.

"He was very tough, but in the end he lost," said Major Mohammed Hassoud from one end of a wooden table on the right side of the windowless room. She noticed the leather straps on the rough surface. "Lift him up."

Khalela felt bile rushing up her throat when she saw that the lower section of Ishmael's body was gone. She leaned over and vomited on the concrete floor. The soldiers put Ishmael's remains in a plastic bag and carried them out of the room.

"Hydrochloric acid. It eats down to the bone."

With tears in her eyes, Khalela managed to get to her feet and looked contemptuously at Hassoud.

"It is indeed amusing. You see, when we first brought him in here, he spat in my face when I asked him his name. His stare was as defiant as yours is now. He became a little more agreeable after his toes were in the chemical. By the time he was up to his ankles in it, he was telling me everything I wanted to know. When the liquid reached his knees, he begged me to put a bullet through his head. He finally passed out from the pain when we immersed him down to his waist. I guess he died soon after that."

Khalela noticed she was quivering, but it wasn't fear. It was anger.

"You see, I know about your friends out there. I know your name is Khalela. I know about someone named Dalton, an American pilot shot down by our superior Air Force. I know about Abdul and the thirty other Kurdish guerrillas who butchered our soldiers in a village south of here. A team is on the way to wipe out your friends. In another hour, you will be all alone."

Khalela blinked twice in silent astonishment, trying to conceive of the kind of pain that had to be inflicted on Ishmael for Hassoud to know those things.

"So, my dear Khalela, are you going to force us to do something like that to you, or are you going to be a little more cooperative than your friend?"

She didn't respond.

"Very well, then. Take off your clothes." Hassoud's hairy face seemed hard, cruel, and pitiless.

She studied the scarred nose and cheeks, gazed into his eyes. "Why don't you come and try to take them off yourself, you ugly butcher?" There was silence. She noticed all five guards in the room staring at Hassoud.

Hassoud tilted his head and began to laugh. He was soon joined by the guards, who laughed even harder. A few moments later, he raised his hand.

"Enough!" Hassoud shouted. The laughter halted. Hassoud, his head still lifted high, looked condescendingly down at Khalela. "Is ugly the only word that comes to mind when you look at me? Perhaps you need to see more of me, Khalela."

Slowly, the Iraqi major unbuttoned the top of his uniform and showed her his chest. Khalela gasped. The man was disfigured.

"I have been given the face and the body of a devil, my dear friend. The Kurds did this to me." He buttoned up the shirt. "That is enough of the show. You and you, rip off her clothes!"

Instinctively, Khalela dropped to a crouch and threw a side kick at the guard on her right. Her heel landed in his groin. The guard folded over and silently rolled away. The other three guards trained their weapons on her, but

Hassoud lifted his right hand, palm open. They lowered the weapons.

The second guard also dropped to a crouch and smiled. Khalela tried a knife hand to the throat but the guard blocked it and slapped her across the face with the back of his hand. The blow sent her crashing against the wall.

She landed on the floor, and before she could react two other guards had her pinned down. One held her arms, the other her legs, and a third guard tore off the shirt of her camouflage fatigues before ripping the white T-shirt in half. One of the guards grabbed both breasts and squeezed them hard. A second reached for her pants.

"Stop!" commanded Hassoud. "Bring her over here!"

The guards laid her face up on the wooden table and strapped her wrists and ankles to the sides. Hassoud came around. "You're indeed a very attractive woman. What a waste." He pulled out a knife and slowly moved the edge up and down her torso.

Khalela wished they would just get it over with. The mental anguish of waiting was probably worse than the physical act itself. As she felt the cold edge making its way around her breasts, Khalela saw her sister. Saw the Arabs in a circle pushing her around. She heard Suleima's scream. Heard her shouts. *Oh, God, please. No, please, stop!*

Hassoud lowered the knife and tucked it in between her body and the pants she still wore. Then in one swift move, he yanked the knife upward, ripping her pants. She kept her eyes closed and turned her head. Hassoud's hand softly stroked the inside of her thighs. She heard the other soldiers break into a laugh when Hassoud moved his hand up until it came in contact with her pubic hair, slowly inching a finger inside her dry vagina. She shivered and clenched her teeth.

It's going to happen now, she thought. *It'll soon be over with.*

The hand was now softly massaging her stomach, fingers circling around her belly button. It moved to her breasts, caressing them for a few seconds. Then it was gone. Khalela waited a few extra moments before opening her eyes and staring at Hassoud. The other soldiers were also looking down. Their intentions were clear.

"What a waste, Khalela. What a waste indeed. Bring the machine," she heard Hassoud order. The soldiers did not respond right away.

"Are you deaf?" Hassoud snapped. "Get me the machine, *now!*" The soldiers quickly left the room.

"We will not kill you as quickly, Khalela. Ishmael was a savage; he deserved a savage treatment. You and I are not savages. We are civilized and should behave as such. All we want to know is where you come from and what you were doing with the Kurds. Poor Ishmael passed out before he could tell us."

She didn't respond.

"Tell us what government you work for!"

Khalela simply stared into Hassoud's eyes.

"As you wish. But know this, you *will* talk. One way or the other, by the time you leave this room, whether under your own power or by us dragging your limp body, you will have told us everything we want to know. It is just a matter of how much pain you are willing to endure in the process."

Khalela ignored him. Somehow she knew they wouldn't break her. She prayed to God that her strict Mossad training would help her withstand the pain she was certain would come from "the machine." *You will take the pain, Khalela,* she told herself. *You will take it time and time again. Suleima took it long ago. She sacrificed herself for you. Now you must do the same for your people.*

Lieutenant Kevin Dalton couldn't bring himself to leave the area without learning what had happened to Khalela and Ishmael, although as several men in the guerrilla group—starting with Abdul—had pointed out to him, they were probably dead by now. Kevin had repeatedly tried to convince them, through gesturing, to attack the complex from several angles using the RPG antitank weapons and machine guns they had brought with them, but they all rejected the idea, indicating that the Iraqis had too many soldiers and too many bases nearby.

For the entire night and most of the morning, Kevin had been scanning the small building where the guards had taken Khalela and Ishmael after they left the truck. He still had not seen either one come out. Now Abdul was pointing in the direction where they had parked the Rovers behind some sand dunes several hundred feet away.

Kevin understood. The Kurds had serious concerns about either Ishmael or Khalela cracking during an interrogation and telling the enemy about the existence of a guerrilla group outside the complex's gates.

In addition, he reflected while inspecting the surroundings, there were really not that many places to hide in case the soldiers came looking for them.

Kevin looked at Abdul, shook his head, and pointed the index finger of his right hand at himself and then at the ground where he stood. He knew he couldn't leave until he was certain Khalela was dead. Besides, he didn't have anything to lose. Getting back across the border only meant a court martial, a fate he would accept only after he had learned the fate of the woman he now knew he loved.

Abdul approached him and handed him a Kalashnikov and several magazines. The Kurd then took his canteen and hunting knife and also gave them to Kevin, who smiled and nodded.

Then, before Kevin could react, Abdul embraced him. Kevin, caught off guard, didn't know how to react, finally opting for a few pats on Abdul's back. When the Kurd released him, Kevin saw tears in Abdul's eyes.

"Good-bye, my friend, may God be with you," he said to him.

Abdul put a hand to Kevin's shoulder. "Good-bye . . . pilot Dalton." He then turned and followed the other Kurds who were already walking toward the vehicles.

A few minutes later, Kevin watched the small caravan of Kurdish guerrillas drive away. Suddenly, a low *whop-*

whop sound made him train the binoculars on the far hills to his left. His middle finger rotated the adjusting wheel, trying to bring the image into focus. A cold chill filled him when two Hind-D attack helicopters came into plain view, flying in the direction of the caravan.

"Oh, Jesus!" was all he could mumble as each of the five vehicles went in its own direction. The helicopters broke formation and went in pursuit. He noticed how the choppers approached at nearly ground level and briefly popped up to fifty or so feet before unloading a shower of rockets on the Kurds.

Three vehicles exploded right away; the other two managed to zigzag their way through the inferno and emerged undamaged. The helicopters turned and came back for a final pass. This time, Kevin heard 20mm cannons and saw the cloud of dust that followed their deadly trail. The cloud quickly moved toward the vehicles. One Rover flipped the moment it came in contact with the bullets. The second crashed against a sand dune. Three rebels got out, but didn't make it far before they too were gunned down.

Kevin lowered the binoculars and closed his eyes. The entire episode had taken less than a minute. *Bastards!*

A sound behind him made him reach for the Kalashnikov and spin around, his finger fixed on the trigger.

"Abdul! You dumb shit! I could have killed you!"

Abdul didn't respond. The Kurd still had tears in his eyes.

Kevin looked at the two huge sacks and the large backpack his friend was carrying, and he noted several green cylindrical RPG-7 shoulder-launched rocket warheads sticking out of the top of one.

"RPG," said Abdul, dropping the sacks and moving the back of his right thumb across his neck.

Kevin nodded. "Tonight."

Over a hundred feet below the surface, Dr. Radsul Sakkar, followed by Risha, inserted his magnetic card into a slot in the wall. The red light above the steel door

turned green and the door automatically slid to the side.
He stepped inside the computer room: the heart of
Allahbad. The door automatically closed behind him.
Usually, he was the only one allowed inside the room.
The computers, all IBM 3033s, worked laboriously at
controlling everything inside the underground complex,
from the delicate climate control system to the automatic deployment and launch of missiles. Nothing was left
to human error. Four computers worked in parallel; a
fifth one did nothing but check the results of the other
four.

Sakkar walked to the large console in the center of the
circular room. Risha stood quietly behind him. Next to
the console was a scale map of the underground missile
deployment tunnels. *Thirty missiles, thirty twenty-kiloton warheads,* thought Sakkar. Each with enough
energy to wipe out an area the size of Baghdad. Sakkar
typed a few commands on the keyboard, and the large
computer screen responded by displaying a map of Iraq
and surrounding countries. At the bottom of the screen
he read the words: View: A, B, or C. Current is B.

Sakkar had gone through the exercise many times.
After all, he had programmed the different target combination scenarios himself. He placed the cursor under *A*
and hit the return key.

Instantly the screen came alive with lines propagating
from Allahbad to thirty different locations in the map.
Scenario A, designed to take out only military installations in the region from Israel to Oman, would leave the
area virtually defenseless to an Iraqi combined air/land
assault with tanks and planes. Scenario B destroyed only
major military installations and most key cities. Scenario C, by far the most destructive of all, would take out
only a few strategic military installations, most large
cities, and most of the region's oil installations. The
system operated by default in scenario A, the scenario
where Iraq would start the attack. But Saddam Hussein
had ordered it changed to scenario B. Sakkar had also
been ordered to hold launches until all thirty missiles
were deployed, and then wait for final confirmation. The

reason for the order was simple. Once a missile left the underground complex, Allied forces would know exactly what Allahbad really manufactured and launch a counterstrike. Although Allahbad had been built to survive such an attack, it would be safer to wait for all the missiles to be ready prior to launching any of them. Sakkar estimated Allahbad to be less than a few days away from having all missiles ready. In the meantime, if the Allies somehow bombed Allahbad, and if by some miracle the underground lab was threatened, the computer system would override all other inputs and go directly to scenario C—the immediate launch of all deployed missiles. Scenario C worked by priorities. The first targets consisted of major cities in Israel, Saudi Arabia, Iran, and Kuwait. Oil installations followed, with a few military targets as a last priority. Sakkar knew that if scenario C ever occurred, Tel Aviv, Riyadh, Kuwait City, and Tehran, would be destroyed, since the first few missiles would launch in their directions. In addition, the world would most certainly suffer a major oil shortage far beyond that which the Iraqis had created during the 1991 Gulf War. This shortage would last for years, until the oil manufacturing facilities in the region could be repaired and brought back to normal production levels.

Sakkar typed a few more keys and placed the system in a self-test mode. This required the systems to leave all control settings at their current positions for a fraction of a second to perform an internal hardware test. Upon completion of the short built-in test, the system went back to its normal duties. Because of the speed of the computers, the test finished so quickly that Sakkar couldn't see any difference in the system's operations. The message *SYSTEM OPERATIONAL* flashed on the screen. Satisfied, he hit the return key once more and the screen went blank.

Sakkar turned and stared into his subordinate's eyes.

"Soon, Doctor," Risha said with a fierce commitment that impressed Sakkar himself. "Soon we will be able to give our country what it needs to prevail."

SALMAN ASAD AIR BASE, SAUDI ARABIA. NEAR IRAQI BORDER.
Day Four. 1145 Local Time.

Lieutenant Chico Delgado's Tomcat touched down gently. Commander John McDeere taxied it next to the canopy protecting an F-117A from the midday sun. Delgado had never seen a Black Jet up close before.

The moment the canopy of his Tomcat was raised, Delgado reached down and flipped open the built-in steps and ladder before the puzzled Air Force crew could figure it out. He stepped down and stared at the unorthodox shape of the black bird.

"Let's go, Chico," he heard McDeere say.

"I'll be right along, sir." Delgado said, still looking at the F-117A.

McDeere shook his head and slowly walked back toward Delgado. "Listen. Perhaps I wasn't clear enough about this back in the carrier. Allow me to tell you that we're doing this thing by the numbers. I don't want you roaming around this base causing trouble and sticking your nose where it doesn't belong. I don't want anything, *anything*, to go wrong either on base or in the air. If you want to look at this plane, go ahead, but don't touch anything, don't screw around with anything, and don't embarrass the Navy. I want us to come out of this mission smelling like a rose. You follow?"

Delgado felt like taking a swing at the large McDeere. Not only had his CO questioned his competence, but he also had the boldness to lecture him in public, and at an Air Force base of all places!

Delgado was furious. He knew he could take him. As big as McDeere was, Delgado knew he could easily take him. The Hispanic lieutenant had knocked down larger guys during his *barrio* days. *Each man's gotta a pair of soft and sensitive nuts, fragile knees, and two temples. And you, Commander John all-I-care-for-is-my-career McDeere, ain't no different. Just one swing and you would drop like a fucking fly, man. Just one kick and you'll be crawling all over the tarmac picking up your balls. Just one shot, asshole. One shot's all I'm asking for.* But

Delgado knew that option didn't exist. He settled for a "Yes, sir," muttered between clenched teeth.

McDeere turned around and walked toward the base's command post.

Fuming, Delgado went back to his examination of the Black Jet. He noticed the sagging set of flaps on the inboard edges of the wings and decided that they had to be hydraulically boosted.

He moved closer until his face was inches from the smooth black surface of the sagging flap and softly rubbed a hand on it. *Fuck McDeere and his rules.*

The black skin felt soft, unlike the hard aluminum panels of the Tomcat.

"That's RAM, bud. Ain't it neat?"

Startled, Delgado turned around and faced a tall and large Air Force pilot wearing a pair of eel-skin cowboy boots. The East L.A. native noticed the pilot's thick mustache lifting as the man gave him a wide grin.

"Excuse me, sir?" Delgado asked after noticing the silver insignia of a lieutenant colonel on his shoulders.

"I said, that's RAM—Radar Absorbent Material."

"What's it made out of?"

"Heck, who knows. I just fly 'em, not build 'em. But I heard someone said once that they use some sort of polyurethane material that's got damned good properties for absorbin' radar."

"So I guess underneath that's just like any other plane, eh?"

"Yep. You got it. It flies just like the rest of 'em birds, except no one can detect ya at night. Pretty cool, ah?"

"Yes, sir," Delgado said. "Oh, I'm Lieutenant Chico Delgado."

"Howdy, Chico. I'm Lieutenant Colonel Richard Kramer, but call me Longhorn."

"Longhorn?"

"Yep. Don't go by that bullshit of sir or nothin' like that."

Delgado smiled. "No problem, Longhorn."

Kramer pulled out a pack of chewing tobacco. "You chew?"

"Ah, no thanks."

"Good for you, Chico. Stuff is nasty." He took a healthy dip and inserted it in his cheek. "You fly that Tomcat in here?"

"Backseater."

Kramer laughed. "Well, Chico, I gotta tell you. I think you would look pretty damned funny out there tryin' to find this bird on your radar. With this baby I can come right up to your ass and you wouldn't notice me till I was bitin' you."

Delgado smiled again. "What about the funny shape? I guess it's necessary, huh?"

"You bet. I'll buy you a beer if you can find a single large flat surface on this bird. It ain't got any."

"I believe you. That way radar will only reflect in one direction."

"Yep. And the unavoidable long straight edge of the forward wing's covered by RAM. And that's not even the best part of the design. Here, let me show you the engine exhausts."

Delgado shook his head and smiled in disbelief as he followed Kramer to the back of the plane. *Where in the hell did you come from, buddy? You're all right.*

While listening to the humming of the portable air-conditioning unit that Draper had already had installed in the tent, Robert Bourdeaux looked outside through the clear plastic window and recognized Colonel Kramer. He was walking around an F-117A with a Navy pilot.

"Well, Bob . . . I can call you Bob, right?" Before Bourdeaux could even nod, Draper continued. "Good. What would you like, Bob? Iced tea or water?"

Bourdeaux let it go. Draper was impossible. He slowly turned his head and looked up at the airman holding a tray of glasses filled with tea or water. He snatched one with water. "Thank you, airman."

"You're welcome, sir."

Bourdeaux was sitting at one end of a table for six, Draper at the other, Halston to one side. The meeting had not started well. The silver-haired general-turned-undersecretary had heard about the two failed rescue attempts for the downed F-14 pilot. Draper had been very blunt. First he criticized Lieutenant Kevin Dalton's actions for disobeying a direct order from his carrier, which, as Draper had put it, had caused an investment of millions of dollars in equipment and training to go down the drain. Draper had said that he would like to get his hands on the hotheaded pilot and called him a typical example of what the Navy *didn't* want their pilots to be like. Then Draper had subtly criticized Halston for not sending in enough firepower to cover the rescue attempts. He did it with the elegance of a full-fledged politician. Not really hammering at Halston, but positioning Halston so that the colonel had to admit openly that he'd screwed up.

"Sir," Bourdeaux interjected in Halston's favor, "with all due respect, all rescue operations have incredible risks attached, especially in daylight. All the colonel did—"

"I'm sorry, gentlemen," Draper said. "I didn't mean to make a big deal of it. What's done is done. Obviously someone around here thinks Colonel Halston's very capable to do the job, otherwise he wouldn't have it. I do hope, however, that you people think twice before sending in another rescue team just for the hell of it, especially during the day. I think I might mention this to President Clinton in my next report. Perhaps we could have a quick change of policy with regards to CSAR. Then again, maybe not. After all it's none of my business, but I do hate to see good men go down because of an insubordinate pilot. Well! I guess it's your choice, Colonel." Draper briefly smiled at his own comment and waved a hand in the air while he took a sip of his iced tea.

Bourdeaux gritted his teeth and forced his mind to find the necessary patience to squelch the overwhelming desire to tell Draper to go straight to hell. Somehow Bourdeaux succeeded and remained silent. He glanced briefly at Halston, who kept his eyes trained on his plate.

Draper motioned the airman to leave the trailer. The airman nodded, turned and left. "Let's see what the U.S. Armed Forces is serving our brave soldiers today. Ah!

Fried chicken and french fries! Why don't you start, Colonel?"

Halston glanced at the tray and snagged a chicken leg.

"Tell me, gentlemen," Draper began, "exactly how is it that the F-117 tricked the Iraqis last night?"

"Simple, sir," Halston responded. "It flew over their facilities and released short, controlled bursts of chaff. The incident must have confused the living hell out of them."

"Yes, how interesting. . . . Care for some fries, Colonel?"

"Ah, no, sir. Thank you."

"Bob? Fries?"

"Please." Bourdeaux reached out and grabbed a handful.

"So, is that the same principle we'll use tonight?"

"Yes, sir," continued Halston. "We'll get more details during the brief—"

"Have the Navy jets arrived yet?" interrupted Draper.

Halston lowered his gaze.

"Just watched them land," said Bourdeaux while holding a fry in his right hand. "Although I hate to take F-14s away from the ships."

"Yes, yes, I know," Draper interrupted. "It was my idea. Look at it another way. Chances are Desert Star will get a lot of publicity, so it would be better if it was a coordinated effort between the Air Force and the Navy. That way both branches of the armed forces will get equal credit and recognition."

"I guess so, sir," responded Bourdeaux as he stuffed the fry in his mouth and chewed it hard and fast.

"Good. I'm glad we're in agreement. I want *our* operation to go perfectly. All's in place, then?"

"Yes, sir. All we have to do now is wait for nightfall."

Thirty minutes later, Bourdeaux and Halston left the tent in silence. *I'm going to kill that bastard,* Bourdeaux thought, coming to terms with the fact that Draper had been able to infuriate him more than anybody else he knew. *Well, I should have known the asshole would have reacted like that to the helicopter incident.* Bourdeaux sighed, realizing the helicopter had been one of those unavoidable incidents. He knew Halston had been taking a chance with the rescue mission. If it had been successful, then Halston would have only been reminded that he was doing his job. But since it failed—and lost a chopper and crew—Halston had been told he was an idiot for failing to anticipate problems. It had always amazed Bourdeaux to see people rendering judgment on his activities after the fact. *Idiots!* he thought. *They are all a bunch of arrogant bastards who have no idea how hard it is to plan and execute a successful mission!* Bourdeaux had little patience for those who were quick to criticize bad missions. *Where were they during the planning stage?* he asked himself. *What right do they have to complain and second-guess decisions?*

Bourdeaux approached his tent. His head was throbbing again. Draper definitely knew how to push his buttons. *He's the master of them all.* He decided he was not going to fight Draper on this one. It appeared as if the old Silver Rat had thought this one out quite thoroughly. He looked at Halston silently walking next to him.

"Fuck him, Pete. Don't let him get to you. Don't let the bastard screw with your mind."

Halston smiled. "Are you kidding me? He's mild compared to some of the officers I've had the displeasure of crossing my path. Don't you worry about me, pal. My skin's thicker than a Bradley's. That asshole will come and go, and life will go on. I, however, will wait until he's gone before trying to do something else about Dalton. That's if something can be done about him. My bet is he's a POW by now."

Bourdeaux relaxed a bit, buoyed by his friend's attitude. "Possible. But you know you're right about how to handle Draper. I'm letting him get to me. Say, you sure seem to be in pretty good spirits under the circumstances."

Halston grinned. "Let's just say that my personal life's taking a turn for the better."

In spite of all his problems, Bourdeaux managed a thin

smile. He felt happy for his old Air Force buddy. "That's great. Glad to hear it. Like I said, she looks like a great gal."

"She is."

Bourdeaux's face turned a bit more serious. "How are you gonna handle the fact that she's under your command?"

"She's gonna transfer out of CSAR in a week, as soon as I can get another pilot. She's moving to noncombat helicopter support. Based here, of course. It's all set up."

"Great. I'm glad it's gonna work out. Well, I'm off to bed. It's going to be a long night." With that Bourdeaux walked into his tent.

ALLAHBAD PROCESSING COMPLEX, SOUTH OF AN NAJAF, IRAQ.
Day Four. 1300 Local Time.

Khalela's body arched up toward the ceiling. She felt as though her soul was being torn from her as several hundred volts ran through her body. It lasted but a second. The current stopped and her back crashed against the rough surface of the wooden table. She stopped screaming. The pain began to ebb. She had nearly bitten through the piece of rubber Hassoud had pushed in between her teeth to prevent her from accidentally biting or swallowing her tongue. It tasted foul.

She felt disoriented for a few seconds until Major Hassoud's hairy face slowly came into focus. The pain from the alligator clips, one on her left nipple and another one on a toe of her left foot, seemed negligible compared to the brutal, uncontrollable fury that had momentarily taken control of her body.

"That is just a taste of what is coming next, Khalela. There are seven settings on this machine. I have seen men survive the first five, only to become vegetables after the sixth. I just gave you a one-second taste of the first setting, and that was using relatively dry spots on your body." He removed the rubber from her mouth.

"Tell me, who do you work for?"

You will not break me. You will not break me. You will

not break me, she silently told herself. Khalela heard Suleima's scream in her mind. Never once did she tell them about Khalela. Not once. She had begged for mercy. She had pleaded for her dignity, her honor, her life, but never told them about her younger sister. Suleima had taken the ultimate punishment that a woman can receive. The ultimate violation of privacy. The ultimate act of deranged men. One by one they came, forcing themselves inside her while screaming death and shame to Israel and its people. *No,* Khalela thought, *you will not break me, you bastard. Resist. Resist. Resist.*

"There is no use in delaying the inevitable, my dear Khalela. You will have to tell me."

Khalela remained silent, her gaze fixed on his.

Hassoud took a knife and brought it closer to her. Khalela followed it down to her belly. The glistening skin on her stomach flinched at the contact with Hassoud's cold knife. He smiled and reached for the alligator clip on her nipple and slowly opened it. He put a finger to his tongue and wet it with saliva. Then softly, he rubbed it around the redness of the bruised nipple.

"It will make a much better contact." He placed the alligator clip over the nipple and let it snap in place. Her body tensed again and a light moan escaped her lips. Hassoud did the same to her toe. "Again, Khalela. Who do you work for and what were you doing in the complex?"

Khalela saw Suleima. Saw the Arab soldiers. Heard her scream, her pain, her agony. *Never! I will tell you nothing!*

Hassoud secured the rubber piece in her mouth and reached for the knob in the machine. "Listen for the click, Khalela."

She followed his hand as he began to turn the black knob. *Resist. Resist. Resist.* The click came, as loud as a gunshot. Then everything went out of focus.

SALMAN ASAD AIR BASE, SAUDI ARABIA. NEAR IRAQI BORDER.
Day Four. 1305 Local Time.

Colonel Peter Halston smiled when Amanda Green walked into his tent. It seemed as if they couldn't get enough of each other since the day before. Like a couple of kids hiding from their parents, they would sneak around just to have a few private moments.

Without saying a word, they kissed.

"You wanted to see me, sir?" she whispered while nibbling his left ear.

He caressed the back of her neck with his hand while hugging her tight with the other arm. He enjoyed the feeling of having her breasts pressed against his chest. "As a matter of fact I did, Captain. We need to head out to the communications tent. There's something I want to show you."

Amanda pulled back a few inches and gazed into his eyes. "And what might that be?" She kissed the tip of his nose.

"It's a surprise."

"Do I get a hint?"

"Nope."

The two of them walked side by side and entered the communications tent, where they headed for the last station on the right, next to the dark green table where Bourdeaux and Halston usually went over satellite photos. The radio operator, a sergeant, looked up at them.

"Ready?" asked Halston.

"He's been on hold for fifteen minutes, sir."

"Sorry. I got sidetracked. Official duties."

Amanda chuckled lightly. The sergeant looked at them questioningly. Halston ignored him and motioned the puzzled sergeant and the other two operators in the tent to take a quick break. He then reached for a headset and put it on, adjusting the microphone to his lips. After reaching down and flipping a switch on the control panel, he said, "Are you still holding, sir?"

"That's right. Where's my daughter? I was told she

would come to the phone," came the voice through the headphones.

"She's right here, sir," responded Halston while Amanda gave him a curious look.

Without another word, Halston handed the headset to Amanda. She looked at it for a few seconds before putting it on. She said, "Hello, this is Captain Green." A moment later, a tear ran down her cheek.

▪ 13 ▪

NIGHT CREATURES

'Tis now the very witching time of night,
When churchyards yawn and hell itself breathes out
Contagion to this world.

—William Shakespeare

ALLAHBAD PROCESSING COMPLEX, SOUTH OF AN NAJAF, IRAQ.
Day Four. 1845 Local Time.

Dressed in one of the Iraqi uniforms the Kurds had captured at the village, Kevin Dalton crawled slowly over the uneven, sandy terrain. The throbbing in his leg remained steady, reminding him that he had been shot just over forty-eight hours before. The early evening sky still showed a light hint of orange and the sand had barely begun to release its heat, but the surroundings had grown dark enough as far as Kevin was concerned. Abdul had wanted him to wait just a little longer, until the area was completely swallowed by the night, but Kevin had refused. In his mind, every second counted. *Every damned second . . . That is, if she's still . . . Dammit Kevin! Stop thinking that way!* he cursed at himself. *She is alive and well. You just need to get to her!*

The thought made him move more quickly, ignoring the pain from his wounded leg. He would worry about that later. *Priorities, Kevin. Priorities.* He approached the south end of the chain-link fence, looked to the other end and saw that Abdul had reached it as well.

His hands now moved in unison. Although he had never done this before, Kevin surprised himself at the ease with which his fingers molded the C-4 plastic explosive Abdul had stolen during the raid on an Iraqi supply post a few days back. He carefully pressed it against one of the wooden posts that supported and insulated the electric fence. Any poor bastard touching the fence itself, Kevin estimated, would be exposed to what appeared to be a thousand volts. He shifted his gaze away from the thick electric cables connected to the top of the fence and continued his work.

His back ached every time he twisted to apply pressure against the explosives. The pain, however, didn't seem quite as intense as the one from his bruised and bloodied knees, particularly since he had to kneel while working. He ignored it all as he used the tip of his fingers to mold the edges of the plastic. Satisfied, he inserted two wires into the C-4, one at each end of the oval-shaped charge.

Slowly, he moved toward Abdul and stopped two posts later, where he repeated the process. He continued alongside the fence, applying a charge to every other post until he met Abdul halfway.

Abdul took the wire leads from Kevin and tied them to his own. Then the two of them moved back behind a sand dune, where Kevin watched his Iranian friend connect the main wires to a digital timer. The giant Abdul set it to go off in fifteen minutes. Next he handed Kevin a sack containing four RPG warheads and a launcher unit.

Kevin slung his Kalashnikov across his back, opened the sack, and inspected the now familiar warheads and launcher unit that Abdul had shown him how to use an hour earlier. With that, the Kurd smiled, put a hand to Kevin's shoulder, and walked to his self-assigned post. Kevin did the same.

Surrounded once again by a sea of darkness, Colonel Longhorn Kramer kept his Black Jet ten thousand feet above the sand at a comfortable 300 knots. Range to target three zero miles.

Thirty miles to the west of the F-117A, Lieutenant Chico Delgado watched Commander John McDeere lead a formation with three other F-14As as they flew at a mere fifty feet over the rugged terrain. He was not that excited about the altitude, but stealth was the key to the success of the mission. The Tomcats were to act as a decoy by dispensing chaff miles away from the real objective.

Delgado sat back and stared at the blank display in front of him. All was quiet. All emitters had been secured to deprive the Iraqi defenses of any chance of detecting them.

Delgado shifted his gaze outside, toward the earth. He couldn't see a thing, but knew the desert sands were close . . . too close. For a brief moment, his thoughts drifted back to Kevin. Going against his CO's orders, Delgado had asked about Kevin at the base. A female helicopter pilot had told him about the two failed rescue attempts and about the disappearing Guard beacon. Nothing after that. The helicopter pilot thought that Kevin might have been captured.

He frowned, wondering what had happened to his friend. Then his curiosity slowly switched to disappointment and finally hate for McDeere and the others who had turned their backs on Kevin. *They had no right,* thought Delgado. *No right to render judgment unless they had been there at the time.* But none of them had been. None of them had experienced the probable wave of confusion that had flooded Kevin's mind the moment Lancaster's craft was shot down. Delgado himself could only attempt to imagine it. They simply heard it on the radio and were quick to pass judgment, having all the time in the world to analyze the situation. *Problem is,* reflected Delgado, *when you're going the speed of sound and the enemy is on your ass, you ain't got all the time in the world to sit down and carefully analyze the situation over a damned beer.*

Delgado knew well that in this business split-second

decisions make or break everything you've worked for so hard most of your life. It could all be gone in a second. The quick and the dead, separated by a hair. The dreams, the friendships . . . the love. All gone in a supersonic hell that always loomed over every man who had ever set foot in a fighter.

"Random chaff in thirty."

Delgado's thoughts were interrupted by the monotone voice of McDeere over the ICS. *Asshole.*

"Ready for chaff dispensing whenever you are," Delgado responded as the formation began a steep climb to five thousand feet. For this mission, instead of Phoenix missiles, the forward belly station carried an expanded chaff adapter, which contained more chaff than the F-14A would normally carry.

He looked outside one last time. *Vaya con Dios, Crackers.*

Kevin Dalton reached his position with ten minutes to spare. He dropped the sack on the sand dune overlooking the front of the complex, pulled out the plastic canteen, and took two swigs. He replaced the cap and pulled out one of the RPG warheads. He grabbed a long green cylinder containing the rocket propellant and screwed it into the warhead. He did the same to the other three warheads until each had a rocket unit safely attached.

He then sat next to the warheads and uncovered the nosecap on each one. This, he learned from Abdul, was something usually done only after inserting the assembled round into the launcher unit, but in this case they didn't think they would have the time to do it to each unit after the firing started.

After uncovering all four nosecaps, Kevin carefully removed the safety pins and replaced the covers. He checked his watch. Five minutes left. He took an assembled round and loaded it into the muzzle of the launcher unit.

Kevin got up, lifted the fifteen-pound weapon and rested it on his right shoulder. The weight felt right. He looked through the sights and centered them on the front of the warehouse, which looked to be roughly three hundred yards away—well within the range of the RPG for a stationary target.

He lowered the weapon and checked his watch. Still a couple of minutes left. Kevin removed the magazine from the AK-47 and briefly inspected it. *Full.* He jammed it back in place and set down the rifle next to the RPG.

Bringing the night-vision binoculars up to his eyes, Kevin inspected the front of the complex one last time. First he inspected the gate. *Nothing different,* he thought as he brought four soldiers into focus by the entrance to the complex. Next came the warehouse. He noticed that the large door was only partially open—*What?*

He heard it again. This time he was determined to find the source of the quiet jet engine noise.

He lay on his back and trained the binoculars at the sky. *Nothing.* He could still hear it. *Damn! What is that?*

Colonel Longhorn Kramer nudged the control stick forward and put the Black Jet into a shallow dive.

He checked his watch and opened the bomb bay doors. Kramer cringed inwardly, knowing that the moment the huge doors under the flat underside of the fuselage were open, his jet would no longer be totally invisible to the enemy. If anyone happened to be scanning this particular sector of airspace, the Black Jet ran a risk of detection.

"In the name of Allah! General Manesh!" shouted Fassan.

Once again, Manesh bolted off his cot and raced to the radar screen.

"Range and speed?"

"Five miles from Allahbad, speed four hundred knots and increasing!"

"What is going on? Is this equipment malfunctioning?"

"No, sir. We carefully checked it after yesterday's—"

"Get on the radio to Allahbad! Hurry, there's hardly any time!" He rushed out the door.

Drenched in sweat, Major Mohammed Hassoud removed the alligator clips from Khalela's nipple and toe and powered down the generator. After another one-hour session and over a dozen "treatments," the woman, whom Hassoud still only knew as Khalela, had finally passed out from the pain.

"We will have to wait a while before we can continue. Wait until she wakes up, unstrap her, and give her something to eat."

"What about some clothes, sir?" asked one of two guards in the room.

"No. I want to lower her self-esteem."

"If humiliation is what you want, sir, could we—"

"Any of you two lay a hand on her and you will follow the Kurd Ishmael in the barrel. Is that understood?"

Both guards' eyes opened wide. "Yes, sir!"

"That woman is a fount of information. I can feel it. I want to keep her alive and well for as long as possible. It's going to take some work to break—"

"Major Hassoud!" A guard came running into the room.

"Yes, what is it?"

"We're under attack, sir!"

"What are you talking about?"

"We just got a call from the air base, sir. Planes are on the way."

"Again? All right, sound the alarm!"

"Yes, sir!"

"And you two remember what I said about her. Just keep your eyes on her, nothing else!"

"Yes, sir!"

Hassoud raced outside the room, down the short narrow hall, and out of the building.

That's one of the bastards! Kevin thought, using the powerful night-vision binoculars to get a better view of one of the soldiers that had taken Khalela away the night before. *Yes, it's you all right—*

Kevin heard the quiet jet noise again. He trained the binoculars to the sky. This time Kevin saw it: a dark silhouette against the star-filled sky. The craft approached at a shallow angle at around four thousand feet. *What in the world . . . lo and behold, it's a damned F-117! It's one of ours!* he thought.

The entire compound came alive with sirens and spotlights. Once again he watched as the compound's side doors swung open and dozens of soldiers raced for the antiaircraft equipment.

He checked his watch. Thirty seconds left.

Kramer made his first pass at four thousand feet. The automatic laser designator mounted on the starboard side under the fuselage was already fixed on the large warehouse by the front of the complex. The moment Kramer released his first Paveway II, the laser finder electronics in the bomb automatically sent the appropriate commands to the control surfaces, which guided the 2000-pound bomb to the spot marked.

"Holy cow!" yelled Kevin when the center of the warehouse exploded in an orange ball of fire, briefly illuminating the skies.

The C-4 charges went off. Kevin watched the fence collapse with a shower of sparks as the high voltage came in direct contact with the ground and created a short circuit. The lights in the compound flickered for a moment and then went out. A few seconds later, yellow emergency lights came on. Under them, Kevin watched a Shilka antiaircraft armored vehicle moving away from the compound, directly toward him.

Kevin brought the RPG launcher unit to his shoulder, trained it on the vehicle and fired.

The five-pound projectile left the launcher with a bright blast and quickly accelerated to nearly four hundred feet per second as it made its way toward the Shilka. Kevin held his breath as the river of smoke streaked in the direction of the vehicle and veered off to the left.

Shit!

He loaded a second round, aimed and fired. The projectile remained on course, but the vehicle managed to turn hard to the right, missing the round by a few feet. The Shilka now moved parallel to the fence, away from Kevin.

Cursing his bad luck, Kevin slung the AK-47 across his back and grabbed the launcher unit and remaining warheads. He ran toward the complex, which by now was in total chaos.

He snapped his head up when another blast shook the compound, leveling the plant behind the warehouse.

Kevin stopped, inserted a projectile into the already hot muzzle, aimed and fired.

The warhead blasted away and hurtled after the Shilka, striking it in the rear and causing a loud explosion. The vehicle continued moving, but it appeared to be out of control. It stopped by the fence.

Kevin left the last RPG round behind, clutched the Kalashnikov and ran for the section of the gate that had collapsed, reaching it a minute later. He saw Abdul running toward him. Kevin motioned him to stay back. Because of Abdul's size, they had not been able to fit him into any of the captured Iraqi uniforms. The Kurd continued running in his direction.

A huge ball of flames erupted from the far side of the complex, now totally ablaze.

Kevin raced past the destroyed vehicle and toward the small building next to the warehouse, praying that his four-day stubble would help him blend in better. But it really didn't matter at this point, he reflected as the thundering sound from nearby explosions rang in his eardrums. He glanced backward and spotted Abdul by the fence. Again he waved him away and pointed to the hill left of the complex. Without waiting for a response, Kevin reached the front door and opened it, looking in every direction before going inside, then closed it behind him.

A relatively narrow and barely illuminated hall extended along the entire length of the short building. Kevin quickly counted six doors, three on each side. He approached the first one and put an ear to it, but couldn't hear a thing over the commotion outside. He tried the knob: locked. He tried the next one across the hall: locked, too. *Damn!*

He continued to the third door. The knob turned. Kevin paused and took a deep breath, not sure how to play it. If anyone asked him a question, he would have to shoot. On the other hand, he could just jump in and start shooting. He exhaled and made up his mind.

He slowly pushed the door open and limped his way inside, left hand on his stomach, head down, right hand gripping the Kalashnikov.

He spotted two guards behind a table where— *Khalela!*

The guards looked in his direction and said something. Kevin moaned and pressed his stomach even harder. The guards stepped to the side and walked toward him. *Now!*

In one swift move, Kevin brought the weapon up and unloaded a dozen rounds. Both guards were propelled against the back wall by the impact.

Still clutching his AK-47, he raced to the side of the table. *Animals!* he thought as he saw Khalela's naked body.

Kevin held his breath once more as he put two fingers on her wrist and felt for a pulse. *She's alive!*

Controlling the overwhelming desire to just hold her tight, Kevin quickly set the Kalashnikov on the floor, unstrapped her and lifted her from the table, setting her gently next to his weapon. Another explosion rocked the compound.

Almost frantically, he stripped the limp body of the guard that was the closest to her height. The uniform was bloodstained, but it didn't matter. In fact it was better that way, he thought.

He guided her feet into the pants, pulled them up, and fastened the belt. He put the shirt on, buttoned it up, put the boots on, and grabbed a green cap that had fallen off a guard. He tucked her long, black hair under the cap and pressed it firmly down on her head. Snagging the AK-47 and strapping it across his back, Kevin pulled Khalela up and ran his left arm across her back. With his right hand, Kevin grabbed the Model 39 tucked in the small of his back.

He started moving toward the door when an officer appeared in the doorway clutching a pistol. Kevin recognized him as the same one who had left the building earlier.

The bearded officer, whose hair fell right to his eyeline, leveled the handgun at Kevin.

"See you in hell, you bastard!" Kevin snapped back as he trained the Model 39 on the Iraqi. Before either one could fire, two huge arms crashed against the officer's side, sending him flying across the room.

Abdul!

The officer kept his grip on the pistol and turned it on Abdul, who was already lunging at him.

The gun went off once, twice. Abdul reached the officer, yanked the weapon from his hand and embraced him in a bear hug.

"Aghh!"

The hairy officer arched back and screamed as Abdul tightened the powerful lock. The sickening noise of snapping bones preceded the officer going limp. Abdul released him and slowly walked back toward Kevin, who was still holding up Khalela.

As Abdul got closer, Kevin noticed two bullet wounds, both in the stomach. The large Kurd fell to his knees, opened his arms, and stared at the ceiling mumbling something Kevin could only guess was prayer.

Abdul then looked at him. "Pilot Dalton . . ." He collapsed.

Kevin laid Khalela gently against the wall, reached down, and felt Abdul's wide wrist for a pulse. There was none. Kevin closed his eyes in mourning, but quickly opened them as another blast shook the building. It seemed a lot closer than the others.

"Good-bye, my friend." He picked Khalela up with both arms, and raced outside.

* * *

General Abunnasr Manesh had leveled off at ten thousand feet and accelerated to 700 knots when all four targets disappeared from his screen.

"Fassan! What is going on? The targets disappeared again!"

"Don't know, sir— For the love of— Sir, check your screen again!"

"What in the world are you talking— Where did they come from?"

"Don't know, sir. Targets are just appearing and disappearing from my screen like ghosts."

"Range to new targets?"

"Two zero miles, heading one one six, five hundred knots."

Manesh threw the control stick to the left and applied full power. He eyed the radar screen and saw several targets. "Got them!"

Thirty miles east of the complex, the F-14s completed their chaff run and turned back toward Saudi Arabia.

One of the targets disappeared from Manesh's screen. He mumbled a few obscenities as he trained his craft on the remaining targets. They also disappeared less than a minute later as their speed decreased to a standstill and slowly faded off his display. His screen was blank once more.

▪ 14 ▪

THE PATHS OF GLORY

The paths of glory lead but to the grave.

—Thomas Gray

SALMAN ASAD AIR BASE, SAUDI ARABIA. NEAR IRAQI BORDER.
Day Four. 2100 Local Time.

The mood was that of victory as Robert Bourdeaux stood behind the video crew and quietly watched General Kenneth Draper put on his show. They stood roughly thirty feet from him, away from the limelight. General Draper had ordered the planes arranged in a semi-circle with their noses pointing to the center of the circle, where he stood on a podium wearing a freshly starched set of fatigues and a cap. Bourdeaux noticed that Draper had even gone to the extreme of placing the F-117A in the center, flanked by two Tomcats on each side to further promote the flavor of a true Air Force/Navy effort.

"Damn, Bob," Halston mumbled, "I don't think anyone at Hollywood could have staged this better."

"No shit. This guy should run for president. Man, I'd probably even vote for the bastard."

Both turned their heads toward the reporter interviewing Draper.

"At exactly what time did the bombing begin, General Draper?" asked the reporter.

Draper shifted his gaze to the camera. His face was set in stone as he related the entire mission. His voice was slow, his words measured. He praised the pilots who had participated in the mission and called Desert Star the best air mission he'd seen in years. When asked about the informal reports from some of the pilots that other sections of the complex had blown up from what appeared to be a ground attack, Draper graciously denied it and firmly stated that Desert Star was strictly a bombing mission.

"What about the missiles, sir? Was there any type of confirmation on their destruction?" asked the reporter.

"Have you ever seen the damage that a single two-thousand-pound Paveway II bomb can do? The place is still in flames, and it'll continue to burn for several days. Also remember that they're in the middle of the desert. The closest river is miles away. By the time the dust settles, I doubt we'll be able to tell a car from a building."

Halston turned to Bourdeaux. "I don't think that will be the case," he said.

"I know," responded Bourdeaux. He knew that, as in the West, Allahbad and other Iraqi processing centers were tied directly into main water lines. They usually had more available water pressure than that of a fire hydrant. In Bourdeaux's opinion, the fires would be out by sunrise. *Just in time for a KH-11 pass.* Bourdeaux checked his watch. "We'll know in six hours when our satellite makes its first daylight pass."

"Yep," confirmed Halston. "If our original assumption was correct about that big warehouse building, when the flames subside, we should be able to tell if there were any rockets in the place."

"Well," Bourdeaux said, "according to Colonel Kramer, one of his bombs hit dead center over the warehouse. I would expect to see a huge craterlike hole in its roof in those photographs tomorrow. I tell you, it would be interesting to see how Draper would react if those photos prove that his Desert Star mission did nothing but destroy a milk facto—"

"Excuse me, gentlemen."

Bourdeaux and Halston turned around and faced a slim, clean-cut, Hispanic-looking Navy pilot.

"Yes, Lieutenant?" Halston said, acknowledging the pilot's rank.

"Could I talk to you in private for a few minutes, Colonel? It won't take longer than that. Promise."

Halston looked at Bourdeaux. "Be right back, Bob."

"All right."

Halston walked several feet away from the crowd.

"Sir, my name's Chico Delgado from the *Ranger*. I'm a good friend of Lieutenant Kevin Dalton. We were crewed together up to the day he went down."

"Hmm . . . were you involved in Desert Star?"

"Yes, sir."

"Well, I'm sure General Draper shook your hand, but I want to congratulate you, Lieutenant. That was one heck of a job you all did last night."

"Thank you, sir. I appreciate the compliment." Delgado lowered his gaze.

Halston smiled. "There's something else on your mind, Lieutenant. I can tell. What is it?"

"It's about Lieutenant Dalton, sir."

"What do you want to know?"

"May I speak frankly, sir?"

Halston blinked twice and narrowed his eyes. "Ah, sure. I suppose so."

"Well, sir," Delgado started, looking both ways, "over at the *Ranger*, no one's sayin' much about what happened to Crackers . . . that's Lieutenant Dalton, sir. When I say no one, sir, I mean people like Commander John McDeere, my CO. A few other officers are acting the same way. It looks like they're hopin' the situation's just gonna fade away if no one brings it up, almost as if they're ashamed of the whole thing. But the fact of the matter's that most of the pilots are gettin' pretty pissed off about all the secrecy."

"That's fascinating, Lieutenant, but what's that got to do with me?"

"The rumor around the base's that you tried to rescue him twice. Any chance you can give me more details?"

"I'm not admitting that I have the information you're asking for, but let me ask you this. If I *did* have that information and gave it to you, what would you do with it?"

"I would like to share it with other concerned pilots and put their minds at ease. Tell them that the situation's being handled properly; that if anyone's gotta chance of findin' him it's you, sir."

Halston nodded. "Well, I guess it's only fair to you and the other pilots to know as much as we know about Dalton's whereabouts. Let's go for a short walk."

BAGHDAD.
Day Four. 2130 Local Time.

Quietly studying a wall map of Iraq inside his bunker, Saddam Hussein pointed to a village a few miles east of Allahbad. Three of his generals slowly nodded in understanding.

"Do it immediately, and take the bodies to Allahbad," Saddam said.

One of the generals, a thin, bearded fifty-year-old with grayish hair, began to say something, but stopped. Saddam raised an eyebrow.

"Yes, General Mojgani?"

The officer hesitated for another second before saying, "Great One . . . could we . . . could we spare the children?"

Saddam dropped his gaze to the hardwood floors of the rectangular room and sighed. He was surrounded by sentimental fools, by soft men without the nerve to do what was right for Iraq. The Allies had just attacked Allahbad, and all General Mojgani could think of were some stupid children? *Incredible!*

"General Mojgani?"

"Yes, Great One?"

Saddam unholstered his Makarov, leveled it at the startled general, and fired once in his face. The other two generals jumped out of the way as Mojgani's faceless body arched back, crashing against the dark wood-paneled wall.

In seconds, six of Saddam's personal bodyguards stormed the room, Kalashnikovs leveled at the two stunned generals standing next to Mojgani. The Iraqi leader motioned his bodyguards to leave the room and take the body with them.

Without another word, Saddam holstered the pistol and pointed his finger back at the village on the map. The two generals quickly nodded. Saddam then pointed to the door. The generals left immediately.

THE WHITE HOUSE.
Day Four. 1600 Local Time.

President Bill Clinton sat back in his leather chair and sighed in relief. Allahbad had been hit hard, and still Saddam had not retaliated with nukes. With a growing sense of confidence, the president read Draper's report once again and smiled. Everything seemed to have gone perfectly. It appeared as if the CIA had been correct in targeting Allahbad.

However, in front of Clinton sat a somber director of Central Intelligence, Craig Kettler, who did not want to concede that the mission had been a success until he had gotten KH-11 verification of the damage done to the site.

Clinton saw the director's point, but he also agreed with Draper's comments on the powerful bombs dropped dead on target. *No*, the president decided. *The mission had to be a success, after all, what could possibly survive such an attack?*

ALLAHBAD PROCESSING COMPLEX, SOUTH OF AN NAJAF, IRAQ.
Day Five. 0035 Local Time.

General Abunnasr Manesh reached the compound shortly after midnight. By that time most of the fire was already under control. He stormed into the compound's temporary command post, a tent in front of what was left of the complex's warehouse. In there he found a young guard sitting behind the controls of a radio. He snapped to attention.

"Who is in charge here, soldier?" he fumed.

"I am," said a young captain, getting up from a chair on the far side of the tent. "I'm temporarily in charge until help comes from—"

"Help has arrived, Captain. I'm General Manesh. I'm in charge of the defense of this sector of the country. I'm relieving you of your command immediately. From now on, you'll report all activities directly to me. Is that clear, Captain?"

"Yes, sir!"

"Now, do you mind telling me what in the world happened here?"

Ten minutes later, a furious Manesh walked outside the tent. His friend, Major Mohammed Hassoud, had been killed and nobody seemed to know how it had happened. All they knew was that Hassoud had been in the process of interrogating two prisoners. After the bombing raid, Hassoud was found on the floor with a broken back next to a huge man no one could identify. There were also two soldiers in the room, both shot dead. There had to be a logical explanation. Was there a relationship between Hassoud's death and the bombing? Or was it merely coincidence? Perhaps the prisoners used the bombing raid as a distraction and overpowered Hassoud and the two soldiers. But who was the large man? No one saw him come into the compound. Was he the one who broke Hassoud's back? There was also the issue of bullet holes in the wall, but none of the weapons in the room had been fired.

Manesh rubbed his eyes. So many questions, and no one in the complex seemed to know the answers. He raised his eyebrows. At least the underground facility was still safe, according to the young captain. Doctor Sakkar, the chief scientist, had reported no serious problems down there. The operation was proceeding as scheduled. There had been a minor blackout during the bomb raid, but electricity had been restored an hour later. There had been no casualties among the scientific community.

Manesh watched several soldiers unload the bodies of women and children from a truck. They had been massacred just a half hour ago in a nearby village by Iraqi troops under orders from Baghdad. Their purpose was to generate enough dead civilians to start a propaganda war against the Allies. Manesh shook his head. Sometimes his government acted quite irrationally. The bodies of the villagers—close to a hundred of them—were lined up on the left side of the warehouse under the mercury lights. In addition, the death toll from the bombing had reached almost fifty men, mostly soldiers, who Manesh noted had been stripped naked and dressed in civilian clothes for the cameras. A video crew was already on the way from Baghdad. *Insanity!*

Manesh walked toward the warehouse. The captain had said that during the bombing nobody had been able to spot the attacking craft. He walked past the warehouse and approached the fallen chain-link fence. More questions, he reflected. The fence had collapsed not from bombs but from plastic explosives. Was the attack a combined assault? Possible, he admitted, remembering the captain's story about the destroyed Kurdish caravan traveling in four-wheel-drive vehicles. In addition, there was the digital timer found a hundred feet from the fence. It was possible that some of the rebels had not perished during the caravan incident, or perhaps not all of them left in the vehicles. Some may have stayed behind. Was that connected with Hassoud's death? Was Hassoud interrogating Kurds? Perhaps, he conceded, but the bombing contradicted the story. *If it was before the rescue, I could understand that, but bombing during the rescue? Why risk it and kill your own people?* In order to get some answers, Manesh had sent troops in every direction to root out anyone that looked suspicious and also to look for tracks. Whoever did this could not be too far away, he decided while staring at the workers fixing the fence. At least the young captain had enough sense to prioritize the repairs. The electric fence had to be operational immediately. Without it, the large complex was too vulnerable.

He headed back to the command post. He wanted to give Saddam an update on the situation.

BAGHDAD.
Day Four. 0050 Local Time.

Saddam Hussein slowly hung up after listening to the update from General Manesh. Although Allahbad had been hit, the underground facility remained fully operational. In fact, in a few hours another missile should be deployed.

The attack had been unfortunate, but now he felt even more certain of the success of Allahbad. The chances of the Americans hitting the complex again were negligible. Actually, after the American media got ahold of the film footage of the dead civilians planted at the factory, American public pressure would keep Clinton from attacking the complex again.

Saddam smiled at his good fortune. Clinton was indeed making life easier for the Iraqi leader. By destroying the factory on the surface, the American president had actually made Allahbad a safer place for the development of Iraq's nuclear weapons program.

SOUTHERN IRAQ.
Day Five. 0100 Local Time.

In spite of the enormous pain in his wounded leg, Lieutenant Kevin Dalton walked for most of the night carrying Khalela in his arms. He would stop every fifteen minutes, and after carefully laying her down on the cold sand, he would sit down next to her, massage his leg and briefly close his eyes. Then he would get up, pick her up, and continue south, guided by the stars alone. His body ached badly. It seemed as if every time he inspected his body he found another cut or bruise. But something else had slowly happened to him. His body wounds no longer seemed to matter as much as they had two days before. None of them were fatal. He would recover.

The night was cold, quiet, almost peaceful, except for the noise from sporadic explosions. These had slowly faded away while he put as much distance between himself and the compound as his exhausted body would allow.

He kept Khalela's face close to his. Her steady breath against his cheek was the only source of pleasure that he could rely on to keep his legs moving. To keep the agonizing pain of his gunshot wound from stopping him. He couldn't afford to stop just yet. He had to continue. Had to get away from this place. And so he went, step after agonizing step, holding the woman he loved close to him. Once in a while, a light moan would escape her lips. She would shiver and brace herself like a child, only to slowly relax her body in response to his warm embrace and soft whispers in her ear.

"You're safe, Khalela. You're with me now. It's going to be all right," he repeated over and over again whenever her body shuddered.

Two hours before sunrise, drenched in sweat in spite of the desert's cool temperatures, Kevin got as far as he humanly could. He looked around, saw several large rocks to his left, and walked toward them. He selected a spot in the center, shielded in every direction, even from the sky, and sat next to Khalela under a ledge that protruded from the largest rock.

Kevin checked his plastic canteen: it was half full. He unscrewed the cap and took a small gulp, which he rolled around inside his mouth before swallowing. Then, leaning over, he put a hand behind Khalela's head and lifted it gently as he brought the lip of the canteen to her lips. He put a few drops on her lips and smiled. They parted, welcoming the refreshing liquid. He let her have a few more drops, and she slowly ran the tip of her tongue in between her lips.

Kevin put a few drops of water on his hands and softly stroked her forehead and cheeks. She moved her head from side to side and inhaled deeply. He brought the canteen to her lips once more. This time she took a small sip, paused, and took a second sip.

Satisfied, Kevin screwed the cap back on the canteen and replaced it on his belt.

He carefully moved her to the side and put an arm around her back, letting her rest her head on his shoulder before he fell asleep.

SALMAN ASAD AIR BASE, SAUDI ARABIA. NEAR IRAQI BORDER.
Day Five. 0545 Local Time.

Lieutenant Chico Delgado leaned back against the nose
wheel of his Tomcat and stared at an orange sun slowly
looming over the dusky horizon. He checked his watch.
It was barely six in the morning.

"Howdy, Chico. What're you doin' up so early?
Couldn't sleep?"

Delgado turned around and faced a smiling Lieutenant Colonel Richard Kramer. "Hey, Longhorn. Got up
an hour ago and couldn't go back to sleep."

"Couldn't sleep from all th' excitement of the mission?"

Delgado waved his right hand. "No, no, it's nothin'
like that, man. Last night was a piece of cake."

"Oh, so it's somethin' else, then?"

"Yep. Guess you can say that." He sighed.

"Feel like talkin' about it?"

"It's a long story. You don't wanna—"

"Heck, there ain't much else to do 'round here anyway." He sat next to Delgado. "So tell me. What's
botherin' ya?"

Delgado ran a hand through his hair and shook his
head. "It's a buddy of mine . . . my frontseater, Lieutenant Kevin Dalton."

"Oh, is that th' poor son'a bitch that got shot down a
few days back?"

"Yep. You heard what happened?"

"Just that he went after some MiG when he wasn't
supposed to and now he's in a shitload of trouble."

Delgado laughed. "That just about wraps it up. He's in
a shitload of trouble all right."

"So, where's he now?"

"No one knows where he is. He was last seen next to a
river a few hundred miles from here. Close to the area
was dispensin' chaff over last night."

"You mean he's still out there?"

"Either that or he got captured."

"C'mon! With all 'em fancy choppers we got, couldn't

we use a couple of 'em to go and search for the poor bastard?"

"Colonel Halston tried twice, but they ran into some bad luck. Two Pave Hawks got shot down."

"Well, shit! Try again! What's th' matter with these people?"

"*Mierda!* That's what I say, man, but truth of the matter's that none of those *pendejos* seems to be givin' a shit 'bout him."

"I just can't fuckin' believe that. Why didn't Halston send a third party after this guy?"

"He wanted to, man, but that *hijo de puta* Draper gave him so much shit about the first two failed attempts that Halston canned the idea until he made contact."

"You're shittin' me."

"No, man. Honest-to-God truth. Draper threatened to elevate the issue on any more rescue attempts. The *pendejo* Draper didn't use those exact words, but that was the message he conveyed to Halston."

"Well, that guy ain't gonna last out there. For all we know he's already a POW, or he's . . . ah, shit, sorry, Chico. Didn't mean to . . ."

"Don't worry about it, man. I understand." Delgado glanced at the horizon once more. The sun was almost fully up. He frowned. Part of him, the logical side, told him that Kramer was right. There was a good chance Kevin had died from exposure if the Iraqis had not gotten to him first. His emotional side, however, refused to listen to logic and desperately struggled to hang on to the hope that Kevin, by some miraculous circumstance, had managed to survive and escape capture.

"You okay, partner?"

"Man, I hope those *pendejos* make up their minds quick." Delgado rubbed his hands together. Temperatures were in the fifties. He ran his hands over his exposed forearms.

"So do I, pal, I hate to . . . Say, what in the hell is that on your arm?"

Delgado looked at Kramer, who pointed to his forearm.

"Oh, that's a tattoo of a bulldog's head."

"Shit, I can see that. Why a bulldog?"

Delgado smiled.

SOUTHERN IRAQ.
Day Five. 0900 Local Time.

For Kevin Dalton, the MiG-29's cannons blasted so
close to him that he jumped in his sleep. Then Khalela's
voice made all the pain go away.

"Kevin? Wake up, Kevin, you're shaking. Kevin? Are
you all right?"

The sun's piercing beams stung his eyes as he slowly
opened them. The light . . . it was too bright.

"Kevin, it's me, Khalela. Are you all right?"

The words again. Softly spoken by her. Slowly, Kevin
opened his eyes and saw the dark silhouette of her face.
She momentarily blocked the sun.

"Khalela . . . Khalela! You're awake!" He bolted up
too fast and got dizzy.

"Lie back. If you did what I think you did last night,
you had better go extremely easy on that leg."

Kevin looked down and saw the bloodstained sand
around his leg.

"You bled a lot last night. You could have died during
the night," she said.

Kevin noticed she had torn off the left leg off his Iraqi
uniform and used the cloth as bandage.

"You always come in handy," he said with a grin.

"Well, you almost killed yourself last night."

"I had to . . . wanted to do it."

She stared him in the eye. "Kevin, all I remember was
the—"

"I know. I saw it."

"You mean you actually saw me strapped to—"

"Yes."

"What happened?"

"I'll tell you everything, but before I start I need
something to drink."

She picked up the canteen, unscrewed the cap, and
brought it to his lips. He smiled.

"What's so funny?"

He didn't answer and took a few sips. Then he cleared his throat and began to speak, his voice calm and serene. He told her everything from the moment he saw her being taken away to the moment he laid her down next to him and fell asleep. Her intelligent eyes never left his. The more he talked, the deeper her stare became. When he finished, she turned away.

"You dumb American!"

Kevin was shocked. "What? What are you—"

"Why did you do it? Don't you know there can never be anything between us?"

Kevin was taken aback by her words—so direct, so cold, so straight to his very soul. "Why do you say that? I did what I did because I happen to care a great deal about you and because somehow I know deep inside that you also care about me. Because I know you would have done the same for me. Now, you tell me what's so bad about that!"

"What is so bad is that you are right. I do care about you, even though it kills me to say it!" For the first time Kevin saw tears rolling down her face. She quickly turned away.

He got up and slowly limped toward her, hugging her from behind. Kevin put his lips to her ear. "Why? What's the big deal? You're a person, too. You have a right to have feelings like anyone else, and right now those feelings are for me. I know that. It shows in your voice, in your smile, in the way you look at me—"

"Stop it, Kevin! You do not understand!" She tried to pull away, but he held her even tighter.

"No. I'm not letting you go. You're stuck with me whether you like it or not. I love you, and there's nothing you or anyone else can do about that. We may never get out of this, so I want you to know how I feel. Those are my feelings. *My feelings.* Do you understand that? And they tell me—" Suddenly Kevin realized she wasn't fighting him anymore. She leaned her head against his shoulder and placed her arms over his.

Slowly, Kevin turned Khalela around and placed both hands on her face, mesmerized at her natural beauty. He gazed into those light green eyes and lost himself in them. She closed them as his lips gently met hers.

▪ 15 ▪

MISSILES

Risha Hassan approached Dr. Radsul Sakkar with her latest collection of completed progress reports. Three additional missiles had been deployed. Sakkar was pleased. The operation was going smoothly in spite of yesterday's attack. It was imperative that the remaining missiles be deployed at once. Sakkar felt certain that a fully functional Allahbad would have a dramatic effect in the course of Iraq's history. *The enemy will definitely think twice about continuing their savage bombing if Iraq proves to the world that it has the means to launch a devastating nuclear strike.*

Sakkar nodded approvingly as he flipped through the pages. Most of the stations had reached phase four of the six required before deploying a missile. He signed each page and gave the stack back to Risha, who smiled and walked away.

He headed for the cafeteria on the other side of the assembly line, where breakfast was served starting at seven sharp. His stomach growled at the thought of tea and fresh fruit. He had not eaten a thing since lunch the day before.

Colonel Peter Halston left the monotone humming of the air-conditioning unit inside the undersecretary of Middle-Eastern Affairs' tent. It had been the only sound in the room after Halston, during the course of a discussion on the bombing mission, had casually mentioned his plan to send a new search party after Lieutenant Dalton to Kenneth Draper. The Air Force general had mumbled a few incoherent words and turned around.

Halston squinted as he stepped away from the tent into the bright morning sun, frowning at Draper's attitude. The general had pretty much told him to do as he pleased, but warned him that if more people were lost in the process, their blood would be on Halston's hands. *In the process?* Halston thought, trying his best not to get too upset. Draper would be out of his hair soon.

He reached for his sunglasses and quickly put them on as he walked toward the communications tent.

"Pete!"

Halston turned around and saw Robert Bourdeaux running toward him with a large envelope.

"Yeah, Bob? What is it?"

"Just got new satellite photos from NPIC."

"And?"

"You want to be sitting down when you see this. I'm still trying to figure out how to explain it."

Both men walked inside the communications tent and headed for the table in the rear. Bourdeaux sat on one side, opened the envelope, and searched for a photograph. Halston was seated across him.

"C'mon, I was just looking at it." His index and middle fingers went through the inch-thick stack of eleven-by-fourteen shots. "Oh, here it is." Bourdeaux pulled a photo from the bottom of the stack.

"All right, this is Allahbad as of six o'clock in the afternoon yesterday. Notice all the activity and the trucks entering and leaving the complex. Also, most of the trucks drove straight into the warehouse."

"All right. I take it these are the trucks and the large warehouse you're talking about, right?" He pointed at small dark rectangular objects in what appeared to be a road of some sort that ended in a large black rectangle in the center of the complex.

"Exactly. Now, notice that there is no other way to access that warehouse but from the front. There are buildings on each side and the processing plant in back."

"Got it. So?"

"Well, the next set of photos are still from roughly the same time frame. I have twenty of the shots taken in a thirty-minute lapse. In them I counted a total of fifteen large trucks going into the warehouse and driving out. That's fifteen in thirty minutes. Quite a few, if you ask me."

"What are you getting at?"

"Bear with me. I'm almost there. A couple of hours later, our boy goes in and boom! Blows the place to pieces. Then morning comes, our KH-11 goes snap, snap, snap, and *voila!* Guess what we get?"

Halston exhaled impatiently as the CIA analyst pulled another photo from the stack and set it in front of the colonel. Over seventy percent of the warehouse was now exposed, revealing—

"Nothing! The warehouse's empty!"

"Yep."

"Where are the rockets? What about the cargo that those trucks had been constantly delivering to the warehouse?"

Bourdeaux nodded at Halston's reaction as he himself searched for a reasonable answer. *What if they were using the trucks to circulate cargo? Maybe they brought in raw material of some sort and drove out with assembled products.* Bourdeaux quickly discarded that as a possibility, realizing no one could be that efficient. It was impossible for him to believe that the trucks came and went without leaving something in that warehouse. Warehouses exist to store inventory. Besides, he remembered the people at NPIC informing him about how they had tracked the route taken by the trucks. They all had returned to the coast, where they loaded back up with boxes. *So, where did the cargo go?*

Bourdeaux opened his eyes and noticed a grin on Halston's unshaven face. "Pete?"

Halston grinned broadly. "All right, Bob. I think I know where all the hardware is."

Bourdeaux snagged the bottle of Tylenol and swallowed two caplets without any water. "Why do I feel that you're about to tell me something that's going to upset me?"

"I think that we're just scratching the surface here, and I literally mean scratching the surface. I think that warehouse's just a place to secretly unload trucks."

"Yes, and . . . ?"

"I think that after unloading, their shipments are taken . . . underground."

Bourdeaux raised an eyebrow. "Either that, or . . ."

Halston nodded. "Or we bombed the wrong target."

Bourdeaux inhaled deeply, closed his eyes, and rubbed the tips of his fingers against his forehead.

Suddenly, Bourdeaux opened his eyes. "Shit! I got it!"

Halston looked at him quizzically. "Huh?"

"If you're right, Pete, and the Iraqis have gone underground with their project, then we should be able to tell based on the level of activity and the materials hauled to the site during its construction."

Halston regarded him for a few seconds before saying, "But, Bob, Allahbad is several years old."

Bourdeaux smiled. "Ol' buddy, the NPIC keeps archives of everything collected by those KH-11s. All images are stored in disk or backed up to magnetic tapes. They have records going back to the early sixties." He began to walk toward the communications tent.

"Where are you going?" asked Halston.

"To make a call. I'm gonna get the satellite records for the period when Allahbad was built, and also when the other milk factory near Baghdad was built. That will give us a reference. If indeed there's something below the sand, we should be able to tell."

THE WHITE HOUSE.
Day Five. 0930 Local Time.

"So, where are the missiles?" asked President Bill Clinton as he stared at the KH-11 photos spread on top of his desk.

CIA Director Craig Kettler slowly shook his head. "We don't know, Mr. President. The warehouse appears to be empty."

Studying the director through half-shut analytical eyes, the president suddenly felt cold. The implications of missing the missiles were quite complex. Several possible scenarios unraveled in his mind. One was the possibility of Allahbad being nothing but an elaborate diversion by Saddam to keep Clinton looking in the wrong place. This meant that the Iraqi leader had succeeding in fooling everyone, and that the actual nuclear development was being held elsewhere. *But what about the CIA data?* The director had given him a brief from Bourdeaux, summarizing how the cargo of numerous trucks had been unloaded inside the warehouse and probably taken to an underground facility.

He checked his watch and waited for Draper's call. President Clinton never made a decision without first listening to all his advisors.

SOUTHERN IRAQ.
Day Five. 1730 Local Time.

Kevin Dalton and Khalela Yishaid walked silently side by side under an overcast sky. He had wanted to wait until nightfall before advancing, but after listening to what she had discovered at the complex, Kevin decided that they had to reach the border immediately to warn his people of the terrible miscalculation made when bombing the Allahbad facility.

Kevin frowned as his mind slowly accepted the facts. He now believed that the bombs had little chance of destroying the facility. According to Khalela, the Iraqi laboratory was too deep. She had also mentioned a service elevator. . . . Kevin's lips curved upward. *Elevators . . . perhaps there is a way.* According to what Ishmael had related to Khalela before the Iraqis captured them, the elevators stopped working the moment the alarm went off and the shaft was automatically blocked, thus isolating the lab from the outside world. Kevin decided that there had to be some control mechanism that rolled some sort of steel plate across the shaft. *How thick can that plate be?* he asked himself, realizing that even if it was a few feet thick, it would definitely be easier to penetrate than trying to blast through dozens of feet of concrete. *A few well-placed bombs, and bingo—we could reach the bottom. . . .* Kevin stopped walking.

"What is it?" she asked as they reached the first few trees. The Euphrates was only a mile or so away.

"I think I heard something behind—"

"Qatala!"

Kevin spun around and was welcomed by the stinging pain of a stone striking him on the shoulder. "Aghh!" He fell to his knees.

There were several Iraqi women behind them with rocks in their hands staring at him defiantly. Kevin grabbed the Smith & Wesson Model 39, held it up in the air and slowly laid it on the ground.

"Khalela, tell them we're the good guys."

"No use. All they see is the uniforms."

"Dammit, try!"

Khalela spoke a few words in an apologetic tone, but the response from the women was unanimous.

"Qatala!"

"What in the hell does that mean?"

"To kill."

Kevin got to his feet and walked in their direction.

"Kevin wait! Don't do—"

"American! I'm an American! Friend! Khalela, translate!" Kevin continued walking toward them as Khalela spoke. The women took a few steps back.

Suddenly a woman threw a rock at him. He ducked in

time. Another rock. "Aghh, shit!" Once more he fell to his knees. His right thigh was burning. Khalela ran to him.

"No, Khalela! Stay back!"

Once more he managed to get up to his feet and put his body in between the women and Khalela as a rock hit him on the forehead. Disoriented, he fell with his hands on his face.

Khalela grabbed the Model 39, flipped the safety, and pointed it at the woman.

"Don't shoot them, Khalela!" he screamed as blood covered most of his face.

The women stepped back and just stared at them. Kevin sat up and crawled back toward Khalela. "If they . . . think we're the . . . bad guys it can only mean . . . they're villagers, probably Kurdish . . . sympathizers. We can't . . . can't shoot them." Pain hammered his head. He began to feel light-headed and everything began to spin slowly.

One of the women took a step forward. Khalela leveled the automatic at her. The woman raised her hand. She clutched a stone. Khalela tightened her index finger on the trigger.

"No!" A voice came from behind the group of women. Kevin spotted the shape of a young girl running in their direction. *"Sadiq, sadiq!"*

Kevin saw through blood and tears the face of the raped girl they had rescued back at the village. She leaned down, embraced him, and started to cry.

Khalela lowered the Model 39. The women dropped their stones. Kevin's vision grew cloudier until he blacked out.

SALMAN ASAD AIR BASE, SAUDI ARABIA. NEAR IRAQI BORDER.
Day Five. 1740 Local Time.

"What is this about an underground lab? Are you serious?" Draper asked in a soft tone, a hint of concern in his voice.

Bourdeaux didn't answer right away; he wanted to be

in full control of himself. Then he cleared his throat and began explaining to the undersecretary that all the information collected to date tended to support that theory. There was no other plausible explanation than that the weapons were underground. Otherwise, where else could the cargo on those trucks be going? In addition, Bourdeaux told him about how Halston had checked with the base's explosives experts. They believed there should have been a lot of burned, twisted hardware in that place. But, as Bourdeaux indicated with his finger, the photographs showed an empty warehouse. Before Draper had a chance to say anything, Bourdeaux continued and pointed out that adjacent buildings had been leveled during the bombing. Their exposed interiors revealed nothing of significance. In summary, all Desert Star had accomplished was the destruction of an empty warehouse and a milk factory. Bourdeaux closed with a mention of his current project with the NPIC, pulling archives of the region to compare the construction of Allahbad with that of a dairy products plant near Baghdad.

Draper remained silent for several moments. Bourdeaux placed all the photographs back inside a plastic bag.

"I'll discuss this with the president shortly."

"I've already sent my analysis to the CIA. I believe the director is briefing the president as we speak."

"Well, the president's entitled to hear the opinion of everyone involved. The way I see it, you approached this administration with what was in my opinion a weak theory about Iraqis building long-range missiles in that factory. You only had circumstantial proof, nothing concrete. Not even one photograph of an actual missile. But the president and everyone down the line believed your story enough to send an F-117A to blow the place apart. Now here we are. We followed your hunch and destroyed Allahbad, and now what? No missiles? All we've got is a destroyed milk factory. You know what that means, right? The only weapon at Allahbad is a missile loaded with propaganda warfare. I'm certain that in another day or so the first photos of the destroyed Allahbad will make their way to Western papers, and if the Iraqi government does at Allahbad what it has done at other destroyed targets, civilian casualties will be high. Now, for proven military targets that's acceptable, but for a milk factory? Do you realize what kind of embarrassment that would be for the Clinton administration? Not counting the fact that we have now telegraphed our intentions to Saddam. If he is assembling nukes elsewhere, he will definitely be on full alert now."

Bourdeaux was fuming. The Silver Rat was doing what he did best: turning the tables. Tactically switching sides at the first sign of trouble. He was about to respond when Draper raised his right hand, palm facing Bourdeaux.

"Enough, Bob."

Relax, Bob. Breathe. In. Out. In. Out. Don't let the fucker get to you. Draper had played him like a grand piano. He knew the old man would go to the president and remind him how much against an air strike Draper had been from the start—particularly if the Iraqis made a big deal out of the incident. *Why? Why must this happen to me? This is exactly the kind of shit I tried to prevent from happening. Damn that bastard! Relax. Relax. Keep your cool. Don't blow it. There's a way out of this.*

Draper checked his watch. "Now, if you don't mind I would like discuss this matter with the president."

Without another word, Bourdeaux turned around and walked outside. The tarmac was still warm, even an hour after dark. He reached the communications tent.

Halston approached Bourdeaux. "Well, how did it go in there?"

Bourdeaux sighed.

THE WHITE HOUSE.
Day Five. 1000 Local Time.

The president hung up the phone. Draper's position was radically different from that of the CIA. The undersecretary firmly believed the United States had made a serious mistake in bombing Allahbad, soon to be made public by

Saddam Hussein. In addition, Draper encouraged the president to direct the CIA to continue looking for a suspicious complex, because somewhere out there Saddam Hussein was probably assembling his nukes. Draper also conveyed his fear that an Iraqi nuclear retaliation for the destruction of Allahbad was very possible.

The president shook his head at the difference of opinion. While waiting for Draper's call, the president had a short phone conversation with his secretary of state, who had told him that the Iraqi delegation had walked out of the talks when they got word of the attack. Tariq Aziz had warned the secretary of state that the United States had drawn first blood, and that Iraq was in a position to respond in kind. The secretary told Clinton it was wise not to act immediately, as suggested by the CIA, until the agency had more pieces of the puzzle. He also warned the president to get ready for a strong Iraqi propaganda war. The secretary felt that Saddam Hussein would waste no time in using the destroyed complex to his full advantage.

Clinton compressed his lips into a tight frown. Did the United States bomb the wrong target? Or was Allahbad an underground facility? Was Saddam going to retaliate? When? How? Where would he attack first? Tel Aviv? Riyadh? Kuwait City? Should America strike Allahbad again? Perhaps they should carpet bomb the entire zone outlined in Bourdeaux's map? Or was the map itself a fake? What if Draper was correct in his guess that the Kurds were double agents? Then again, what if Bourdeaux was the one with the right facts? What if the missiles were there all along, hidden beneath the surface of the desert? What if the historical data Bourdeaux and the NPIC were pulling from archives of the region showed that Allahbad was indeed an underground facility? Then again, what if the data showed just the opposite?

Possibilities. There were all sorts of possibilities. And while everyone in his administration played out the different scenarios, presented their points of view, collected more information, and claimed to have the right answers, the president knew that somewhere out there Saddam Hussein was about to become the leader of the world's newest nuclear power. And so far the Clinton administration had not done a damned thing to stop him.

SOUTHERN IRAQ.
Day Five. 1900 Local Time.

Kevin woke with a pounding headache. He briefly scanned the murky room before closing his eyes again. A single candle burned next to the bed. He massaged his right temple with the tips of his fingers and felt the bandage on his forehead. He lifted his head and saw a new bandage over his leg wound. He wore only his underpants. His knees were skinned again, and the pain from the bruises on his back would not go away. He sighed. His body was in bad shape.

He tried to remember the last thing he had seen before that stone had knocked him out. He closed his eyes and visualized the face of the young Iraqi girl approaching him after he had fallen. Then he remembered Khalela lowering the automatic before he blacked out.

He moved his legs to the edge of the bed and managed to sit up. The bruises on his shoulder and leg were not as bad as he first thought. He ran his fingers over them. There was something on them—some sort of clear cream. *Perhaps some Kurdish miracle medicine?* Suddenly, his vision tunneled and he became dizzy. Quickly he lay back down on the bed, realizing that he had probably lost a great deal of blood between the leg and the head wound.

He shifted his gaze to the dark side of the room, where he guessed the door was. Someone had just come in.

In the flickering candlelight, Kevin watched Khalela slowly approach him. Her face glowed in the yellowish light. Her eyes were fixed on his.

"Khalela, how long have I—"

She brought a finger to her lips as she stopped by the end of the bed.

Kevin slowly moved to the side to let her sit down on the edge of the narrow bed, but instead she just stood there staring at him. Kevin reached down for the blanket to cover himself.

"No, Kevin."

He stopped and looked back at her. She was unbuttoning the shirt of her blood-stained Iraqi uniform with a look of careful thought on her face. She let the shirt fall by the side of the bed. Next were the pants, falling to her ankles.

Kevin was taken aback by her beauty. The enchantingly soft curves of her body moved in his direction. Slowly, carefully, she lay next to him. Her body was inches from his. She put a leg over him and pulled him closer. Kevin felt her against him and was overwhelmed by her warmth. Close, very close. Her body against his. Her lips meeting his. Softly at first, a mere brush, then with growing intensity as they explored one another.

For minutes they moved in unison. The sound of their own passion was the only reality inside the room. Kevin let it all go, pushing all logical thoughts aside as Khalela's slender frame shivered under him. Nothing mattered any longer for Kevin Dalton. Nothing. The MiGs, the gunshot wound, the missiles, the burning Pave Hawks, McDeere, Campbell, Lancaster. Khalela seemed to drain all of it away, drawing him closer, holding him tight. Her hands caressed his back. Softly rubbing fingers circled around bruises Kevin had received what now seemed like a lifetime ago. Kevin struggled to absorb it all. He wanted to remember every detail: the flickering candlelight, her tender lips, her firm, yet soft body. All in so much contrast with the nightmare that had been his life since he'd pulled the ejection handles, yet all so very real. He was here, now, today. The woman he loved, only a stranger yesterday, melting her body with his in a rapture he prayed would never end. He wished he could freeze time, remain like this forever, live in an imaginary world lit by the yellowish glow of that candle, but he felt the end coming. Kevin had not been with a woman in months and was not able to control his body, quietly shuddering as he reached climax. Khalela felt him and hugged him.

They lay there in silence for a long time. Her head rested against his shoulder as her fingers played with the hairs on his chest.

"Kevin?"

"Yes?"

"Nobody has ever saved my life before, except once when I was very young."

"Well, let's call it even, then."

"No, you do not understand. It was not my idea to save you from those choppers. It was Ishmael and Abdul who asked me to help you. They were planning to take you back to their CIA contact and trade you for weapons."

"Ishmael and Abdul," he mumbled. "I'm going to miss those two."

"Pay attention," she snapped, and she gently pulled on his chest hairs.

"Ouch! All right, all right. You have my undivided attention."

"Like I was telling you, I did not volunteer to—"

"I know that, Khalela, and you shouldn't feel bad about it. You didn't know who I was."

"But wait, there is more. At first I even questioned Ishmael if it was a good idea to take you with us. I was opposed at—"

Kevin rolled on his side and looked down into her eyes. "Don't you know that I love you? It doesn't matter what happened before. I was a stranger to you, and you to me. What I did back at the complex was because I loved you and couldn't bear the thought of you dying. I had to save you or die trying. Do you understand now?"

She nodded. Kevin saw a smile. It was followed by a few seconds of silence.

"Khalela?"

"Yes?"

"You do know I have to go back and warn my people about—"

"Why? From what you have told me, you do not want to go back. Come with me to Israel. No one will bother you there."

"I can't do that . . . not just yet anyway. Look, I'm sure the information that we have is worth something to the CIA."

"Why take the chance when you could just as easily come with me?"

"Because it's not right. I have to face the consequences of what I did. I can't run away from it forever. I chased that MiG after being told to knock-it-off. I did it because I felt in my heart it was the right thing to do. Now, again, I must follow my heart. I must go back."

She nodded as a single tear rolled down her cheek. He brushed it away with his lips. Khalela pulled him closer.

"I love you, Kevin Dalton."

Again, their bodies became one, but with familiarity now. Once more, Kevin fell away from the chaos that was his life. Her smell, her touch, her eyes—he knew it would all stay with him forever as her warm body moved with a hungry intensity. Kevin felt in control now. He stared at her. She closed her eyes and tilted her head as a soft moan escaped her lips. Slowly, he continued to build her up to a climax until he felt her quiver from an uninhibited joy that suddenly engulfed him, too. It could have been minutes or hours. Time was in suspension. Her body eventually relaxed. He eased himself alongside her body. She closed her eyes and her breathing steadied. Kevin, too, slept.

Time passed. Kevin heard her speak. Puzzled, he opened his eyes and looked at her. Shivering, Khalela had tensed in her sleep.

"Oh . . . please, don't . . . Suleima . . . oh, God."

Kevin rubbed a hand against his five-day stubble. *Suleima?*

She continued to quiver.

"Khalela, wake up. Wake up. You're dreaming."

Khalela opened her eyes and inhaled deeply. In the dark, her eyes found his and, placing her head on his shoulder, she quietly wept.

Kevin was taken aback. *What is this? Who is Suleima?* Respecting her privacy, Kevin simply rubbed a hand over her hair, shoulders, and back as Khalela continued crying for another minute. Slowly, she pulled away and sat up, rubbing her wet eyes and staring at him once again. Her long hair fell over her shoulders, grazing her breasts.

My God, you are gorgeous, Khalela.

"Feel like talking about it?" he asked. She closed her eyes and nodded.

Kevin pulled her back down. She turned her body sideways, placed a leg over his, and rested her head on his shoulder. Her hands curled up in front of her face, fingers toying with the hairs of his chest.

As he stared at the wooden ceiling, Khalela began to speak. Her voice seemed distant, monotone, cold. He learned about Suleima, her late sister. Kevin closed his eyes and listened. Listened to her pain, her sin. Understood the memory Khalela had carried with her from that horrid day long ago. Understood the fire that drove her: the fire of retribution, of guilt, of anger. Slowly, her voice dropped to a whisper, then her words became sporadic, until finally Kevin felt her breathing steadying.

He lifted his head and noticed her closed eyes. She had fallen asleep. He did the same.

SALMAN ASAD AIR BASE, SAUDI ARABIA. NEAR IRAQI BORDER.
Day Five. 2200 Local Time.

Once again, Robert Bourdeaux sat across from Colonel Peter Halston in the deserted mess tent. He rubbed his forehead and stared into his friend's bloodshot eyes. Bourdeaux was mad at himself. He felt there was something he should be able to do, but what? Draper had him pinned down. All Bourdeaux could do was continue collecting and analyzing data until he got a response from the White House. The NPIC was making some progress pulling out all the tapes from the satellite image archives, but that was just the first step of a long, tedious task. Operators still had to load the images into the computers, pan to the areas of interest, zoom in, and electronically clean them up before they could be of any use to Bourdeaux. Image enhancing was a science in itself. Computer operators trained specifically for this task would adjust the amount of contrast between the objects of relevance and their backgrounds, sharpen all images out of focus, eliminate glare from reflections of the sun, enhance shadowed objects, and sometimes even combine pictures taken in the infrared and visual spectrums to enhance certain patterns. This was an enormous task, even for the army of people assigned by the director of the CIA under presidential order to work on this. According to his contact at the NPIC, the first set of shots would be ready for the analysts in the morning.

At least there had not been any nuclear attacks yet, which could either mean that Saddam had not yet assembled his nukes, or maybe he just wanted the Americans to sweat it out for a while longer.

Frowning, Bourdeaux shifted his gaze to the entrance and spotted Delgado and Kramer. Amanda Green and Orlando Delaney, the Apache helicopter pilot, were also with them. All four looked in his direction. He waved them over.

Halston and Bourdeaux went through a few introductions.

"Don't think I've met you, Colonel," said Kramer, extending his hand toward Halston. "Name's Richard Kramer, but call me Longhorn."

Bourdeaux couldn't help but smile.

"Pete Halston . . . Longhorn," he responded, getting up and shaking Kramer's hand.

"Pleasure to meet ya, Pete."

"Bob, this is Lieutenant Delgado," Halston said.

"Yeah, I remember you from yesterday evening," Bourdeaux said, pumping Delgado's hand.

"Nice to meet you, sir."

"And I take it you two have already met Captain Green?"

"Hell, we're all good buddies. Right, sweetie?" said Kramer.

Amanda looked at Halston, shook her head, and closed her eyes.

"And I believe all of you know Captain Delaney?" asked Halston. Kramer, Delgado, and Bourdeaux shook his hand.

Amanda sat next to Halston. Delgado, Kramer, and Delaney sat across the table on Bourdeaux's side.

"Sir," Delgado started, "has the decision been made to continue with a search?"

"It was left at my discretion, Lieutenant," responded Halston. "Right now, I'm leaning toward continuing."

"In that case, sir, I would like to be granted permission to stay here for a few days and help out."

"You're not under my command, Lieutenant. You'll have to get authorization from your CO. That's Commander McDeere, isn't it?"

"Yes, sir. But I can tell you right now he's not gonna go for it. Not only is his position clear on this issue, but he needs a RIO to fly the jet back to the *Ranger.*"

"In that case, there's not much I can do."

"Sir?" Delgado asked with a slight grin.

"Yes, Lieutenant?"

"You wouldn't authorize a sick pilot to leave base if the flight surgeon grounded him, right?"

"That's right, Lieutenant, I—You want to stay that bad?"

"Nothin' else matters right now, except findin' Kevin Dalton, sir. I owe him that much. He saved my life over the Gulf the day before he was bagged. We had two missiles fired at us. He shook them off and knocked down the enemy jet, sir. If he's still alive, we gotta find him and pull him out."

Bourdeaux looked at Halston, who raised his eyebrows and nodded slightly.

"All right," Halston said. "We'll start at the last place we spotted him: the village where we lost the second Pave Hawk."

"Sounds good," said Delaney.

"Very well," said Halston. "But before anybody leaves I want you, Bob, to get me some overhead shots of the area. I want to make sure there isn't going to be a welcoming committee this time around."

"All right," said Bourdeaux.

"Are we all in agreement, then?" asked Halston.

"Yes, sir," responded Amanda as Kramer, Delgado, and Delaney nodded.

"Say, Delgado?" asked Halston.

"Yes, sir?"

"How do you plan to get the flight surgeon on your side? You look healthy to me."

Delgado smiled. "It ain't me that's gonna be sick, sir."

"Oh?"

"It's my CO, sir. Commander McDeere's about to get a severe case of the shits. I'll have to stay, of course, since no one can fly that F-14 back to the *Ranger* except him. Guess I'll stick around till he's better, like a loyal junior officer." Delgado unzipped a pocket in his flight suit and pulled out a clear plastic bag. It was filled with a white powder.

▪ 16 ▪

THE LAWS OF CSAR

Laws are silent in time of war.
—Cicero

SOUTHERN IRAQ.
Day Six. 0700 Local Time.

Wearing a sweat-soaked light brown shirt and pants the villagers had given her in place of the Iraqi uniform, Khalela Yishaid reached a spot halfway up the hill an hour after sunrise. Her wary eyes scanned the uneven, rocky terrain before moving forward one last time. She spotted the small village at the foot of the hill. Arid plains extended as far as Khalela could see, lazily fading away to the horizon in the hazy early morning sky.

She held Kevin's emergency radio in her right hand. He had told her that its range was probably thirty to forty miles on level ground, but could go as far as two hundred miles from a high point. She inspected the black, handheld set and pulled out the antenna. She felt a weight in her right pocket—the backup batteries Kevin had taken from his dead RIO.

Kevin had also explained to her the day before that there were two modes of operation. In the first mode, the small radio transmitted an emergency beacon in Guard, a frequency constantly scanned by American forces—

and also by the Iraqis. In the second mode, the unit behaved like a regular two-way radio. She selected the latter and brought the unit to her lips.

"Any Allied unit. Wolfpack Two One Four Alpha," Khalela said, using the call sign that Kevin had mentioned the day before.

No response.

"Any Allied unit, this is Wolfpack Two One Four Alpha."

She tried a few more times but got no response. If her calculations were accurate, the Saudi Arabian border was around 150 miles away. She switched the radio off and decided to wait until she reached the top before trying again. She shifted her gaze upward toward the summit and estimated it would take her another hour to reach it. She wiped the glistening sweat off her forehead; temperatures had already reached the eighties.

As she kept climbing, Kevin's face grew in her mind's eye. Last night had been special. The smell of him remained with her, fooling her senses into believing she was still lying next to him in the narrow but cozy bed where they had spent the earlier portion of the night silently loving one another. Even after they had fallen asleep, his arms kept hugging her from behind as they lay on their sides. Then the nightmare had returned and she had seen Suleima and the Arabs, but Kevin had quickly woken her up, and she had told him about her past.

She sighed, not believing she had finally shared that experience with someone else. Kevin was indeed very special. He understood the way she felt. Understood her pain. Slowly, she had fallen asleep again. Every now and then, she remembered briefly waking up but quickly falling back to sleep, feeling his warm breath against the back of her neck; his arms tightly wrapped around her chest; a hand comfortably snuggled between her breasts. Hours later she had gotten up, dressed, grabbed the small radio from the belt holster of his pants, and headed uphill.

Khalela knew he had to go back, and in a way she believed she understood his reasoning, which was driven by the same internal fire she had seen in his eyes from the day they had met. It was that passion for doing what was right that had caused her to fall in love with him. A love Khalela knew could not be. She was Mossad, a professional. Just like Kevin, she knew she had to go back to her world. Last night she had allowed her feelings to get in the way of her mission. Now that the professional in her was back, Khalela knew what had to be done.

In his sleep, Kevin rolled to the other side of the bed. It was empty. He quickly opened his eyes and scanned the room.

"Khalela? Khalela, are you here?"

No response.

Frowning, he sat up, half asleep, and picked up his underpants lying next to the bed. There were a pair of brown pants and shirt hanging from a chair across the room. He walked over and put them on.

A noise behind him made him turn around. It was the young Iraqi girl. She was carrying a basket filled with round, thin discs of bread and a few dates. She smiled and extended the basket to him.

Kevin smiled back. He took the basket and placed it on the bed. She turned around and started to walk away.

"Ah, listen . . ." She stopped and turned around. "You don't know what I'm saying, do you?"

She tilted her head and gave him a puzzled look.

"Khalela . . . do you know where she is?" He pointed around the room. "Khalela?"

She shook her head.

Kevin pointed at her. "You know, woman . . . this tall. Long hair . . . Khalela . . ."

The young girl smiled and pointed out the window.

Kevin looked outside the small opening in the wall but saw no one. He shook his head. The girl frowned and walked up to the window. She raised her hand and pointed at the hill across the ravine, then left the room.

SALMAN ASAD AIR BASE, SAUDI ARABIA. NEAR IRAQI BORDER.
Day Six. 0745 Local Time.

Robert Bourdeaux sat across from Halston in the back of
the communications tent going over one of two sets of
satellite images that had just arrived from the NPIC. The
first set was from a KH-11 pass yesterday afternoon.
Bourdeaux and Halston would use those to try to decide
where to start looking for the downed Navy pilot.
Amanda, Kramer, and Delgado would be there shortly
to go over the images.

The second set of photos were selected archived images of the region for a period of two years starting
almost nine years ago. The two-inch stack contained
images for both dairy products facilities which, as it
turned out, began construction at roughly the same time.
The difference, however, was that the facility near Baghdad had been completed two years after construction
started. At Allahbad, only the large warehouse and part
of the plant in back were finished by the time the factory
near Baghdad was already distributing milk and other
dairy products. The images from the past six years had
not arrived yet, but from what he could tell so far,
Bourdeaux saw what seemed to be a nonstop flow of
cement trucks going in and out of Allahbad. And just as
in the recent photos from Allahbad that he had been
analyzing for the past few days, all the trucks drove
straight into the large warehouse and back out. The
photos were spaced out by two weeks, and in every single
shot the area around Allahbad was packed with the
traffic of cement trucks, lumber trucks, and trucks
carrying steel beams and other materials. All going
into the warehouse with full loads and coming out
empty.

"Well, they're either building an underground facility,
or that warehouse has the world's thickest foundation."

Bourdeaux nodded. "Let's wait for the second set of
archived images, and then I'll write another letter to the
director."

* * *

Twenty minutes later, Robert Bourdeaux spoke to the assembled personnel leaning over the satellite photographs on the table in the rear of the communications tent as Peter Halston stared into space, thinking. The colonel had already seen the photos a few minutes ago and simply sat back, letting Bourdeaux give Longhorn Kramer, Chico Delgado, and Amanda Green a lesson in satellite surveillance photograph interpretation.

Bourdeaux showed them several shots of the village and pointed out that the irregularities in the buildings probably meant that they were damaged to some degree, most likely due to artillery shelling. All three leaned over the table when he pointed to several circular shaded areas around the village and told them that those were craters left by shells that had missed the target. Bourdeaux ventured to say that they were no older than a few days. Amanda's report that the village had appeared to be undamaged during the rescue attempt supported the statement.

Bourdeaux leaned closer and ran the index finger of his right hand along the center of a photograph while he explained that the shaded areas represented three houses, none of which had any roofs; only sections of the walls were left. The CIA analyst then pulled out one of three photographs and showed them the particular coloration and shape of a few large craters.

"All right, now compare those craters to these two over here." Bourdeaux pointed at two smaller craters of a lighter shade of gray than the larger ones he had just shown to them.

"Why are they smaller?" asked Delgado as he moved his head back and forth between the two photographs.

"Well, let's take a closer look." Bourdeaux pulled two photographs from the stack. They were enlargements of each type of crater. The large crater had perfectly round edges as well as several contour lines from the edge to the center. The greater the number of contour lines, the darker the crater would look from the air. The lines, he explained, indicated depth, which meant that those craters were created by a very powerful shell. The smaller craters, on the other hand, did not have as many contour lines, which meant they were shallower and gave the impression of being a few shades lighter. The reason for the shallower craters was not a less powerful shell but a different type of shell. One which not only created a smaller crater, but a crater with imperfect edges. Bourdeaux concluded that the shell had to be nonconventional.

He waited for a reaction. Kramer's head snapped up first. The colonel's eyes narrowed and his thick mustache dropped at the ends.

"Where are you drivin' at? You mean nonconventional as in . . . chemical?"

Bourdeaux nodded. "I'm afraid so. Just as a final check, the NPIC did a large-scale analysis of the surface elements in the area."

All three stared at Bourdeaux. "And?"

"Well, why don't you see for yourself." Bourdeaux pulled out a color photo of the village. It looked like an array of bright colors without much distinction between the outlines of buildings and other landmarks. Halston placed a transparency over the photo. The clear foil had the outline of the village drawn on it. The surface analysis photo showed the bluish hues of the large craters and the deep red color of the small craters.

Bourdeaux continued. "If you notice, the leftover elements from the conventional shell, which usually involve a glycerin agent, show up as blue. That's normal. It's also normal to see a defined outline of the color over a light brown background. What's very abnormal is the red coloration of the smaller craters, and the fact that surrounding the crater, the color slowly fades to a light rose, which eventually fades into the light brown shade."

"Yeah, but the fadin' only occurs after a while." Kramer's finger circled the rose-colored areas, most of which overlapped one another.

"That's right. That red coloring indicates the presence of a blister agent."

"Mustard gas?"

Bourdeaux lifted his eyes off the photograph. "Yep."

"Holy cow! Looks like 'em bastards cooked the entire village."

"That's right," responded Bourdeaux. "I definitely advise against going anywhere near that village, which would prove useless anyhow. I doubt there's anyone left there."

Delgado sat on his chair and rubbed his bulldog tattoo. "So, what's next?"

"Good question, Lieutenant," Halston said from behind the group. "We need to seriously reconsider our initial approach of merely following the F-14 pilot's footsteps. I doubt that would get us anywhere." All four turned around and stared at the colonel.

"What about adjacent villages, sir?" asked Amanda.

"Possible," responded Halston, "but there are over two dozen villages in that area. He could be anywhere."

"Damn!" fumed Delgado as Kramer shook his head.

"Hold on," said Halston. There was obvious frustration in his tone. "What about your Kurdish friends, Bob? Do you think they might be able to help out?"

"Sure. They'll help us for the right price, but the problem is that they might not be back for days. I don't think we have that much—"

"Colonel Halston?"

Bourdeaux stopped in mid-sentence as a young sergeant approached them.

"Yes. What is it?" answered Halston.

"You better come over, sir. An F-15 pilot just picked up a Guard transmission from Wolfpack Two One Four."

Halston bolted up as the heads of the other four snapped in the direction of the sergeant.

"What? When did this—" Halston began to say.

"Just now, sir. AWACS is trying to establish comms with her."

"*Her?* Who? What in the hell is going on?" Halston followed the sergeant to the front of the tent, where a bank of several communication radios stood. The colonel grabbed a headset equipped with a microphone as the others gathered around him.

He looked at the sergeant. "Get me the AWACS mission commander on the secure line ASAP!"

The sergeant nodded and moved to speak with one of the radio operators.

Ten minutes later, Halston placed the headset down. "What do you think?"

"Well-handled, sir. You bought us some time to think this through," Delgado responded.

"Personally, I don't like it. I think it could be a trap. So what if the woman knows Dalton's call sign? We all know the Iraqis monitor the channel, too. They could have picked it up from one of the earlier conversations," noted Kramer. "Or what's worse, he could have been captured and forced to reveal that information."

"Perhaps, Colonel, perhaps. But right now that's the best lead we've got," Halston said. "We're gonna have to play it carefully from this point on. It's too strange not to be genuine. I mean, why have a woman make the call if it's a trap. If it's genuine, the Iraqis heard the call too, and they're probably heading in."

"That's right," Delgado added. "And the *pendejos* are a lot closer than us."

Halston rubbed his eyes. They had to move fast.

AMAN BAKISH AIR BASE NEAR AN NAJAF, SOUTHERN IRAQ.
Day Six. 0815 Local Time.

General Abunnasr Manesh drank tea from a cup and watched the large radio unit in front of Fassan Tabriz. The conversation had come through clearly. Although his English was not as polished as it had been when he studied at a British university, Manesh had managed to pick up most of what was said.

He now stared at the radar screen. It showed the origin of the call. He smiled. It was his lucky day. *Payback time.*

SOUTHERN IRAQ.
Day Six. 1000 Local Time.

Khalela followed the same path that she had taken on the way up. It slowly veered down the side of the hill until reaching a small cluster of trees by a shallow river that flowed next to the village. She was puzzled. The conversation had not gone at all how she had expected it to go. *The Americans are getting overly cautious,* she reflected as she emerged from behind the shadow of a large rock and the noon sun momentarily blinded her. She'd had a hard time convincing the Americans that she was calling on Kevin's behalf, even after giving them the call sign that Kevin had casually mentioned to her during the past few days.

The Americans had been reluctant to believe her story and requested to talk to Kevin himself. She had told them that Kevin was hurt and had lost a great deal of blood. She did not think he could make the climb. She was then asked to turn off the radio to conserve the batteries, walk down to the village, and in exactly three hours reactivate the radio. When she had argued that the radio was not powerful enough to reach the border from the village, she was simply told to comply with the request.

Khalela wondered how Kevin would react when he found out what she had done. But she'd had no choice. There was no way she could get Kevin to the border without a four-wheel-drive vehicle. She had to seek help.

She entered the narrow forest at the foot of the hill and began to make her way through the sparse vegetation, emerging on the other side a minute later. The shallow stream was next. Its surface flickered as the relatively strong current flowed around the village. She smiled in relief as her feet came in contact with the cool waters, going up to her knees at the deepest place.

Khalela cupped a handful of water and brought it to her lips. Her mouth was dry and pasty. She drank twice more before she continued walking toward the other shore. The village was less than a hundred feet—

Kevin?

She saw Kevin standing at the edge of the village, looking in her direction. She sped up her pace and approached him.

"You mind telling me what that was all about?"

"Yes, Kevin, but first let us get under the shade. It was a long walk."

Khalela walked past him and toward a large tree in the small clearing in the village. He followed her.

SALMAN ASAD AIR BASE, SAUDI ARABIA. NEAR IRAQI BORDER.
Day Six. 1200 Local Time.

Captain Amanda Green walked by the Apache helicopter tied down on the ramp across the tarmac, roughly a couple of hundred feet from where the Grumman Gulfstream IV transport stood next to a refueling truck. Two mechanics sat on one of the wings, keeping a hose in place.

She gave a quick glance at her Pave Hawk next to the Apache before shifting her gaze back toward the menacing-looking Apache. Captain Orlando Delaney and his gunner, Lieutenant Steve Rizzo, were already performing the preflight inspection, checking all air surfaces, rotors, and the extensive warload under the stub wings. She looked back to the third, and last, Pave Hawk rescue helicopter. Her pilot had already started the preflight.

Amanda frowned. Although they had wanted to send more than just one Apache to cover the rescue, the group had reasoned that the fewer the craft going in the less chance of detection. As a safety measure, though, Halston had requested the support of two A-10s, which would meet the rescue party at the site.

Here we go again. She continued toward her craft.

Orlando Delaney finished inspecting the exterior of the craft and glanced at Rizzo, who was performing a last-minute check to ensure the powerful antitank missiles were safely locked in place.

"Hello, Lieutenant. How does it look?"

"All right. Got four quad pods of Hellfires. Figured the Hellfires could also handle any air-to-air incidents," responded the blond lieutenant, who was almost as slim as Delaney.

The black captain eyed the quad pods of Hellfires, each capable of incapacitating any Soviet-made tank. Two were probably enough for full destruction. The Hellfire could also be used as an air-to-air missile. Although such usage of an air-to-surface weapon was not necessarily recommended by the manufacturer, Delaney knew that the missile would home in on any target being tracked by the Apache's laser designator system. He smiled. Sixteen Hellfires could keep several enemy tanks busy. He climbed up the ladder and pulled the rear door open. Rizzo got in front.

He eased himself into his seat and instantly felt right at home. He belonged inside the Apache. Before glancing at the instrument panel, Delaney put on his helmet and flipped the master switch to power up the avionics and the weapons control system, thirteen embedded minicomputers interconnected through a closed-loop multiplex system. All thirteen minicomputers fed into the heart of the full digital solution of the Apache's weapons system brain, a high-speed hybrid fire control computer.

Delaney connected the helmet display unit to the right side of his helmet and rotated the miniature CRT display and monocular optical relay in front of his right eye to link the integrated helmet and display sighting system to the Apache's TADS, the Target Acquisition and Designator Sight. This would enable the Apache's minicomputers to "see" what Delaney saw, and vice versa. He checked the craft's fuel level and nodded in satisfaction.

Delaney went down the checklist, taking almost twice as long as usual. He didn't want anything to go wrong with this mission. In addition to the warload under the stubwings, the aircraft housed a potent 30mm M230A1 chain gun. The gun, which utilized a rotating bolt mechanism electrically driven through a chain drive, hung unfaired from a hydraulically driven turret under the Apache between the gunner and the pilot.

Delaney finished the preflight check and threw the engine starter. It didn't take but a few seconds for both General Electric T700 turboshafts to come to life. As Delaney watched the engines accelerate past seven hundred RPM, the spring-loaded clutch connecting the main rotor transmission to the turbines slowly began to engage due to the centrifugal force from the rotating turbines. The centrifugal clutch drum applied friction to the main rotor transmission, which in turn began to move the stainless steel/fiberglass rotor blades. He watched the rotating blades slowly melt into a clear disk as he added throttle while keeping an eye on the engine/rotor speed information displayed by the vertical scale instruments located on the left side of the control panel. He advanced throttle to achieve takeoff RPM. Unlike most helicopters, the Apache did not have the twist grip-type throttle control at the end of the collective lever, instead sporting side-by-side throttle handles on the left control console. He glanced over to the Pave Hawk.

From the Pave Hawk's copilot seat, Amanda Green watched Poole add throttle, collective, and rudder while keeping the cyclic centered. The large rescue craft slowly left the tarmac. She spoke into the voice-activated headset of her helmet.

"Hawkeye Zero One, Tango Six Five, airborne."

"Hawkeye," Amanda heard Kramer's heavy Texan accent through her headphones.

Delgado put his headset down and looked at Kramer. There wasn't much they could do but hope Halston's plan worked. He glanced around the noisy, dark interior of the Grumman E-2C Hawkeye and spotted Halston walking down the narrow corridor from the cockpit.

"I just talked to the pilot. We finally made it to twenty thousand. I don't think we'll have any problems reaching him from up here."

"I hope not. Otherwise we'll be back to square one," Delgado said. "How long before we—"

"Five minutes."

"I hope he's there," Delgado said.

"Don't worry about it, pal," Kramer said, placing a hand on the Hispanic lieutenant's narrow shoulders. "If he's alive, he'll be there."

Delgado sat back in a chair facing an incredible array of electronic gear. He knew the Grumman E-2C was a designated AEW, airborne early-warning aircraft. Their sole purpose during combat was as control craft, keeping an "eye" on the overall battle and feeding vital information on enemy forces to the Allies.

The two operators to Delgado's right worked on tracking the Apache and the Pave Hawk.

Halston looked at Delgado. "It's time."

Delgado put the headset back on.

"You know what you want to say?"

Delgado nodded.

Kevin checked his watch and reached for the radio next to the bed before heading outside with Khalela. He flipped it on.

"Wolfpack Two One Four Alpha, is anybody there, over?"

"Crackers, Chico."

Kevin froze. *Chico? How in the—*

"Crackers?"

Kevin put both hands on the radio. "Crackers here."

"What's your situation?"

"Leg wound and minor concussion, but I can walk, and even run if I have to."

"Glad to hear it. I was afraid you were gonna be in worse shape than the Doberman I've got tattooed on my arm."

Kevin narrowed his eyes. *Doberman?* Then he understood and smiled.

"This is not a trap. Nobody's forcing me to contact you. The woman who called earlier is on our side. It's not a Doberman but a bulldog."

"I think we're all breathing a little easier over here now. Be ready to leave in niner zero mikes."

Kevin smiled. *An hour and a half.* "One Four Alpha."

"Vaya con Dios, hermano."

Kevin switched off the radio and together with Khalel walked back inside.

Khalela looked at him. "Crackers?"

Kevin smiled. "We all get nicknames in the Navy. Actually mine's not that bad compared to others. Say, ready for a short helicopter ride?"

"After you."

The young Iraqi commander inspected the villag through the telescopic sights of his T-72 Soviet-mad tank. He spotted a few small houses, but nothing out o the ordinary.

"Hold position. Firing system check."

The driver cut back power to the V-12 diesel engin bringing the 90,000-pound vehicle to a halt two mile from the village. The moment it stopped, the gunne trained the laser rangefinder on the closest house an tested his equipment. The advanced computer system quickly generated a firing solution with over ninet percent first-round hit probability. He repeated the test changing targets. The system responded flawlessly. Satis fied, he gave his commander a thumbs-up.

The commander waited. His instructions were to hol until the rescue helicopters came into view. He ordere the infantry following the tanks to spread out in case a American aircraft spotted the armored vehicles. Withi a minute, the forty soldiers following the tanks in truck and jeeps split in different directions. Two jeeps heade up the hill overlooking the village while others remaine in the clearing but kept a safe distance from the tanks Two trucks loaded with soldiers slowly approached th village from the north. They stopped just under thousand feet from the nearest building.

General Abunnasr Manesh pounded his fists on the table when Fassan Tabriz told him that they could only send one Hind to escort the tanks and infantry. He could not believe that most of the Hinds in the area were grounded due to lack of spare parts.

Manesh screamed at Fassan for a few minutes and ordered him to find another Hind from somewhere and get it airborne immediately, even if it meant cannibalizing parts from another helicopter. He stormed out of the communications bunker only to be welcomed by a rush of hot air. He sighed and raced across the runway. Squinting under the bright afternoon sun, he spotted the Fulcrum peacefully standing inside the shelter. He shifted his gaze to the left and saw mechanics sitting around in a circle.

"I need to take it up immediately!" he shouted as all three ground crew members bolted to their feet and raced toward the MiG.

"You cannot, sir. Your weapons systems are not operational."

"What? Everything was working yesterday! What in the hell is going on?"

"I do not know, sir. During the daily inspection of the system we discovered problems. I am afraid you cannot use the missiles until we get the spare parts from Baghdad."

"For the love of Allah! Is there anything around here that works?"

"The cannon, sir."

"What?"

"The cannon is operational, and we just finished reloading it, or . . ."

"Or what?"

"Or you can use one of the MiG-21s." Manesh glanced at two old MiG-21 Fishbeds neatly parked behind the Fulcrum. He saw that they had a full arsenal of old air-to-air missiles under the wings.

"Both jets have just been through a systems check and are fully fueled. They are ready to go, sir."

Manesh exhaled as his gaze went back and forth between the fast and extremely maneuverable—but under-armed—Fulcrum and the old and slower—but fully armed—Fishbed. *Damn!* Actually, the MiG-21 was a good turning machine, but it still wasn't a MiG-29.

He made his decision and walked toward the Fulcrum. "Remove all of the weapons under the wings, at least that will give me the edge of maneuverability!"

"Yes, sir!"

Manesh went up the ladder and started his preflight check while the ground crew raced back and forth with steel carts quickly unloading the heavy weaponry. He closed his eyes and prayed to Allah that his 30mm cannon did not fail him.

SOUTHERN IRAQ.
Day Six. 1300 Local Time.

"What do you think is going to happen to you, Kevin?" Khalela asked as they both waited by the southern edge of the village.

"Not sure. I guess the Navy's going to bring charges against me for insubordination. I'm also pretty certain that they're going to blame me for the RIO's death."

"What would that mean?"

"Most likely I'll be permanently grounded and given the worst assignments until I decide to quit. Not a very comforting scenario."

"Why not come with me to Israel? We can always use good pilots like—"

"I don't think I can do that, Khalela. I love my country, and by God I love the Navy. The only reason I'm so good at what I do is because my heart, my entire self, is devoted to flying Tomcats. You take patriotism away, and all that's left is mechanical skills without passion, the internal fire that makes me push those birds to the outer limits of their capabilities. The Israeli Air Force is tops, but they're fighting for their country, not mine. Sorry, but I don't think I would be any good in your Air Force."

Khalela put a hand to his cheek. "That's why I love you, Kevin Dalton."

He smiled and blushed.

"I'm glad I—" he began to say, but stopped. Instead, he turned around and faced the southern horizon.

"What is it?"

He raised his right hand. "Wait. Listen. Hear it?"

"Yes, I hear it. They're here."

The dark green beast darted at 150 knots at a mere twenty feet above ground. It smoothly followed the imperfections of the terrain in response to Captain Green's gentle cyclic movements, as she focused her total concentration on keeping her Pave Hawk below radar. Major Poole had given her the controls ten minutes ago.

Delaney's Apache was at her twelve.

Captain Orlando Delaney risked a backward glance and checked that the rescue chopper was at the same altitude. There was no use in his maintaining such a dangerous flight level if the Pave Hawk blew it by flying higher. He grinned. *The Pave Hawk's pilot is good,* he thought as he noticed the rescue helicopter roughly a half mile behind. This time, Delaney was not taking any chances. The landing zone would be clear before that Pave Hawk got anywhere near the place.

He turned his attention back to his craft, barely spotting the blurry outline of the village through the heat wave. He checked his coordinates and smiled. It had taken him ninety minutes to get here from the base, and so far there had been no problems. He wondered where the A-10 contingent was.

"Sandy, Sandy, Dragonfly Niner Two, over."

"Niner Two, Sandy. On station in three mikes."

"Roger, Sandy." Delaney switched to Guard. "Wolfpack Two One Four Alpha, this is Dragonfly Niner Two."

"Niner Two, Wolfpack Two One Four Alpha. We got a visual on you."

"Where are you located, One Four Alpha?"

"South side of the village, at eleven o'clock. You can't miss—"

"Tally. Do you have a Tally, Six Five?"

"Roger, Niner Two," responded Amanda as Poole took control of the Pave Hawk.

Delaney watched the rescue chopper turn toward them as he started circling the village. "Do you have the rescue helicopter in sight, One Four Alpha?"

"Affirmative, Niner Two."

"Start moving away from the—" He stopped speaking when he spotted the bright flashes in the distance.

"Incoming! Clear out, Six Five. Pull out, now! Get out of firing range! One Four Alpha, take cover!"

Kevin grabbed Khalela's hand and raced across the clearing toward the ravine. He felt the earth tremble under his feet as powerful shells impacted the houses on the northern side of the village. Almost immediately havoc set in. Kevin watched women race away from the village with children in their arms.

"Bastards!" He slowed down.

"There is no time for that, Kevin! We must reach the foot of the hill and find cover!" She pulled him forward.

"But the village, the women—"

"They have been taking care of themselves forever! They'll reach another village by night. We can't help them now. Let's go!"

He sped up. As they reached the ravine, he looked back and spotted the rear of the Apache. It was heading toward the source of the blasts.

"Enable laser designator!" Delaney commanded as he turned his head toward the lead tank. TADS automatically projected alphanumeric information and flight symbology onto a combining lens, instantly superimposing it on Delaney's integrated helmet and display sighting system. In a flash he had a target solution with range.

"Target acquired," responded Rizzo as he used TADS

to train the laser gun, mounted on the nose turret of the Apache, on the first tank.

"Select Hellfires!"

"Ready!" responded Rizzo.

"Fire!"

The solid-propellant rocket motor of one Hellfire came alive, thrusting the eighty-pound missile to just under Mach 1 in seconds.

Delaney threw the cyclic left, forcing the Apache into a tight left turn. The nose turret rotated in the opposite direction as it automatically kept the laser trained on the lead tank.

The Hellfire's tracking electronics immediately locked on to the laser and sent corrective electronic pulses to the small servomotors that controlled the tail fins of the five-foot-long missile, making minor flight adjustments in compensation for the tank's sudden evasive acceleration.

Delaney glanced backward and smiled when the twenty-pound warhead blew the turret off the Iraqi lead tank.

"That's a kill, Captain!"

The young Iraqi commander was the first to react after the tank to his left was blown to pieces.

"Clear out! Smoke! I need smoke!"

The driver floored it. The T-72's powerful diesel responded by accelerating to maximum speed. He then injected diesel fuel into the exhaust outlet on the left side of the hull. Thick smoke engulfed the tank.

Delaney watched the other three tanks moving in different directions. One disappeared under a cloud of smoke. He knew the other two would soon do the same.

Delaney selected a new target and fired another Hellfire: another score. He turned to the third tank. Smoke was beginning to cover its rear.

"Niner Two, Six Five. You got a Hind at your six!" Delaney heard the warning call from the Pave Hawk. He looked and spotted a Hind roughly two thousand feet behind and to their left. He applied full power and

dropped to just above the ground. The Hind stayed with them.

"He's getting into firing position!" said Rizzo.

Silently cursing the Hind, Delaney swung the cyclic from side to side, forcing the craft into a tight zigzag. TADS informed him that the port engine was overheating, which meant that even the infrared suppresser system could not reduce the overheated gas plume from the port engine enough to bring it below the infrared lock-on threshold of the Hind's missiles. *Bad news.*

"Missile in the air!"

The Apache's AN/ALQ-144 Infrared Counter Measures jammer, designed to defeat the homing of heat-seeking missiles, kicked in. At that moment, an electrically-heated ceramic block, mounted atop the aft portion of the upper pylon fairing, modulated intense heat radiation away from the craft as the Apache approached a hill at 180 knots. As the IRCM presented the missile with a number of new hot targets, Delaney's hand went to the AN/ALE-39 countermeasures dispensing system. In the following three seconds, ten flares left a box strapped to the outer side of the port stubwing, giving the missile yet another target.

"It's going for the flares!"

Delaney let go of the breath he had been holding. He reached the hill and kept his craft glued to its side as he turned the corner. With the Hind temporarily out of sight, he lowered collective, cut back throttle, pulled back the cyclic, and pushed the right pedal as hard as possible. He slammed against his seatbelt as the chopper nearly came to a halt and spun around. He released rudder and left his craft in a hover less than ten feet over the ground.

He smiled as the Hind came into plain sight at full speed. It dashed halfway across his field of view before the pilot realized Delaney's maneuver. The Hind quickly turned away, but not before Delaney had a laser-homing Hellfire streaking after it.

Delaney watched the smoke trail propagate directly toward the departing Hind. Twenty pounds of explosives hit the exhaust of the left engine. The strong blow pierced through the thick armor and severed the rotor from the shaft. The rotor slashed through the air out of control as the heavy body of the craft plummeted to the earth, exploding on impact.

Suddenly, the blasting started again as the remaining two tanks renewed their bombardment of the village. He also noticed the trucks moving toward the village.

Delaney applied throttle, collective, and cyclic. The Apache hurtled forward. There were two clouds of smoke, each about three hundred feet in diameter. He frowned. There was a tank in each one. "Switch to infrared!"

"Switching!" Rizzo switched control of the Apache's laser target designator from direct-view-optics mode to forward-looking infrared sensor mode. The gunner trained the heat-seeking sensor on the closest cloud. TADS did the rest, automatically training the laser on the heat source in the center of the cloud. "Got him!"

"Fire!"

General Abunnasr Manesh watched the bright flash from the American helicopter. The missile went straight to the center of the smoke cloud. The powerful explosion that followed told him the American missile had found its target. He glanced at the other two destroyed tanks and the burning Hind. His eyes filled with anger as he flipped his jet on its back and pulled the stick, descending and accelerating in full afterburners; his finger caressed the trigger on his control stick.

Manesh saw another flash followed by another missile. The last tank was destroyed. He brought his nose to bear on the offending helicopter and carefully sweetened his shot, bringing the illuminated crosshairs to his quarry. The six-barrel 30mm gun started vomiting rounds at a rate of one thousand per minute. The first burst was off to the right, the second to the left. He smiled as the third burst brought smoke from the rear of the American helicopter. Manesh pulled out of his dive, did a one-eighty, and came back around for another pass.

* * *

"Engine failure. Shutting down starboard engine!"
Delaney glanced back but couldn't see a thing. He eyed
his altimeter. Three hundred feet. "What in the world
fired at us?" he asked, moving his head in all directions
to acquire whoever had fired at them.

"Don't know, Captain. Can't get a visual!"

Delaney headed back to the hill. His craft felt extremely sluggish under the power of a single turbofan.

"It's a fucking MiG!" said Rizzo. "Ten o'clock high!"

"Got it!" He halted the Apache and turned it in the
direction of the incoming MiG.

"Hellfire selected!"

"It's firing!" The MiG hurtled directly for them with
its cannon blasting.

"Fir—" Delaney's words were cut short by the thundering 30mm projectiles hitting the upper section of the
armored canopy of the Apache. The Armorlite glass,
rated to sustain up to 23mm fire, managed to deflect the
first few dozen rounds before collapsing. Rizzo's head
snapped back. A round had pierced his helmet.

"Aghh!" Delaney felt the stinging pain of a bullet
crashing through his right shoulder. Ignoring the agonizing pain, he switched to manual and placed the incoming
MiG in the crosshairs of his helmet sighting system. He
fired.

The MiG broke hard to the left as the Hellfire left the
outboard pylon and accelerated to just under Mach 1.

Manesh put the craft in a vertical climb and began
dispensing flares and chaff. The missile flew past the
decoys. He topped out of his climb at fifteen thousand
feet. The missile was gone. He had outrun it.

Kevin watched the entire episode from the foot of the
hill. He wasn't surprised that the MiG had managed to
escape destruction. The Apache had only been able to
fire a subsonic air-to-ground missile at the MiG. But at
least it had broken the MiG's initial run on the combat
helicopter. The Pave Hawk, which had remained out of
sight the entire time, finally began to come around the

clearing. He watched the wounded Apache also approaching.

"Let's go, Khalela."

"Wait, Kevin. Look!" She pointed at the sky.

Kevin glanced up and held his breath as he saw a MiG-29 with green stripes across the wings.

"Son of a bitch! That's the same damned MiG again!"

"Is that the one . . . ?"

"Yes! That's the same bastard who shot me down!"

Through the dirt and debris that swirled upward as he hovered ten feet over ground, Delaney also noticed the MiG turning back. The rotor wash blasting down through the large opening in the top of the canopy made his movements difficult, as if he were pulling g's. The excruciating pain from his shoulder spiraled up as he pulled back the cyclic and added rudder. The Apache turned around and faced the incoming MiG once more. This time he moved his head in the direction of the MiG. Sensors on both sides of the cockpit detected his helmet's motion and passed the information to the Hughes 30mm chain gun, which swung in the direction of the MiG. Delaney pressed the trigger on the cyclic. The gun started firing at a rate of over six hundred rounds per minute. He mentally kept track of the number of seconds as he quickly began to deplete the 1,200-round ammo box.

Once more he centered the MiG on the crosshairs of his helmet and activated a Hellfire. He saw muzzle flashes coming from the MiG. The ground beneath his Apache boiled with the incoming rounds.

The turret-mounted laser following his helmet sight splashed the MiG with invisible light.

Now!

The missile blasted out of the tube and tracked toward the MiG. Delaney continued firing the cannon.

Manesh released the trigger and pulled hard left. Once more he put his craft into a vertical climb and glanced back as the altimeter shot past fifteen thousand feet. The missile was gone.

He scanned the skies, but could not find it. Puzzled, he leveled off and started his third run.

Orlando Delaney frowned. He knew it was a desperate attempt to take on a MiG using a slow Hellfire, but that was all the air-to-air defense he had left. Once more he watched the MiG coming back, its left wing alive with flashes. He pointed the Apache's nose in its direction, aimed and fired both the machine gun and a Hellfire. His craft trembled suddenly as the last of the 30mm rounds left the red-hot muzzle. The Hellfire continued to track as he kept his sight on the incoming MiG.

Delaney spoke into his radio. "Sandy, Sandy, Dragonfly Niner Two, where in the hell are you, over?"

"Niner Two, Sandy Eight Oh. Be there in thirty seconds."

It was getting to be a tiresome exercise for Manesh. Frustrated, he pulled back on the control stick and applied full power. The MiG projected upward in full afterburner.

"Six Five, Niner Two, over."

"Go ahead Niner Two," responded the Pave Hawk.

"It's now or never. Come into the clearing and pick them up!"

"Roger."

Delaney watched the warning lights on his control panel. Flying single engine, he turned back toward the village.

With the missile gone, Manesh turned around and headed back down to the clearing for the fourth time. The American attack helicopter was slowly flying toward a second helicopter approaching the clearing. He decided to go after the larger helicopter and swung the stick in its direction. He fired.

The world seemed to explode around Amanda Green. As a torrential shower of glass fell on her, she caught a glimpse of Poole hanging limp in his harness, a bullet wound in his chest. The sight was quickly followed by intense pain in her right thigh. She looked down and saw her own blood soaking her flight suit. *Oh, God. I'm hit, too!*

Breathing deeply, she placed her right hand on the cyclic and left on the collective lever while pressing her feet against the rudder pedals—an action that sent a jolt of pain up her body from her wounded leg. She forced her mind to ignore it. She didn't have a choice; she had to keep the Pave Hawk under control as they approached the village.

Just as suddenly as it started, the attack stopped. She scanned the instrument panel and saw a few warning lights, but both turbines were undamaged.

Manesh cursed his bad luck as the last of his rounds left the muzzle of his cannon. He had depleted his load. As he pulled out of the dive, he caught movement out of the corner of his eye. *A-10s!* Two jets were closing in on him.

Cursing his bad luck, he inverted, dove for the ground, and headed home in full afterburner.

Kevin Dalton saw the rescue chopper coming back around just as two A-10s flew overhead. He shook his head, knowing that the subsonic Warthogs would never catch up with the MiG-29. He centered his attention back on the helicopter. This time he didn't say anything, simply pulling Khalela by the hand as he raced forward.

"Wait, where are—"

"This is our chance. Look!" he shouted, pointing to the large clearing north of the village. Several trucks and jeeps were moving in their direction. "Iraqi infantry. Tanks never go anywhere alone! The soldiers will be here in no time!"

They raced away from the hill and toward the chopper, which was hovering between them and the ravine a foot or so above ground. Kevin felt burning pain in his leg as he kicked hard against the sand. He didn't notice when Khalela let go of his hand.

Kevin didn't turn around. His entire self became focused on reaching the helicopter. The gunner started firing its mini-gun over Kevin's head to slow down the approaching Iraqis. Two men dressed in fatigues and holding M-16s jumped out of the helicopter and ran toward him, signaling him to hurry up. But his legs refused to go any faster. The excruciating pain from his gunshot wound slowed him. Sand swirled up and stung his face as he reached the rotors.

"Hurry, hurry!" one of the men yelled as he stepped in front of the chopper, leveled his weapon at the Iraqis, and began firing.

Kevin kicked at the ground one final time and propelled his body up in the air. His shoulder stung as he landed on the armored floor of the craft. He felt disoriented, confused. He stared at the gunner, who wore a helmet with the green visor down.

"All right, let's go! Let's go!" Kevin heard him shout. The two men with M-16s jumped back in the helicopter just as it left the ground. The gunner went back to the mini-gun, spraying the area with bullets to cover their departure.

"No, no . . . we can't go yet," he managed to say, but nobody heard him.

In a frenzy, Kevin shot up and jumped toward the door. One of the soldiers grabbed him in time.

"Easy, Lieutenant. Calm down, you're almost home, sir."

"No, you don't understand. The woman . . . we must wait for the woman!"

"Woman? You mean her?" He pointed at a person running across the stream and into the hills to the west of the village. She stopped briefly and turned.

Kevin stared at Khalela, who raised her hand and waved.

"She stopped halfway and raced toward the river, sir."

"No! It can't be! She wants to come . . . damn! She must come!" The gunner joined the soldier, and between the two of them they pinned Kevin down.

"We can't turn around, sir. This place is too hot!"

Kevin didn't respond. His mind was in turmoil. *Why, Khalela? Why did you do it?* An overwhelming sense of despair nearly engulfed him, crushing the only shred of sanity he had left. But she was gone. She had chosen to stay behind.

"You're going to be all right, Lieutenant. I'm going to take a look at that leg and try to stop the bleeding. Relax. You're safe now."

Kevin barely heard him. It didn't matter. He tried to say that he didn't care anymore, that he wanted to be left alone, but he couldn't. He felt cold, light-headed, alone. The back of his head hit the floor as he stared at the faceless gunner who seemed to be moving farther and farther away down the narrow tunnel that appeared to engulf everything. Then it all faded away, and there was silence.

Gunfire exploded around Orlando Delaney as the ground troops closed in on his hovering helicopter. He had wasted too much time watching the Pave Hawk rescue the Navy pilot. Bullets now ricocheted off the Apache's underside.

"Sandy, Dragonfly Niner Two. Where in the hell are you?" he shouted while throwing the cyclic forward to get away from the guns.

"*We got you covered. Coming around to clean the area!*"

As Delaney watched, the pair of Warthogs made a wide sweeping turn around the clearing before firing their cannons. Suddenly, his cyclic shook, seemingly out of control. Delaney applied maximum friction to his collective and throttle settings and used both hands to try to bring the cyclic under control. He knew exactly what had happened. The rounds had damaged the sensitive electronics of the digital automatic stabilization system, the electronics designed to enhance overall maneuverability by augmenting Delaney's control inputs. Without the enhancing system, Delaney's commands were sent in raw form to the Apache's control surfaces, making the craft harder to control.

The firing continued for a few more seconds until the Sandies got there. Delaney swung the cyclic left and approached a hill. Another group of Iraqis was now firing at him. He lowered to ten feet AGL and began to zigzag until he reached the hill, where he threw the cyclic left and began to make his way up the hillside—*Oh shit!*

Delaney stared in surprise at the Iraqis hiding off the side of a rock up the hillside in two jeeps. The machine guns mounted on the rear of the jeeps were pointed in his direction.

Delaney reacted as swiftly as he could. Since he was running on a single engine, his upward momentum had not been that great, and he managed to get his craft back down the same side of the hill as the firing began. The rounds missed . . . except for a few that somehow managed to reach the port turbine intake, exploding the moment they hit the high-speed blades. In an instant, the sighting system went emergency red with a flashing message to release collective and start an autorotation.

Delaney checked his altitude: one hundred feet. He lowered collective and began to glide toward the foot of the hill at the end of the clearing north of the village. He frowned when he spotted a four-wheel-drive vehicle approaching at full speed. The Warthogs were still busy engaging another group of Iraqi soldiers closer to the village.

"Sandy! Get over here!" he shouted into his microphone as the Apache hit the ground less than fifty feet from the rocky hill. The vehicle came to a screeching halt just ten feet from him, under the decelerating rotor.

Delaney was hurting. His right shoulder stung and continued bleeding. He began to feel cold, weak, dizzy. His vision began to cloud, but he fought it, blinking rapidly and bringing the three soldiers in the jeep back into focus.

The soldiers jumped out of the vehicle carrying automatic weapons. They leveled them at him and signaled him to get out. Delaney pretended to be seriously injured and kept his head down. His right hand slowly moved to the side of his flight suit and extracted a Colt .45 automatic, which he kept hidden out of view from the Iraqis.

Out of the corner of his eye, Delaney spotted the Warthogs circling the area, but he knew they couldn't do much for him with the soldiers standing next to the Apache.

The Iraqis looked at one another, and then two of them climbed up the side steps. Delaney waited a few more seconds. The men reached the last step and were banging on the sides of the bullet-proof canopy. Delaney closed his eyes. His heartbeat rocketed with every blow. For a moment it seemed as if he were back in Willoma. The night surrounded him. White-robed men hammered at the windows of his father's truck as his girlfriend screamed in fear. Delaney felt the gun in his hands. Saw the Klansmen shouting outside. They were going to hang themselves a couple of niggers. *Bastards! You're all a bunch of fucking bastards!*

Delaney opened his eyes and noticed the third man walking to the jeep and pulling out an RPG shoulder-launched antitank unit from the back of the vehicle.

Delaney raised his head and stared back at them with uncompromising defiance. *This is one nigger you ain't gonna get your hands on, motherfuckers!* In one swift move, he reached the canopy jettison handle on the top right hand side of the instrument panel, pulled it and turned it ninety degrees clockwise.

The explosive bolts of the canopy blew both windows and doors outward, taking the two Iraqis with them. The soldiers landed several feet from the craft and remained still. The third man was caught by surprise. He hesitated for a few seconds before leveling the RPG at Delaney, but that was all the time the native of Mississippi needed. Orlando Delaney pressed his finger against the trigger and began to fire just as he had done a lifetime ago in another land and for another reason. Round after round left the hot muzzle of the Colt. Delaney felt his strength leaving him. He was losing blood at a staggering rate, but he could not stop firing. He would not be captured alive. Iraqis or Klansmen: in his tired and cloudy mind, they were one and the same. He refused to be hanged by the Klan. Refused to submit himself to the way white justice had been secretly dispensed in Willoma for generations.

Empty shell casings shot out the side of the stainless steel weapon as his arm grew weaker, too weak to hold the automatic. His vision became foggy, but not before Orlando Delaney saw the last Iraqi arch back and land next to his fallen friends.

Amanda Green saw the downed Apache and swung the cyclic in its direction.

"Sandy, Six Five. Cover me!" she yelled as she maneuvered the Pave Hawk twenty feet over the sand.

"We got you covered, Six Five," came the reply, but Amanda was barely listening. The swirling debris lifted by the massive rotor entered the cockpit through the large opening blasted by the MiG. Brown dust obscured her vision as Amanda maneuvered her craft to within fifty feet of the Apache and touched down. She maintained rotor RPM to allow for a quick take-off.

The two Special Ops soldiers raced toward the Apache, climbed up the side and dragged the unconscious crew out of the helo. They came under fire again. Amanda frantically searched for the source and found it halfway up the hill. The Iraqis were firing down at them. Bullets ricocheted off the side of the helicopter.

"Jesus, Sandy! Get these idiots off of me! Nine o'clock, high!"

"Rog."

As the Special Ops team approached the Pave Hawk and the side gunner sprayed the hill with bullets, both A-10s came around and fired their cannons at the hill. To Amanda's horror, she saw that one of the Special Ops men was down, and the other was limping as he continued dragging an Apache crewman.

The gunner jumped out and quickly dragged the other two in. Thirty seconds later everyone was aboard. She raised collective, added throttle, and inched the cyclic forward. The Pave Hawk headed back toward Saudi Arabia.

Thirty minutes later, Amanda Green began to feel cold. Her right hand shivered as she held on to the cyclic. She continued to lose blood from her thigh wound in spite of the tourniquet she had applied. On top of all that, the main rotor downdraft pounding on her through the broken canopy made her moves sluggish, painful.

She kept her gaze fixed on the southern horizon as her craft cruised at 185 knots fifty feet above the desert sands toward the Saudi border. The A-10s had left to refuel.

She forced her mind to think positively. The border was only forty miles away and closing. *Forty miles, Amanda,* she told herself. If she could only reach the border, perhaps someone would come and meet them halfway and take them the rest of the way. That meant she would have to hang on for about fifteen more minutes.

Fifteen minutes! Jesus Christ, I don't think I can last that long. Her leg continued to bleed. She spoke into the microphone.

"Eagle's Nest . . . Eagle's Nest, this is Tango . . . Six . . . Five. I don't think I'm . . . gonna make it. I'm bleeding . . . badly. I'm getting . . . awfully cold."

"Hang in there, Six Five. You're almost home."

"No," she responded to the monotone voice coming from the base. "I don't think I can . . . I don't . . ."

Robert Bourdeaux and Colonel Peter Halston stood behind the radio operator listening to the conversation on the overhead speaker. Halston, along with Kramer and Delgado, had walked inside the tent just ten minutes before from their short flight.

"You better talk to her, Pete," Bourdeaux said. "She needs to hear a familiar voice."

Halston looked at the crowd now gathered around them. He took the mike away from the radio operator and brought it to his lips.

"Captain Green this is Colonel Halston. You hang in there and keep that cyclic centered. You're almost—"

"Dammit, Pete!" Bourdeaux shouted, startling everyone around them. "Fucking *talk* to her, man! She needs you!"

Halston closed his eyes and inhaled deeply. "Amanda, this is Pete. Listen, you gotta hang on. You have to!"

"I can't hold on . . . any longer. I don't . . . even know if I can . . . set this thing down right . . . here."

"No, Pete!" said Bourdeaux. "Don't let her land there! She's flying right over the damned Iraqis heading south!"

Halston tightened the grip on the mike. "Don't set it down, Amanda! Oh, God, please don't set it down! You're flying right over the Iraqis. Just hang on. You can do it!"

"I . . . I can't, Pete . . . I . . ."

"Dammit, Amanda. Don't you fucking leave me here alone! You hear me? Don't you die on me! Push yourself, dammit! Push! You have a father and mother that love you dearly. You have brothers that care about you! You hold on. Concentrate!"

"Pete . . . it's cold . . . it's so cold . . ."

"I know it is. I know, but you can handle it. I know you can! What's your altitude?"

"Fifty feet . . ."

"Heading?"

"One . . . seven . . . zero."

Halston looked to his right at the radio operator, who gave him a thumbs up.

"You're right on target. Right on target. You're headed straight for a temporary base of Army tanks just south of the border. We have two helos on the way from another base to meet you and bring you here. The flight surgeon and his staff are aboard the choppers."

"Oh, God, it hurts . . . I'm shivering . . ."

Halston felt his heart sinking. Tears welled up in his eyes as he struggled to remain in control, searching for the right words to say.

"You're only ten miles away from the Army base, Amanda. You're almost home. Almost home. Start your descent. You should get a visual on the camp in under a minute. You can make it. I know you can. Please, hang on!"

"I'm sorry . . . I can't . . . longer . . ."

Halston lowered the mike and pressed his lips into a tight frown as his heartbeat pounded inside him. He glanced at everyone in the room. All eyes were on him. He made up his mind and brought the mike up to his lips again. Tears now rolled down his face. "I love you, dammit! Can you hear me, Amanda Green? I said I love you and I need you! I lost someone I loved dearly once, please don't do this to me again! Please . . . *please* come back to me."

Captain Amanda Green breathed deeply, shuddering with pain, as her ears listened to the words of the man she loved. She didn't want to die. *I'm too young, dammit. I can't die yet! He loves me!*

And so Amanda pushed. She looked deep inside and pulled out the unyielding determination to remain alive. She blinked rapidly as her vision began to fog. She couldn't afford that. She needed her eyesight to spot the—*There! I see it!*

A final burst of adrenaline gave her the energy to focus on her landing. Amanda cut back throttle and lowered collective while inching the cyclic forward. The Pave Hawk began to descend. She focused on the base. Tears had filled her eyes and she could no longer read the instruments. She flew on instinct. She felt the Pave Hawk through the cyclic and collective, through the rudder pedals. It became a part of her. Her craft was wounded like her, struggling to return home, fighting to stay together. The Pave Hawk talked to her, told her when to add more power, when to adjust collective or cyclic, when to add just a bit more rudder. Amanda felt something she'd never experienced before. The Pave Hawk was really telling her what to do. Telling her how to take it home. Like herself, it didn't want to perish so close to home after fighting so hard.

And so they went together, machine and pilot. Pilot and machine. The two became one as they flew over the perimeter fence and reached the tarmac, hovering ten feet above the ground before slowly, oh, so slowly, touching down.

Too weak to move, Captain Amanda Green's last impression was a pair of hands pulling her out of the cockpit before all faded away.

▪ 17 ▪

WARNINGS

The defense secretary showed President Clinton the latest advancement of Iraqi troops. It seems as if the Republican Guard detachment had slowed down as it approached the border with Kuwait and Saudi Arabia, finally coming to a halt just fifteen miles from the border. The initial force of American troops in the region had been reinforced with 7,500 Marines, plus additional aircraft, tanks, and the USS *Kennedy* Carrier Group in the Med. But so far there was no sign of Saddam's nukes.

Could this whole thing be just one gigantic bluff to make my administration look foolish in the eyes of the world? No. Clinton didn't buy that. Saddam wouldn't risk another heavy pounding like Desert Storm if he didn't have the nuclear power to back up his moves. Or would he? The Iraqi leader certainly had a history of making the oddest of moves for no obvious strategic gain.

What's he waiting for?

One possible explanation, which Clinton liked most, was that the Iraqi leader didn't have the nukes assembled yet. Another explanation, which he feared, was that Saddam had a few nukes built and was simply building more, positioning Iraq in the world map of nuclear powers.

The CIA had some preliminary data from the NPIC archives that indicated that Allahbad had consumed far more construction materials than the factory near Baghdad, and that it had also taken much longer to build. Those findings tended to support the CIA's theory of an underground facility. Draper, however, still believed otherwise. His secretary of state claimed it was too soon to tell. Defense wanted a second attack immediately. A recent briefing by the chairman of the Joint Chiefs of Staff gave Clinton a good idea of the latest plan of attack should a ground war break out.

But the president didn't want to go to war, simply because there was no need for war. He just wanted to eliminate Saddam's nukes and make the Iraqi dictator crawl back into his little hole in Baghdad.

Clinton decided to wait it out a bit longer, at least until the CIA finished searching through their archives.

On the positive side, the president had just gotten word that the pilot of the downed F-14 over Iraq had been rescued and flown to a base in northern Saudi Arabia, where he still remained unconscious. The president prayed for his quick recovery and for that of the wounded crew who rescued him.

SALMAN ASAD AIR BASE, SAUDI ARABIA. NEAR IRAQI BORDER.
Day Six. 1700 Local Time.

The light became progressively brighter, then went away. The image of a doctor came into focus.

"He's going to be fine, sir. Just lost a lot of blood. He'll feel much better after a couple of transfusions."

"Thank you, Doctor," another voice responded. "Is he conscious enough to understand what we're saying?"

"I doubt it, but you're welcome to try," the doctor

responded as he walked away. His face was replaced by the face of a stranger.

"Lieutenant Dalton . . . Lieutenant Dalton, if you can hear me simply blink your eyes. One for yes; two for no. Got it?"

Kevin blinked once.

"Good. My name is Colonel Peter Halston, U.S. Air Force. Do you remember what happened to you out there?"

Kevin blinked once.

"A woman used your radio to give us your position. Where is she now?"

Kevin didn't respond. He simply stared into space. *Khalela . . . why?* Inexorably, his mind drifted back to the moment he realized she was not in the helicopter. Her touch, her eyes, her smell—it was all gone in a second. Kevin felt alone, cold. He turned his head away and closed his eyes.

Halston slowly shook his head, realizing that Kevin had obviously been under a lot of stress. The colonel decided to wait until the doctors got more blood into him and he'd had a chance to sleep for a few extra hours. Halston began to turn around when he noticed a single tear flowing down Kevin's right cheek. He remembered the Pave Hawk's gunner relating the incident. The gunner had had a hard time controlling Kevin when he made it to the chopper. He'd said that the lieutenant kept screaming about a woman named Khalela. The gunner also indicated that the woman had been running toward the chopper with Kevin, but had stopped halfway and started running the other way.

That's odd, Halston thought. *Why would she do something like that? Especially with the place crawling with Iraqi troops.* Halston wondered if that was the same person he had talked to on the radio.

Halston was curious about how the Iraqis had managed to deploy the tanks, the Hind, and the MiG-29 to the area so quickly. He knew that the Iraqis constantly monitored the Guard channel and would have found the rescue spot, but how did they do it so fast? After all, the rescue team was already airborne and well on its way by the time Delgado had made contact with Dalton. Maybe the woman was responsible. Halston frowned. It certainly would explain why she didn't get in the chopper. *But on the other hand, Dalton could have easily warned us when Delgado asked about the tattoo on his arm, but Dalton came right out and specifically told us to relax, that it wasn't a trap. Unless . . . that woman fooled him, too.* Halston stared at the Navy pilot and tried to put himself in his shoes: injured, abandoned, and alone in hostile ground. Not speaking the language and sticking out like a sore thumb. A woman somehow manages to cross his path, probably pretending to be a Kurd or with some antigovernment group, and offers her help. Suddenly, he has a translator, a friend, someone that could be his ticket out of there. Halston smiled. The story fit the facts, but he decided to wait until the lieutenant came around before drawing any conclusions.

He walked over to the bed adjacent to Dalton's. Amanda was in a similar situation. She had lost a lot of blood and remained unconscious. It had been a miracle that she had managed to bring the craft back in one piece, especially wounded and with a blown canopy. *She's the best.* Delaney, Rizzo, and one of the Special Ops soldiers were still in surgery. Poole never made it; he was dead on arrival. Rizzo, on the other hand, had been very fortunate that the helmet had deflected the round, otherwise he would have been dead on impact.

Halston kneeled down next to her and took her hand. "Thank you, Amanda. Thank you for coming back to me," he whispered.

"Pete . . ." Her eyes opened.

Halston's eyes filled. "Yes, baby. It's me. I'm here with you."

She smiled. "Thank you."

"No, baby. Thank you for coming back to me. God, for a moment I thought—"

She put a hand on his lips. "I know. I love you, too."

He remained with her for ten more minutes before she slowly drifted back to sleep.

Slowly, Halston got up and glanced at the orderly "Call me the moment she comes back around."

"Yes, sir."

Halston left the hospital tent and headed for Draper's tent. The late afternoon sun blinded him. Halston took out his sunglasses and put them on. Kramer and Delgado stood next to a parked Army jeep. He approached them

"How are they, sir?" asked Delgado.

"They'll be all right. We're going to have to wait a few more hours before he's fully conscious. The doctor said he's lost a lot of blood. Amanda's in better shape. I just talked to her for a couple of minutes."

"Can we go in and see them, sir?" Delgado asked in a half-pleading tone.

Halston smiled. "Sure, I guess you guys can go in." He walked past them.

"Well? What does he have to say in his defense?" Draper asked the moment Halston walked inside the tent.

"He won't be saying much until he comes back around, sir."

"Do you have a guard next to his bed?"

"No, sir. Why should I?"

Draper shrugged. "Fine. It's not my place to argue with you on this. The Navy pilot is your responsibility, not mine."

"With all due respect, *sir,* in case you haven't been keeping up with current events, Lieutenant Dalton was the one who turned himself in to us. He is the one that ran *to* the chopper and the one that jumped *in* the chopper. Doesn't that mean anything? Doesn't that give him the right to be treated like the pilot he is until such a time as a military court finds him guilty, if he is found guilty at all?"

Draper didn't flinch. "The only reason I came to this godforsaken base was to make sure Operation Desert Star went smoothly. What you do about other issues is your business."

Halston tightened his fists. *Control. Control. Don't let him get to you, Pete. He's almost out of here.* "You asked for an update on his situation and I just gave it to you. Is there anything else that—"

"That will be all, Colonel."

Halston managed to control his anger and did not storm out of the place. He slowly turned around and walked away.

"Madre de Dios, Crackers. You look like shit! What in the world happened to you out there?"

"Chico . . . hi . . ."

Delgado knelt next to the bed and grabbed Kevin's hand.

"You're gonna be fine. See this?" He pointed at the plastic tube connected to an IV. "You're gettin' lots of blood, man. In a few hours you'll be jumpin' up and down." Delgado saw the hint of a smile on Kevin's bruised face.

"Doubt it . . . but thanks."

"Is there anythin' you need, *hermano?* Anythin' at all?"

"Thirsty . . ."

Delgado bolted up to his feet and glanced at the orderly. "You heard the man. How about some water!"

The orderly walked to the nurse's station, where he grabbed a paper cup and poured water from a plastic pitcher.

"Here you go, sir."

Delgado knelt down and brought the cup to Kevin's lips. "Go easy, man. Just a few sips for now."

Kevin coughed after the first swallow. Delgado looked down to put the cup on the floor. By the time he looked back up, Kevin's eyes were closed.

"The doctor said he's going to be like that for at least another hour, Chico," Longhorn Kramer said from the foot of the bed.

Kramer walked over to Amanda's bed. Delgado followed him. "Hey, I see you're doing better," Longhorn said. "Gotta little color in your cheeks. How're you doin' down there, hon?"

Amanda's lips curved upward. "Are you . . . always so damned . . . cheerful?"

"Honey, where I come from you gotta have a cheerful personality or you'll go nuts."

"That was some serious flyin' you did over there, Amanda," Delgado said. "The gunner from the Pave Hawk told us all about it."

Amanda smiled.

"He also told us about the MiG-29. Sounds like somethin' you would see in a movie. I'm tellin' you, you're goin' up for some serious medals."

"How's . . . Poole doing?"

Delgado looked to Kramer, who took Amanda's hand in his gently before speaking. "I'm sorry, darlin' . . ."

A silent tear flowed down her cheek.

An hour later, Halston and Bourdeaux headed for the hospital tent after receiving messages that Kevin and Amanda were fully awake. The evening air was warm and dry as they walked across the still-hot tarmac. Bourdeaux broke out in a light sweat.

The second set of satellite images from the NPIC archives that had arrived an hour ago contained more of the same: an unusually high number of trucks hauling all kinds of materials into the warehouse over the course of several years. Bourdeaux found it amazing that this facility was never flagged before, but then again, he reflected, during the height of the construction in the mid-eighties, the United States was on Iraq's side in the fight against Iran. At the time, CIA and military analysts could care less about the construction of a milk factory in south-central Iraq. During those years, the Reagan administration had the American intelligence community focused on the Soviet Union, Iran, Libya, Cuba, the war against cocaine traffic, the Contra-Sandinista war, the civil war of El Salvador, and Noriega's Panama.

Nope. Nobody gave a shit about Iraq back then, though Bourdeaux, deciding to write a final recommendation to the director of the CIA based on the second set of archived images he had just reviewed.

Followed by Halston, Bourdeaux pushed the canvas flap open and walked between the two rows of beds. He spotted Delgado and Kramer. As Bourdeaux had ex pected, Halston went to see Amanda first. After a few minutes, the colonel turned toward the U.S. Navy lieutenant.

"Good evening, Lieutenant," Halston said.

"Hello, sir."

"You do remember me, right?"

"Yes, sir."

"Good. Where shall we start?"

"The beginning sounds like a good place to me, sir," responded Kevin.

"Very well, then," Halston said, pulling up a chair. Bourdeaux stood behind the colonel. "We're listening."

Kevin cleared his throat and began. His voice was slow and steady, his words carefully chosen. He described the highlights only, figuring that they would ask questions afterward about specifics.

"Ha! I told you, Bob!" Halston shouted the moment Kevin mentioned the underground facility at Allahbad. "Those bastards are assembling their nuclear missiles down there. Well, I'll be damned!"

The CIA officer slowly shook his head in disbelief. The pilot's testimony was the final piece of data he needed to really point the finger at Allahbad. Bourdeaux turned to Kevin. "That's one hell of a story, Lieutenant, especially your friendship with the Kurds and this woman . . . what's her name again?"

"Khalela Yishaid."

"How do you know she's not the enemy?" Halston asked.

Kevin smiled. "Because, sir, she's Mossad."

"What?" snapped Bourdeaux.

"She's Israeli intelligence. When I met her she was training the band of Kurds on some Javelins they had just—"

"You said Javelins?" Bourdeaux interrupted.

"Ah, yes. They said they got them from someone they called 'the American *Ba'i*.' The American merchant, as Khalela translated it for me later."

Bourdeaux couldn't believe this. "Damn! One of their names wasn't Ishmael by any chance, was it?"

"Yes, it was. How do you—"

"Because I was the one that gave those Javelins t⋅
them. I'm the *Ba'i*."

"You what?"

"You heard me. I'm Robert Bourdeaux. CIA."

"Boy, that's interesting."

"What's that?" asked Bourdeaux.

"Well, sir. The only reason I'm here today is becaus⋅
Ishmael and his Kurdish guerrillas wanted to trade m⋅
for additional weapons. They kept mentioning that th⋅
Ba'i would be very generous when they brought me t⋅
him."

"Going back to the woman, Lieutenant," Halsto⋅
said. "How do you know she was Mossad? She coul⋅
have easily been lying."

Kevin frowned and told them that the thought di⋅
cross his mind at first, but then he had put two and tw⋅
together and realized that she could not have been lyin⋅
First, she was well known by the Kurds, who ha⋅
contacts in a lot of places inside Iraq. Second, she ha⋅
destroyed two Iraqi helicopters and had rescued him⋅
Would the Iraqis let one of their own people destroy tw⋅
craft and crew just to impress an American pilot? Kevi⋅
couldn't buy that. And third, Kevin saw the way she ha⋅
been tortured at the chemical complex when he rescue⋅
her. Khalela was for real. As for the Hinds, the Iraqis ha⋅
simply reacted very fast to the transmission they proba⋅
bly picked up on Guard.

"Then how do you explain the fact she didn't get o⋅
the chopper?"

Kevin lowered his gaze. "She's Mossad, sir. She stil⋅
had a mission," was all he could say.

"All right," Halston said. "We'll go with that for now."

"Ah, Lieutenant?" asked Bourdeaux.

"Yes?"

"Did all the Kurds perish in the ambush outsid⋅
Allahbad?"

"All died during the ambush except for two, si⋅
Ishmael was tortured to death, according to Khalela⋅
Abdul, Ishmael's right hand, was killed by an Iraⵊ
officer while helping Khalela and me escape from th⋅
complex during the bombing."

"Damn! They were good people."

"Yes, Mr. Bourdeaux. They were the best."

Bourdeaux thanked the Navy pilot and left the group. He had a report to write.

▪ 18 ▪

VALUES

SALMAN ASAD AIR BASE, SAUDI ARABIA. NEAR IRAQI BORDER.
Day Six. 2120 Local Time.

Robert Bourdeaux was very surprised. General Kenneth
Draper had not reacted exactly as he had expected.
Draper had listened to him without interruption as the
CIA analyst sat across the table from Draper in the
general's tent. Bourdeaux even saw what appeared to be
true concern in the general's eyes.

"So the pilot also claims there is an underground lab?"

"Yes, sir."

"And you said that you have already sent your recommendation to the director of the CIA based on the pilot's
testimony and the satellite images?"

"That's right, sir."

Draper regarded Bourdeaux for a few seconds. "Well,
let me talk to the president. Perhaps we can all come to
some kind of consensus on this issue."

Bourdeaux smelled trouble. The Silver Rat simply
wasn't this nice. "Ah, yes, General. That will be fine."

Bourdeaux turned around and left the tent. The air
was now cool and invigorating. He breathed deeply

everal times, trying to figure out Draper's game. Rub-
ing his right temple, Bourdeaux spotted Halston,
Kramer, and Delgado standing next to Kevin Dalton. He
approached them.

"Shouldn't you be in bed, Lieutenant Dalton?"

"I feel great. Maybe it's because of all the blood they
umped into me."

"Well, I suggest you don't push it."

"Oh, I won't. I just got up and came outside to get a
reath of fresh air."

"So," Halston asked, "how did it go in there?"

Bourdeaux frowned and shifted his gaze to the row of
F-15 Eagles parked on the far side of the base. "He said
e would discuss it with the president."

"That's it?" asked Halston.

"Yes, but I'm not really certain what to—Oh, there he
goes, probably heading to make his call," Bourdeaux
aid as he spotted Draper and his pilot walking toward
he Gulfstream IV.

"Hmm," said Halston. "Say, guys, I'll be right back."

Bourdeaux watched Draper and the pilot go inside the
Grumman executive transport jet and close the door
ehind them. "Where are you going, Pete?"

"To check something out." With that Halston headed
or the communications tent.

Five minutes later, Bourdeaux watched Draper and
he pilot leave the Gulfstream. Draper walked back to his
ent. Another minute went by, and Halston emerged
rom the communications tent. He held a piece of paper
n his hand.

"Bob, I'm afraid I've got some bad news for you," said
Halston.

Bourdeaux looked at his old Army buddy's hardened
ace. "C'mon, Pete. Out with it."

"Draper just made a secure call to the White House. I
ntercepted and unscrambled it."

"You did what?"

Halston shrugged and looked at his notes. "It's all for a
good cause. Draper told President Clinton that Desert
Star was a disaster. He blamed the CIA, and in particular
you, Bob, for not gathering enough intelligence on the

site prior to the bombing raid. Did you know that the Iraqis are claiming a civilian death toll of over two hundred at Allahbad? Two hundred innocent men, women, and children?"

Bourdeaux blinked twice. "Oh, shit, I didn't know about—"

"It's supposed to be all over the networks," responded Halston.

"That's bullshit," said Kramer. "You know that's all a bunch of Iraqi propaganda horseshit."

"I know that," said Halston, "but you know how the media is about these things."

"Jesus Christ," said Bourdeaux, closing his eyes and massaging his temples.

"There's more, Bob."

Bourdeaux opened his right eye. "More?"

"Yep. Draper stated that Desert Star had given the Clinton administration a large black eye. Draper reminded the president that he had been against the operation from the start, and that he should have never listened to you in the first place. He warned the president against acting on the information provided by the hot headed Navy pilot, and he also said that this kind of impulsive behavior is what got us in this mess in the first place. I imagine the White House is now trying to figure out how to explain this one to the world. This is some mess, Bob. . . ."

"And?"

Halston exhaled. "Shit. Well, here it comes. I'm really sorry, man, but Draper has recommended that you be removed from your current assignment and shipped back to Langley. Sounds like he's trying to get you canned."

Bourdeaux stood in utter disbelief. Draper was making the ultimate move against him and he felt impotent to stop it. He knew the president would pay more attention to Draper's opinion than his own, particularly after the Iraqis used the dead civilians to make themselves look like the victims of a ruthless Allied bombing. The Silver Rat had been around for some time and knew a lot of people in Congress and in the military. Bourdeaux didn't stand a chance against him.

"Damn!" Longhorn Kramer said. "Like they say where I come from, the two-faced bastard borrowed your brandin' iron and is gonna use it to brand your ass when you ain't lookin'."

Bourdeaux nodded. "Yep. You got the right picture, Colonel."

"It's not fair, Bob!" protested Halston. "I think I should go in there and—"

Bourdeaux raised his right hand. He explained to Halston and the others that there was nothing they could do *for* him, but there was a lot they could do *against* themselves if they went to Draper and try to defend Bourdeaux's position. Draper's mind was set and he had already made his move. There was nothing that could change it now. Bourdeaux walked away.

"That bastard Draper," Halston murmured to the others. "Bob Bourdeaux's one hell of a man, and that asshole's about to destroy him. There must be something we can do."

"Hey, what about the fucking missiles?" Kevin asked. "When all the smoke clears after Draper's back home and Bourdeaux back at Langley, the fact will still remain that the Iraqis have managed to build and deploy nuclear missiles. You know if those bastards are crazy enough to have launched Scud after Scud against Tel Aviv and Riyadh during Desert Storm, they won't hesitate to launch a few nuclear missiles if they have them ready. We gotta do something fast."

"But what? You heard Draper," Delgado said. "Desert Star's dead."

"The hell with him. At this point it doesn't matter what I do anyhow. The moment I'm discharged from the hospital, I'm going to be facing that long green table, and you know what that usually means."

"Yep. You can kiss off your flying career and forget about your future in the Navy."

Kevin took two steps away from the group, turned around and faced his audience of three. "Gentlemen, if

I'm gonna be forced to leave the armed forces, I'm going to do it in style, and *truly* serve Uncle Sam in the process."

"What do you have in mind?" Kramer asked.

Kevin smiled.

"Oh, shit," Delgado said.

BAGHDAD.
Day Six. 2230 Local Time.

The Syrian woman slowly undressed and smiled, showing two perfectly straight rows of glistening white teeth. With her light green eyes gazing into his, Saddam Hussein, sitting on the bed of one of his luxury bunkers, also smiled, not in response to the beautiful woman in front of him, but because a fourth missile had been deployed at Allahbad. He now controlled the future of Tel Aviv, Riyadh, Kuwait City, and Tehran. All he had to do was pick up the phone next to the bed, and in ten minutes those four cities would cease to exist.

Soon, he decided. *Very soon.* Another reason for his smile was the attention the world had given to the sixty-second film of the civilians killed at Allahbad. Once again, the predictable Americans and their news media were helping his cause.

The Syrian whore dropped her last garment on the carpeted floor and approached him, her hands reaching for the buttons of his brown uniform. Saddam placed his hands on her tanned hips and stared at her flat stomach.

The phone rang. Glaring at the intrusion, Saddam picked it up. "Yes?"

"Great One, the field general with the southern deployment is requesting further instructions."

Saddam nodded. The deployed forces had stopped short of the border and, with all the Allied activity on the other side, were getting restless. In spite of Saddam's control of the media inside Iraq, horror stories of the 1991 Gulf War continued to circulate among the ranks of his army. *This time around, things will be much different.*

"Tell them I will give them new instructions in the morning."

As scenarios unraveled in his mind, Saddam hung up the phone while the Syrian whore fiddled with the buttons of his uniform. *Soon. Very soon.*

THE WHITE HOUSE.
Day Six. 1300 Local Time.

President Clinton had a serious problem in his hands. On one side, CNN played the massacre at Allahbad over and over again, stirring concern around the country—and the world. Already the White House telephone lines were overloaded with callers from across the country complaining about the killings of innocent civilians. On the other side, he had the CIA and the downed F-14 pilot telling him that Allahbad—the same complex where Iraqi officials claimed hundreds of women and children had perished—had an underground laboratory that was assembling nukes. He had listened to his advisors over and over again. All had given him their honest opinions based on their positions and their experience. All except for Undersecretary Kenneth Draper, who appeared to care more about pointing fingers than about solving this problem. In this case, Draper had stated in no uncertain terms that Bourdeaux was responsible for this disaster.

President Clinton grimaced at the thought of Draper making life very difficult for CIA Officer Bourdeaux, who simply appeared to be doing his job. He would deal with Draper later. Right now it was time for an executive decision.

While leaning against the edge of his desk, the president silently probed his defense secretary, who wore a dark blue suit and sat on one of the sofas.

"Mr. President?"

"I want you to get in contact with General Marshall and coordinate another strike on the facility. Only those who need to know about this second strike should be aware of it. Nobody else. Is that understood?"

"Yes, sir," responded the defense secretary. "But it's going to take some time to set it up."

"How much time?"

"Twelve to twenty-four hours, sir. It took that long to

prepare for the first strike. If all goes well, we should be able to launch the attack by sunset tomorrow night. We'll probably launch it directly from the F-117 base at Khamis Mushait. That way we'll be able to keep it between us in this room, General Marshall, and General Towers, the commander of the F-117 base."

Clinton nodded. "Very well. Get it done."

AMAN BAKISH AIR BASE NEAR AN NAJAF, SOUTHERN IRAQ.
Day Six. 2120 Local Time.

General Abunnasr Manesh watched the technicians remove the faulty electronic modules from his MiG-29 and replace them with brand new spare parts. The missile control system was now operational again, giving his MiG full weapons capability once more. The technicians faced him and gave him a thumbs-up.

"This jet is one hundred percent ready for combat, sir."

"Good. Very good." He walked away.

SALMAN ASAD AIR BASE, SAUDI ARABIA. NEAR IRAQI BORDER.
Day Seven. 0420 Local Time.

With sunrise less than two hours away, Colonel Long-horn Kramer and Lieutenant Delgado walked away from their jets, having verified that both the F-14 and the F-117A were fully fueled and armed.

They headed for the medical tent.

Lieutenant Kevin Dalton had not been able to sleep. The rush of adrenaline through his veins kept him fully awake. He glanced to his right and saw Amanda sleeping peacefully. He nodded his head slightly. In his mind, she deserved to get all the rest in the world after the way she had managed to bring the Pave Hawk and crew back home in one piece in spite of her wounds. On the bed next to Amanda's was Captain Orlando Delaney, also sleeping. The Apache pilot had fended off the MiG and made the mission a success. Kevin only regretted that the green-striped MiG had managed to escape. Across the narrow hall were Delaney's copilot and one of the Special Ops men, both of whom were knocked out with painkillers.

He shifted his gaze to the empty nurse's station. The nurse on duty had gone to the supply room to get more painkillers after Kevin had complained about his leg wound. He sighed. He knew it was just a matter of time before he had to defend his actions. Facing the long green court-martial table didn't bother him as much as it had just a few days ago, but he could imagine how the senior aviators sitting at that table would slowly take him apart. He knew the questions that would be thrown at him. *What in the world were you thinking, Lieutenant? How could we ever trust you again with a multimillion dollar jet? Your ego killed a fine officer. What do you have to say for yourself?*

He frowned. There were more pressing issues going through his head at the time. Khalela, for one thing. He had temporarily managed to suppress some of his feelings for her and replace them with the logical understanding that she didn't belong in his world. She was Mossad, a highly trained operative; he a pilot in name only about to face the consequences of . . . *Dammit, I still feel that I was doing the right thing at the time!* he thought, his face contorted with anger. Although he had only known Commander DeWayne Lancaster for just under two years, he had had a lot of respect for him. Lancaster had helped him a lot, especially during his first months at NAS Miramar. His encouraging words and impeccable example as a true naval aviator had reinforced Kevin's desire to become the best. Kevin thought of the green-striped MiG. He was fixated on it. He didn't care what it took and would trade anything—short of a chance of seeing Khalela again—to meet that MiG again in a Tomcat. In his mind, the MiG's action had violated all the established codes of aerial combat.

He pressed the tips of his fingers against his temples, massaging them. He knew that any way he looked at it, the fact still remained that he had disobeyed a direct order from McDeere, and because of that he had been shot down and his RIO killed. He knew that would be the way the court would also see it.

Sighing, Kevin looked to his left at Commander John McDeere, sleeping peacefully after taking a strong pain-killer for a severe stomach virus. Kevin smiled. Delgado was really something else. Kevin owed Delgado one for knocking McDeere out of commission before Kevin arrived at the base. The last thing Kevin needed right now was an earful from his commanding officer.

A noise to his right made him lift his head from the pillow.

"Shh, easy, Crackers, or you gonna get us all in trouble."

Kevin got up. "All right, Chico," he whispered. "We only got a few minutes before the nurse comes back and sees an empty bed."

"Don't worry about that. In a few minutes it won't really matter. Let's go."

Kevin followed Delgado out the back entrance. Outside, they joined Kramer, who had the stolen gear of another Tomcat pilot, one roughly the same size as Kevin. The trio quickly moved toward their jets.

Robert Bourdeaux heard the jet engines and recognized the distinctive sound of the Tomcat. There weren't supposed to be any F-14 missions at this time. Puzzled, he got up, put on his shoes and walked outside. He spotted an Air Force sergeant staring at the F-14 after-burners accelerating down the runway.

"What's going on, Sergeant?"

"Don't know, sir. Sure is pretty, though. Always loved those Tomcats."

"Shit." Bourdeaux headed for the communications tent. A minute later, he found Halston sitting behind the radio gear.

"Pete, we gotta talk."

"What's up?"

"I don't know what's up. That's why we gotta talk."

Halston followed Bourdeaux outside.

"A Tomcat just took off. Do you know why?"

"I'm afraid so, Bob. It's Dalton and Delgado. Kramer left a couple of minutes ago in his Black Jet."

"What? Dalton's in the hospital! What in the hell's going on? And what do Delgado and Kramer think they're doing?"

"Well, you could talk to them, though I doubt they'd answer." Halston grinned.

Bourdeaux regarded him for a moment. "Pete, do you know what's going on?"

"They're going to Allahbad."

"Are they out of their minds? Pete, are you involved in this?"

"Ah . . . yep. I guess you can say that."

Bourdeaux turned as he heard footsteps. It was General Draper. He wore a robe and slippers.

"Bob, I hear an F-14 just took off. What's the story?"

"Lieutenant Dalton just left in an F-14."

"He what?"

"You heard me, sir. He just took off."

"Where does he think he's going?"

"Allahbad."

Bourdeaux watched Draper's face redden and then quiver as he tightened his fists and stormed inside the communications tent.

"That son of a bitch!" He turned to Halston. "I should have put him in the brig! What does he think he's doing? Hasn't he done enough damage already? Dammit! This is exactly the kind of shit I was trying to prevent from happening! Who's in the backseat?"

"Lieutenant Delgado, but it's too late for that now," responded Bourdeaux.

"Dammit! They're about to ruin everything!"

"Are they, sir?"

Draper locked eyes with Bourdeaux. "What did you say?"

"I said, is he really going to ruin everything?"

"What's that supposed to mean?"

"Have you thought of the fact that maybe he *is* right? That perhaps there *are* nuclear weapons at Allahbad?"

"I've had just about enough of your insolence, Bob!

Halston, I want you to get on that radio and call them back now!"

Halston looked at Draper and smiled. "Sorry, sir. But I'm afraid I'm in on this as well."

"What? Do you realize the implications of your actions, Colonel?"

"Yes, sir. I do."

"In that case, you're relieved for insubordination!" Draper turned to Bourdeaux. "Bob, I want you to talk to Lieutenant Dalton and order him back right now!"

Bourdeaux picked up the microphone and brought it to his mouth. He stopped.

"Bob! This is your last warning. You either call or I'm going to—"

"Here, sir," Bourdeaux said, handing the mike over to Draper. *"You* want him to turn around, *you* talk to him. I'm CIA, not Air Force. I'm not allowed to talk on that radio, but even if I could, I wouldn't because I'm getting canned anyway. Right, General?"

Draper blinked twice and gave Bourdeaux a half-puzzled look. He then looked at Halston, who raised his eyebrows.

"I'm in charge of communications, sir," the Californian responded.

Draper snatched the mike from Bourdeaux's hands. "You, you—both of you just made the worst decision of your careers!"

Kevin Dalton pulled back throttles to forty percent and kept the craft below one hundred feet above ground. He smiled broadly behind the oxygen mask. It felt good to be flying again, even if it would be his last hop.

"Wolfpack Two One Six, this is General Draper," Kevin heard over a secure channel.

"Shit, Crackers. That's the asshole from CENTAF," Delgado said over the ICS.

"It was bound to happen sooner or later, Chico."

"What are you gonna do?" asked Delgado.

"Guess I'll talk to the guy." Kevin switched a knob on his radio. "Wolfpack Two One Six."

"One Six, I'm ordering you to turn the craft around immediately or face the consequences."

"Negative."

"Return to base or I'll vector F-15s to shoot you down."

"Sorry, sir. A lot of people died to get the information that I passed to you yesterday, and you've chosen to close your eyes to what I have seen at Allahbad. I can't. Millions of lives are at stake!"

"It's of no use anyway, One Six. You're only carrying air-to-air missiles. They won't do you any good."

"Lieutenant Dalton's stores won't, but my cargo will, sir," interrupted Kramer.

"Who's that?" Draper asked.

"This is Longhorn. I got two Paveways and I know where to put them."

"Christ, Colonel! Do you realize the consequences of what you're doing?"

"Sure do, sir. Somebody's gotta do it."

"You bunch of lunatics! I order all of you to RTB right now!"

"Say again. You're broken."

"Don't hand me that bullshit!"

That was all Kevin cared to hear from the general. He deselected that frequency and switched to the squadron frequency. "Everybody still up for this?"

"Listen, pal. The only reason that I'm a lieutenant colonel at thirty-five's because I've always taken chances. Otherwise I wouldn't be more than a captain."

"Besides, Crackers," added Delgado, "not much else to do around here."

Kevin smiled. "Thank you, guys. Now let's get down to business."

"ETA to target two zero mikes," he heard Kramer say.

"Concur," responded Delgado.

Kevin glanced outside and saw the orange light coloring the horizon. Sunrise was minutes away.

ALLAHBAD PROCESSING COMPLEX, SOUTH OF AN NAJAF, IRAQ.
Day Seven. 0545 Local Time.

Dr. Sakkar approached Risha across the corridor between two red-fuming nitric acid tanks. Another missile would be deployed in an hour. Sakkar smiled. It seemed that every time he assigned Risha to assist a missile crew, their rocket got deployed next.

THE WHITE HOUSE.
Day Six. 2147 Local Time.

The phone interrupted a late meeting in the Oval Office, where the defense secretary and the chairman of the Joint Chiefs of Staff presented the plan for the raid on Allahbad to the president, the secretary of state, and the director of Central Intelligence.

The president, sitting behind his desk, picked it up on the third ring.

"Yes?"

"Mr. President," one of his aides said, "I have Undersecretary Kenneth Draper on the line. He claims he needs to talk to you about a matter of national security."

Jesus. What now?

"All right, put him through." The president pressed the speaker box button on his phone.

"Mr. President?" the voice of Draper crackled inside the Oval Office.

"Yes. What's wrong?"

"I'm afraid we have a serious problem in our hands, sir. It involves the Navy pilot Lieutenant Kevin Dalton. He just stole a Tomcat and is heading for Allahbad. I just tried to convince him to turn around, but he switched me off. An F-117, piloted by the same officer who flew the initial strike, also went along with Dalton, sir."

Clinton leaned back in his chair, interlocking his fingers in front of his face while closing his eyes. He opened them a second later. Blank stares from his staff bombarded the president. Clinton didn't flinch. "How long ago did they leave?"

"Minutes ago, sir. We're still in time to stop them."

The president's eyebrows rose a trifle. "And how, Mr. Draper, do you propose we stop them?"

The line went silent for a few seconds. "Ah . . . I recommend vectoring F-15 interceptors to shoot them down, sir. There is a squadron of them flying an exercise a hundred miles east of here. You can't let them get to the facility, sir."

"Mr. Draper, are you recommending that I order F-15s to shoot down our own planes?"

"Mr. President, I—"

"I want you to report back here immediately, Mr. Draper. And I expect your resignation on my desk within forty-eight hours."

The president hung up. The room went silent.

"Well," Clinton said, "looks like our plan is now a backup." The president turned to the defense secretary. "Get ahold of General Marshall. Explain to him what the Tomcat and the F-117 pilots are doing, and ask him to have rescue teams ready."

"Yes, sir."

With his staff still wearing startled looks, Clinton got up, walked to a window behind his desk, and gazed out at a star-filled sky.

May God be with you, Lieutenant Kevin Dalton.

SOUTHERN IRAQ.
Day Seven. 0545 Local Time.

Under the light of a single gas lamp, Khalela Yishaid sat across the rustic table inside the murky room and looked at the two senior Mossad operatives. She felt nauseated and drained from lack of sleep. Since their arrival in the small village five hours ago, the senior operatives had gone through an extensive debriefing of her mission, all of which had been recorded on the portable tape recorder now rewinding.

"I'm glad that you made it, Khalela. For a while we were worried," said Colonel Hassin Abaraka, the older of the two, still dressed like a villager.

She glanced at him and then stared blankly out the window.

"Yes, Hassin, I did make it. That young Iraqi officer who told you about the plutonium shipment couldn't have been closer to the truth."

Hassin laughed. "That was *your* idea, Khalela. I just played the role, remember?"

Khalela nodded. "Yes, I remember."

"What do you think is going to happen to the American?"

She lowered her gaze. "I'm not sure. He may never fly again."

"He's lucky if he gets just that. In our Air Force, the punishment would have been a lot more harsh. We have no room for insubordinates."

Khalela didn't respond. Somehow Hassin's comment seemed cold.

"Khalela, are you all right?"

Khalela realized that although Hassin was showing her compassion, she was being evaluated for future suitability. A subtle trap. She could be removed from the Mossad based on her next few words. Oddly enough, she didn't care. Her feelings for Kevin weighed as heavily as her deep dedication for the Mossad.

She finally lifted her eyes. "Yes, Colonel, I'm fine. Just tired. I feel like I could sleep for a week."

"And you shall. You have done a terrific job."

"I wouldn't have come out of it alive if it hadn't been for the American pilot."

"You did what an operative is supposed to do: create contingency plans in case something goes wrong. In my opinion, this Lieutenant Dalton was a contingency plan. You used him wisely."

Khalela felt confused. A week ago she would have agreed with Hassin, but now it was different. She actually felt guilty about having tricked Kevin the day before, but the professional in her said that she had made the right decision. She was Mossad, a highly trained operative for the service of Israel. Her country had spent a great deal of time and money training her to do what she did best, and now it was time to pay it back. The problem was that she only now understood the price tag associated with her job.

"Yes, Colonel, I did use him," she responded, getting up and walking toward the window, hoping that Hassin did not notice the feelings she had developed for Kevin. Feelings that now consumed her. *Oh, dear Kevin, I hope you understand why I had to do it.*

SOUTHERN IRAQ.
Day Seven. 0600 Local Time.

Delgado had kept his radar dark until the last moment. Flicking the AWG-9 power switch forward, his Tactical Information Display—the most powerful air-to-air radar in the world—came to life, flooding the air ahead of the Tomcat with energy. Immediately, Delgado saw tracks appearing on the TID.

"Two . . . no, three bogeys, Crackers! Zero eight zero at one niner miles, five hundred feet at six hundred knots."

"They're making a run into the zone."

"Not for long. Select Sparrow."

"Sparrow selected."

As Kevin moved the control stick to the right, he watched the Black Jet fade away in the murky sky. Kramer would continue to Allahbad and make the pass by himself while Kevin kept the skies clear of enemy craft.

"General Manesh! Look!"

General Abunnasr Manesh jumped off the cot before even opening his eyes. He stumbled across the room and struggled to focus on the radar screen. He saw several contacts on the radar screen near Allahbad.

"Again? What is going on? Who are they?"

"These three are ours, sir. They are MiG-21s from a base in Salman Pak. They were just flying inside the no-fly zone to create a disturbance. This fourth one came out of nowhere. It must have been flying below fifty feet."

"Can you contact our fighters?"

"As you wish, General."

Manesh grabbed the microphone from Fassan's hand. "This is Bakish Wind. You have single contact heading north. One five miles."

"Do you want us to intercept, over," reported the MiG's pilot.

"Take no chances. I repeat, no chances. Shoot when in range. Is that understood?"

"Yes, sir!"

Manesh handed the mike back to Fassan and raced outside.

Kevin Dalton felt safe at his low altitude. He knew that even if the extensive ground radars managed to detect the low-flying Tomcat, any interceptors would find it impossible to track him in the ground clutter. He also knew the Iraqis would be hesitant to get down in the weeds to look for him.

The TID still tracked three bogeys and assigned firing order priorities to each. Now it was just a matter of time before they were in range. Kevin knew his Phoenix and Sparrows could outrange the best of what the Iraqis could dish out.

"Almost . . . got trackin' on all three targets."

"Fire on priority one target!"

The missile rack locking mechanism released an AIM-7F Sparrow III. The missile glided under the Tomcat for a second before the solid-propellant rocket accelerated it to Mach 4. Kevin saw the bright flash under the craft followed by the river of light. The semi-active radar guidance system housed inside the 500-pound missile homed onto the reflected energy of the MiG illuminated by the Tomcat's fire control radar.

A few seconds later, Kevin saw a distant flash above the horizon. It contrasted clearly against the orange-stained sky.

"One down. Tally, MiG-21. Four o'clock high."

Kevin frowned. "Don't waste the missiles, Chico! Switching to guns!"

Kevin closed on the MiG, lined it up in the sights of his heads-up display and fired a short burst. The tracers were off to the left. He adjusted, but the MiG went for a dive. Kevin stayed with it. A short left and right turn and he had it in his sights once more. Floating his F-14 up to the MiG, Kevin fired another burst.

With the MiG filling his windscreen, the 20mm cannon came alive, spitting rounds at the Iraqi jet. Kevin kept the pipper on the MiG as it went into a steep climb, followed by an inverted dive and left turn. He fired two-second bursts until he spotted smoke coming out of the MiG's tail.

"Good shootin'!" Delgado said.

"Where's the third bogey?"

"High three o'clock."

Kevin turned his head to the right and spotted it: a silvery shape reflecting the early-morning sun's rays. "Got it!"

"Someone's got us locked. Break port *now!*" shouted Delgado.

"Not a MiG-21!" Kevin grunted under the heavy g-load as he racked the 60,000-pound fighter around. The g's continued to hammer him as he forced the F-14 into an oblique turn.

"Chaff, flares!" Kevin said as he watched the altimeter dash past ten thousand. He threw the stick forward. The negative g's gave him the sudden feeling that his stomach was being jammed against his throat as he leveled off and followed with a tight left turn.

"It went for the chaff!"

"Where's the bogey?"

"Tally, single at four, low, nose away. Looks like it's runnin' away."

"We'll see about that!" Kevin pulled the F-14's nose around to cut off the MiG's escape and got a visual in thirty seconds. He selected an automatic radar mode.

"Good lock!" cried Delgado.

Kevin centered the MiG's tail in his pipper and hosed off another Sparrow. The 500-pound missile overtook the MiG. Eighty-eight pounds of explosives with continuous rods tore off the tail of the MiG with a bright flash seconds before the Iraqi jet disappeared in a ball of flames.

"Mayday, May—!" Manesh heard the MiG's pilot scream over the radio before it went dead. He cursed out loud into his mask as he rolled his MiG off the cool tarmac. He remained below fifty feet above ground.

Kevin Dalton pulled back throttles as he resumed course to Allahbad. Soon the seemingly destroyed complex came into view through the hazy morning sky. He put his craft into an easy right turn.

"Talk to me, Chico," Kevin asked over the ICS.

"Nothin'. Scope's clean."

Kevin scanned the skies for Longhorn Kramer.

With the deafening sound of sirens piercing his eardrums, the young captain in charge of defending Allahbad raced for one of the surviving Shilkas parked in front of the complex.

"You, in there!"

The private sitting next to the Shilka's radar dish and searching the skies with field binoculars snapped his head in the major's direction.

"Yes, sir?"

"What are you waiting for? There's an air strike on the way!"

"That's what we heard, sir, but we can't get a reading . . . wait, there it is!" He pointed at a black shape darting toward the complex. The private and the major disappeared through the round main door on top of the armored vehicle and closed it. The Shilka accelerated away from the complex.

"Get radar lock, quick!"

"It's up to the computer, sir!"

While the Shilka was still moving, the gun dish radar searched, detected and locked onto the incoming craft. It then automatically sent the appropriate control signals to the four water-cooled cannons on the front of the vehicle. The self-propelled Shilka abruptly came to a full

top before the power-operated turret rotated ninety
degrees and the 23mm cannons each opened fire at a
cyclic rate of one thousand rounds per minute.

Kramer put the Black Jet in a gentle dive and reduced
throttles as he opened the bomb bay doors. He activated
one Paveway.

Through the HUD, he trained the laser designator on
the spot in the warehouse where Kevin and Halston had
told him the service elevator was located. He locked the
laser and released the Paveway.

His craft trembled as several rounds blasted through
the sensitive skin of his jet. Kramer spotted the muzzle
flashes and realized his mistake. Quickly, he rolled the
jet over so that the opened bomb bay doors pointed away
from the Shilka, and he pulled the control stick aft. The
laser designator automatically kept the beam dead on
target.

The Paveway immediately locked onto the laser,
crashed through the warehouse roof and went off.

Sakkar fell back from the blast that shook the entire
structure.

"What in the hell . . . ?"

Smoke quickly started to fill the large cavelike room.

"A bomb, Doctor. It crashed against the elevator shaft
plate!" screamed Risha, running toward the elevator
doors, which had been blown open by the shock wave.

"Did it pierce through?" he asked, bringing a handkerchief to his face.

"Can't tell, Doctor."

"Open the vents! Get this smoke out of here, quick!"

"But, sir. That would expose us to—"

"Dammit! Open the vents! We don't have a choice! We
must get the smoke out of here."

Smoke was getting thicker.

"Calm down, Doctor. We're all right."

"You don't understand, Risha. We can't have smoke or
a fire in here. The computer system will start the firing
sequence automatically! We have to wait until we get all
the missiles deployed!" He dropped to his knees and

dragged her down. The smoke was getting out of hand.
"Quick! The vents! Get the smoke out, out!"

The young captain felt the earth tremble from the
powerful bomb going off below ground level. He turned
to his gunner.

"Why did you stop firing? It is getting away!"
"Lost the signal, sir. The system is malfunctioning!"
"Then go manual, dammit!"
"Yes, sir!"

The gunner flipped the manual override, rotated the
turret and elevated the guns, but the aircraft was already
out of range.

Longhorn Kramer watched in surprise as two huge
camouflaged circular doors on the field next to the fence
slid open, revealing a pair of wide tunnels.

Kramer smiled when he spotted the smoke coming up.
"They're damned vent holes! That Paveway hit the
jackpot! You were right, Crackers! Gonna go around for a
second pass!"

"We got you covered from up here," responded Kevin.

Kramer went up to two thousand feet and enabled the
second Paveway. A red light blinked over the CRT
display.

"Son'a bitch! Fuckin' release mechanism's malfunc-
tionin'!"

Three thousand yards away, the Shilka's gunner had the
Black Jet centered in the crosshairs of his sighting
system. Although the range of his guns was under two
thousand yards, he aimed at a spot slightly above the
craft to compensate for the bullet drop. He fired.

Alarms went off inside the cockpit. Kramer watched his
control panel light up like a Christmas tree. "Whatta
hell? Mayday, Mayday! Bastards hit my left turbofan!
Losing hydraulics!"

Kramer pulled out and felt the power loss as he
struggled to get his F-117 away from the Shilka. His

ontrol stick shook violently as he forced the jet into a
ight turn. Kramer grabbed the stick with both hands
nd completed the turn and climb. Three more blasts.

He felt the excruciating pain as a round managed to
reak through the bottom of the fuselage. Burning debris
lasted through his left thigh. "Aghh . . . shit!"

Another round punctured the fuselage and exploded
nder the cockpit. The CRT blew up under the pressure.
he shock wave jammed him back against the seat.
Kramer felt the debris crashing against his chest and
ouncing off his visor. Suddenly a stinging pain came
rom his legs. He looked down and saw that the bottom
f his flight suit was smoking. The heat from the round
urned him. Smoke quickly filled the cockpit.

With the smell of burning flesh filling his nostrils,
Kramer struggled to get the jet back under control and
lanced at the analog instrumentation. Most of the
auges appeared operational. He put his right hand on
is leg and felt the wound. It was bleeding, but the bone
vas not shattered. He could still press it against the
udder pedals, which he did as he turned the craft
round.

Kevin was shocked to see smoke inside the F-117's
ockpit. He tried to use the radio but got no response.
Now he watched the crippled Black Jet turn around.

"Where does he think he's going?" asked Delgado.

"Don't know. The bastard's crazy."

Kramer approached the complex at 300 knots, the
maximum speed he could reach with a single turbofan.
He watched the Shilka's turret turning in his direction
and smiled. He pushed the control stick forward and
eached under the seat.

Kevin yelled, "Oh, shit!" as the F-117 dove directly
oward the ventilation tunnels. He followed the black
hape from two thousand feet all the way down to three
undred.

Pull up! What are you waiting . . . ?

Kevin's eyes opened wide when he realized wha Kramer was trying to accomplish. He held his breath an prayed.

The canopy blew out of sight as Kramer felt the powerfu blast from the solid-propellant rocket under the seat. H felt the g's crushing down on his shoulders as he hurtle higher and higher. His vision narrowed until all wen dark.

Sakkar heard a light engine noise. It came from th ventilation holes. At first he thought it was the sound c jets flying overhead amplified by the concrete tunnel Maybe enemy planes making a second pass. He turne his head toward the elevator shaft expecting a secon blast, but it never came from that direction. He turne around and froze in disbelief as a huge black objec crashed through the steel grill over one of the emergenc ventilation tunnels. Then fire engulfed him.

"Madre de Dios! Look, Crackers!"

"Sweet Jesus!" Kevin stared at the powerful column of fire that boosted out of the tunnels and toward th clouds. The blast had been severe. Suddenly it appeare as if the earth underneath the complex opened an swallowed the entire site. Most of the structures disap peared in seconds as the ground trembled and a colossa rift engulfed men, equipment . . . everything.

"Have you ever seen . . . ?"

"Only in an earthquake back in L.A. What in th world was under there?"

"Don't know, but . . ."

"A parachute! It's Longhorn!"

"Well, I'll be damned! That crazy cowboy!"

Kevin made a final pass over the collapsing comple and rocked the wings of the Tomcat.

"Shit, Crackers. What's that on the ground at thre o'clock?"

Kevin moved the stick to the right and banked th craft. He saw four small explosions, all within a fev hundred feet of each other.

"I don't know. Maybe a fuel line to the base, or something like—"

"Crackers! They're missile silos!"

"What? You're imagining . . ." Kevin went quiet as flames spewed out of each hole.

"Contact on the nose. Two miles, fast! Tally!"

Kevin shifted his gaze toward the contact. It moved across the sky before he had a chance to blink. "It's that MiG again!"

He looked back at the ballistic missiles slowly lifting off. He knew that in another thirty seconds they would be out of reach. Instinctively, he pushed full throttles and afterburners and put his craft into a shallow dive and activated the cannon. He eyed the fuel gauges. Ten thousand pounds left.

Kevin came in from the north at 650 knots. He put the pipper on the closest missile, just barely clearing the silo. He fired three short bursts. Nothing. The missile continued to climb. Kevin adjusted his fire and tried again. Four two-second bursts. *Blow, dammit!* The missile disintegrated and went off in a bright cloud.

"Great shot. Tally. Single. Seven o'clock low!"

Kevin frowned as he spotted the MiG a few thousand feet behind him.

"Locked. He's got us locked!"

"Fuck him! I'm going for the missiles!" Kevin said, knowing that doing so would give the MiG a great position in a dogfight. But he didn't have a choice; he had to stop the nuclear missiles. Kevin did a one-eighty and came back around for a second pass at the ballistic missiles.

"Select Sidewinder."

The radar locked and the Sidewinder seeker head slaved to the closest heat source and began buzzing.

"Good lock. Shoot!" said Delgado.

Kevin released it, and the 180-pound missile reached is target a few seconds later.

The resulting explosion created a larger ball of flame, momentarily reaching up to the sky. *Two more to go.*

"MiG's got us locked . . . missile in the air! Break to port!" warned Delgado.

Kevin pumped chaff and flares and threw the Tomca into a wickedly tight turn. He leveled off, pumped mor decoys, and rolled the plane onto its back before divin

"Missile went for the flares! Tally. Bogey at our six! Delgado said as Kevin leveled off fifty feet above th ground. He silently cursed the MiG as he watched th last two ballistic missiles, roughly a thousand feet abov him, quickly gather speed.

As the MiG came around, obviously trying to ge behind the Tomcat, Kevin Dalton knew that he had t try to reach those missiles, even if it cost him th dogfight. And so he did, jamming the throttles to fu power and entering a vertical climb in full afterburner

"The MiG's at eight o'clock low," said Delgado.

"The hell with him. I'm going after the missiles!"

The Tomcat rocketed toward the heavens, toward th silvery shapes of the missiles Kevin could not allow t reach their target, but the ballistic missiles had alread gone supersonic. Kevin glanced at the informatio painted on the HUD. His indicated airspeed was onl 500 knots and dropping as he thundered above te thousand feet. He would not be able to get close enoug to use the cannon.

"Dammit. They're getting away! Select Sidewinder!"

"Trying, trying!"

A moment later he heard the infrared buzzer going of and he released a Sidewinder.

The heat-seeking missile streaked upward as its elec tronic brain tracked one of the ballistic missiles.

Kevin watched as the Sidewinder's contrail closed i on the large missile, until the 180-pound missile went o with a bright flash.

As his indicated airspeed dropped to 375 knots, Kevi Dalton waited for something to happen, but the Ira missile continued its upward drive. Then he understoo The hottest part of the ballistic missile—where th Sidewinder had locked on—was several feet below th missile's nozzle. The twenty-five-pound warhead ha done nothing to the rocketing nuclear missile.

"Select Phoenix!" Kevin ordered.

"Wh—what?"

"Dammit, Chico. Give me a Phoenix!"

"Won't work! The system's not designed for—"

"Fuck the system. You get me a lock! Bastards are getting away!"

Delgado exhaled as he put the AWG-9 into Pulse-Doppler Single-Target Track (PDSTT), a mode which concentrated all of the power of the AWG-9 antenna onto a single long-range target at ranges of up to seventy nautical miles, giving range, range rate, and angular data. The software running through the system was not designed to track ballistic missiles accelerating past Mach 2. Delgado just hoped that using the AWG-9 system in PDSTT mode would give him his best shot. He was right. The Tomcat's powerful tracking radar locked onto the ascending missile.

"I'll be damned. Gotta lock, Crackers!"

Kevin released a Phoenix as his airspeed dropped below 200 knots.

The Hughes AIM-54 Phoenix missile left the underside pallet and hurtled skyward. Since the Iraqi missile was only one mile away, the Phoenix automatically switched to its own internal target-acquisition program.

The amber stall lights came on: airspeed 120 knots. "Shit!" Topping out at nineteen thousand feet, Kevin inverted and dove to avoid entering a spin, but not before he saw the third Iraqi missile burst in midair as the Phoenix struck the nose section.

The last missile was now a distant light in the morning sky. Kevin watched it as he leveled off and searched the sky above him. *I'll never catch it.*

"Tally. Single at our six!" warned Delgado.

Kevin glanced at the MiG behind them. He had let him get too close, and he knew it would be very difficult to get the Iraqi off his tail. He executed a series of tight turns, dives, and climbs to no avail. The MiG remained at his six o'clock.

"Can't shake him off!"

The MiG opened fire.

Kevin cut left, but not before a river of bullets ripped

across the starboard wing, creating small clouds of white debris. He broke left and checked for cautions. *None.*

"The MiG's closing again!" Delgado yelled as they dove below ten thousand feet at Mach 1.

"Bastard's trying to get an angle—" Kevin's words were cut short by the thundering blast from the MiG's cannon. An image flickered in his mind. It was of Lancaster's head snapping forward as the canopy was blown to pieces. Then there were the visions of him running away from the cannons and toward Abdul. The ground around him exploding with bullets as his Kurdish friend waved him over to the cave. Khalela screamed for him to hurry. Kevin remembered kicking his legs against the sand until they would not go any faster, then he had jumped.

Another river of bullets blasted across the port wing. Kevin threw the stick to the left and placed the craft in a tight turn, pulling maximum g. He watched the vapor pouring off the wingtips as he sank into his seat. His vision tunneled and his limbs tingled. His G suit inflated, keeping his blood from accumulating in his legs. Fighting the hammering g's, Kevin followed the evasive move by pushing the stick forward. Now the g's turned negative, ferociously pushing him up against his restraint harness. Blood rushed to his face and the world changed to palettes of red as the capillaries in his eyeballs inflated. The pressure eased. He glanced back. The MiG could not keep up momentarily, but soon was on his tail again.

Kevin eyed the fuel gauges once more: eight hundred pounds. He had consumed a great deal of fuel by using burners. He was now flying on fumes, probably not enough to keep him airborne for ten minutes, much less enough to make it back. He pulled back throttles.

"What are you doing?" Delgado screamed.

"Get ready to eject, Chico!"

Kevin watched the MiG position itself behind them.

"Let's do it, Crackers!"

"Not yet! Wait." He reduced throttles even more.

"Madre de Dios. Why are you slowin' down? He's right

on our tail! I can see the bastard's face! Let's get outta here!"

Kevin eyed the airspeed indicator: 500 knots. Too fast. "Get ready, Chico!"

The MiG opened fire.

"Eject us both on count!" ordered Kevin.

"You're fuckin' crazy, man!"

Kevin reached for the air brakes lever, the flap lever, and the landing gear handle. The first few rounds pierced through the canopy. Several more ripped across the aluminum layers of the starboard wing. Bits and pieces of the wing washed away in the slipstream.

"Madre de—"

"On count! Three . . . two . . . one . . . now!"

Kevin slapped the landing gear down and pulled up all air brakes and lowered flaps as the canopy was blown up.

He felt the windblast crashing against his chest. His body was thrown up, to the side, and flipped upside down. The g's pushed down on him with titanic force. Again he watched in a blur as the sky and desert changed places, but his senses were quickly clouded by the extreme pressure. His vision narrowed and his limbs tingled. His mind hung at the edge of unconsciousness but he refused to fall into it, holding on until his ears registered the sound he so desperately hoped he would hear. Suddenly his body was further propelled through the air as the shock wave from the midair collision reached him. In spite of the harrowing pain, Lieutenant Kevin Dalton managed a thin smile.

His last conscious feeling came from the jerk of the deployed parachute. It temporarily shielded his eyes from the brilliant morning sun.

Then there was peace.

Bourdeaux watched the operator sitting at the controls of the MIM-104 Patriot tactical air-defense system furiously typing commands on the keyboard.

"Got one missile from Allahbad on a ballistic trajectory to Riyadh, sir! Looks like our guys could only nail three. One got away!"

"Range?" asked Halston.

"Sixty miles and closing. It'll be within our reach fo thirty seconds in exactly twenty seconds."

"Engage!"

"Yessir! Range fifty miles. Speed Mach 1.3. Visual i fifteen seconds!"

Halston ran outside. Bourdeaux went after him. The both scanned the skies.

"There! See it, Bob?"

Bourdeaux shifted his gaze to a bright point in the sky "Got it!"

Four Patriots left their red-hot M-901 launch station The operator wasn't taking any chances. The dark con trails streaked through the morning sky as the 2200 pound missiles blasted to Mach 3. The rivers of smoke continued in an intercept trajectory with the bright spo Bourdeaux had spotted several seconds before.

One bright flash. Quickly followed by two others Three Patriots had reached their target. Dark, smokin debris began to fall back to earth in the distance Bourdeaux silently followed it all the way down to abou five hundred feet—

Robert Bourdeaux instinctively brought both hands t his face to shield them from the brightest flash he'd see in his life, and the sudden realization of what that mean sent a chill through his tired body.

The flash. The blinding flash that resulted from nucle ar fission. The incandescent outburst of light from chain reaction started in a one-kilogram, sphere-shape plutonium core after being compressed to half its size b a perfectly symmetrical implosion of high explosiv plastic. As the HEP increased the density of the plutoni um 239, a neutron initiator collided against a singl plutonium atom with a force large enough to split it i half, releasing a small amount of energy in the form o light and heat, as well as releasing a few more neutrons which in turn collided with other plutonium atoms causing further fission, which released more neutrons The multiplication, which took close to eighty genera tion to absorb the plutonium mass, was over in one millionth of a second, producing the energy equivalent to 20,000 tons of TNT.

"Shut your eyes! Don't look at the light!" Bourdeaux shouted at Halston as he dove for the cover of a truck, but by that time the initial flash had ended. Slowly, he shifted his gaze at the sky and saw a rapidly developing fireball rising up to the sky roughly fifteen miles away. The ball reached about two thousand feet in height before cooling off, forming the familiar mushroom-shaped cloud with a column of smoke and dust.

"Everyone reach cover!" Bourdeaux shouted. The size of the mushroom told Bourdeaux that the warhead had been no larger than twenty kilotons, which meant that with ground zero over fifteen miles away, the thermal and shock wave that should soon reach their position would be mild. He was right.

Even though the sound was intimidating, the wind and heat that soon engulfed them was a mere fraction of the inferno that had been the square mile surrounding ground zero, where the blast wave, heating the air to incandescence, had moved outward in all directions at an initial velocity greater than the speed of sound. Soon a second blast wave reached his position from the opposite direction as cool air rushed back to fill the partial vacuum created by the explosion. Radiation effects this far away would be almost negligible.

With the mushroom still visible in the distance, Robert Bourdeaux got up and looked back at Kenneth Draper, still wearing his robe and moving slowly away from a truck. He felt a hand on his shoulder and looked to his right. It was Halston, and he wore a mask of disbelief.

"Jesus, Bob. The bastard already had them."

In spite of the shock, for the first time in days Robert Bourdeaux, CIA Operations Officer, smiled broadly. "That's right, ol' buddy. He *had* them."

BAGHDAD.
Day Seven. 0725 Local Time.

The phone rang. Then it stopped. Then it rang again.
The Iraqi leader crawled over the warm body of the
Syrian woman sleeping next to him and picked up the
phone. He froze after hearing the news.

Impossible. It was simply impossible.

Cursing his luck, Saddam pressed a fist against his
mouth while listening to the voice of one of his generals.
Allahbad had been destroyed, and what was worse, one
of the missiles had been fired and it had gone off near the
border with Saudi Arabia. The secret was out.

The Syrian woman rolled over next to him. Giggling,
half asleep, her hands reached down for his groin.

Saddam, still holding the phone to his ear, grabbed the
Makarov, cocked it and, after abruptly getting up, fired
twice into the woman's chest.

Three of his bodyguards stormed the room, the general
on the phone shouted, and Saddam, naked, dropped the
weapon. The woman, convulsing, coughed up blood and
foam before going limp.

"Great One! Are you all right?" asked the general on
the phone.

Saddam exhaled. "Yes."

"But the shots, the noise!"

"Do not worry."

"Yes, Great One."

Saddam hung up and motioned his bodyguards to
clean up the mess. He grabbed a robe next to the bed and
put it on as a young major walked into the room, briefly
looked at the naked woman being dragged away by the
bodyguards, and snapped to attention.

"Great One. I have a message from the field general of
our deployed forces. He is requesting further instructions."

With his mind still trying to absorb the events of the
past thirty seconds, Saddam Hussein closed his eyes,
muttering through his teeth, "Tell him to pull back."

EPILOGUE

For the first time in his life, Robert Bourdeaux walked into the Oval Office. A smiling President Clinton, dressed in a dark gray suit and maroon tie stood up from behind his desk, quickly walked around it and met Bourdeaux in the middle of the light blue carpeted room, right over the embroidered presidential seal. They shook hands.

"This is a real honor, Mr. President."

"No, sir. The honor is mine," the American Commander in Chief responded, blue eyes gleaming at Bourdeaux.

"Thank you, sir," the CIA officer responded.

The president had plenty of reason to smile. Saddam Hussein had quickly retreated, stopped all flights over the no-fly zone, and given U.N. teams unconditional freedom of movement and inspection inside Iraq after it became evident that his nuclear project had come to an embarrassing end. All the nations of the world were enraged at the news of Saddam firing nuclear missiles at

Tel Aviv, Riyadh, Tehran, and Kuwait City. Had it not been for the Americans, their intelligence agency, and their military equipment, the Middle East would be embroiled in war now. But as it turned out, Saddam's short-lived nuclear empire had fueled an unprecedented peace process in the region.

"Mr. Bourdeaux, you have done your country—and the world—a great service. Your work saved the lives of millions, and for that I salute you."

Bourdeaux felt overwhelmed and also uncomfortable. Flattery made him feel uneasy, *and coming from the president himself!* He settled for a simple, "Thank you, Mr. President."

Clinton, still smiling, slowly shook his head. "No, Mr. Bourdeaux. Thank *you.*"

RIYADH, SAUDI ARABIA.
Day Twelve. 1500 Local Time.

Lieutenant Kevin Dalton looked out the hospital window, watching local merchants sell their goods at the downtown bazaar. Taxis made their way through the crowded street to the complaints of pedestrians slamming their hands against the hoods and screaming words Kevin hoped he would soon never have to hear again.

He put down the copy of the *Washington Post* he'd just finished reading for the third time. Iraq had pulled back all its forces after the nuclear blast, and the peace process was in an upswing again. The Clinton administration had managed to avoid a war, but peace had come only after several brave men had lost their lives. Men like Lancaster, Ishmael, Abdul, Poole, and others.

Casualties of war. Kevin swallowed the lump in his throat that came whenever he thought about his RIO. The rescue team had found Chico Delgado's broken body still strapped to his seat. The parachute had never opened. The seat had malfunctioned. A one in a million chance and it had happened to Delgado. *Chico.*

Longhorn Kramer had been luckier. He was in a room two doors down, where doctors had him drugged with morphine. His legs were covered with scar tissue.

Kevin reached for a white envelope on the nightstand. He opened it and removed a folded sheet of paper. It had the presidential seal on the top of the page. His eyes read the handwritten note from President Bill Clinton calling him the last of the true heroes. In addition, all charges against him had been silently dropped.

How ironic, Kevin thought as he watched a tall nurse walk into his room. Her back was to him. One day he was an insubordinate outcast, the next he was a hero. But even under Kevin's new status, Commander John McDeere had requested for Kevin to be transferred to another air wing. Kevin sighed.

"Morning," he said, noticing that the nurse was not the old woman who had been taking care of him for the past few days.

"Hello, Kevin." She turned around. The face, the eyes, the smile: it was all there once again. "I came to thank you for what you did."

Kevin raised his eyebrows. "Khalela? What are you—"

"Shh, not so loud. So I guess you did it."

"It had to be done. I didn't see anyone else signing up to do it."

"My government is grateful for what you did. We believe our nation was the primary target for the missiles at Allahbad. Although we would never publicly acknowledge our ties with you, I was instructed by my government to personally thank you for destroying those missiles. You saved a lot of lives. If we can ever be of service to you, all you have to do is ask."

Kevin turned his head and stared out the window once more.

"I am sorry about your RIO. I heard that—"

Kevin shifted his gaze back to Khalela. "He was a good friend. I'll miss Chico. But you, Khalela . . . why did you do it? Why didn't you come with me? I was crushed, alone. I *needed* you."

"I am sorry. You do not know how hard it was for me to do what I did at the village." She walked up to the side of his bed.

Kevin put his hand on hers. "Somehow I knew you'd be back."

"I cannot stay long, Kevin. I came to say thanks and also to say good-bye."

Kevin stared into her magical light green eyes, gleaming with bold intelligence. "Why, Khalela? Why must you punish yourself and me this way? I love you and I know you love me, otherwise you wouldn't be here right now. I want you to stay with—"

"It just cannot be. Please understand. It would not work. Our worlds are too different, and my country needs me now more than ever. Perhaps one day . . ."

Kevin kissed her hand. "You will always have a special place in my heart, Khalela Yishaid . . . perhaps one day."

She gave him a warm smile and leaned down to kiss him on the cheek. Kevin softly pressed the side of her face against his.

"Good-bye, Kevin Dalton."

He didn't respond. Instead he simply closed his eyes, once more letting her overwhelming warmth caress away the pain. Her touch, her smell, her soft hair brushed against his tears. For one last time, Kevin Dalton surrendered himself to the soothing comfort of her nearness.

RETRIBUTION

■

R.J. PINEIRO

Coming in. . .
FROM TOR/FORGE

THE STAND

Laws are silent in time of war.
—Cicero

SOUTHERN IRAQ.

The Teledyne Ryan BQM-145A Unmanned Aerial Vehicle separated from the solid rocket booster assembly after reaching the apex of its parabolic flight. The single static-thrust turbofan jet engine kicked into life, providing 970 pounds of thrust, and propelling the composite-skin craft to five hundred knots. The UAV's twelve-foot-span wings tilted to the right as the American-made craft turned to a northerly heading in response to its inertial navigational systems receiving constant updates from the Global Positioning System stored in the probe's center fuselage.

Twenty miles to the south, outside Kuwait City, Lieutenant Colonel Diane Towers sat inside a large rectangular tent with the ten surviving pilots of her flight group. Tired but otherwise in good enough health to continue flight operations, Diane readied herself to strike back with decisive force on this cool and windy night. Her mission was to take out a large Iraqi air base, which military intelligence believed would support the initial strike against General Oliver Grogan's 52nd Tank Regiment just south of the border with Kuwait.

Diane's mission was particularly critical because General Grogan's forces were vastly outnumbered and reinforcements would not arrive in time before the Iraqis struck. According to her recent radio conversation with the sixty-year-old general, the 52nd would have a chance of containing the initial wave only if the United States had air superiority over the battlefield.

As Diane's eyes drifted to her new wingman, Major "Blue Jeans" Levi, the seasoned lieutenant colonel decided that this time things would go differently.

Although temperatures had already dropped well into the fifties, the cool, refreshing weather had no apparent effect on Diane, whose penetrating eyes remained glued to the large color projection screen, which, divided into four windows, displayed in real time the data collected by the UAV's sensors. The upper left window showed the probe's position in relation to a built-in color map of northern Kuwait and southern Iraq. Next to it Diane saw a real-time image from the probe's image-intensifier visual camera. Below that window, she saw the equivalent infrared image of the surveyed area. The lower leftmost screen displayed telemetry data, consisting of altitude, speed, fuel, and a number of other operating parameters. Both visual and infrared data were stored on tape for later analysis.

Diane looked at the position marked on the map on the screen, the place which a KH-11 satellite had identifed as the location of the air base. Under different circumstances, the satellite data would have been sufficient for Diane and her team to commence the air strike, but not on this cool night. Not after hearing the news that the *Kennedy* would not be able to launch any planes, its crew still battling the damage sustained twelve hours ago. Diane needed to confirm the satellite data because she knew she would only have one shot at striking the Iraqis. Once her squadron became airborne, she would have to reach and destroy the Iraqi air base immediately, before the Arabs detected them and got their MiGs airborne. According to the CIA and the satellite data, the base had over seventy-five MiG-23s and many more MiG-29s being fueled and armed to provide air cover for

Republican Guard divisions poised to strike General Grogan's forces in Kuwait. The general would be facing a formidable invading force as it was, even without the support of the MiGs. And reinforcements seemed unlikely to arrive for the next several hours. C-5 Galaxy transports were due to arrive in Kuwait hauling another twenty thousand troops by noon, but they wouldn't do General Grogan any good during the morning battle.

If those MiGs got airborne before Diane could destroy them, the Marine Corps lieutenant colonel and her team would be hopelessly outnumbered in aerial combat. But stealthiness was her team's credo. Striking at night in their Hornets was what this group of leathernecks did best, and tonight, Diane would put all the hours of practice and hard work to the ultimate test.

"How long before the probe reaches the target, Blue Jeans?"

"Just a couple more minutes, ma'am," responded Major Levi, without taking his light brown eyes off the screen.

Diane nodded while focusing on the upper right window. The image, thanks to the half-moon and the advanced optics of the sensoring lens, which amplified the available light to enhance the viewing resolution, gave an amazingly clear picture of the terrain. She briefly eyed the infrared underneath.

"What's the optical resolution of this thing?"

"If anyone's smokin' inside a hangar on that base, I reckon we oughta be able to see him from the IR signature," Levi said, pointing to a satellite photo next to the screen.

Diane took in a deep breath of cool air. It was already one o'clock in the morning, and it was going to be a long night. She tilted her head and glanced at Levi. "How hard is it for the Iraqis to detect the probe?"

"Hard's catchin' a runnin' chicken, ma'am. The UAV's too small, and it's coated with the latest radar-absorbent stuff. That, plus the fact that it's black, and it has a high-bypass turbofan, sure in hell makes it damn near invisible at night."

"Let's hope so," Diane said. "The last thing we need is

for those Iraqis to figure out our plan and launch an early attack on Grogan."

Diane Towers crossed her thin but firm arms and briefly closed her eyes. She felt weary and nauseated from lack of sleep and also from the residual effects of the radiation dose she had endured. She now wore a Marines baseball cap to hide her thinning hair, and her flight suit was zipped all the way up to her neck. She didn't want anyone to see the purple blotches that had taken over most of her upper chest. The tissue in her gums had also begun to decay, resulting in very painful toothbrushing sessions and a lot of blood, which she also found in her urine. She had come close to informing the squadron flight surgeon but decided against it. The surgeon might ground her at a time when her country needed her most. She would deal with the effects of the radiation later. Right now she had a mission to fly.

For the past thirty minutes the group had listened to Major Levi's detailed briefing on the SAM installations surrounding the Iraqi air base, and of the forces on the base itself. Now the probe was finally about to reach the target and hopefully confirm their satellite data.

"We're there," Levi said. Diane opened her eyes and studied the rapidly changing image on the screen.

The UAV's sharp nose bit into the air at four hundred knots while maintaining a shallow left turn. With the quiet turbofan now on idle, the eighteen-foot-long, honeycomb-structured plane slowly descended from five thousand feet while its Advanced Tactical Airborne Reconnaissance System's electro-optical and infrared sensors scanned the valley underneath. As the craft's passive wings—a design derived from NASA's super-critical wing design for better range and fuel economy—maintained a steady fifteen-degree angle of bank, the sensors went to work, providing real-time images of the terrain below. The instant the UAV reached an altitude of one thousand feet, the constant-motion elevons, located outboard of the two vertical fins, became flush with the streamlined design, leveling out the probe. The single rudder, located on the left fin, stopped the shallow turn and pointed the nose to a westerly heading. The turbofan didn't kick in right away. The craft glided for another minute at the rate of thirty feet forward for every foot of altitude—another advantage of the NASA wing design. The moment the Global Positioning System told the inertial navigation system that the craft had reached the three-mile mark from the target zone, the turbofan accelerated, but not to full throttle, just enough to maintain a two-hundred-knot escape velocity without losing any more altitude. At the ten-mile mark, the single engine's low hum increased to a mild whine as airspeed jumped to five hundred knots and the remote probe headed home.

"That was fast," said Diane.

"Yep, but sure was long enough," Major Levi responded as he approached the small portable control console built into a metallic briefcase, and replayed the fifteen seconds of low altitude surveillance in slow motion. The visual and infrared images confirmed the KM-11 data. Warm turbofans told them the planes had been flown recently, most likely in war exercises. In addition, the short aerial pass also revealed four underground fuel storage tanks, from which a number of hoses currently serviced dozens of fighters. Thermal images of about a hundred men moving around the parked fighters further confirmed the satellite data. The base was indeed getting ready for a morning assault.

"All right, Blue Jeans. Looks like the satellite data was accurate."

Levi ran a hand through his close-cropped brown hair and continued, covering in fine detail the numerous SAM batteries surrounding the base, as well as additional detail on the air base itself.

"Thanks," Diane said, checking her watch before getting up and scanning the group, mostly young pilots, but their age was not to be confused with the training and combat time they had under their belts.

"All right, gentlemen. We'll be flying top cover for General Grogan's 52nd Tank Regiment. Although we'll be carrying a full load of ammo for the cannons and a couple of air-to-airs, most of the load we'll be hauling are air-to-muds. Make no mistake, SAM facilities and the air base are where your ordnance goes. You must unload all of the bombs on the targets before engaging Iraqi MiGs, which I know will be a headache if they get airborne before we get there, although I'm sure the Iraqis will have some jets already on patrol. The timing here's critical. Our intelligence believes the Iraqis will attack the 52nd at dawn and aren't expecting an American strike tonight. Those MiGs on the ground are loaded with fuel and ammo for the morning. This is our best chance, so hit hard and decisively. Just as during our practice runs, we'll work in five sections of two. Blue Jeans, you'll be my wing. The rest split as we discussed before." Diane checked her watch once again. "If you have to go and relieve yourselves, do it now. Let's move out."

The pilots, already wearing their G suits and life vests, and carrying their helmets and oxygen masks, got up and headed outside. A few stopped by trees at the edge of the clearing to urinate, well aware that few things in this world were as uncomfortable as a full bladder in high-g situations.

Diane slowly walked to her single-seat version of the F/A-18 Hornet. Her ground crew finished up last-minute details to get the thirty-three-thousand-pound fighter-bomber ready for action, a task that involved filling up empty fuel tanks, replenishing the single 20mm cannon's magazine, securing missiles and bombs onto stores hard points under the short wings, and doing a number of "tweaks" to the avionics. The ground crew resembled a well-orchestrated play, with each of the five members performing his duty with grace and a high degree of effectiveness. There could be no mistakes here. No missiles left unsecured. No jammed cannons. No malfunctioning avionics. The Hornets had to be perfect for battle. Perfect to fight an enemy armed with the latest Russian technology.

The ground crew chief approached Diane. "Your plane is ready, Colonel."

The crew chief handed Diane the acceptance form and

a pen. The lieutenant colonel grabbed them and began her walkaround, carefully examining all control surfaces, weapons, and panels. Satisfied, Diane signed the form and passed it back to her subordinate before climbing up the special ladder rolled up to the F/A-18.

Diane strapped herself into her seat, plugged the combination oxygen-intercom lead, which fed her mask communications system, into the connecting block on the left side of the seat, and threw the jet fuel starter switch. At once, the auxiliary power unit housed in between the pair of turbofans came to life, bringing the generators on line to provide enough electrical power to allow Diane use of the intercom and cockpit instrument displays.

Instantly feeling at home, Diane went down the pre-taxi checklist, verifying functionality of the central CRT, the radar, and the color map. She threw the Heads-up Display switch and confirmed that the projected telemetry and symbology data on the canopy matched that of the CRT. After adjusting the brightness of the HUD, Diane used the auxiliary power unit to engage the starboard turbofan while her eyes scanned the engine-related data shown on the upper right corner of the CRT. The low whine grew into a steady whirl. Diane kept the throttle on idle and started the port turbofan. She shut down the auxiliary power unit and turned her attention to the control surfaces' checks. Outside, her ground crew moved in harmony once more, visually checking the response of the ailerons, elevators, rudder, and flaps, reporting the results to Diane through the intercom system.

Diane enabled the Built-In Test Equipment, a program in which the onboard computers automatically examined all avionics and weapon systems. BITE came back green, and Diane dialed in the mission's Identification Friendly or Foe code into the transponder, permitting the other Hornets to "interrogate" her Hornet and verify it as a "friendly."

Diane placed both hands against the canopy so that they could be clearly seen by the ground crew as they removed the safing devices inhibiting accidental missile firing. The moment the crew backed away from the F/A-18, she activated the radio and spoke into the small microphone built into her oxygen mask. "Strike Leader. Radio check."

"Five . . . two . . . four . . . three," came the response from the other teams.

The ground crew chief walked in front of the Hornet, snapped to attention, and saluted Diane. The Marine Corps lieutenant colonel saluted back.

With the brakes released and a gentle push of the side-by-side throttles to her left, Diane taxied her jet clear of the trees and toward the short runway. Levi followed her. Together they made the first "section" of their flight group.

Diane let her wingman catch up, and the pair rolled onto the runway. After a power check and a quick exchange of hand signals to indicate that all was well, both Hornets hurtled forward under the power of their turbofans. Diane slowly advanced the throttles to build up forward airspeed without much concern about the rapidly approaching sand dunes at the other end of the four-thousand-foot-long runway.

She broke ground as her airspeed continued to increase.

120 knots . . . 170 . . . 210 . . .

Diane leveled off at two thousand feet holding 320 knots and put on her night goggles, instantly turning the world around her into a palette of greens.

"This is Strike Leader. Stay close. Stay low," Diane said as she inched the centerstick forward, dropping down to two hundred feet, hugging the desert floor. Levi's Hornet flew slightly behind her and to her right. The color map told Diane the exact range to the Iraqi air base.

"Roger," she heard Levi respond.

Diane checked her mission timer clock. *Right on time.*
Speed 320 knots. Perfect. Everything seemed perfect. The jet was a work of art, the product of two decades of American engineering targeted at creating the ultimate advanced tactical fighter. In it, Diane knew she was

nearly untouchable and almost invisible, especially if she maintained this altitude.

As an ocean of infrared-stained sand rushed under her, Lieutenant Colonel Diane Towers allowed herself the simple pleasure of briefly gazing at the crystalline sky, the adrenaline boost from the mission forcing her mind away from her decaying medical condition.

"Pickin' up some fast movers, Lead," reported Levi from Strike One One Seven. *"Three MiGs at your two movin' in a parallel course in the opposite direction at fifty thousand. I reckon they can't see us while we're so close to the ground."*

Diane quickly checked the optical radar to the right multifunction display, confirming Levi's finding. The MiG trio flew too high for their lookdown radars to pick out their Hornets from the ground clutter. Although the MiGs were pounding the region with E-band radar energy, their searching beams were way too wide to pinpoint Diane's squadron. They were simply doing a large-area sweep. "Confirmed, One Seven. This is Strike Leader. Be aware of three MiGs thirty miles east of the target. Ignore unless they narrow their beams. Your ordnance's spoken for."

Diane heard confirmation from the other four elements of her group while keeping an eye on the optical radar for any sign of disturbance from the enemy fighters. She could hear their radars making a sweep every thirty seconds.

Beep . . . beep.

The MiGs continued their flight until disappearing from the screen a minute later.

Just as suddenly, Diane's radar warning receiver told her she was being "painted" on E-band by another radar. The narrow beams indicated that in spite of the Hornet's low altitude and speed, somehow the Iraqis had detected her, were currently tracking her, and had probably passed the information on to the nearest SAM systems and the air base.

"Hot damn!" Levi said over the radio. *"Bastards found us, and right over the sand!"*

Diane nodded. "This is Strike Lead. All elements to Mach one point five. The mission is a go. Lock in your targets and unload your stores before the Iraqis get here. Repeat, lock in your targets."

"*Roger,*" came the unanimous response from the other elements, which Diane had spaced by twenty miles to maximize the chance of the elements reaching the target. Her plan would have to change now. She had to drop her load to give the Hornet the maneuverability necessary to engage with the fast and highly maneuverable MiG-29s adequately.

"*Incoming missiles! Two, no . . . three!*" reported Levi as Diane pushed full throttle and climbed to three thousand feet while tracking the incoming SAMs on the optical radar, which showed the tracking vectors of the Iraqi missiles.

"Got them. Follow my lead, One Seven. Countermeasures!"

"*Confirmed, Lead.*"

As the pair of Hornets got within fifty miles of the base, Diane activated the electronic countermeasures and chaff dispenser system. The missiles, less than five miles away, approached them head-on. On the night vision goggles, the SAMs looked like shooting stars in the distant sky, almost blending themselves with the real ones. At a closing rate of almost Mach 4, the missiles grew dangerously large.

The internal countermeasures system released two dozen five-foot-long Mylar strips coated with a microfilm of aluminum oxide. At the same time, the powerful ALE-905 system began to electronically pound the homing brains of the Iraqi missiles to provide them with a hundred virtual targets.

"Chaff released. Break!"

As the cloud of chaff washed away in the slipstream, Diane pulled the sidestick to the left while pushing full power. The g's tore at her as the jet cut left at great speed. Her G suit inflated to prevent her legs from becoming pools of blood, but even that didn't keep her upper extremities from tingling because of lack of circulation as her vision narrowed. The ensuing shock wave from the combined explosion of three warheads inside the cloud of chaff pushed her jet even harder to the right.

"One Seven, Leader. Damage report?"

"None, Lead!"

Diane cut back throttles and leveled the wings. She briefly checked her radar as it began to make wide sweeps searching, acquiring, and tracking ground targets, which were then passed on to the fire control computer. In an instant, over a dozen targets, labeled according to a priority system based on the highest probability of kill, peppered the Heads-up Display.

"One Seven, Strike Lead. Drop them as you see them."

"Targets acquired. Going shoppin'."

As Levi broke right, heading for the targets within his area of responsibility, Diane pulled the sidestick back and the Hornet went vertical to five thousand feet. The g's remained with her as she flung the stick forward, and the negative g's took over, pushing her upward against her restraining harness. Blood rushed to her head, making her eyeballs feel ready to explode. With the world turning shades of red, Diane forced her disciplined mind to ignore the g's and scan the information painted on the HUD. Throttles at half settings—540 knots—Altitude 5,200 feet.

Pushing the nose over to a forty-five-degree angle, Diane heard her two tail sensors going crazy. Someone had sneaked up behind her and was trying to get a lock. *Too bad.* She pushed full throttles and the Earth filled her windscreen.

A single depression of a red button on the sidestick, and one HARM antiradar missile left in a blaze before she began pulling on the sidestick. The g's hammered her as she kept up the rearward pressure. The Hornet jerked back up into the murky sky. A fiery ball of flames behind her told Diane the HARM had reached the SAM system.

The tail warning momentarily stopped. The goggles gave her superior vision for a night air-to-air engagement. Perhaps the MiG hadn't been able to pull up as hard and had lost her in the darkness. It didn't matter. She climbed up to three thousand feet and followed a new vector to the next SAM emplacement, which she locked in moments later. Once more she dropped on it like a hawk, releasing her second HARM from the rightmost underwing pylon, and a few seconds later she verified the secondary explosion.

Once more the tail sensor went crazy. Its high pitch told her the pursuer was close. Real close. Diane still couldn't engage in a dogfight, not with ten thousand pounds of explosives under the wings. She noticed the increased aerial activity near the air base twenty miles away. Blips began to appear on the radar.

"This is Strike Lead, sky's getting dirty. Drop your loads before the MiGs get airborne."

"Roger."

Ten miles. Diane pressed full power and the Hornet rushed past Mach 1.5. Nine miles. Eight . . . seven . . . six . . . five.

With the threat temporarily lost in her supersonic wake, Diane eased back throttles as the base loomed in plain view thanks to the goggles, which also told her of the half-dozen MiGs that had just gotten airborne, and the many more taxiing into position on the crowded air base.

Diane dropped to five hundred feet while decelerating to six hundred knots. She armed the dozen Snakeye smart bombs on the multiple ejector racks under both wings as the fire control computer calculated her firing solution.

Antiaircraft fire broke out from several places at once, resembling streaks of lightning to the NVGs, filling the sky with light beams reaching out for her. Feeling the slight vibration on the stick from the explosions of near misses, Diane popped up to seven hundred feet and gave the system a few more seconds to achieve total lock. The symbology projected on the HUD told her that twelve ground targets had been identified, and in the following second, she pressed the release button on the sidestick and pulled up as she flew right above the base.

The g's pounded her. With her vision narrowing, Diane saw thin streams of vapor pouring off the wing roots as the pressure blasted against the composite surface of the Hornet.

The Snakeyes continued their ballistic trajectory. Multiple explosions turned the night into day as fighters went up in flames, creating instant havoc.

Her Identification Friendly or Foe system detected Levi's Hornet as it made its pass over the blazing airfield. Antiaircraft fire had decreased significantly, and that suited her just fine, Diane decided, as she rolled her craft to get a better view of Levi's run.

Unlike Diane, Levi flew in at treetop level—a necessary approach owing to the nature of his stores. Levi carried one large cluster of cratering munitions, which contained a shaped charge designed to drill through the runway to allow a second charge to detonate below the surface. The resulting craters made airfield repair specialists truly earn their pay. In addition, her subordinate carried two Rockeye II cluster bomb dispensers, designed to go off fifty feet above the airfield. The resulting shrapnel could damage an area the size of a football field.

Levi maintained his low approach at high speed until reaching the edge of the airfield, where he popped up to three hundred feet and released his load. Inflatable "ballute" tails stuck out the back of the bombs to increase drag and give Levi a chance to get away from the ensuing inferno.

As the runway, surrounding planes, and ground crew disappeared behind a sheet of fire, Diane saw two fighters closing in on Levi's tail.

"Leader to One Seven. Got two MiGs on your . . . one of them just fired, Blue Jeans! Two, three missiles. Get the hell out of there!"

Diane hadn't finished speaking when Levi's Hornet went vertical a fraction of a second after releasing a cloud of chaff. Two missiles went under, the third remained locked on her subordinate's tail.

Diane pushed full throttle and went after the two MiGs following Levi, who rolled his craft and executed an inverted loop after popping more chaff and a cluster of infrared flares. That did it. The last missile went astray, but the MiGs stayed with him.

"Can't shake them bastards!"

"Hang in there, Blue Jeans. I got them."

Diane followed the inverted caravan down to five hundred feet, where her subordinate leveled off and pulled the tightest loop Diane'd ever seen. Both pursuing MiGs overshot the loop, losing the Hornet in the dark. Diane smiled as the Iraqi pilots obviously realized they had been outperformed.

The MiG-29s simultaneously executed a vertical corkscrew to five thousand feet, and Diane took pursuit with Levi now glued to her starboard wing.

"Bastards sure are fast," she heard Levi say as the MiGs split in a Y at the apex of their ascent. Both Hornets remained with the left MiG as it tried to go supersonic, but to do so, the Iraqi first had to push full afterburner to achieve the required supersonic transitional speed, and when it did, Diane locked a Sidewinder heat-seeking missile on its white-hot nozzles.

She fired and followed the river of smoke as it sprinted across the sky at Mach 4.

A cloud of infrared flares left an underside pod of the MiG-29, but it was too late. Although the Iraqi fighter hurtled downward to attempt fooling the missile into the floating countermeasures, the missile's infrared homing unit had too good a lock on the afterburning tail. Diane saw the missile detonate alongside the starboard aft fuselage section. The blast effect peeled the vertical fin, along with the starboard elevator, causing an immediate loss of control. The MiG-29 rolled and pitched nose-downward as an explosion in the aft fuselage caused fragments of the warhead to penetrate into the fuselage, impacting the turbine blades with disastrous results. The thrown blades, still rotating at thousands of revolutions per minute, shredded nearby fuel lines. The engulfing fire that followed quickly spread to the wings as the burning fuel moved toward the main tanks. The MiG broke apart in midair just seconds before striking the ground.

Diane saw no ejection.

"Strike Three to Lead. MiGs, MiGs. Three at my six o'clock! Bastards are right on my tail! My wingman just disengaged with a downed turbofan!" Diane heard the lead pilot of the group's third section shout over the radio.

"Confirmed, Strike Three. Coming back around. Got an approach vector. Be there in twenty seconds," Diane responded as she turned into the vector and pushed Mach 2 with Levi glued to her side.

"I don't know if I can hold them, Lead. The bastards . . . oh, shit. Missiles! Two closing at Mach four!"

"Get out of there!"

"Chaff's out!"

Diane saw the air show in the distance. The two missiles followed the Hornet as it tried to lose itself in the ground clutter. It worked. The missiles went astray in a cloud of chaff, but the pursuing MiGs kept the pace. Diane played the throttles and sidestick to close the gap. One of the Iraqis broke left.

"Stay with the two on Strike Three's tail, One Seven!"

"Lead, Lead, the third's loopin' around," said Levi. *"He's gonna try to—"*

"I know, One Seven. I know. Just stay with the two MiGs. Strike Three, Lead, over."

"Lead, can't get them off my tail!"

"Relax," responded Diane as she unsuccessfully tried to saddle in for a missile shot. "I'll clear them for you. Too close for missiles. Switching to guns!"

Strike Three executed a vertical corkscrew and the two MiGs followed. Diane pulled on the sidestick and added throttle to go vertical and float her fighter right up to the left MiG-29, before lining up the craft on the HUD's crosshairs and pressing the trigger to the first detent.

The 20mm cannon kicked into life, firing rhythmic bursts of ten rounds each every two seconds. The NVGs allowed her to see the bursts as strings of light projecting toward the MiG. Diane used the luminous beams to adjust her fire, and watched in satisfaction when the MiG's left turbofan began to smoke as the caravan reached forty-five hundred feet.

Diane's tail sensor went red again as the third MiG-29

completed the loop and tried to get a lock on her Hornet.

"Gotta move, Lead. The bastard's going to get an angle on my ass," Levi said.

"Break hard left, Strike Three," Diane told the pilot of the lead Hornet. "Get him when he overshoots. I have to take care of a MiG on my tail."

"Confirmed, Lead," responded Strike Three's pilot.

"Okay, One Seven. Stay with me. Let's see what this guy can do."

The pair of Hornets left the tail of the MiG following Strike Three by executing an inverted dive. Suddenly, instead of following Strike Three, the second MiG joined the one following Levi and her.

"Lead, now we got both of 'em bastards on our butts!"

"We have to separate, One Seven. Break left on count!"

"Roger, Lead."

Diane pulled out of the inverted dive and broke hard right while applying full throttle. Eight g's blasted on the composite skin of the F/A-18 as Diane forced the Tactical Fighter to the outer envelope of the design. The trick worked again. The Iraqi overshot the turn and came out of it five hundred feet ahead of Diane, who managed to fight the high-g-induced tunnel vision enough to lock him in the crosshairs and fire, but the MiG-29's pilot anticipated Diane's attack and broke left just in time. The Iraqi then inverted and shot straight down. Diane followed and switched to missiles. In order to pull out of the dive and maintain that forward airspeed, the MiG would have to use afterburner. Diane smiled when the MiG-29 rolled out and started a tight right turn and climb in full afterburner.

Diane heard the loud buzz of the heat-seeking head of her second missile, and fired. The Sidewinder left in a blaze and closed in at Mach 3, got momentarily lost in a cloud of infrared flares left behind by the departing MiG, but quickly reacquired and closed in for the kill. This time, the missile disappeared into the MiG-29's right exhaust, and a second later the entire sky in front of

Diane became a ball of bright NVG green light as the Iraqi fighter blew from its core out.

After making a sharp right turn to avoid the burning debris, she scanned the radar for signs of Levi, who had already taken care of his MiG-29 and was returning to her side.

"Good shooting, One Seven."

"Ditto, Lead."

Diane verified that the remaining craft in the area were friendlies. "Leader to Strike group, Leader to Strike group. Confirm touchstone on red, over."

"Three . . . Four . . . Five . . . Two."

All SAM systems had been destroyed. The base was in flames. All enemy fighters that had managed to get airborne had been downed. General Grogan would have air superiority during the initial Iraqi attack in the morning.

The trip back took only ten minutes as the Hornets cruised in a straight line at Mach 1.3, depleting nearly ninety percent of their fuel by the time their landing gear struck the metallic surface of the portable runway.

Under the dim lights of the temporary base, Diane taxied her Hornet back to the shelter, where the ground crew chief already waited with his team and the rest of the pilots. Diane performed a tight 180 turn using the rudder pedals, leaving her jet on the clearing with the tail facing the desert. A diesel tower with a nosewheel adapter came around and pushed the craft into the temporary shelter, which had a roof made of heavy camouflage mesh over a waterproof canvas.

As the ground crew chief pulled the ladder out from the left side of the fuselage, Diane powered down, lifted the canopy, and unstrapped herself. On the ground, Levi ran to join the other pilots, who cheered their victory.

Diane removed her helmet and quickly put on a green cap to hide her thinning hair before climbing down the ladder. The small crowd surrounded her.

"Yes, Colonel, we really did it to them this time, didn't we?" one pilot said.

Diane, helmet in hand, rubbed her eyes and said, "It's too early to call it a victory, isn't it? Particularly with half of the Republican Guard heading this way."

Smiles vanished in a flash as most of the pilots lowered their gaze. Levi glanced at Diane, who simply raised a fine eyebrow while tilting her head.

"Gentlemen, no one celebrates in this place until that maniac is back in his little shithole in Baghdad. No one. Today we just scratched the surface. It's going to take a lot more flawless, top-notch flying to keep those Iraqis at bay, and I can tell you it's not going be easy. Today we lucked out. The timing was just right. Another ten minutes and we would have found ourselves fighting dozens of Iraqi MiGs instead of the few that managed to get airborne before we got there. Tomorrow this place is going to be swarming with Air Force planes on their way from the States. But before that, we have another sortie coming up to support General Grogan. I suggest you get something to eat and grab some sleep before reporting to the briefing tent. Dismissed!"

The pilots looked at one another, half in disbelief, half in bitter understanding of their commander's words, before slowly walking away from the makeshift shelter.

Diane remained behind, standing next to the F/A-18C as the ground crew began to haul carts loaded with 20mm ammunition and missiles. As she watched it in silence, Diane's prayers went to General Oliver Grogan, who somehow had to hold back the Iraqis until reinforcements came. Defeat meant the imminent loss of Kuwait, and the beginning of another long and arduous campaign to eject the Iraqis from a country that never belonged to them in the first place.